Insatiable

Insatiable

Virginia Henley

A SIGNET BOOK

SIGNET
Published by New American Library, a division of
Penguin Group (USA) Inc., 375 Hudson Street,
New York, New York 10014, USA
Penguin Group (Canada), 10 Alcorn Avenue, Toronto,
Ontario M4V 3B2, Canada (a division of Pearson Penguin Canada Inc.)
Penguin Books Ltd., 80 Strand, London WC2R 0RL, England
Penguin Ireland, 25 St. Stephen's Green, Dublin 2,
Ireland (a division of Penguin Books Ltd.)
Penguin Group (Australia), 250 Camberwell Road, Camberwell, Victoria 3124,
Australia (a division of Pearson Australia Group Pty. Ltd.)
Penguin Books India Pvt. Ltd., 11 Community Centre, Panchsheel Park,
New Delhi - 110 017, India
Penguin Group (NZ), Cnr Airborne and Rosedale Roads, Albany,
Auckland 1310, New Zealand (a division of Pearson New Zealand Ltd.)
Penguin Books (South Africa) (Pty.) Ltd., 24 Sturdee Avenue,
Rosebank, Johannesburg 2196, South Africa

Penguin Books Ltd, Registered Offices:
80 Strand, London WC2R 0RL, England

First published by Signet, an imprint of New American Library,
a division of Penguin Group (USA) Inc.

ISBN: 0-7394-4637-1

To my editor, Laura Cifelli,
who shares my passion for history

Chapter One

She hesitated only long enough to turn her back, then, with impatient fingers, she drew off her velvet cloak and dropped it onto the padded couch. She lifted her skirts, untied the tapes of her voluminous petticoats, stepped out of them and threw them atop the cloak. Then she unfastened her costly gown, baring her back all the way down to her saucy curved bottom.

Catherine Seton Spencer was cursed with impulsiveness. Desire often rose up in her so passionately that she banished all caution and gave in to an irresistible urge. She and her companion had stolen away from the Queen's Court by way of the river, and the bustling London streets filled her with reckless excitement. The gaily painted signs of the various establishments, offering everything from horoscopes to rooms rented by the hour, were designed to lure patrons inside.

Her companion, who had been eager and overbold, now cautioned, "You may regret this whim. Then you will blame me."

"'Tis not a whim! You dared me and I cannot resist a challenge."

"You've never done this before. There'll be pain and blood."

"The first prick is bound to be painful. I'm no coward! Let's get it over with."

When the man stroked the small of her naked back, she glanced down at what he held in his other hand. "It looks alarmingly long." Fear added to the thrill. "How much time will it take?"

"Only about twenty minutes. Hold still while I get it in."

Lady Catherine closed her eyes and gritted her teeth. Once she got past the pain of the initial thrust, the corners of her mouth lifted in a smile, and when he was finished, she gave a shout of triumphant laughter.

She dressed quickly and the couple quit the establishment without a backward glance. "Don't you dare tell the gentlemen I got a tattoo, Bella, or I'll pull your ear inside out! If my name is bantered about the Court, my reputation will be sullied."

Lady Arbella Stuart laughed. "Don't you think meeting gentlemen for a secret rendezvous will sully our reputations?"

"Who will know, pray? We are wearing our vizards and we only agreed to let them escort us to the play."

"It's to be staged in the yard of the Bull and Bear. Naturally our escorts will have reserved a private room upstairs so we may watch from the window."

"Bella, you've done this before!" Catherine accused. She was surprised and more than a little envious. She didn't like anyone to steal a march on her in the skillful game of husband hunting.

As they made their way along Thames Street, Arbella, brimming with worldly knowledge, pointed to a tall building. "That's a famous brothel frequented by the courtiers."

"Ohhh, I'm curious as a cat! I'd give my eyeteeth to see what goes on in there."

"What a shocking thing to say!"

"I frequently have thoughts that would shock the devil himself. I want to know what men enjoy women doing to them."

"But they are . . . *whores.*" Arbella whispered the wicked word. "Gentlemen wouldn't want a lady doing those things to them."

"Would they not?" Catherine let go a peal of laughter. "Wherever did you get such quaint notions? I doubt they came from your grandmother, the infamous Countess of Shrewsbury. She's had four husbands and must have been lusty both in and out of bed!"

"Cat Spencer, that's a wicked thing to say! My grandmother, Bess, is an old lady and a veritable *dragon* regarding my morals. I was glad to escape from Derbyshire and come to Court."

"I warrant Bess knows all the tricks females can get up to with the opposite sex. Speaking of which, here come our escorts, panting at the thought of having us to themselves for the afternoon." She smiled beneath her mask. "Let's keep them at a cool distance."

•   •   •

Patrick Hepburn, Lord Stewart, masked the relief he felt that this was the final day of a four-month tour of duty patrolling the Middle March of the Scottish Borders. He commanded fifty moss-troopers, all Hepburns, Stewarts, Douglases and Elliots who had pledged their loyalty to him and his father before him. If he let down his guard and allowed them to see he was eager to be home at Crichton, they would be off like a pack of hounds from hell, seeking their own beds and the lasses who warmed them.

Patrick dismounted and handed his horse's reins to Jock Elliot, his captain. He held out his hand to the Warden of the English Middle March. "Well met, sir." He grinned affably. "I like a man who is punctual." He liked Robert Carey for other reasons. The tall redhead was the living image of a gallant Elizabethan: brave, intelligent and naïvely honest. His father, Lord Hunsdon, was a bastard of the late King Henry Tudor and Mary Boleyn, making Robert cousin to Queen Elizabeth.

"Your lordship, it is an honor to deal with you." Though tall, Carey had to look up at Hepburn, who was six foot four in his stocking feet and far more in spurred leather boots.

Both men were unbelievably young to command such tough, hardened Borderers—proof they'd earned their men's loyalty. Between the two of them, they'd managed to keep the Scottish and English Middle Marches fairly quiet for the past four months. Of course there had been clan raids, where beasts and goods had been lifted, but burning and murder had been kept to a minimum.

This meeting at the Border was for the purpose of exchanging prisoners. Jock Elliot gave Lord Stewart a list of the English they'd taken, along with their offenses, and Hepburn handed it to Carey. With a curt nod he turned his captives over to the warden. All had been stripped of anything of value, including their mounts, and those from wealthy families had also pledged ransom in exchange for their freedom. Prisoners held at the medieval nightmare known as Hermitage Castle were not just willing—they were eager—to offer gold for their release.

Robert Carey handed over his own list and watched ruefully as his grinning Scots prisoners eagerly crossed to their own side of the Border. "The wily buggers had little of value jingling in their pockets. I'm hard pressed to pay my men."

Patrick grinned. "Ask your cousin for a raise."

"Raise?" Robert snorted. "I was appointed warden for a year and I've not seen one crown of my five-hundred-pound fee. At the end of May, when I've served my twelve months, I intend to go to London to collect my due."

"Royalty is notoriously tightfisted." Patrick thought of King James's parsimony. Scotland's monarch had no standing army. He relied on his nobles to raise men and arms at their own expense to keep the country safe. "You must devise other sources of income." The grin was wiped from his face as he examined the list. "This says Sim Armstrong raped a woman. If you've proof, why didn't you mete out punishment?" His black brows drew together in outrage.

Robert, keeping his voice low, said, "His brother's a Scots warden. A harsh sentence would likely mean retaliation with fire and sword."

Patrick nodded and walked down the line of men Carey had just turned over to him. "Armstrong. The English warden has put your fate in my hands. Any complaints?"

Armstrong, nicknamed Bangtail, grinned. "None, m'lord."

Hepburn turned to Jock Elliot. "Hang him."

The Scot's curses, protests, pleas and struggles were ignored as the moss-troopers seized him and carried out the order. By the time Hepburn returned to Carey, Armstrong's legs had kicked for the last time and his corpse swung slowly in the breeze.

The English warden was grateful. "You'll share a bottle with me, Patrick, before you depart?"

"It would be my pleasure, Robert."

A short time later, as Sir Robert and his troopers departed, Hepburn swung up into his saddle and addressed the two dozen men who'd been released to him. "Think yourselves lucky you were caught by Carey. Most English wardens make no distinction between thieves and murderers and would've hanged you out of hand." He watched them steal furtive glances at Armstrong's corpse and was satisfied they'd learned a lesson today. He accepted that they had few scruples about stealing, but murder and rape would not be tolerated on his four-month patrol of the Borders.

He raised his head like a stag scenting the wind and grinned at his moss-troopers. "Home, lads!"

With a great shout they galloped off, driving before them the

English horses they'd taken. They left their fellow Scots on foot without a moment's compassion. If they were careless enough to get caught, they deserved to walk home.

As they rode north over the rolling moors and past swift streams, they knew spring had arrived. Patrick scanned the familiar hills dotted with sheep, and his dark eyes reflected the deep and abiding love he had for the Borders. Riding through Liddesdale and Teviotdale and up into Midlothian he mourned the loss of the vast tracts of land that had once belonged to his father. *Regret the loss, but never let it make you bitter, Patrick. Bitterness blackens the soul.* His father's words came back to him as if he had uttered them yesterday instead of ten years ago. That's when Francis Hepburn Stewart, the infamous Earl of Bothwell, had offered to go into voluntary exile, forfeiting titles, lands, castles and manor houses in return for a pardon from the Crown and on condition that his only son and heir retain Crichton Castle and its holdings.

Patrick had been forced to leave boyhood behind that day. "I hate King James!" he had sworn, as the vengeance of a man full grown rose up in him.

"Nay, lad, my own reckless acts brought about this pass. As you well know, James V was grandsire to both of us. When I flaunted my power, Jamie believed I was plotting to replace him on the throne. He feared my power so he stripped it from me. Never forget that the king is *omnipotent.* He can *take* whatever he wants. But always remember you are blood relatives, and that same all-powerful hand can also *give* if you are shrewd enough to cultivate his friendship and his trust. And remember too there is one thing he can never touch."

Patrick knew he wasn't speaking of Crichton, owned by generations of Hepburns. The castle wasn't the only thing he'd inherited from his father. Psychic ability, visions and uncanny supernatural powers that sometimes allowed him to foretell the future had been passed down through the Royal Stewart bloodline. It was an amazing gift. It was a formidable curse.

On the spot Patrick promised that someday, someway, he would gain enough power over King James to make him *give* far more than he had ever *taken.* Each day thereafter for a full year he'd sworn it, vowed it, pledged it like an oath, until it became a part of him. Now, a decade later, on this last day of April, he knew he was a match for any man breathing. Lord

Patrick Stewart threw back his head and laughed. Poor Jamie didn't stand a chance!

In London, the two young couples watching the play through an upstairs window at the Bull and Bear applauded as the actors took their final bow. Lady Catherine and Lady Arbella stepped back from the window, removed their masks and helped themselves to the refreshments their escorts had ordered.

Cat flashed a smile at Henry Somerset after she bit daintily into a sweetmeat. "I'm particularly fond of almonds, Hal."

"Then try some of this almond-flavored wine." He poured them each a glass and closed the distance between them until they were standing only inches apart.

Cat studied her escort's handsome face with its closely clipped golden beard and shapely lips. "No wine, Hal, it steals the senses. Bella and I must get back to Whitehall before dark."

He captured her hand and murmured, "Don't go back tonight. Stay with me, Catherine. I'll get us a private room."

Cat looked pointedly at his hand with its polished nails and heavy gold ring on the little finger, then deliberately pulled her hand from his. "I am both shocked and offended that you dare ask such a thing. I am not a serving wench; I am a lady," she said with cool disdain. "I came to see the play, not for dalliance."

In the opposite corner, Arbella was indulging in a passionate kiss with auburn-haired William Seymour. "I'm dying to stay, Will, but I know Cat will never agree. She wears her virginity like a badge of honor. I'll come alone next time," she whispered.

Shortly thereafter, the ladies made their way to the river to catch a water barge that would carry them back to Whitehall. The frustrated gentlemen made their way to the nearest brothel.

As twilight descended on the fine spring day, Lady Catherine and Lady Arbella climbed the Old Palace Water Stairs and with trepidation hurried along the path that led to Whitehall Palace. Escaping from Court earlier in the day had been great fun, but returning undetected now seemed fraught with risk. When they gained the long hallway that led to the ladies' quarters, both girls heaved a sigh of relief. It proved to be a mistake.

"*Mistress* Arbella! *Mistress* Catherine!" The elderly dragon in charge of the young maidens of the Queen's Court purposely addressed them without the courtesy of their titles. "You have been absent the entire day. Where have you been?"

"We didn't leave Whitehall, Lady Throckmorton!" Arbella said defensively.

Dear Lord, Arbella is such a wretched liar, she will get herself banished from Court. Catherine sank into a graceful curtsy. "Please do not blame Arbella, my lady; it is entirely my fault. She was helping me learn my lines for the masque we are soon to perform for Her Majesty. I have no talent for playacting." She swept dark lashes to her cheeks, conveying humility. "We are fortunate to have someone who cares so much about our welfare. I humbly apologize for causing you worry, my lady."

"You are wearing cloaks and masks and appear to be returning from somewhere," the dragon persisted.

Catherine raised her lashes. "We are returning from the chapel. The acoustics in the gallery are perfect for delivering lines, in spite of the bone-chilling cold."

Lady Throckmorton pressed her lips together. "You'll be late to the Privy Chamber for dinner. Can you not hear the summoning trumpets? If your thoughtlessness makes me tardy, I shall have a word with your mother."

As the dragon flew off, Arbella took Catherine's hand. "Thank you for drawing her attention from me to yourself."

"It was nothing. I have my mother to protect me, and I don't want you to be sent from Court. I'd have no partner in crime!"

In Scotland, by the time Lord Stewart neared Crichton, the only moss-troopers who still accompanied him were Hepburns. For the last few miles Patrick had felt a growing unease. His calloused hand rubbed the prickle at the back of his neck.

Jock Elliot noticed the gesture. "Danger, my lord?"

"Nay, but there's something amiss. We'll secure these horses in the upper pasture by Fala Water, then I'll handle the trouble."

They herded the horses past the castle's orchards to the fields beyond. A cry went up and the Hepburns who inhabited and served Crichton hastily gathered in the Great Hall to welcome home their laird. When the horses were pastured, the saddle-weary men rode into the sprawling stables and turned their mounts over to young grooms. Then, grim-faced, Patrick strode beneath the stone arch carved with Hepburn roses. His spurs struck sparks on the flagstones as he entered the Great Hall.

His cousin David, who captained Crichton's garrison, stepped forward with a broad grin on his face. "Welcome—"

"Oh, I saw the *welcome* you had waiting for me in the upper pasture." He surveyed the young faces brimming with self-satisfaction and watched their smirks flee as he crashed his powerful fist on the oak table. "Splendor of God! You haven't the brains to pour piss from your boots! How long have the Earl of Winton's cattle been grazing on Crichton pasture?"

David's eyebrows rose in surprise. "What makes ye think they're Winton's?"

"Christ, I don't *think,* I *know*! His beasts are unique. They are prize longhorns, bred special. Now, instead of taking my pleasure in Edinburgh tomorrow, I have the distinct honor of returning that herd up to Seton and lying through my teeth to the Earl of Winton." He paused. "You may accompany me, David."

All at Crichton knew Patrick's hot temper flashed like lightning, followed by a deafening roll of thunder, then cooled and dissipated as quickly as it arrived. The men remained wary for a time, treading softly; not so the women. The younger females worshipped him; the older ones adored him. He was never harsh with the fair sex; rather, he was protective, generous and appreciative of all they did for him. In return they made sure his kitchens were spotless, his meals bountiful and served on time, his bed linen immaculate and his shirts sewn with loving hands. His moss-troopers' wives flirted openly with him, while their daughters practiced their cajolery. All the Hepburn and Stewart women, whether nubile or ancient, vied with one another for his attention and approval.

Patrick loved them dearly and was wise enough to treat them all like sisters, particularly when they behaved provocatively. After the evening meal, as he sat with his long legs stretched to the fire, his favorite deerhounds sprawled at his feet, a young second cousin snatched a jug of ale from a servant and hurried to his side to refill his tankard. As her glance slid across his wide, muscular shoulders, she licked her lips and tossed back her red hair. "Patrick, I saw the fine horses you brought today. I'm old enough for a mount of my own. Would you be generous enough to give me one for my birthday?"

"You are a saucy wench, Jenny Hepburn, and the answer would be *no* even if it was your birthday. I intend to sell the English horses back to the English." When he saw her lips pout prettily, his big hand ruffled her hair. "Tell your father I said you could have a sure-footed pony. He can cut one from the herd that wintered on Fala Moor."

The seductress vanished. Jenny's eager young face shone with hero worship. "Thank you, Patrick!"

As Hepburn stood up and stretched his shoulders he saw the head steward, who was in charge of his household, approach with a sheaf of papers clutched in his hand. Patrick nodded his head in the direction of the library. He cursed good-naturedly and knew he'd have a couple of hours of Crichton business to attend to, approving everything from supplies for the brewery to a tally of his tenants' rents, which his bailiff had collected. It was a constant battle between income and output, and he hoped he would never have to mortgage Crichton again to pay his men. The dogs followed at his heels and flung themselves down before the library fire. Like the castle's human inhabitants, they knew that all was right with their world now that the master was home.

Next morning, by break of dawn, David Hepburn had assembled the young reivers who had lifted the longhorns so successfully only a sennight ago. As Patrick joined them for the trek north, he noted with amusement that they showed little remorse. Still, it was enough that they were being forced to swallow their pride—no small feat for Borderers.

The five-mile journey presented few problems but produced some ripe curses from the men as they herded the longhorns across Tyne Water. Winton Castle lay on the far side of the river, atop a rise in the fertile land. Pastures filled with cattle ranged as far as the eye could see, all owned by Geordie Seton, the irascible Earl of Winton. Seton land stretched all the way to the sea, and Patrick silently admitted that he coveted every acre.

The earl spied them from half a mile away and came at full gallop. Now almost sixty, he had once been a handsome man with a head of thick, jet-black hair, which had now grown sparse and gray. His once fair skin was florid and wind-chapped. "God's wounds, Hepburn, I never thought to see those beasties again. I intended to send men out searchin' as soon as the calvin' was done, but cowherds are no match fer bloody, thievin' raiders! Where did ye find 'em?" he demanded angrily.

"I spotted them yesterday on my way back from Border patrol. The cattle are distinctive—I knew immediately they were yours, Lord Winton," Patrick replied truthfully.

The wiry Seton would not let it go that easily. "I thought we were safe this far from the Border. I suspect it wasn't the bloody English. I believe these reivers were Scots!"

Patrick saw David Hepburn stiffen and he felt the alarm his men were experiencing. "You are right, your lordship. They were Scots," he confirmed, relishing the discomfort his words provoked.

"I knew I was right! It was the bloody Armstrongs, wasn't it?"

His ruddy face turned a shade of purple. "I demand that ye arrest them! I intend to lay charges at the next Border Wardens' Court. I'll go to the king if I must. I want justice!"

"I dispensed immediate justice. I hanged Sim Armstrong."

"By Christ, ye ha' my admiration and my thanks fer returnin' the herd." His eyes narrowed in thought. "I've always bin against payin' protection money, thinkin' it a form of blackmail, d'ye ken? But now I believe the time is ripe to loosen the purse strings. Bring yer horse to the stable and come up to the castle, Patrick. We'll draw up an agreement."

With a straight face Patrick asked, "Do you mind if the lads look around? They've a keen interest in your cattle."

When the two men dismounted, the disparity in their height was marked. The earl was short of stature, and as Patrick followed him from the stable he tried not to stare at his bowed legs. *Holy God, his mother must have rocked him on a barrel!*

When they reached the library, the earl sent a servant scurrying for whisky, and Patrick was thankful he had a hard head for liquor. They agreed on a price for a year's protection for the vast herd, which numbered more than two thousand. "How and when did you start breeding the Seton longhorns, my lord?"

"It was twenty-odd years ago. Lord John Spencer, an English noble with a large estate in Hertfordshire, came to look at my Highland cattle. He had some French Charolais that were good milk producers but didn't thrive, and he was lookin' to breed them with my sturdy beef cattle. Fortunately, they lent themselves well to crossbreedin', and these unique longhorns were the result. The experiment turned out so well we both decided to breed them."

As Winton wrote out the agreement he became loquacious.

"There was a price to pay. My daughter, Isobel, deserted me to become Lady Spencer. She's not visited Seton once in over two decades."

"She must have found Hertfordshire to her liking."

"Wheesht, not Isobel! She cajoled him into buyin' her a house in Richmond and used his sister's connection as lady-in-waiting to Queen Elizabeth to get herself an appointment. She left John to his cattle breedin' and deserted him for Court. When he died two years back I don't think she grieved much. He was just a steppin'-stone to Isobel." Geordie tossed off his second whisky. "My one great regret in life is havin' no son, no male heir to inherit all this. My younger sisters have sons, but I was damned with only a daughter. God's passion, but lasses can be a curse to a mon!"

"Females will always take the bit between their teeth unless they are controlled with a firm hand." Patrick signed the agreement and pocketed half the fee. The other half would be paid if the Seton longhorns went unmolested for a year. Satisfied with the morning's business, he bade the earl good-bye and left him to his whisky and his regrets.

As Patrick entered the stable to get his horse, a cat crossed his path, and suddenly the dark interior became illuminated by a dazzling light. The vision that appeared before him was a female in full, naked glory. She was standing before a mirror, which presented him with an unimpeded view of both her back and her front at the same time. She was small, with a tiny waist and delicate limbs, yet the swell of her lush breasts told him she was a woman full grown. He gazed at her alabaster skin with the admiration of a man who truly appreciated female flesh. When he finally raised his eyes, he saw that she was not completely naked, after all. She wore a frilly white neck ruff that emphasized the exquisite beauty of her face and contrasted with the profusion of black, shining curls that were piled high on her head.

Patrick stared in fascination, missing no finest detail. Her heavy lashes formed dark shadows on her cheekbones. When she raised them to examine herself in the mirror, he saw that her eyes were the color of amber with glittering gold inclusions in their depths. For one brief moment her eyes looked directly into his and left a physical impact. Not only did his heart miss a beat, but his unruly cock began to throb as it hardened and lengthened.

His hot gaze slowly lowered, licking over her delicious curves like a candle flame, and came to rest on her round bottom. He suddenly blinked in disbelief. At the top of her left bum cheek sat the image of a saucy black cat. "A tattoo, begod!"

Chapter Two

W hen Catherine looked over her shoulder to view the reflection of her back in the mirror, she gasped. "God in Heaven! What on earth possessed you to do such a reckless, shocking thing? You must have been mad! The whim of a moment has indelibly marked you for a lifetime!" As the lasting consequences of her action sank in, she stopped speaking in the third person. "Marked *me* for a lifetime."

She rubbed her fingertips over the tattoo, but the pert little cat sat immovable. "I shall be able to keep it hidden from Mother, but what about Maggie?" Her despair deepened. "She has eyes like a hawk. I've never been able to keep a secret from her for more than a day." Maggie was the serving woman her mother had brought from Seton when she left Scotland to marry Lord Spencer. The Scotswoman had been Baby Catherine's nurse, mothering her far more than Isobel had ever been inclined to do. Maggie was a formidable force to be dealt with. Because Cat loved and respected her, she also feared her disapproval.

"What's this of secrets?" Maggie entered the bedchamber carrying a garment she'd just finished stitching.

Catherine snatched up her petticoat and backed up to the mirror. "Maggie, I thought you'd be at dinner!"

"Well, ye thought wrong. I wanted to finish yer costume for the masque. Seeing ye're undressed, ye might as well try it on."

"No, no. I'll try it later."

Maggie eyed her curiously. "What's this of secrets?"

"I have no secrets from you," Catherine denied.

"Well, ye're right there. I know ye and yer bold-faced friend, Arbella Stuart, went into London yesterday."

"Oh, Maggie, how did you know?" Cat whispered.

"This wretched old palace has only one advantage—its proximity to London. I know the city draws ye like a lode-stone."

"We went to see a play," Cat confessed. "It was wonderful!"

"I warrant ye didn't attend unescorted, either."

"Well . . . no. Henry Somerset and Will Seymour offered us their protection. There; now I've confessed everything."

"No' quite everything, Mistress Impulsive. What the hell is that black thing on yer arse?"

She spun around and realized Maggie had seen her naked back in the mirror. "Oh, Maggie, it's a tattoo! What am I to do? I've ruined my body and spoiled any chance I had of a noble husband."

Not if I know aught of men. It will make ye more desirable. "Come now, my wee lass, there's no point in weeping, wailing and gnashing yer teeth. What's done can't be undone. It hasn't ruined ye for marriage. Ye're beautiful and ye're an heiress. The highest in the land will seek ye for their bride. Come, slip on this costume ye designed and we'll see how it fits."

Obediently Cat raised her arms, and Maggie lifted the silvery costume of Cynthia the Moon Goddess over her head. "Ye don't really wish to marry a foppish courtier, do ye, love?"

"Of course I wish to marry a courtier. I would never see him otherwise. I don't want a marriage like Mother had. They lived apart because Father had no interest in Queen Elizabeth's Court, which was, and still is, Mother's whole existence."

Isobel Spencer had become Mistress of the Queen's Wardrobe and had instilled such a love of fashion in her daughter it had inspired Catherine to try her hand at designing dresses, gowns and costumes. It did not take long for Her Majesty to notice her lovely creations and demand that she design exclusively for the queen's person, with the exception of her own wardrobe, of course.

"But I don't want it to become *your* whole existence. This isn't the real world; it's make-believe. Ye should be learning how to become an efficient chatelaine and run a great household, not pretending to be a moon goddess."

"Maggie, the Tudor Court is the hub of the kingdom's affairs. The queen is a magnet who attracts the greatest men of our time to her service. Ministers of state, senior officials of her household and peers of the realm gather about Elizabeth, making the Court the center of political, social and cultural affairs. Everybody who is anybody comes to Court for part of the year."

"Part of the year is fine, but ye should spend more time at yer home in Hertfordshire, living a normal life."

"But I've lived at Court since I was a child. I love the beautiful fashions, the dancing, the entertainments, moving from palace to palace. Court will give me the opportunity to make a great marriage. If I were stuck on a farm in the country I'd never get to meet the most eligible gentlemen in England."

"Oh, aye, we're tripping over elegant young courtiers, but the queen is a selfish old woman. She's madly jealous of other females' youth and beauty and keeps ye all out of reach with her false reverence for spotless maidenhood. She demands that men pay homage to only her. The courtiers are *her* gentlemen. Elizabeth believes she owns them, heart and soul."

Catherine laughed with delight. "But that is what makes it all so much fun. The challenge of making one of the queen's devoted gentlemen fall in love and completely lose his heart and soul to me is utterly irresistible."

Patrick, flanked by his faithful captain, covered the eight miles from Crichton to Edinburgh in less than an hour. Darkness covered the ancient city, but Hepburn, familiar with every wynd and alley, easily found his way to the stables of Holyrood Palace. A coin slipped to a groom who was an Elliot clansman assured the pair that their horses would be royally housed. They made their way to the kitchens at the rear of the palace and gained easy entrance. Lord Stewart's face was as well known to the guards as his easy generosity, while Jock was a favorite among the kitchen wenches, who were eager to supply food and other favors to a man who wore the Hepburns' famous horsehead crest on his doublet.

The pair parted company as Patrick took a staircase leading to the upper reaches that housed the many suites of the courtiers. The flickering torches offered scant light, but he could have found his way blindfolded to the wing that held the private bedchambers of the queen's ladies. He scratched on a paneled door and felt a stab of pleasure at how quickly it was opened.

"Patrick! I expected you last night." The tall blonde pulled him into the room, giving him no chance to escape, and quickly shut the door. Margretha, who had been only fifteen when she accompanied Queen Anne from Oslo, still had a fascinating Danish lilt in her voice after more than a decade at the Scottish Court.

"Gretha, you know only unavoidable business would keep me from you." He drew her into his arms and kissed her deeply.

As she lifted her arms about his neck, her loose robe fell open, and when he pressed her against his powerful body she sighed with undisguised pleasure. "It's been so long, Patrick."

Amused that she had been awaiting him almost nude, he teased, "Have you been undressed since last night in anticipation?"

Her hand slid over his huge bulge. "Cocksure devil. I attended the queen all day."

"I brought you a present, but you'll have to find it."

She squeezed his erection. "I think I did."

"Explore farther. Better yet, let's explore each other."

His hands disappeared inside her robe to glide over her high, pointed breasts. He heard her gasp of pleasure as he rolled a nipple between his thumb and forefinger to make it erect, then dipped his head to suck it into his mouth.

Margretha forgot the present, forgot everything except the feel and taste and scent of the man whose foreplay rendered her limp with need. Hepburn was not only the largest male she had ever lain with; he was also the most satisfying lover she had ever had. With urgent hands she drew him toward the bed. "Hurry, Patrick!"

"Hurry?" he puzzled, as she pushed him down and began to undress him. "There's little pleasure in haste, Gretha. We have all night." He shrugged from the doublet she had unfastened and retrieved a small package from its inside pocket. He stripped off his clothes while she unwrapped a pair of beaten silver bangles.

"They're lovely, my lord. Allow me to thank you for them."

"Allow me." He slipped a bracelet over each wrist, then laid her back against the pillows and raised her arms above her head, holding her captive in a blatantly submissive position. The fingers of his other hand trailed down the curve of her belly and began to toy with the curls between her legs.

She arched against his powerful hand. "Now, Patrick, please!"

"You don't want to play? I have a new game," he teased.

She moaned. "I'm slick with need. Take me now."

His fingers told him that she was indeed wet and wanting. Her need was so great that she hadn't even removed her robe. "I'm not cruel enough to make a lady beg." He straddled her and plunged up inside her with a powerful thrust. Then he freed her wrists and cupped her breasts so that he could feel them bounce as he moved in and out with long, vigorous strokes.

As her palms caressed the heavy musculature of his chest and shoulders, she tried to hold back the scream that was building in her throat. When his demanding mouth covered hers she could hold back no longer and climaxed with a convulsive shudder and a cry that he took into his own mouth.

Though he had not spent, he paused for a moment so that she could enjoy the sensual ripples spreading inside her before he resumed the mating dance that would take her to new heights of arousal and satisfaction.

Unbelievably, the door opened and someone entered the room. Margretha slid his hard cock from her sheath, and he sprang from the bed to confront the intruder.

"Your Majesty," Gretha said softly.

As his bedmate covered her nakedness with her robe, Patrick suddenly realized why she had not removed it and why she had urged him to hurry. She had been expecting this visit from the queen.

"Leave us." Anne of Scotland waited quietly in the shadows until she and Patrick were alone. Her eyes frankly assessed his naked body bathed in candlelight. "You are the living, breathing image of Francis," she murmured wistfully.

In that moment he realized that his father had been the queen's lover. It shocked him, yet he knew it should not, for it answered so many questions. As she stepped forward into the light he forgot his own natural state as his eyes examined and appraised her. At almost thirty, she maintained a statuesque figure and voluptuous breasts that made her still attractive, but at seventeen, when his father first laid eyes on her, the nubile young Dane must have proved irresistible.

"Lord Stewart . . . Patrick . . . I need a favor."

"I am yours to command, Your Majesty."

"The king wishes to see you privately."

Christ, so much for discretion. Does the whole bloody Court know I've come to fuck Gretha? He remembered that he was naked and reached for his clothes.

"James has been so dumpish and melancholy lately"—Anne hesitated—"ever since his last letter from Queen Elizabeth. She is such a cruel bitch! Please, Patrick, tell him what he wants to hear. 'Tis the only thing that will lift his spirits."

Patrick nodded his understanding as he dressed. "Lead on."

He followed the queen past the bedchambers of her ladies-in-waiting. He'd been entertained in some of them, but not all; his taste in women was discerning. She took him past her own suite of rooms and the audience chambers, stopping outside the private apartment of the king. She opened the anteroom door, spoke to the guard and quickly departed.

The guard opened the inner door and announced, "Lord Patrick Stewart."

The king, who had been sitting at an oak table strewn with papers, stood up and came forward to greet his visitor. "See that we're not disturbed," he told the guard. James Stuart was not a fashionable man. He wore a shabby fur robe spotted with wine stains. His sparse auburn beard and sad brown eyes gave him the look of a hunting hound. Though he looked older than his thirty-five years, he could be moody and petulant as a bairn. "Patrick, lad, I've bin waitin' hours, nay, months—where've ye bin?"

Patrick went down on one knee. "Patrolling the Borders, Sire."

The king spoke with a heavy Scottish brogue, and his words were indistinct, as if his tongue were thick. It gave the impression that he was dull-witted, but Patrick knew his intellect was sharp. When he felt James tug on his doublet, he stood up.

"Pour us wine and come and sit. I don't like ye towerin' o'er me. What I say tonight must be kept privy. Is that understood?"

"Always, Sire." He handed the king a goblet of golden Rhenish wine and took the chair opposite him before the fire.

"I want tae know my future. I want ye tae foretell it fer me."

"My father was charged with witchcraft. I'm not foolish enough to dabble in the dark arts, Sire," he said carefully.

"Wheesht, lad, we both know that was a trumped-up charge by his enemies. He had the *sight* and prophesied fer me many a time. I know ye have the power; dinna pretend wi' me, Patrick."

"You want me to draw up your horoscope, Sire?"

"Horoscope, my arse! I want tae know if she'll name me her successor." He went over to the table and snatched up a letter. "The old bitch has dangled it in front of me fer years tae keep me in grovelin' submission. The minute I reach fer it, she snatches it away and laughs at me. Then she looks down her long, haughty nose, takes up her pen and rebukes me as if I were her lackey. She murdered my mother and constantly adds insult to the vile injury!"

Tell him what he wants to hear. It was perfectly clear to Patrick that James wanted to hear that Elizabeth would name him successor to the English throne. Not only did he want it and need it, he *lusted* for Elizabeth's crown. "May I hold the letter?"

James placed it in his hand. "Read it if ye must."

Without reading it, Patrick saw Elizabeth's words in his head: *Let not shades deceive you. I will have no rascal to succeed me. Ambition can turn to dust or smoke.*

The Queen of England was clearly warning him against intrigue, and Patrick immediately knew that James was guilty. "Sire, you involved yourself in Essex's rebellion, offering him support. Though he was her favorite, she put him to death for treason."

James snatched the letter from him. "I did no such thing!"

Patrick knew the king was lying, but he realized he must tread warily. "Sire, Elizabeth is telling you that she is suspicious of you and is warning you against further intrigue."

"I could write a letter that would dispel all suspicion and pledge her my loyalty and devotion, but there's none I can trust tae deliver it into her hands. I am surrounded by spies who carry tales. I wouldn't dare give it tae Nicholson, her English ambassador tae Scotland. He blackens my name every chance he gets, hintin' that I'm in league wi' the Pope."

"I know a man you can trust, Sire. The Warden of the English Middle March is Robert Carey. I've had dealings with him and know him to be a man of honor. He was knighted for his service in France; moreover, he is the queen's cousin."

"Elizabeth has more cousins than fleas on a hound, and the degree of intermarriage is scandalous. Robert Carey is one of old Hunsdon's brood, if I'm not mistaken."

"You are seldom mistaken, Sire. All the Carey brothers have been Border wardens at one time or other, and Robert's sister is wed to Lord Thomas Scrope, Constable of Carlisle Castle.

Robert served under him as deputy of the West March before he became Warden of the Middle March a year ago, so he's lived on the Scots' Border for some time and is a strong advocate for peace between our two countries. I could arrange for you to see him, Sire."

"Would he not serve Elizabeth's interests before mine?"

"Not if you pay him well for his services. He was once a loyal attendant at Court, but it was a way of life that ruined his pocket. He escaped from Court to serve on the Border; however, I happen to know that his warden's fee has never been paid."

"Bring him tae see me wi'out delay. I am in need of an English faction who will be loyal tae me. Now, stop yer evasive tactics and tell me what ye foresee in my future."

Patrick smiled wryly. "You are tenacious as a terrier, Sire."

"That's because it's like gettin' blood from a stone. I must know, Patrick! I'm livin' in purgatory. Will Elizabeth name me her successor, or will I have tae fight a war and take the Crown of England by force? Be assured that I *will* invade England in defense o' my hereditary rights! And if I do fight the English, will I then have tae fight Spain, which wants a Catholic on the throne?" James was working himself into a passion. He wiped the spittle from his mouth on his sleeve. "Above all, I need tae know how much longer Elizabeth will live. Sometimes I fear it will be as long as the sun and the moon!"

"She is not immortal, Sire."

James licked his lips. "England is wealthy beyond the imagination. Her English nobles live lavishly, while we in Scotland live in penury, and all my nobles are impoverished. It's like havin' a feast spread out before a starvin' mon. Patrick, I need tae know how much longer Elizabeth will live!"

This is the first time he has ever dared put his thoughts into words. He is desperate for any glimmer of knowledge.

"Look at my poor, paltry crown and compare it with hers!" James pointed to an alcove where his crown sat on its velvet cushion. The king did not keep it with the sword of state and silver-gilt scepter but had removed it to his chambers so he could wear it whenever he felt the need.

The firelight reflecting in Patrick's wine suddenly glinted off the gold crown in a red flash, illuminating the alcove with shimmering light. Above the crown of Scotland's king, another crown, far more glorious, encrusted with huge diamonds, pigeon-blood rubies and other precious jewels, floated above the simpler crown.

James stared at Patrick intently. He could tell that the dark Stewart was experiencing a vision of some sort. He held his breath, prepared to wait until his kin came out of his trance, but impatience won out. "What do ye see?" he whispered.

The spell was broken. The vision vanished. Patrick was far too shrewd to reveal all he had seen. *Tell him what he wants to hear.* "You will wear both crowns, Sire," he assured the king.

"I knew it was my destiny! But, Patrick, ye do no' tell me *when* or *how*. Why do ye keep it from me?" he demanded petulantly.

"It is the great fundamental political question: Who gets what, when and how?"

James took his meaning immediately. "Ye know I will reward you handsomely, Patrick. What is it ye want?"

"The same as you, Sire: my hereditary rights."

"The lands your father forfeited have been granted tae others. All his castles were mortgaged tae the hilt, and the new owners have paid off those heavy debts. I canno' restore them tae ye."

"Land and estates in England equal or greater in number and size would suffice, along with an earldom," he bargained. He could read James's mind. The king was tempted to agree to anything in exchange for what Patrick could foresee and prophesy. "I want no *false* promises, Sire. I want your sacred pledge."

"I canno' take estates from the English nobility and grant them tae ye, wi'out them risin' up against me," James said truthfully. "There is one way," he added thoughtfully, determined to learn all that Patrick could portend. "If ye prophesy correctly *how* and *when* I become King of England, I will give ye a wealthy heiress."

"Marriage?" Patrick considered the idea for the first time and was tempted to refuse. He'd have none select a wife for him, especially not James Stuart. "You drive a hard bargain, Sire. If you give me my choice of *any* English heiress I desire, I think we can draw up a bond. I'll need the pledge in writing, Sire."

"I will gladly give ye any heiress that takes yer fancy. In return ye must tell me exactly when Elizabeth will *die!*"

"I would need to be in the queen's presence and look into her face to know that, Your Majesty."

"Then ye will accompany Robert Carey tae Elizabeth's

Court." The king stood up. "I was goin' to invite ye tae the hunt tomorrow, but ye will be leavin' fer the Borders in search of Carey. Tonight I know ye hunt other quarry." His hand rubbed across his groin in a crude male gesture. "In my experience, *coitus interruptus* makes the cock grow harder."

Long after Margretha fell asleep, replete and exhausted from the passion she had expended, Patrick lay wide awake. He had been of two minds whether he would return to her chamber or not, then decided she had been guilty of only a small deceit. All females dabbled in deception, a character flaw that paled when measured against male duplicity. His restless thoughts began to prowl. Though physically he remained beside her, mentally he withdrew. Fleetingly, he thought of tonight's vision, brought on by the sight of the crown. His visions were always initiated by a *trigger,* such as the black cat in the Earl of Winton's stable. He visualized the cat now, hoping to conjure the female, but she remained elusive and refused to materialize. Her exquisite beauty, however, was indelibly engraved upon his memory. He pondered who she was and why he had envisioned her. He was certain he had never encountered her in his past, for such a wench would be unforgettable. One thing was certain: If he ever met her in the flesh, so to speak, he would recognize her instantly. His body stirred, and he cursed his rampant appetite that could be whetted by his own sensual imagination.

To ease the hungry ache and cool his blood, he forced his mind to more practical matters. He would likely find Carey at Bewcastle, the English Border fortress. If he left immediately he might be able to bring him for an audience with the king tomorrow night. He decided the fastest way for him and Robert to get to London was by ship. This fit in well with his plans for the English horses. He would transport them in the hold of his bark, the *Hepburn Rose.* With a fair wind and any luck, the voyage could be made in two days.

Patrick slipped from the bed and dressed quietly so he would not disturb Margretha. It wasn't gallantry that prompted him; it was expedience. He didn't know when he would see her again and he couldn't abide clinging good-byes.

Chapter Three

*C*at Spencer tried to open the door quietly so she would not disturb her mother. It was past midnight and she was slightly unsteady on her feet from the wine she had consumed.

"Where on earth have you been until this hour, young madam?"

"Mother, I thought you'd be *asleep*."

"Dear heaven, you're flown with wine! If Her Majesty learns of this we could both be banished from Court." Such a fate was Isobel Spencer's worst nightmare. She equated it with being buried alive. "Tell me instantly where you have been."

"I was only in the next wing. Philadelphia is back from Carlisle, so I was visiting with her and her sister Kate."

"You should use their titles. Philadelphia, Lady Scrope, is a baroness, and Kate, Lady Howard, is the Countess of Nottingham. I will not have you show such disrespect to the queen's favorite ladies, who have served her faithfully for more than twenty years."

Cat rolled her eyes. Philadelphia and Kate, two of the Carey sisters, had the huge house next to theirs in Richmond. She had known them since she was a baby and had spent more time with them, playing and romping about the garden, than she had with her mother. They would fall down laughing if she used their titles.

"Beth was there too. We were having a little party."

"You must address your father's sister as *Aunt* Beth. Naturally she was there; she's married to their brother George."

"I don't know why you didn't join us."

Isobel sniffed. "I didn't join you because I wasn't invited."

Cat immediately felt guilty. "Never mind; we'll all be together at Richmond next week. We won't have to worry about etiquette and the strictures of the Court. We can laugh and gossip and have as much fun as we like." Because Richmond was convenient to the queen's residences of Whitehall, Windsor, Hampton Court, and Richmond Palace, the Spencer and Carey ladies spent two days every fortnight at their country homes along the river Thames for a much-needed respite from their Court duties.

"A young lady should aspire to something higher than gossip and fun. You are at Court to serve Her Majesty the queen. I am most disappointed in you, Catherine. Get to bed."

Glad to escape, Cat immediately obeyed. Before sleep claimed her, she contrasted her mother's cold nature with that of the other ladies she had grown up around. Kate was the eldest of ten Carey offspring, who were cousins to the queen, and, though she had the exalted title of countess and was married to Lord Admiral Howard, everyone felt comfortable in her presence. Kate had a motherly quality about her that encouraged others to confide in her. She was the sweetest, kindest lady Cat had ever known. Her warm brown eyes, gentle smile and understanding ways endeared her to all, especially the queen.

Her sister Philadelphia was the beauty of the family. She was the only one who had not inherited red hair. Dark gold tresses and lovely pale skin set off the flamboyant fashions she liked to wear. She was witty and outgoing, loved to laugh and was an inveterate matchmaker who never tired of introducing Cat to the eligible young gentlemen of the Court, with a view to marriage. By contrast, Cat's mother, fearing Elizabeth's disapproval, shared the queen's rigid views that the younger ladies of her Court remain unwed. Catherine knew that technically she was a ward of the Crown since her father had died while she was still a child. The Court of Wards had made her mother trustee for the estate in Hertfordshire until she came of age. But as Cat climbed into bed she smiled a secret smile. *I turned twenty last month. In less than a year I will no longer be a minor. When I come of age I shall receive my legal inheritance and be free to marry whomever I wish, without either my mother's or the queen's consent!*

Patrick Hepburn and Robert Carey watched the sailors set the square-rigged canvas of the foremast as the ship left the Firth of Forth behind and headed into the open sea. They had become firm friends and allies in the last few days since Robert had agreed to carry secret correspondence between the monarchs of Scotland and England. His brother would patrol the Middle March along with his own, since the late spring and summer was usually a peaceful time in the Borders. "My father has a few ships, but no barkentines."

"The only thing fancy about her is her name, the *Hepburn Rose*. She's an old workhorse that gets the job done. My father took a couple of Spanish treasure ships with her. It paid for the new wing on Crichton Castle."

"The Earl of Bothwell was a pirate?"

Patrick grinned. "A pirate, an outlaw and a thief. I never need worry about him. He leads a life of luxury in Florence."

"Speaking of luxury, you will find Elizabeth's Court extravagant beyond reason. Its opulence is the result of obscene indulgence. Most courtiers are in debt up to their eyeballs."

"During the year I attended Cambridge University I visited the Court upon occasion. James Stuart lives like a pauper by comparison. Most Scots nobles are impoverished, including myself. I appreciate your inviting me to stay at Hunsdon Hall, Robert."

"It's an enormous house along the river in Richmond, quite handy to the Royal Court. Two of my sisters and my brother's wife, Beth, use the house when they can escape their duties to the queen. They'll be in their glory having two bachelors under their roof."

"Are you sure they won't mind the dogs?"

"They are English ladies—they care far more for the company of hounds than the company of their husbands! And the hunting in Richmond is marvelous."

Patrick laughed. "No wonder you remain a bachelor!"

"Actually, I have been contemplating marriage lately. A year ago, I met a most alluring widow from Northumberland who was visiting in Carlisle. Not the least of her attractions is her wealth. Marriage would certainly solve my money problems."

"If and when James becomes the King of England and Scotland, there will no longer be a Border, and you will be out of a job. Marriage is likely in the cards for both of us, my friend."

"God's fury, I never thought of that. It could be a long time in the future though. Knowing my cousin Elizabeth, I warrant she is not ready to relinquish this world for the next anytime soon."

Patrick Hepburn kept a wise silence. When he'd had the vision of the two crowns, he had seen a pair of female hands holding the crown of England far too possessively to bestow it on another.

Late that night, as the ship cut smartly through the waves of the North Sea on its way down the east coast of England, Patrick sat down with a chart and a pen to calculate their arrival time at the Port of London. He was pleased to learn they should be ready to dock tomorrow before dark. He stripped, climbed into his bunk and tucked the warm blanket across his naked limbs. Then he reached for paper and pen, jotted down the number of horses he had for sale and multiplied it by the price he hoped to get. He was satisfied with the total, and his restless mind moved on, contemplating his visit to London. Absently, he sketched the horse-head symbol that was on the Hepburn crest, then beneath it he began to draw the outline of a small cat. The corners of his mouth lifted in a smile. "Why not?" he asked himself, deliberately making the cat ink black. As his dark eyes stared through the latticed window of his cabin, he did not see the outline of the quarterdeck or the velvet black sky hung with stars; he saw instead the tantalizing female who was slowly but surely becoming the object of his desires.

She was abed, fast in the arms of Morpheus, and Patrick guessed that while she slept it would be a simple matter to capture and control her spirit. He focused intently upon the exquisite features of her face. His gaze lingered on the dark crescents that shadowed her delicate cheekbones, then moved to her lush lips, soft with sleep. "Come to me." Though his words were whispered, they were totally compelling.

Her lashes slowly lifted, and he stared deeply into amber eyes flecked with shimmering gold inclusions. She pushed back her covers, slipped from the bed and floated toward him. Patrick could feel his heart thudding in his chest, his blood coursing thick and hot through his veins.

At last she stood before him in the cabin, wearing the most delectable nightgown he had ever seen. It was made of pristine white silk that clung to the curves of her body and was fastened with a dozen tiny bows that marched down the front from neck to knees. His mouth went dry at the thought of undoing them, one by one. She began to sway in time with the rocking motion of the ship, and as she moved, he saw that the silk was so sheer he could discern her rosy nipples through the fabric and the dark shadow of her pubic curls between her legs.

His pulse beat wildly in his throat and the soles of his feet, as his cock lengthened and hardened, and throbbed with a need to bury itself deep inside her. As he stared, mesmerized, she slowly lifted her arms and unfastened the ribbon that tied up her hair. The shining black mass came tumbling down to her tiny waist, and with a sensual flip she tossed it back over her shoulders.

Her body began to move in a rhythmic, undulating dance that matched the ship's motion. Her movements, capturing the wild, free spirit of the sea, became sensual and hypnotic. As she began to spin and turn with total abandon, her black cloud of hair flew about her shoulders until it became a mass of disheveled curls. Then she threw back her head and laughed with uninhibited delight.

Patrick, fully aroused, wanted her beside him in the bunk. He hungered to taste her, longed to feel her beneath him, yet first he wanted to see her naked. He reached out a powerful hand, but the moment his fingertips brushed the delicate silk, her image began to fade. "No!" he cried as she vanished into thin air.

He cursed out loud, knowing he would not be able to conjure her back. He should have known that her spirit was too ephemeral for physical contact, at least this first time. The corners of his mouth lifted as he stooped to retrieve her ribbon from the cabin floor. Had the saucy wench left it behind deliberately? Was it a sign that she wished to return? Patrick decided that whether she wanted it or no, he would compel her presence again soon.

Maggie pulled back the heavy brocade curtains, allowing the May sunshine to flood the room. "Ye overslept, my wee lass."

Cat sat up and shielded her eyes from the bright light. "Oh, I had the strangest dream. I was aboard a ship and I was afraid of the sea. To keep my fear at bay, I began to dance, and suddenly my fear was swept away and replaced by a wild recklessness. I laughed in the face of danger!"

"Yer bedclothes are in such a tangle, they look like they've been tossed about in a storm at sea. Too much wine, I warrant."

Cat put her hand to her head. "You are right, Maggie. Now, where the devil did my hair ribbon go?" She searched among her pillows, but the ribbon seemed to have vanished. "I must hurry . . . no time for breakfast. I have an appointment with Her Majesty to discuss some new designs for chamber robes."

"Lady Catherine, I swear you are the most elegant young female to grace our Court. Your taste in clothes is exquisite, your posture is perfect and your grooming is impeccable." Elizabeth delivered her compliments in a voice that sounded displeased.

Cat sank down in a reverent curtsy. "I try my best to emulate my queen in all things."

Elizabeth was flattered; her petulance dissolved. "Rise, child, you know there is no need to stand on ceremony with me."

Cat smiled sweetly. She knew just the opposite. Waiting until she was invited, Catherine sat upon a low stool at Elizabeth's side so she could elaborate on the designs she had sketched. As the queen had aged, her taste in clothing had become progressively more exaggerated and fantastic. "This chamber robe is loose, for comfort, Your Majesty; the motifs are honeysuckle and butterflies embroidered in silken thread. The material could be either cambric or fine lawn. The sleeves are quite elaborate. I've designed them with frilled cuffs at the wrist to show off your beautiful hands, madam. These are removable, of course, so they may be washed and starched. Separate trailing sleeves that cascade to the floor are attached to the bottom of the cuffs. If you raise your arms, the sleeves will appear to be fluttering, transparent wings." She held her breath as she awaited the queen's approval or rejection.

"Your design captures my essence of fragility, Mistress Spencer. I like the ethereal quality of the garments you fashion and notice you always manage to contrive that look for yourself. It also lets the world know that we are extremely fastidious."

"Your praise is too generous, Your Majesty."

"Pish! A lady thrives on praise. Show me the other sketches."

Cat went over the other chamber robes, and when Elizabeth

voiced no criticism it gave her confidence. "I took the liberty of designing a new concept for a ruff, Your Majesty. It is fan-shaped, to be worn with low-cut gowns. It stands upright to frame the back of the head, rather than encircling the neck. I thought it would show off your lovely hair, madam, to say nothing of your magnificent collection of jewels."

"I like it! I warrant the French have nothing like this. Take it along to your mother. My Mistress of the Wardrobe will know which needlewomen to trust with this intricate design."

"Thank you, Your Gracious Majesty."

Cat found her mother in the Queen's Wardrobe, where she supervised a staff of thirty seamstresses plus a dozen females who did nothing but clean and refurbish Elizabeth's lavish garments. The chambers occupied an entire upper floor of White-hall, with separate rooms for gowns, shoes, wigs and jewelry.

"I hope you didn't offend Her Majesty in any way, Catherine." Isobel could never hide the fact that the queen was the center of her universe and her daughter's well-being came a distant second.

No, Mother, I didn't fall down laughing at her flaming orange wig nor tell her that her skin is as wrinkled as an elephant's scrotum. "Her Majesty seemed delighted with my designs, and she has complete trust in your judgment to choose the right needlewomen for the job."

Isobel preened. "Did she truly say such a thing?"

"She did indeed, Mother. Her Majesty sang your praises and informed me that she could not manage without you."

In the afternoon, Cat joined her friend Arbella for a stroll that took them past the cockpit and the archery butts to Whitehall's tennis courts. The warm spring weather had brought most of the courtiers outdoors. Some of the gentlemen who were athletically inclined enjoyed playing sports and had gathered a female audience, but for the most part it was a fashion parade where secret assignations were made.

"Good afternoon, ladies." William Seymour, wearing a jaunty short cape and satin breeches, winked at Cat, then doffed his feathered hat and in doing so managed to pass Arbella a note. The two ladies kept on walking until they came to the tilt-yard, where they sat down in the empty stands.

"Is it a poem? Hal Somerset wrote one for me after the play."

"No, Cat, it isn't poetry. Will is asking me to meet him secretly one night next week . . . alone," she confided breathlessly.

"Oh, Bella, you will refuse him, of course?"

"Refuse him? I don't want to be an old maid. I'm older than
you, Cat. Someday William will be the Earl of Hertford. We are
certainly well matched, since we are both in line for the throne."

Arbella Stuart had royal blood. Her late father was the great-
grandson of King Henry VII.

"If you do meet him alone, you must be very careful to keep
it secret, Bella. The queen must never learn of it." The danger
involved stirred Cat's excitement.

"I shall need a plausible excuse to be away from Court."

Eager to help, Cat said, "I go to Richmond for two days early
next week. You can say that I have invited you to join me. It's
no lie, since I invite you this very minute."

Arbella sighed with relief. "You are such a good friend, Cat.
Your thoughtful invitation solves my dilemma."

Patrick was grateful that Hunsdon Hall would be fully
staffed with servants; it eliminated the necessity of bringing his
own. He had, however, brought a steward to buy cargo for the
return voyage. Patrick had decided on hops for the brewery and
a supply of golden Rhenish wine, favored by King James. He
knew he would make a tidy profit when he resold the wine to
Holyrood Palace.

The morning after the *Hepburn Rose* docked, the horses
were unloaded and taken to a livestock auction house near the
London docks. Robert accompanied Patrick to the sale.

"I understand you breed horses at Crichton. Did you keep
any of the mounts you took from your prisoners?" Robert
asked.

"No, I find English horses don't tolerate our harsh climate
well. I prefer wild horses that have wintered in the Lammermuirs. Each summer I go in search of a wild stallion that has his
own string of mares and bring some of the herd back to Crichton."

"One of my brothers breeds horses on our Hunsdon lands in
Hertford. Perhaps we should acquire one of your stallions for
stud. Would you like to ride up there one day?"

"I'd love to. Horses are a passion of mine. Hertford's only

twenty miles from London, isn't it?" Patrick smiled. "How the devil can you cry poor when your family owns so many properties?"

"They are all in Father's name. My brother George will be the next Lord Hunsdon. I'm the tenth child and will inherit little, apart from his royal blood, of course," he added mockingly. "You have royal blood, Lord Stewart. What's it worth these days?"

Patrick grimaced. "About the price of bat shit, I believe!"

Robert doubled over with laughter. "Well, at least horseflesh is bringing a high price today."

"The English army is in short supply of mounts because of the fighting in Ireland last year. I knew I'd get a good price. Let's celebrate tonight. Who serves the best food in London?"

"Friar's Folly: sumptuous fare, fine wine and painted ladies!"

"I assume they have gaming?"

Robert grinned. "Any games you fancy, from dice to dancing round the Maypole!"

Struggling with a large portmanteau, Lady Catherine stepped from the early-morning water barge at the Richmond landing. "No, Maggie, I can manage it myself."

"I'm sure it's no' necessary to cart baggage about, lass. Yer wardrobe at the house is already full to bursting."

"A lady can never have too many clothes, Maggie. I have also brought a dozen designs that I sketched for Philadelphia, but unfortunately she could not get away from Court this morning. Mother said she would wait and accompany her and Kate tonight."

"Humph, if Isobel can drag herself away from the queen!"

"Oh, just smell the May blossom! I vow, this is the prettiest time of the year, when all the trees come into bloom."

They took a shortcut through the gardens of Hunsdon Hall, where the lawns were carpeted with daffodils and the thrushes were busy gathering caterpillars to feed to their nestlings. "I adore birds. They have a special place in my heart."

"Ye adore every creature in nature, even the crawling, biting things that were put on earth to plague us. Ye used to think dragonflies were fairies!"

"Shakespeare often writes about Fairy Land, so it's not beyond the realm of possibility," Cat said blithely, holding the door open for Maggie. "Mmm, smells like Mrs. Dobson is baking apple tart." She removed her cloak. "I'm going straight to the kitchen to steal an apple for Jasmine."

"Ye should change yer clothes before ye ride yer palfrey. I'd best go upstairs and make sure yer mother's bed is aired. Ye know how damned fretful she can be."

Ted Dobson, the gamekeeper, had seen them arrive and came to the door. "Hello, Maggie. Will you tell Lady Spencer I have a good supply of quail for the queen? And by tomorrow I may have a crate of ruffed grouse. The woods are overrun with game at the moment."

"Thank ye, Ted. My lady asked that I remind ye." She picked up Catherine's bag and headed toward the stairs.

"Oh, no, you don't," said Cat. "You carry the apple and I'll take the bag."

"Ye're no bigger than a cricket!"

"Ah, but I make up for it with stubbornness." Cat pried Maggie's fingers from the handle and hauled the bag upstairs.

Maggie opened the wardrobe in Cat's chamber and took out her hunter green riding dress. "Now, where are yer boots?"

Cat hung the dress back in the wardrobe. "Maggie, I'm not riding. I'm just taking the apple to Jasmine and saying hello."

"But ye can't go to the stables in that pale yellow gown, lass; ye'll ruin it."

"When was the last time I ruined a gown, or even dirtied one?"

Maggie looked at the lovely picture Cat made in the delicate gown with its matching pale yellow ruff and shook her head in wonder. Even the black curls piled atop her head were held neatly in place by a yellow hair ribbon. "I give up, lass; off ye go."

Cat picked up the apple. "Rest, Maggie; it's your day off."

When she entered the stables, she walked a direct path to the box stall where her white palfrey was munching some fragrant clover hay. "Jasmine, my lovely girl. I'm so glad to see you . . . did you miss me? See what I've brought you." She held out the apple.

The small horse tossed her head and nuzzled Cat's hand before her lips picked up the apple from her palm.

She stroked her horse's neck, then threaded her fingers

through the blond mane as she murmured soft words of praise. Cat lifted her head as a strange, low noise caught her attention. It sounded like soft clucking mixed with tiny barks. She left the stall to track down the creatures that seemed to be in distress. When she came upon the wooden crate filled with gray feathers, she bent close to examine the contents. "Oh, no!" she cried in alarm as she saw the white tufts on the little game birds' heads and realized they were quail. They were packed so tightly they could move only their heads, and she realized with horror that the crate held about thirty.

Without hesitation, Catherine put a packsaddle and leading rein on Jasmine, then, struggling, with great determination, she managed to lift the crate and strap it securely onto her palfrey's back.

She was quite aware that the quail were a gift from her mother to the queen; Isobel sent them every year. Cat smiled grimly, her pretty gown forgotten. "Not this year! I am taking you back to the woods where you belong."

When Patrick Hepburn and Robert Carey arrived in Richmond, they stabled their horses and carried their luggage into Hunsdon Hall. Servants immediately came forward to take their bags. "Ah, Barlow, my guest, Lord Stewart, needs the services of a valet while he's here. Would you oblige him?"

Barlow bowed with deference. "It would be my pleasure, sir. I shall take the liberty of unpacking your garments and refurbishing your formal clothes for Court, Lord Stewart. You probably desire hot water to shave twice a day, and you must tell me if you prefer wine or whisky. If you have any special needs, do let me know."

"I would like my deerhounds to share my chamber, Barlow."

"Your dogs will be no problem, my lord."

As Hepburn and Carey made their way upstairs to the north wing, Patrick said, "I made the right decision leaving Jock Elliot in charge at Crichton. The rough devil would never fit in here."

"London servants do have a certain polish that Borderers lack."

"I think I could use some of that polish myself, Robert."

When the two men went back downstairs, a tall, slim, attractive lady, whose hair was the color of burgundy, greeted them.

"Why, Robert Carey, as I live and breathe! I had no notion you would be here in Richmond." The lady's face lit with genuine pleasure as she held out both hands to him.

"Lady Widdrington . . . Liz . . . the pleasure is all mine." He raised her hands to his lips. "Allow me to introduce my friend Patrick Hepburn, Lord Stewart."

Her lavender eyes swept him with an appraising glance. "Hepburn is an infamous name, my lord."

"I am delighted to make your acquaintance, madam." His intuition immediately told him this couple had been on intimate terms. "I assume you are the lovely lady whom Robert met in Carlisle last year?"

"And how do you know that? Are you a warlock, as rumored?"

Patrick did not deny the rumor. "I know it simply because he never stops talking about you," he said gallantly.

Liz looked inordinately pleased. "Your sister Philadelphia invited me to London. I've never been before. She's been on duty at Court all week, and she and your sister Kate can't be here until tonight. Richmond is such a delightful place . . . especially now."

Patrick waggled suggestive eyebrows at Robert. "This must be Providence . . . a heaven-sent opportunity to renew your acquaintance. Unfortunately, I have other plans. I intended to go hunting the moment I arrived. The dense woods of Richmond are reputed to teem with wild game. I'll be gone most of the day." When he saw the roses bloom in Lady Widdrington's cheeks, Patrick knew she had taken his point.

He went upstairs to change into clothes he used for hunting in Scotland. He donned leather breeks and boots and replaced his shirt with a sheepskin vest that left his arms bare. He ran his hand over his bristly chin and knew he needed a shave, but decided he would do it tonight when he returned to the hall. He strapped on a wide leather belt that held both his hunting knife and dirk.

The dogs, already excited at the prospect of a hunt in new territory, followed Patrick to the stables and waited impatiently as he resaddled Valiant. He kept them in check until they entered the forest, then almost immediately they tore off after a hare they spotted. The Scottish deerhounds were trained to take down large stags, and Patrick had high hopes of returning with venison.

Suddenly a scream rent the air. It was the unmistakable cry of a woman, and the hair on the nape of Hepburn's neck stood on end.

He tightened his reins and with his knees quickly guided his big black hunter between the trees to the clearing where the dogs had found their quarry.

"Satan! Sabbath! Heel!" One of his deerhounds had been standing with its enormous paws on the female's shoulders, and when it removed them the impact knocked her down.

Patrick was out of the saddle in a flash. He ran over to the small girl and lifted her to her feet. "Are you all right, lass?" He was about to examine her for broken bones, when she raised black-fringed lashes and stared at him in utter outrage through amber eyes flecked with shimmering gold.

Patrick's heart jumped into his throat. "Cat!"

Chapter Four

*C*atherine, who had been feeling triumphantly self-righteous as she watched the last tiny quail flutter off into the dense undergrowth, suddenly became aware of a pair of enormous, shaggy beasts rushing toward her. When one of the monsters stood on its hind legs and planted its great forepaws on her shoulders so that its huge head towered above her, she feared wolves were attacking her and a scream of terror was torn from her throat.

When a male voice, deep and authoritative, ordered the animal to heel, its heavy forepaws pushed her to the ground in its rush to obey its master's command. She instantly realized they were not wolves but massive hunting hounds, and her fear was replaced by hot fury. Then a powerful arm reached down, lifted her into the air and planted her feet on the ground with such force that it jarred her teeth together.

With utter outrage she stared at the dark giant whose sheer size overshadowed everything in his presence, including her—especially her! The uncivilized brute not only had the audacity to speak to her; the lout had actually called her *Cat*!

She recoiled in horror, her gorge rising at the thought that he had actually touched her. "How dare you speak my name?" Her breasts rose and fell in indignant agitation. His dark visage was so threatening that she took a step backward and held her pale yellow skirts away from him so that his loathsome presence would not contaminate her. The baseborn creature was garbed in leather and wore a filthy sheepskin that branded him a primitive savage. She had never encountered such a coarse, unsavory barbarian in her entire life. He was completely different from all the other men of her acquaintance. He was oversized, overbold and overbearing. "You are trespassing, you uncivilized lout. These woods are the private property of the Spencers and Careys. You had best leave at once before I call the game-keeper and have you arrested." The wild-looking devil was gawking at her clothes as if he had never seen a lady in a fine gown before. "How does a violent ruffian such as you know my name?" she demanded.

Patrick's black eyes narrowed as he assessed the delicate fe-male who stood before him. He had known she would be ex-quisite, but she was far smaller than he had expected and vain beyond belief. She thought her ethereal beauty made her so spe-cial that the opposite sex should fawn upon her and grovel at her dainty feet. "I know far more about you than your name, wench."

"Wench?" she cried in outrage. "You will address me as Lady Catherine, you rude, repulsive brute." Her glance traveled from the bulging muscles of his bare arms to his unshaven jaw, and she shuddered at his unkempt appearance.

"I will address you as *Hellcat,* you spoiled little bitch!"

"Spoiled?"

"Spoiled, selfish and brainless to boot," he added with relish.

"*Brainless?*" she gasped, offended to her core.

"Only an imbecile would wear a gossamer gown and ruff into the woods. You care naught for the man who provided the money for it, and even less for the poor drudge who must clean and repair it."

"You offensive swine! You are so ignorant you do not real-ize you owe me an abject apology for the attack of your wolfhound."

"Wolfhound? These happen to be Scottish deerhounds, the finest, most prized hunting dogs on earth, *Hellcat!*"

"You're a Scot," she said with loathing. "That explains everything. I have been told what uncouth, uncivilized brutes Scots *men* are. You and your savage beasts had better begone before you are arrested for trespassing in these private woods."

Without another word, Patrick Hepburn picked her up and set her down upon her white horse, clenching his jaw in anger when he saw her recoil at his touch. "You are the one who is leaving. Get the hell home where you belong before I tan your arse." He slapped her palfrey's rump and watched with satis-faction as the dainty little horse kicked up its heels and fled.

He stood staring after her long after she had gone, his dark brows drawn together in consternation. Then, all at once, he threw back his head and his laughter came rolling out in a torrent of pure male glee. He had finally met the female of his visions. Her name was Cat and that was the reason she'd had the saucy creature tattooed on her bottom. "Before I'm done with you, little Hellcat, I intend to tame you. The day will come when you won't disdain my touch. You'll purr when I stroke you," he vowed.

Robert Carey silently blessed Patrick Hepburn for his omniscience in leaving him alone with the divine widow. He would never have a better opportunity than this to begin an overture. A year ago in Carlisle, he had managed a few furtive fumbles in various alcoves, but the place had been overrun with northern troops who patrolled the Borders, and the degree of privacy necessary for complete intimacy had been nonexistent.

"My sister Philadelphia must have a crystal ball. Until a week ago I had no notion that I would be coming south."

Liz laughed. "Philadelphia is a determined matchmaker, and she did promise I'd have my pick of potential husbands if I came to Court, but I assure you, Robert, she did not have you in mind."

"Then Providence has sent me so you don't make a drastic mistake." He closed the distance between them and slipped an arm around her. "Welcome to Richmond, Liz. Let me give you a tour of Hunsdon Hall." With a firm hand at her back he guided her to the main staircase, determined to begin their exploration upstairs.

Liz did not demur; rather, she aided and abetted Robert's plan. "You are just the man I need. Would you help me with something?"

As she entered her chamber and walked to the window, she glanced back over her shoulder, using the age-old gesture to lure a man to his destiny. She placed her hands on the window sash. "It seems to be stuck. I cannot open it."

Robert's arms came around her and he covered her hands with his. His lips brushed against her ear. "Some things are better done in tandem," he whispered suggestively. The sash lifted with ease. His arms closed about her waist and he pulled her back against his hard length.

Liz turned about in his arms and lifted her mouth for his kiss.

Once his lips took possession of hers, his tongue began its dalliance, teasing, tempting and luring her into a giving mood. Liz soon became breathless with desire, and Robert's body was aroused long before he began to undress her. Excitement built in both of them as their garments came off. By the time he lifted her to the bed he was rampant with need. As he knelt above her on the bed her lavender eyes widened in surprise. "You are already rigid."

Her words brought home to him the knowledge that she had been married to a much older man, and it suddenly occurred to him that though she was a widow, Liz might not be as sexually experienced as he had assumed. "Yes, but there's no hurry, sweetheart, if you are not fully aroused yet."

Liz blushed. "No, no, Robert, there is no need to wait."

He straddled her and then swept his hand down her slim body, caressing her breasts, her belly and her soft thighs. Before he entered her, his fingertips slid into her cleft to make sure she was dewy moist. Robert rose up above her, separated the burgundy curls on her mons with his thumb and forefinger, then plunged down with a heartfelt moan of pleasure. It had been a long time since he'd savored a beautiful woman, and Robert set a slow, rhythmic pace to draw out the mating, rather than gallop to the goal.

"I'm sorry, Robert." Her whisper was so low, he wondered if he had imagined it.

"Sorry?" He hadn't the vaguest notion what she meant.

"You are having difficulty . . . you cannot spend," she said softly.

"Sweetheart, of course I can spend. I want to wait for you."

There was a long silence, while he scythed in and out, then finally Liz whispered, "I don't know what you mean."

He brushed his lips across her brow, then looked into her eyes. "I want to bring you to climax first—then I'll spend."

She gazed up at him. "Women don't spend, Robert."

He stopped, mid-stroke, and stared down at her in disbelief.

"Oh dear," she murmured, realizing her ignorance. "I'm afraid I don't know how."

He gathered her close with a little shout of joy. "My darling, Liz, it will give me the greatest pleasure to teach you how." He withdrew gently and crossed the room to lock the door. When he returned, he climbed on the mattress and reached high to pull the curtains of the bed closed. He slipped down beside her. "First we shut out the whole world. Intimacy demands complete privacy, and we are going to become extremely intimate before we leave this bed, my love."

Robert drew back the covers so that he could make love to her with his eyes. His gaze moved slowly from her lashes to her lips, along the column of her throat, then down across the swells and hollows of her lovely breasts. He slowly licked his lips and smiled with delight as her nipples became ruched. He blew on them and watched them tighten into rosebuds, then he blew on her navel and the burgundy curls upon her high mons. He hadn't even touched her, yet he knew her body was starting to respond.

When he finally touched her with his hand, she arched up from the bed. He cupped her mons with his palm and began to describe the things he was going to do to her; then he told her how it would make her feel. "You have a little bud at the top of your cleft. When I encircle it and stroke your bud, it will engorge with blood and make you feel hot. If you let me continue you will become wet and lubricated. If I keep up the pressure of my fingertips and increase the speed, your pleasure will build in its intensity to a little climax, and your bud will open like a flower. Now bend your knees a little and open your thighs. That's it! Are you ready, sweetheart?"

She licked her lips nervously. "Yes, please."

As the pressure of his fingertips continued, she became fever hot and wasn't sure she could bear the intense sensitivity, but then, as he'd promised, she became moist, then slick, and she began to writhe with pleasure. When the little climax burst, she came up off the bed and clung to him. "Robert! Robert!"

He held her tightly and rubbed her back until she relaxed. With his lips against her ear he murmured, "Now I'm going to pleasure you again with my finger up inside your sheath. Each time I draw it out I stroke your bud until it finally explodes."

Liz was panting with excitement. "You don't mind teaching me?"

"Mind? I think I've died and gone to heaven. Now, open for me."

Once Catherine was safely back in the stables she realized that the only sin the massive deerhound had been guilty of was overfriendliness. The unsavory, uncivilized giant in charge of the dogs was another matter entirely. His overt maleness suddenly made her afraid as she realized she could have been in grave peril. *How did such a brute know I was called Cat? And when I challenged him, he said he knew far more about me than my name!* She could not report him to Dobson, because she had released the gamekeeper's quail, but she certainly intended to alert the male servants at Hunsdon Hall that there was a vile, dangerous devil lurking in the woods and warn them he was armed with vicious-looking weapons.

Cat hurried inside to seek out Maggie. "You were right. I should never have gone into the woods alone today. There was a vile poacher who laid hands on me. He was at least seven feet of brute strength. I know he was uncivilized because he was a *Scot!*"

"Ye had me going fer a minute, lass, but there's no need to make up stories about how ye got yer dress torn."

"His deerhound did that. *Satan,* I believe he called it!"

Maggie studied her for a minute. "The devil did it? And I suppose the devil spirited off the crate of quail that Dobson managed to snare?"

"No, I was the one who did that, Maggie. The poor little birds were suffocating to death. He wore a sheepskin!"

"The devil? I warrant that's because he was a Scots devil."

"You're not taking me seriously," Cat accused. "You don't even believe me!"

"Oh, I believe ye; thousands wouldn't. Better remove the dress so I can repair it, and I recommend a bath while you're at it, if ye intend to dine with the ladies at Hunsdon Hall tonight."

Catherine overcame her frustration by assuring herself that the odious brute was probably miles away by now. She polished off a dish of apple tart, and then took her bath. She refused to allow the disturbing encounter to ruin her visit to Richmond, and as she soaked in the scented water, her apprehension began to dissolve.

An hour later the incident was almost forgotten as Catherine surveyed a dozen sketches of fashionable gowns she had designed. She couldn't decide which creations Philadelphia would like best, so decided to let her make her own selection. As she absently gathered the sketches from the floor and slipped them into a leather case, her thoughts had already moved on to what she would wear this evening.

She opened her wardrobe and pushed aside all the white dresses. Being away from Court gave her the opportunity to wear more daring colors. Cat had a keen fashion sense, however, and knew what styles and colors flattered her and gave her the ethereal look that set her apart from the other young ladies who attended the queen.

She decided to wear the lilac velvet whose sleeves were slashed to show cream satin under-sleeves. Its low-cut bodice and stomacher that came to a point were decorated with tiny seed pearls, and Cat knew that somewhere she had a ruff that was edged with the same cream-colored beads. Outside the front door there was a lilac bush that was just coming into bloom. She cut two small bunches and put them in water. By the time she was ready to fasten them into her hair, the lilac blossoms would be open.

When Catherine heard her mother arrive, she went downstairs. "Mother, I'm so glad you decided to come. Time away from your demanding Court duties will do you good."

"I consider them an honor, not a duty, Catherine." Her mouth tightened. "Your gown is far too low-cut for a maiden. I do not approve. Don't let me catch you wearing it at Court."

"Of course not, Mother." *I wouldn't dream of letting you catch me wearing it.* "Did you all come down together?"

"Yes, apparently Philadelphia is entertaining a guest from Carlisle. Lady Widdrington is a widow visiting London for the first time. Poor soul! I know what it's like to be widowed. We must do our best to dispel her loneliness and make her welcome."

Cat spotted Maggie and sent her a desperate signal.

With uncanny Scots intuition, Maggie discerned her dilemma. She greeted Lady Spencer and drew her toward the kitchen. "Come and see what Cook has baked. Perhaps ye could take some to Hunsdon Hall tonight."

As soon as the kitchen door closed, Catherine ran upstairs to get her sketches. She would have to smuggle them next door. If her mother saw them, she would forbid her from designing for Philadelphia because it might displease the queen.

•   •   •

The first person Catherine encountered at Hunsdon Hall was Beth Spencer, her father's plump, blond sister, who was married to George Carey. "Hello, Aunt Beth."

"Catherine, don't you dare call me *aunt;* it makes me sound positively ancient!"

Cat dimpled. "Sorry, Beth; it was Mother's idea."

Beth rolled her eyes. "She has more rules and regulations than the queen herself. I shall have a word with her."

"Cat, darling, you look exquisite as usual." Philadelphia kissed her cheek. "I warrant this is one of your own designs."

"Yes, it is. I've brought you a dozen sketches. You can decide for yourself which you like."

"How lovely. Let me introduce you to my friend Liz Widdrington. Liz, this is Lady Catherine, who has designed some of the queen's most spectacular gowns."

"I'm delighted to meet you, Liz. Please call me Cat. You have such beautiful hair. I've never seen that unusual shade before."

"Why, thank you. I like to think of it as burgundy. I have to be careful about the colors I wear, so they don't clash."

"It's evident you have a keen fashion sense and know exactly what suits you. Your jade velvet truly compliments your hair."

"I am surrounded by beautiful ladies."

Cat spun toward the familiar voice. "Robert! I had no idea you would be here. You look so . . . rugged. Patrolling the Borders has given you a tan. You have quite lost your fashionable courtier's pallor."

"Thank God for that. At the English Court you can hardly tell the males from the females."

"Oh, I think you underestimate our little Cat. I've taught her an infallible way to tell the males from the females, as well as the men from the boys." Philadelphia's laugh was most suggestive.

Robert kissed her cheek. "I think your bawdy sense of humor is the reason you are my favorite sister."

"Ah, so Philadelphia is your favorite, is she?" Kate swept in and playfully boxed her brother Robert's ear.

"My favorite sister, after *you,* Kate!" Robert said, laughing.

Cat looked at them all fondly. She always felt extremely happy when she was in the midst of this warm, loving family.

"Ah, here comes my guest now," Robert announced. "I won't tell you who he is—I want you to guess."

Cat's head snapped up and her mouth fell open as a tall figure stepped into the room. He was bathed and shaved, and a fine linen shirt had replaced the sheepskin, but the uncivilized brute male was still evident beneath the thin veneer of respectability.

Every head in the room was turned toward him in undisguised admiration. Philadelphia held out her hands to him. "It's as if the legendary Earl of Bothwell himself were standing before us."

Cat watched in amazement as the dark devil took Philadelphia's hands and gallantly kissed them. "My father could never deny my paternity, I'm afraid. You must be Lady Scrope. Though I've not had the pleasure of meeting you before, I've had dealings with your husband on many occasions."

"My condolences, Lord Stewart!"

"Your droll wit is exceeded only by your beauty, my lady. I would be honored if you would address me as Patrick."

"This is my sister Kate Howard, Countess of Nottingham, though we don't hold that against her."

Kate placed her hands in his. "Welcome to London, Patrick. I must confess that when we were girls, my sister and I were both madly in love with your father. When he visited the English Court as Admiral of Scotland we sighed over him, and then we dreamed of him for months after he left."

"He's an earl's son?" Cat asked Liz in disbelief.

Robert introduced his brother's wife. "Allow me to present Lady Carey, who is more like a sister than a sister-in-law."

Cat's plump aunt turned kittenish when Patrick kissed her fingers. "Please call me Beth, your lordship."

"You met Liz Widdrington this morning, Patrick," Robert continued, "so let me introduce—"

"The gamekeeper's child. We met in the woods." Patrick's black eyes flicked over Catherine with scant interest, but he gave Robert a broad wink to show that he was jesting.

Cat was stunned. With his first three words he had managed to insult her twice. To add injury to his insults, he had made everyone laugh at her. She suddenly realized that he was paying her back for the insults she had heaped upon him this morning.

Robert took her hand and drew her forward. "The most exquisite gamekeeper's child in Richmond, Catherine Seton Spencer."

Patrick nodded politely but deliberately placed his hands behind his back, refusing to touch her. Though he immediately turned away from her and gave his attention to the other ladies, Cat consumed his thoughts. *Catherine Seton Spencer! No wonder my first vision of her came while I was at Seton. She's the Earl of Winton's granddaughter, and heiress to his lands. Splendor of God, Destiny has taken you by the hand today, Hepburn! And didn't Robert mention a niece who'd inherited Spencer lands in Hertford? 'Tis a match made in heaven.* Patrick grinned as he felt the beauty's eyes furiously boring a hole in his back. *Or perhaps a match made in hell. Either way, I have no complaints!*

Catherine linked her arm through Robert's and drew him aside. "His father may have been an earl and an admiral, but your friend is unrefined, uncouth and uncivilized."

"As a matter of fact, he is better educated than most gentlemen of the English Court. He attended the universities of Edinburgh, Cambridge and Rome."

"Ah, is that what makes him so damned arrogant?"

"No, I believe that comes from confidence in his own ability, coupled with his royal blood. And I'd far rather have him as my friend than my enemy, Catherine."

Cat shuddered. "Well, I'd rather have him in Scotland."

Robert grinned at her vehemence. "Most ladies find him irresistible."

"Thank God I'm not a lady!"

"Speaking of ladies, what do you think of Liz?"

"I think she's extremely attractive."

"Well, she certainly attracts me."

"Then go and put your brand on her before the *irresistible* Lord Stewart stakes his claim."

"If I didn't know better, I'd say you were obsessed with him."

Once he left her side, Cat felt a little forlorn. She watched from afar as the attractive widow welcomed Robert's solicitude, while the other three ladies in the room basked in the attention of the dark, devilish Scot. She was used to being the center of attraction when she visited Hunsdon Hall. Tonight, however, she felt almost invisible. Cat was actually relieved when her mother arrived, but Isobel too ignored her and joined the circle of ladies clustered about the loutish lord from Scotland.

She saw her case of sketches lying forgotten on a table and decided to whisk it up to Philadelphia's bedchamber before her mother's eagle eye spotted it. She managed to slip from the room unnoticed but could not resist the impulse to crash the door closed after her.

Patrick smiled with satisfaction. *My strategy is working. The little hellcat just slammed the door to get my attention!*

Chapter Five

$\mathcal{F}$or Catherine, dinner was an exercise in frustration as the two male guests received the lion's share of attention. Kate directed the servants to proffer the dishes to Patrick and Robert before serving the ladies. Cat had a dainty appetite and was astonished at the amount of food the Scot consumed. All at the table were having a marvelous time eating, laughing and conversing—all except Cat, who sat in silence, making no effort to hide her dislike and disapproval. Unfortunately, no one seemed to notice.

Philadelphia invited their guests to attend the Court masque on Saturday evening but made no mention of the fact that Cat had designed many of the costumes and was to play the role of the Moon Goddess, Cynthia. The impulsive need to say something outrageous suddenly overwhelmed her. Cat drained her wine glass and narrowed her eyes to slits. "Lord Stewart, I hope you are aware that sheepskins are inappropriate attire at Queen Elizabeth's Court?"

A hush descended and all heads turned toward her.

"Lady Catherine, I regret that my sheepskin offended you when we met in the woods this morning." The heads swiveled toward him.

"It was not the sheepskin that offended me," Cat said sweetly. "It was the wolf in sheep's clothing. Did you have a successful hunt, my lord?" All present awaited the answer.

"I sighted my quarry, but instead of moving in for the kill I deliberately allowed it to escape. The undersized doe was so afraid, she presented no challenge to a seasoned hunter."

Undersized, am I, you insulting lout? "I quite agree it would be more sporting to pick on something your own size. Trouble is, you are unnaturally large. Perhaps not quite a giant, but I would certainly describe you as a *bruising brute.*"

Kate interrupted before Cat decided to scratch his eyes out. "Why don't we go into the other room for an after-dinner drink? I believe we have some fine Scotch whisky."

The men got to their feet and allowed the ladies to lead the way. Catherine swept past Patrick with her chin in the air.

"Hellcat." He spoke softly so only she could hear.

"Hellhound!" she retaliated, loud enough for all to hear.

Isobel Spencer was incensed at her daughter's show of bad manners. She gripped Cat's arm and squeezed cruelly. "You will make your excuses and leave immediately," she hissed.

Cat blushed warmly and cursed her impulsive tongue. As the drinks were being poured, she said, "No more wine for me, thank you. I shall bid you all good night, if you will excuse me."

"Of course, darling." Philadelphia gave her a speculative look. "We shall see you tomorrow."

"Sweet dreams, Lady Catherine," Patrick said softly.

She looked across the room. Their eyes met and held for a moment. His were challenging; hers were defiant. *Go to hell, Lord Bloody Stewart!*

Hours later, Patrick stood at his window staring across at the house next door, absently fingering a length of white satin ribbon. His senses were still saturated by the scent of the lilac she had worn in her hair. Catherine Spencer rejected everything about him: his size, his looks, his clothes, his manners, his personality and his nationality—especially his nationality. How ironic that he found everything about her utterly irresistible: her size, her beauty, her clothes, her impulsiveness, her reckless courage and her inheritance—especially her inheritance. His mouth curved in a rare smile. *She is the challenge of a lifetime!*

In spite of her fastidious aversion to him, Patrick had complete confidence in his ability to make her his wife. It made little difference to him that she would be unwilling. He was much closer in his quest than he had been a week ago, for now he had met and marked his prey. All he had to do was lure her to his bait and capture her unaware. The taming could come later.

"Sweet dreams, Lady Catherine," Patrick said softly.

• • •

Cat hovered on the edge of sleep. Nothing had gone as she had expected tonight. That was the fault of the intruder, of course. It had been a great shock to see him at Hunsdon Hall and jolting to learn that he was the son of the *Devil Earl,* as the infamous outlaw Bothwell was called. She was amazed that Robert counted him a friend. If he wasn't careful, the devious swine would pluck the lovely widow from under his very nose and devour her.

When she was sent home, Cat had intended to catalog her grievances to a sympathetic Maggie so that she could pour soothing balm on her wounds, but her champion had been abed and Cat's conscience wouldn't allow her to disturb her old nurse.

Upstairs, she had kicked off her shoes, then leaned on the windowsill and gazed down into the darkened gardens. Already she regretted her impulsive tongue, which had banned her from being with the people she loved best. It would have been far better if she had smiled sweetly and ignored Patrick Hepburn. Her brows drew together. *How the hell do you ignore a seven-foot barbarian?*

In spite of her dejected mood, she had carefully hung her gown in the wardrobe. It was one of her favorites and there would be little satisfaction venting her spleen on the delicate creation. Cat had put on her nightgown and crawled into bed determined that tomorrow she would be on her best behavior, no matter the provocation, and tonight she would indeed have sweet dreams!

As Cat hovered on the edge of sleep, she heard a faint scratching at her bedchamber door.

When she investigated, she saw that it was the Scottish deerhound that had been exuberantly overfriendly with her in the woods. She went down on her knees and slipped her arms around its dark, shaggy neck, delighted to have company that found no fault with her. "Oh, you are such a dear, sweet boy. You have come to make me feel better!"

The huge animal gave a sympathetic whine.

Cat sat back on her heels. "Sabbath, is that your name?"

The dog sat back and looked at her expectantly.

"I've always wanted a dog, but Mother would never permit it."

The hairy hound got to its feet, began to leave, then changed its mind and came back, as if refusing to go without her.

Needing no words to communicate, Cat followed it.

At first the garden seemed so dark that she placed her hand on the tall deerhound's back and followed it trustingly. The perfume of the night-scented flowers drenched the spring air, and as she breathed in deeply she became light-headed, almost intoxicated by the smell. She heard the sweet musical notes of a nightingale, which seemed to transform the garden into an enchanted, magical, otherworldly place. At first, she only felt his presence. Then, as her eyes adjusted to the indigo shadows, she saw his tall, dark shape beneath the copper beech. "Sabbath brought me to you."

"Satan brought you." His voice was deep, mesmerizing.

"It is said that Satan always supports the Scots."

"That is a legend."

"I believe in legends and so do you, Lord Stewart." She stepped closer and gazed up at him. "You keep your hands behind your back so you won't be tempted to touch me."

"If I touch you, the dream will dissolve."

"Then may I touch you?"

"It is your dream, your choice . . . you are free to do anything."

"I've never seen anyone like you before."

"I know. Therein lies the fascination."

Her glance slid over his wide, muscled shoulders. "Are you aware that sheepskins are inappropriate attire?"

"If it offends you, Lady Catherine, you are free to remove it."

The impulse to touch him became too strong for her to resist. With reckless daring she went up on tiptoe to push the sheepskin vest aside to reveal his naked chest. She watched enthralled as the primitive garment slid down his arms and fell to the grass of its own volition. Then she remembered that it was her dream and that she could make anything happen. The realization sent a shiver of excitement slithering down her spine.

She reached up and allowed her fingertips to rest on the great slabs of muscle that covered his upper torso, then she traced their outline, slowly drawing her fingers down across his ribcage. "Your body is hard and smooth as marble."

"You have no idea, Hellcat."

She laughed up into his dark face. "Why do you call me that?"

"Because it is a perfect fit."

She licked her lips. "We are not a perfect fit, however. My ear only reaches your heart." Impulsively she pressed her ear against his chest and felt the slow, steady, powerful beat within.

She rubbed her cheek against his firm flesh and breathed deeply. "Mmm, you smell of leather." She became aware that her own heart was racing wildly, and suddenly she stepped back from him. "If this is my dream and I am in charge, why have I no control over my own heartbeat? Mine races while yours is slow and steady. That tells me you are the one in control, Lord Bloody Stewart—in control of yourself and in control of me, you dominant devil!"

"That's the way it should be between a man and a woman, Cat. That is the way it will always be between you and me."

"There is no you and me, Hepburn. There will never be anything between us other than hostility and hatred."

"You are quite wrong. There is already defiance and desire."

Cat's fury exploded. Impulsively, she stood on tiptoe and raked her nails down his cheek, then took to her heels and fled.

In the morning, when she awoke, the details of her strange dream were still with her. She was thoroughly disgusted with herself. How could she possibly have been attracted to him, even in a dream? The very idea repulsed her. He was the most odious, loathsome male she had ever met, and she vowed to avoid the vile devil like the plague.

Since she had little desire to visit Hunsdon Hall today, she decided to go riding. Both she and Jasmine would benefit from a good gallop. She put on the hunter green riding dress and a starched white ruff. She twisted her hair into a French knot and secured it with ivory pins and pale green ribbon. She couldn't understand why Maggie had allowed her to sleep late. She usually drew back her curtains at the first light of day, then helped her to dress.

As soon as Cat opened her bedchamber door, the tantalizing aroma of fresh-baked scones met her nostrils. *It's May . . . perhaps the strawberries are ripe.* She ran lightly down the stairs, found the dining room empty, so followed her nose to the kitchen. She swung open the door and stopped dead on the threshold. Patrick Hepburn was holding court before Mrs. Dobson and Maggie.

"Oh, yer lordship, ye make me so homesick for Seton."

"Perhaps I'll smuggle you aboard and make off with you, Maggie."

"Damnation!"

The exclamation made Patrick turn to look at her, and she suddenly went icy cold as she stared at the scratch on his cheek.

His eyes were amused as he touched his face. "Just a cat scratch. No permanent damage."

"Too bad! A scar might improve your looks."

Sheathe your claws, Hellcat.

Catherine stared at him in horror. She had heard his thoughts as clearly as if he had shouted the words. *Dear God, can he read my thoughts? Am I still caught fast in my dream?*

She realized immediately that she was awake and chided herself for being fanciful. Nevertheless, she could not dispel the strange sensation that she was caught fast in something ephemeral, like the gossamer silk threads of a cobweb.

"I can see that I disturb Lady Catherine, so I'll be off."

"Please don't delude yourself," she said sweetly.

"Thank you for the hares, Lord Stewart." Cook bobbed a curtsy.

"It was my pleasure, madam. My deerhounds are forever on the prowl for game. Just last night they brought me a rare bird—"

"Good day, Lord Stewart." Their eyes met in a challenge of wills, and again she heard his thought: *I don't dismiss so easily!*

He left through the kitchen door, as familiar with the house as if he had always lived there.

Maggie gave Catherine a long look of speculation. "Now, there's a *real* man for ye."

"Not for me, thank you. At last I realize why Mother married an Englishman." Cat gave a delicate shudder and changed the subject. "Is it my imagination, or do I smell strawberries?"

"It's no' yer imagination. We had a huge basketful, but the wee laddie polished them all off," Maggie said fondly.

"Wee laddie? He's a bloody giant! How could you give him all our strawberries?" She recalled his gargantuan appetite from last night. "Never mind; I'll have one of your lovely scones instead."

"A chance is a good thing." Maggie and Mrs. Dobson exchanged a merry glance and went off into peals of laughter. "I suppose we couldn't resist mothering him."

"I have a similar urge. I can hardly resist smothering him!" Cat settled for bread and honey. "Thank heaven he is back from hunting. The woods will be safe once more."

Before she made her way to the stables, her glance traveled over Hunsdon's lovely garden. She blushed as her eyes rested on the copper beech tree. *That's where I behaved so wantonly.* She assured herself that it had only been a dream. *What about the scratch?* her inner voice persisted. *A coincidence,* she concluded.

Cat decided that she would ride through the woods to a glade where bluebells grew in great profusion. The scent of the wild hyacinths coupled with their vivid color had drawn her every May since childhood. Once upon a time she hadn't been able to resist picking handfuls of the lovely blooms with the sticky stalks, but as she grew older she realized it was better to leave them growing so they would reproduce and be there forever.

As Cat rode through the trees she talked to Jasmine, her white palfrey, as if the animal could understand her. She praised her and patted her neck, never doubting that the little horse knew she was loved. "I shall tether you to a tree before we get to the glade, Jasmine. You might be tempted to nibble the bluebells and I fear they may be poisonous."

Cat dismounted and tied her reins to a young oak. She could see the heavenly color of the glade through the trees and breathed in the heady fragrance with appreciation. As she approached the sunny clearing she saw someone, and when she got closer, Cat realized that it was Robert Carey. She opened her mouth to call out his name but stopped as she realized that he was not alone. Robert was talking with someone she could not see. She concealed herself behind some mulberry bushes in case his companion was Patrick Hepburn. If it was, Cat intended to withdraw quietly before they spotted her. She watched Robert sink to his knees.

Then she saw a head emerge from the sea of bluebells and the distinctive burgundy-colored hair told her it was Liz Widdrington.

"I couldn't wait to have you beneath me again."

Cat not only heard Robert's words clearly, she heard their underlying intensity and knew immediately that this was a romantic tryst. She was both shocked and fascinated, for though she had a vivid imagination, she had little experience in sexual matters between men and women.

Cat was well aware that she should not be here watching and listening to such a private and intimate interlude, but if she moved they would undoubtedly hear her as clearly as she could hear them. On the other hand, if she remained perfectly still, though, it was unlikely they would see her, since her hunter green riding habit blended with her surroundings.

"It feels deliciously wicked making love outdoors," Liz said.

"I'll make you feel wicked before I'm done, sweetheart."

"Undress me, Robert; I want to lie naked in the flowers."

How flagrantly reckless she is! Cat wondered if this was what being in love did to a woman and she suddenly envied her. She heard Liz's abandoned laugh and realized how irresistible it must be to a man. *She's a widow. Robert isn't the first man with whom she's lain.* Once again Cat felt envious.

"Open for me, that's a good girl. Now wrap your legs high about my back."

Cat's eyes widened as she watched two long, slim limbs arise from the carpet of bluebells and Robert sink down between them. *She isn't a good girl at all; she's decidedly bad, and he can't get enough of her!*

If their conversation had been prurient before, the noises they now made were positively erotic. Cat blushed hotly, and suddenly she became aware of the feel of her undergarments brushing against her breasts and her thighs.

"That's it, stay with me, sweetheart," Robert gasped as their gyrations became almost frenzied.

Liz's cries reached a crescendo and were followed by a long moan of pleasure.

Cat found that she was almost panting. *They copulated before my very eyes!* All was now quiet, as the couple lay spent. Cat wondered if she could make her escape without being detected. Then she heard Robert's voice. "Will you marry me, Liz?"

Liz's voice was languorous. "Darling, I thought you'd never ask."

Cat felt her insides begin to melt. *Ahh, he proposed and she accepted. What a lovely bride Liz will make.* She sighed, thinking how romantic it had been to make love in a glade of bluebells. Quietly, she withdrew from the mulberry bushes and with great care made her way back to Jasmine.

As she rode home she realized that though she had been shocked initially, she had received a valuable education this morning. One thing she had learned was that both male and female gave and received pleasure when they mated. The idea thrilled her.

When she returned, she took Jasmine to the Hunsdon stables and asked one of the grooms if he would put her in their outdoor paddock for the rest of the day. She went home to change her clothes. The day had turned almost sultry and she definitely needed something cooler than velvet. Her cheeks felt flushed, but that might not be from the weather alone, she decided.

Cat chose a cambric dress in a shade of peach. Embroidered brown silk pansies with amber beads at their centers were scattered upon its bodice and sleeves. She took down her hair and brushed it, then tied a peach satin ribbon about her head to keep her abundant tresses from her face but allow dark curls to cascade down her back. She critically surveyed her appearance in the long mirror and decided she looked far too young with her hair down, but before she had a chance to change it, she glanced through her window and saw Arbella Stuart walking up from the river. Cat hurried outside to meet her on the path.

"Bella, I know I invited you, but I never expected that you would actually come to Richmond. Is everything all right?"

"Everything is marvelous." Arbella was breathless with excitement. "I couldn't wait to talk and thought it best to come up-river so we could be seen returning to Whitehall together."

Cat took her small bag. "That is probably wise. Appearances are everything with so many spies about the Court."

When Catherine walked in with Arbella, Isobel and Maggie looked up in surprise, so Cat quickly explained. "I invited Bella to Richmond to spend the day with me. I'm so sorry I forgot to mention it."

"Lady Arbella is welcome here anytime," Isobel said graciously. "How is your dear grandmother?"

"She is very well, thank you, Lady Spencer."

"Catherine, you must take Arbella next door to meet the

other visitors. We are invited to an early supper before we go back downriver tonight. Lady Scrope has a widowed friend from Carlisle staying at the hall, and Philadelphia's brother Robert Carey is here too. His guest, Lord Stewart, is a distant relative of yours, I believe."

"Patrick Hepburn is related to you?" Cat asked, surprised.

"I suppose he must be." Bella drew her brows together. "Lord Stewart is related to King James and, of course, my father and the king's father were brothers. I would love to meet him."

"I doubt that," Cat said dryly.

Isobel immediately pounced on her daughter. "I will not tolerate another display of yesterday's appalling manners, young madam! Lord Stewart and I had a delightful conversation when we met. He was gracious enough to bring me a message from my dear father, Gordon Seton, whom I haven't seen in over twenty years."

Maggie interjected, "Lord Stewart told yer mother how much ye reminded him of yer grandfather, Geordie!"

"But my grandfather is a Scot. How could I be like him?"

"I remember Father being an extremely handsome man with jet-black hair, the exact same shade as yours. Though he was willful as the devil himself," Isobel added.

"Come to think of it, the resemblance is uncanny," Maggie said with a straight face.

"Then have no fear. I shall conduct myself with the gracious manners I have inherited from my grandfather, the Earl of Winton."

Cat's smile was serene. She knew she'd had the last word in that little encounter. She took Bella upstairs and put her in the bedchamber next to her own. "I thought we'd never get away from them. I'm bursting to learn what happened to you last night."

"Well, I'm not sure I should divulge such intimate—"

"Shh!" Cat put her finger to her lips. "Walls have ears," she whispered. "Let's go out into the garden where none can overhear."

They found an ideal spot on one of the wooden garden benches beside the fishpond, where orange and black carp glided to the surface to catch insects. "Tell me everything," Cat implored.

•   •   •

Since Robert had left Patrick to his own devices while he dallied with the wealthy widow, the Scot took refuge from the household of females in Hunsdon Hall's library. He scanned the bookshelves and thumbed through pharmacopoeias of herbal remedies, books of poetry and texts of astrology. There were some plays, prayer books and histories. He opened a history volume and found a genealogical table for the Carey family showing they were descended from Mary Boleyn. Someone had scratched out her husband's name, William Carey, and replaced it with Henry Tudor. Patrick chuckled. *All ten Carey offspring are proud that their father, Lord Hunsdon, is a bastard of the late King Henry!*

Suddenly, his brows furrowed as he noticed that the year of Hunsdon's death was listed after his name. The year was 1602, which was this present year. When he looked again the date had disappeared and the space was blank. Patrick realized he had experienced a premonition that Hunsdon would die sometime this year. Robert's brother George would become the new Lord Hunsdon, and his plump blond wife, Beth, who was here at the hall, would become Lady Hunsdon before the year was over. He closed the volume with a snap and wondered if he should share the knowledge with Robert or keep it to himself. Patrick knew that death had its own foreshadowing and wondered if he would have as much luck portending when Elizabeth would depart this vale of tears.

Patrick glanced through the French doors of the library that opened onto the garden and was mesmerized by what he saw. The beauteous Catherine, wearing yet another exquisite creation, was sitting by the fishpond. She was having an animated discourse with another young woman he did not know. More to learn who Cat's friend was than to eavesdrop on their conversation, he listened in to their voices.

"No, we didn't dare meet at his family's London mansion. He took me to the gatehouse instead."

"Oh, Bella, I hope no one saw you."

"Only a couple of servants, and Will swore them to secrecy."

"Arbella, you know how servants gossip!"

That must be Arbella Stuart, Patrick realized. *She looks years older than Catherine, but Cat looks far younger than she really is.*

"How long did you stay?"

"All night, of course."

"Bella, you didn't sleep with him?" Cat sounded dismayed.

"We didn't do much sleeping," Arbella said smugly.

She was playing the whore with someone called Will. Patrick had no interest in Arbella's morals, only Catherine's.

"Did Will make love to you, Bella?" Cat was breathless.

For answer, Arbella gave her a self-satisfied smile.

Cat sighed, remembering the lovemaking she'd witnessed earlier in the day. "Then he asked you to marry him!"

Bella's smile vanished. "No! But I feel sure he will, very soon. Perhaps next time."

Patrick chuckled at his little hellcat's naivety.

"You will have to elope. Do you think Will Seymour will agree to a secret wedding?"

Splendor of God! The two devious little bitches are dabbling in something that could get them thrown in the Tower! A marriage between William Seymour and Arbella Stuart would fuse together two of the existing claims to the throne. Elizabeth will run mad, and poor King Jamie of Scotland will shit himself! For long minutes Patrick pondered what he must do. *Calm down, Hepburn. At the moment Seymour is only fucking her and likely has no intention to make her his wife. He couldn't be that bloody reckless!*

Nevertheless, Patrick decided that for their own good he must keep his eye on this pair of foolish female plotters.

Chapter Six

*L*ady Widdrington has agreed to become my wife!" Robert made the announcement as the assembled company was sitting at dinner.

"Let me be the first to congratulate you, Robert." Patrick smiled at the blushing Liz. "I wish you every happiness."

Isobel Spencer shared the queen's narrow view that widows should not remarry, but Robert's sisters and sister-in-law were delighted that the baby of the family was embracing matrimony and had managed to catch himself an attractive widow who was financially secure. Moreover, he would not be burdened by children from her first marriage, so there appeared to be no disadvantages to the match whatsoever.

"Oh, Liz, let me touch you for luck," gushed Arbella. "In the 'Merry Month of May,' love seems to be everywhere!"

Cat gave Bella a sharp kick beneath the table and asked a question to divert attention from her indiscreet friend. "Have you decided where you will be wed, or when?"

"Liz would like to be married in her own church at Widdrington, in Northumberland. We haven't set a date yet, but I won't wait long." Robert's eagerness made the ladies' hearts flutter.

"I am desolate that we must return to Court tonight, but I suppose if left to your own devices you will no doubt find some way to amuse yourselves," Philadelphia teased.

The fragrance of bluebells filled Catherine's senses and she blushed profusely, but Liz laughed and said, "Tomorrow, the men will likely hunt all morning, and then we must ready ourselves for Court. Will there be dancing after the masque?"

"Oh, absolutely. The queen seldom dances herself these

days, but she enjoys watching her courtiers take the floor." Kate rolled her eyes. "I have to stay up until she's ready to retire."

"Since you are her principal Lady of the Bedchamber, it is your duty to do so," Isobel pointed out.

Kate smiled. "Quite right, Isobel. It is an honorable duty and I would be a selfish ingrate to complain."

Arbella eyed Patrick. "I hope you dance, Lord Stewart."

Cat laughed aloud as she pictured his enormous spurred boots clumping about the dance floor. Their eyes met and she saw that his were filled with amusement. She wondered if he had read her thoughts or if he was still thinking about her *sheepskin* remark.

The Presence Chamber at Whitehall was filled to capacity. The courtiers, arrayed in their finery, vied with one another in the splendor of their garments and costly gems. Her Majesty, however, enthroned upon the dais, outdid them all. Tonight she wore white satin, dramatically slashed with black and encrusted with jet beads, pearls and diamonds. Her red wig was adorned with ostrich feathers and black lace. Elizabeth believed that her external magnificence propagated her image of royalty and power and emphasized her essential femininity in a world dominated by men. If her raiment and jewels bedazzled the eyes of her courtiers, she assumed they would never notice that she was old and wrinkled.

Tonight's masque was based upon John Lyly's play *The Woman in the Moon,* which was a favorite at Court. Lyly wrote to entertain, not instruct, and his romances were written for the gentlewomen of England. This particular court comedy, drawn from mythology, was florid and rich in simile. The story of Endymion, a Greek shepherd boy who adored his heavenly mistress, Cynthia, the Moon Goddess, but was unfaithful and became entangled with not one but *two* earthly loves, was daringly risqué.

Lady Catherine, adorned in her costume as Cynthia, the Moon Goddess, represented the queen, who no longer took an active role in the masques. Cat wore a wig whose red-gold tresses fell below her waist. Her gown of sparkling silver tissue over flesh-colored silk made her costume appear transparent. She sat upon a huge glittering crescent moon that was elevated against a backdrop of black velvet to represent the night sky.

The other players had to look up to her when they delivered their lines, as she cast her pure, cool, innocent light down upon them.

Patrick Hepburn's glance was drawn to Catherine almost against his will. As well as being exquisitely beautiful, she was a wise little minx. Perched high on the crescent moon, she drew every eye, and her lack of stature went unnoticed. He knew she loved attention and easily discerned that this need arose from her mother's cool indifference toward her. Isobel's deliberate disinterest, coupled with the separation from her father, made Cat feel unloved. His own boyhood experiences ran parallel with hers.

With difficulty he pulled his gaze away from her, telling himself that he would have the rest of his days to admire her loveliness. Tonight he must concentrate his full attention upon Elizabeth. It might be his only chance to observe the queen close up. The darkness of the Presence Chamber allowed him to maneuver through the throng unobserved as he advanced toward Her Majesty. She, of course, was well lit, along with the masquers. Once he got close, his great height allowed him to stand against the wall and look over the heads of those in front of him.

Patrick focused his mind upon Elizabeth Tudor, forcing all else from his thoughts. The voices of the performers and the laughter of the audience receded. His concentration intensified and deepened until he was in a trancelike state that oftimes produced visions. Gradually, he began to hear far-off music and recognized it as a dirge. He felt icy cold and knew his senses were telling him that a period of mourning was coming. As he stared unblinking at the queen, he saw the ostrich feathers upon her head turn into black plumes that adorned the head of a black, riderless horse. Four more black horses followed, drawing an open chariot upon which lay a leaden coffin. Its black velvet trappings were emblazoned with the arms of England and France. Patrick had no doubt that he was envisioning Elizabeth's funeral procession.

Suddenly, the long room was filled with tumultuous applause and his vision faded away and was replaced by the sight of the players taking their bows. As the myriad candles of the Presence Chamber were lighted, Patrick could hardly believe that a whole hour had passed in what seemed like but a brief moment.

He blinked in disbelief as a figure clad in white satin and gold lace lifted Lady Catherine down from her crescent moon and led her toward the queen. The blue boar embroidered on his left shoulder identified the dandy as Edward de Vere, the dissolute Earl of Oxford, and a Court favorite whose effeminate garb and gestures disgusted Patrick. When Cat smiled up at the fop, he felt the urge to run him through his narrow shoulders.

"You played your part to perfection, my dear Catherine. The resemblance between us is uncanny." The queen looked pleased.

Catherine went into a graceful curtsy. "Thank you for your generous praise, Your Majesty." She turned and gave Oxford her hand so that he could lead her onto the dance floor. Everyone she passed stopped to praise her performance or compliment her delicate silvery gown, and she rewarded each with a radiant smile.

"You draw every eye, Lady Catherine," Oxford complimented.

"Only when I am on your arm, my lord," Cat said graciously. Tonight's performance had been an unqualified success, and happiness bubbled up inside her. As they waited for the musicians to begin the first coranto, Cat's curious glance swept around the chamber, and she counted at least a dozen courtiers who would be eager to partner her tonight. Then she had a sobering thought. What on earth would she do if the loutish Hepburn asked her to dance? She decided that she would decline graciously and tell him she had promised the dance to another.

Out of curiosity, she began to look for him. She saw Robert Carey, resplendent in Tudor green, partnering his bride-to-be, who wore a fashionable gown of rose brocade. The chamber was crowded and she had almost given up her quest when she spotted him. The Scot was dressed in a black velvet doublet and tight black hose. The frill of his snowy white shirt showed only an inch above the collar of his doublet. His elegant attire made the other males look gaudy by comparison. Cat missed a step as she realized that admiring females, all openly flirting with him and competing with one another for his attention, surrounded him. Many were older, sophisticated Court beauties, among them, Lettice Knollys and Douglas Sheffield. *Both are married and both are strumpets!* She averted her eyes and concentrated on the quick running steps of the coranto.

The dissolute Oxford bent close to whisper an invitation. Quite used to fending off his lascivious advances, Cat smiled sweetly. "Would your wife be joining us?"

"I fear not, puss. Three in a bed can be amusing, but not when two of them are wed to each other."

The moment the dance ended, Charlie Blount, Lord Mountjoy's son, shouldered Oxford aside. "Lady Catherine, your beauty haunts me heart and soul, O thou fair Moon so close and bright."

"You flatter me, Charlie, though the words are not your own."

As she matched her steps to the rhythm of the lavolta she was surprised to see Patrick Hepburn join the dancers. She watched him surreptitiously and saw that his movements were lithe and fluid, with an animal-like grace. When he lifted his partner higher than any other lady, his great strength was obvious.

When the partners rotated, Cat was passed into the waiting arms of Henry Somerset. "I thank you for the poem you sent me, Hal."

"Your beauty almost blinds me tonight, Cat. Will you let me take you to see another play on Wednesday?"

"It's extremely difficult to get away from Court," she said doubtfully, and then rewarded him with a smile as he began to beg. He swirled her high in a silver arc, and the moment her feet touched the dance floor she saw that her next partner would be Patrick Hepburn. A feeling of panic engulfed her. She felt she would scream if he touched her. The mannerless lout had not bothered to seek her out and compliment her on her performance. He had neither greeted her nor even glanced her way this evening.

As she changed partners and stood before him, she felt unreasonable anger surge through her because she had to put her head back to look up at him. *Why are you so bloody tall?* She waited for his compliment, which never came. She noticed the emblem on his black velvet doublet. The solid silver horse head had an emerald eye. *Horse's head indeed—horse's arse would be more apt!*

With disdain she reached up and tapped it with her finger-nail. "Have any spat upon the emblem of your outlawed father, Bothwell?"

"None dare. I always carry a knife." His grin was wolfish.

"Tell me, Lord Stewart, did you enjoy the masque?"

His dark glance swept her with amusement. "Not really. I don't much care for idolatry. Your queen has made you addicted to *heroine worship*. Don't expect it from me, Lady Catherine."

"I should slap your face," she hissed furiously.

"It is beyond your reach, Hellcat."

With chagrin, she saw that it was. She had managed to scratch him once, but that had been in a dream. Hadn't it?

The final measure of the lavolta reached a crescendo. His large hands easily spanned her tiny waist, and he swept her up so high that her silk petticoats as well as her ankles were revealed for all to see. He held her motionless in the air with sheer brute strength, compelling her to grasp his wide shoulders for support. Her amber eyes flashed golden fire as she gasped with outrage, and, as if relenting, he lowered her toward the floor.

Before her feet could touch, however, he swung her up again, demonstrating that he was the one who was in control.

Fury had almost choked her by the time he released her. "I shall repeat your disrespectful criticism to Her Majesty the queen."

"No need, *ma petite*. I shall inform her myself." He gave her a curt nod of dismissal and made his way to the dais. Going down on one knee he made a gallant bow to Elizabeth and made no move to rise until she crooked her finger. As protocol dictated, he respectfully waited until she addressed him first.

"I often welcomed the admiral to my Court, and now I welcome you. What brings you to London, Lord Stewart?" she asked bluntly.

"Mundane trade, Your Majesty. Your fair city is the trading center of the world. I came to sell horses and buy wine, in an effort to replenish my empty coffers."

"Speaking of wine, you must join me in a glass." Elizabeth signaled to a maid of honor sitting on the dais beside a small table that held refreshments. She was there to serve the queen and also taste the monarch's food and wine for poison. The young lady filled two glasses and brought them over with a linen napkin.

"Allow me, Your Majesty." Patrick took the first glass from the maid of honor, tasted it, wiped the rim with the linen, and then proffered it to the queen. "Since you enjoy sweet wine, I'll take the liberty of sending you some casks of Canary tomorrow."

Elizabeth tapped his broad chest with her fan. "I warrant you enjoy taking liberties, Hepburn, as your father did before you."

Patrick smiled into her eyes. "I must confess that I do."

"Bothwell and I dealt well together. He was ever a staunch Protestant and a strong bastion against the Catholics who sought to rule Scotland."

Taking care not to stare, he saw that her face was a cobweb of wrinkles in spite of the heavy white maquillage and red rouge. Despite the magnificent wired and padded gown he could see that beneath the jeweled satin, the royal body was emaciated. He was glad that he had not made the mistake of offering to partner her in the dance. She was far too frail for such physical exertion. Her spirit alone was keeping her alive. Yet he could clearly see that her spirit was amazingly strong. Strong enough to demand adulation. Strong enough to vent her temper should something or someone dare to displease her. Strong enough to imprison someone in the Tower of London, or sign a death warrant with her delicate but still imperious, all-powerful hand. Above all she was strong enough to resist naming a successor to her Crown of England.

When Patrick finished his wine, he stood up to leave. Many courtiers hovered below the dais waiting their turn to pay homage to their sovereign queen.

She eyed his great height and breadth with approval. "I admire a man who is both big and bold. I should like to see you perform in the joust. We always have a grand tournament to celebrate my Accession Day. I invite you to take part, Lord Stewart."

"It will be my honor, Your Majesty, to return in November." As he bowed before her he wondered if she would be alive in November.

Patrick found the Presence Chamber stifling hot, and the heavy perfume of the courtiers, both male and female, was cloying. Without seeming to hurry, he walked a direct path to the end of the chamber. His dark eyes sought out Lady Catherine's silvery costume before he went outside. She was dancing with a young noble named William Herbert, who was heir to the great earldom of Pembroke. The moment Patrick's glance touched her, she made a great show of deliberately turning her back upon him. He smiled with satisfaction. It was obvious the little hellcat's eyes had been following him for some time.

Outside Whitehall Palace, Patrick found the air cool and fresh, yet still nothing like the air of Scotland, which was as pure and heady as fine wine. He strolled down to the river and stood watching the lights on the barges as his mind went over every detail of what he had learned about the Queen of England tonight. His vision had shown him her funeral yet had not revealed *when* that fateful and momentous event would take place.

Psychic abilities aside, what do your gut instinct and plain common sense tell you? he asked himself. *Less than a year—nine or ten months, but no longer.* He shook his head and smiled at her courage and her stubborn spirit. He could not help but admire her and admitted he would not be surprised in the least to see her celebrate her November Accession Day one last time.

With reluctant steps he returned to the festivities. Courtesy demanded that he dance with the ladies he had met in Richmond.

Just as he was about to ask Liz Widdrington, she was whisked off on the arm of a fashionably garbed courtier. "Who's the dandy?" Patrick asked with a grimace.

"That's William Seymour, a dissolute young opportunist, like most here at Court," Robert replied. "My sister Kate presented me to Elizabeth, who immediately asked why I'd deserted my post. I told her I could not bear to be away from her sight. My answer must have pleased her. She assented to a private audience tomorrow after chapel. The queen may be my cousin, but she sometimes puts the fear of God in me. I think it would be in my best interest to attend the church service."

"Better you than me," Patrick said with a grin. He turned to find Arbella Stuart at his elbow and knew she wanted him to partner her in the dance to make William Seymour jealous. He bowed gallantly. "Would you do me the honor, Lady Arbella?"

As they moved together in the sprightly galliard, Arbella puzzled, "My lord, if we are both related to King James of Scotland, why are our names spelled differently?"

"Stewart was the ancient spelling of Scottish rulers since 1371. When King James's mother, Mary, married the Dauphin, she discovered that the French pronounce the letter *w* as a *v,* so she changed the spelling to Stuart so it would sound the same."

"How clever she was!"

"She married a Hepburn," he said wryly. "How clever was that?"

"Mary managed to catch three husbands, so I would call her exceedingly clever, Lord Stewart."

Patrick suddenly sensed her overwhelming fear of becoming an old maid. "Elizabeth never lost her head over a man." It was a subtle warning, but Arbella seemed oblivious. When the dance ended, they found themselves standing next to Lady Catherine and her partner, who was resplendent in puce satin.

"Oh Cat, the play was so romantic and you were the loveliest Moon Goddess ever. Don't you agree, Lord Stewart?"

"Certain people become strangely affected by the moon. The word *lunatic* comes from the Latin word *luna.*" He looked pointedly at Cat's satin-clad dancing partner. Though she pretended to be angry, he could see that his words had secretly amused her and she raised her fan to hide her laughter.

Douglas Sheffield sauntered up and she boldly slid her arm through Hepburn's. "Patrick, I believe the next lavolta is ours, though if you've had a surfeit of dancing I could show you the gardens."

"My dearest lady, how can I refuse your generous offer? I shall be delighted to see whatever you wish to show me." Though he did not look directly at Cat, he knew that her smile had fled.

Elizabeth did not withdraw from the Presence Chamber until two in the morning. Many courtiers stayed on to dance and gossip, but Isobel Spencer signaled to her daughter that she must retire to bed. With an envious glance at the older women, who were free to stay until dawn if they so desired, Cat followed her mother.

She removed her wig and costume quietly so that she would not disturb Maggie. Though the evening had been a great success, Catherine felt subdued. As she lifted the covers, she wondered in which strumpet's bed Lord Bloody Stewart would end up. By what she had seen he could have his pick, yet for the life of her she could not fathom the attraction.

Catherine tossed and turned for an hour before sleep claimed her, and just before dawn she began to dream. She was in a large chamber filled with beautiful women in exquisite gowns. There was music for dancing, yet there were no male courtiers present to partner the women. Then a lone man stepped down from the dais, and she saw that it was Patrick Hepburn. He moved from female to female, searching for a partner who would please him above all others.

When he stopped before her and gazed down at her, Cat knew she was the one and it filled her with joy. The other ladies faded away, until she and Patrick were alone in the center of the chamber. She looked up longingly at his mouth, wanting him to kiss her.

"It is beyond your reach, Hellcat."

"Then lift me up," she invited temptingly.

He slid his hands beneath her bottom cheeks and linked his fingers together so she could sit upon his palms. He raised her slowly until their lips were inches apart, then his mouth claimed the kiss for which they both hungered. She clung to him breathlessly as he withdrew his lips and whispered, "I know a place where bluebells grow. Will you come with me, Catherine?"

She suddenly awakened, and for a moment her sense of loss was devastating. Then she realized she had been dreaming. Cat shuddered with revulsion. *Even in a dream, how could I possibly be attracted to him? Patrick Hepburn is loathsome to me!*

In Whitehall's chapel, Robert Carey sat with his sisters Kate and Philadelphia for the Sunday morning service. The music, truly lovely and uplifting, soared up to the rafters of the vaulted ceiling. Then Bishop Bancroft walked from the altar to the pulpit to deliver his sermon. He began by lecturing those who broke the sanctity of the Sabbath by playing bowls on God's day. He moved on to condemning vanity and castigated those who decked out their bodies too finely, flaunting their silks and satins and allowing themselves to become slaves of fashion.

Robert, who had kept his eyes on Elizabeth since she arrived in the chapel, saw her lips press together and knew that the bishop's railing against magnificent garments was not going down well with her. He heard the queen clear her throat, a sign for the bishop to move on. Sadly, the next subject the churchman chose was duty.

"Both those in low and high places have a clear and pressing duty to those who come after them. So that our beloved England does not fall into chaos and religious strife, it is the duty of the highest in the land to name a successor to the throne."

"Silence, sirrah!" Elizabeth jumped to her feet in outrage. "That subject is forbidden . . . *forbidden,* do you hear me?"

Robert, with the letter from James burning a hole in his flesh beneath his doublet, wanted to sink through the chapel floor.

"I am in no mood to sign my death warrant, good Bishop. If you wish to keep your place in my church, or *any* church, you will never touch on this banned subject again." She stalked from the chapel with the agility of a woman in her prime.

"She'll need a deal of soothing," Kate concluded. "I'll do my best to calm her before your audience, Robert. But don't be late. Tardiness is another thing that infuriates her."

Robert knew that his sister believed the audience was to remind the queen that he had not been paid. Only Hepburn knew that he carried a letter from the King of Scotland. He devoutly hoped that James was not crass enough to ask outright that Elizabeth name him her successor—at least not in this first letter.

Elizabeth kept him waiting in the anteroom of her Privy Chamber for almost two hours before he was admitted to her presence. He went down on his knees before her and suddenly realized he had not brought a jewel or other costly gift with which to appease her. He waited for permission to rise, but the queen did not give it.

"So, Cousin Robert, you bring a woman to my Court uninvited and flaunt her before all. Does this female have a name?"

Her words shocked him to the core. He was a man of almost thirty; surely he did not need anyone's permission to court a woman? "Her name is Lady Widdrington, Your Majesty."

"A wily widow. Next you'll be sneaking off to marry without my consent." Her tone warned that he should deny such an accusation.

He suddenly saw Liz through the queen's eyes. Elizabeth could not bear the fact that Liz was young and pretty, with glorious burgundy-colored hair, and that he was sexually attracted to her. *The old harridan is seething with jealousy. She'll keep me on my knees until I swear Liz means nothing to me.* Robert opened his mouth to protest and started to get up from his knees.

"Remain where you are, sir, and address me only when I give you permission to speak. Lady Widdrington is not welcome at my Court. Never bring her here again, Sir Robert. Do I make myself clear?"

"Perfectly clear, Your Majesty."

"You may withdraw," she said with icy finality.

Chapter Seven

*T*he audience was a disaster from beginning to end! It was impossible for me to give her James's letter," Robert told Patrick as they walked along the Thames at Richmond. "The hideous old bitch kept me on my knees the entire time and forbade me to speak. She was consumed by insane jealousy the moment she spotted me with Liz last night. She has forbidden her the Court."

Patrick, who had experienced a sense of foreboding all day, nodded his understanding and allowed Robert to continue.

"Elizabeth had a temper tantrum in chapel this morning when Bishop Bancroft touched on the subject of the succession. I knew I was sunk long before I had my audience with her."

"The bishop would not dare approach the subject unless he had been instructed to do so by the power behind the throne."

"You mean Robert Cecil, her Secretary of State?"

"Precisely. We need an appointment with Cecil."

"My father should be able to arrange that, but he will expect me to tell him why I need to speak with the secretary."

"Cecil controls the Treasury. Your warden fees are overdue."

"I'll go to Blackfriars tonight and speak with Father. I should have visited him the first day I arrived in London."

"Tell him you've been paying court to a lady. Why not take Liz with you and introduce Lord Hunsdon to your future wife?"

"Judas! How am I to tell Liz that she's forbidden the Court?"

"Emphasize that Elizabeth is jealous of her beauty. Any lady would be flattered to learn that a queen envies her. I am sure that if you let Liz know you are ready to defy your sovereign majesty for her, she will be the happiest female alive."

"Perhaps I should not tell her she is forbidden the Court. I find it difficult to deceive a woman," Robert admitted.

Patrick laughed. "If you intend to take a wife, you will need to practice deceit. In any case, Liz hasn't been forbidden the city of London. The streets are filled with fabulous shops, theatres and eating houses. Ladies have a mania for shopping."

"I'll do it! I shall take Liz to Father's house in Blackfriars tonight. Will you come too, Patrick?"

"I'll come to London, but I'll sleep aboard the *Hepburn Rose*."

William Seymour, without a servant at his heels, made his way from the Thames water stairs to the New Temple, where many London goldsmiths were housed. They did a brisk business selling precious metals, jewelry and plate, but also made handsome profits from money lending. Before Seymour could enter the goldsmith's shop of Isaac Abraham, the door opened and his friend Henry Somerset stepped into the street. "Hal, don't tell me you are buying a jewel to lure Lady Catherine to her deflowering?"

"Not bloody likely," Somerset said grimly. "I'm here for the same reason you are, Will; to borrow money against my inheritance."

Seymour's false smile vanished. "I hope you were successful!"

"Not at the first two goldsmiths I approached. They refused me on the grounds that I had already exceeded my limit on earlier loans. Bloody Jews ought to be run out of the country!"

Seymour glanced at the sign above the door. "Abraham came through for you?"

"Not without charging me an arm and a bloody leg. The old thief wanted twenty percent and finally settled for eighteen when I told him I would shortly become the Earl of Worcester."

"But your father's in the best of health," Seymour protested.

"Yes, worst luck! But Abraham took me at my word."

"Then this is where I shall start."

"I'll wait for you. I spotted a jeweled dagger in a shop at the far end of the Temple that quite took my fancy."

When the two met half an hour later, Henry Somerset commiserated with his friend. "I can see by your dejected look that you were turned down."

"The name Seymour is like a bloody millstone around my neck. When I mentioned I was heir to the Earldom of Hertford,

Abraham reminded me that my father stood in line before me and that it would be a donkey's age before I became an earl. The devil of it is that he's right. Father is in no danger of sticking his spoon in the wall, and my obstinate grandfather may outlive us both!"

"Cheer up. Perhaps you'll win at primero tonight."

"I've lost two thousand in the last fortnight and have no way of paying off any of my gambling debts."

"Christ, William, you're down to your last resort: marriage! Still, I can't feel sorry for you when I think of all the wealth Arbella will come into when her harridan of a grandmother is six feet under. The Countess of Shrewsbury owns half the land in England, and the old bitch must be close to seventy."

"Seventy-five, actually," Seymour acknowledged morosely. "You're right, Hal. I'm afraid I have no other choice."

Patrick read the message from Robert Carey confirming that arrangements had been made for him to meet with Cecil at his offices in the Savoy Palace on Wednesday afternoon. Since no mention had been made of Hepburn being included, Robert thought it best that they meet outside the Savoy.

When the two met at the appointed time, Robert said, "Your advice regarding Liz was right. My father approves of her wholeheartedly and wants to see me married in his lifetime."

Patrick gripped his friend's shoulder. "Then do it soon."

Robert looked into Hepburn's dark eyes and understood his meaning. He had been shocked to see how much his father had aged. He tried to lighten the mood. "Liz is off shopping today with a pair of Hunsdon footmen in tow to carry her purchases."

"You are uneasy about this meeting with Cecil," Patrick said bluntly.

"I am," Robert said earnestly. "My audience with the queen went so badly, I'm afraid of saying the wrong thing to Cecil. Perhaps you should see him alone first?"

"We will see him together. A united force of two against one guarantees that we will prevail."

Robert was relieved. "You always exude confidence, Patrick."

Busy as he was with affairs of state, Robert Cecil did not keep them waiting. Within thirty minutes they were ushered into his inner office, which was lined with books and journals.

It had no less than three desks, all piled with files, papers and documents.

"Sir Robert, thank you for granting me an appointment on short notice. May I present Patrick Hepburn, Lord Stewart? My father did not tell you his lordship would accompany me today, because he did not know. This meeting is strictly confidential."

Cecil indicated that they should sit. "I have learned to expect the unexpected, gentlemen."

"You were High Steward of Cambridge the year I attended." Patrick sat down immediately. He had no wish to tower over the slightly built statesman with the deformed shoulder, whom the queen addressed as *little man*. The sobriquet was appallingly insensitive, and Patrick divined that though Cecil served Elizabeth better than any minister who had come before him, he could have no love for her. "At the beginning of May, King James asked me to find an honest and honorable man whom he could trust to carry a letter to Queen Elizabeth. I recommended Robert Carey."

"With all due respect, my lord, though Her Majesty the queen is my cousin, she made it impossible for me to deliver the letter that the King of Scotland entrusted to me. Lord Stewart concluded that we should seek your counsel," Carey declared.

Now that Patrick was in Cecil's presence, he could tell that the man who sat before him had one of the greatest intellects he had ever encountered. He studied the hooded eyes as he tried to merge his mind with Cecil's and realized he would have only partial success. Sir Robert was too clever, too shrewd, too guarded, to allow another to share all of his thoughts.

"If I took the letter from you, it could be construed as secret communication with the King of Scotland."

"There are only four people who know of this letter, Sir Robert, three of whom are in this room," Patrick stated. "More harmonious relations between the two realms would benefit both countries and both monarchs and be advantageous to you personally."

"It would certainly be in the King of Scotland's best interests to be named as the Queen of England's successor. But Elizabeth is my sovereign and I am her loyal servant. I cannot deceive her."

"Making plans for the good of the State, in an area of policy in which the queen herself has steadily refused to give guidance, is not conspiracy; it is statesmanship," Hepburn insisted.

Carey spoke up. "I would not dream of asking that you deceive Her Majesty in any way, Sir Robert. All I ask is that you personally deliver James's letter into Elizabeth's hands."

"As the queen's Principal Secretary, I will accept the letter."

With relief, Carey took the well-sealed envelope from his doublet and handed it to Cecil. "Thank you, my lord. You have removed a heavy burden from my conscience."

Cecil nodded. "Give my regards to your father."

"Lord Hunsdon made the appointment so that his son could collect his warden's fee, which has been in arrears for a year, but I fear that Robert is too polite to broach the subject."

The corner of Cecil's mouth lifted. "While you do not suffer from a surfeit of politeness, Lord Stewart."

"No, Sir Robert, I have learned to ask for what is owed me."

"I'll have one of my clerks prepare a draft for your fees, Carey, if you will come this way."

"I think we should leave separately," Patrick said decisively.

Hepburn waited patiently until Robert Cecil returned alone to his inner office. He had decided to persuade him to become James Stuart's ally. "Sir Robert, I am not speaking treason; I am speaking truth when I tell you that Elizabeth Tudor does not have years to live. It would be prudent to enter into communications with King James. Do not allow your illustrious career to be jeopardized by the queen's death. Approach James and safeguard your position in the state. It would be a simple matter for a man of your intellect to gain his trust and then guide him. Jamie already considers you the king here, in effect."

"Are you asking me to entrust you with letters?"

"No. Robert Carey is your man. Though his integrity would prevent him from reading them, the letters should be written in cipher. Carey would guard the correspondence with his life. His warden's post will allow him to travel between London and the Scottish Border without comment. The king trusts him." Patrick urged, "Demonstrate to James that he can trust you, too."

"Thank you for coming, Lord Stewart, I will give your suggestions some thought."

Patrick stood, shook Cecil's hand and delivered his clincher. "If you do not soon forge a bond with James, your rivals will.

Once the great northern Border lords learn of Elizabeth's frailty, they will rush to offer the king their friendship and support."

Hepburn left the Savoy and walked toward the river. He noticed two elegantly dressed courtiers emerge from Worcester House, which was directly behind the Savoy Palace. He immediately recognized William Seymour, Lady Arbella's lover, but pondered over the identity of Seymour's companion. It didn't take him long to deduce that it was Worcester's son, Henry Somerset. Patrick's instincts urged him to follow them and he seldom ignored his intuitive senses. The men hailed a river craft going westward and Patrick took a wherry sailing in the same direction.

When they disembarked it was an easy matter to follow the fashionable pair along Thames Street. A crowd was gathering at the *Bull and Bear Inn,* and Patrick concluded that since it was Wednesday afternoon, they were likely there to attend a play.

When he spotted the two exquisitely dressed females wearing vizards waiting outside the inn, he was not the least surprised. He lengthened his stride and closed the distance between himself and the two couples in less than a minute.

Feigning surprise, Patrick bowed gallantly. "Lady Arbella, this is an unexpected pleasure. If I'd known you enjoyed the play, I would have offered to escort you." He made a point of ignoring Catherine, who stood fuming behind her mask.

"Lord Stewart!" Arbella lowered her vizard and deliberately tried to provoke her escort's jealousy. "Allow me to present William Seymour. Will, this is Patrick Hepburn, a Stewart kinsman of mine. I'm sure you noticed him at Court on Saturday evening. His great height set him apart from the other gentlemen."

Seymour narrowed his hazel eyes and stared up at the man he suddenly suspected of being his rival. "How do you do, Hepburn? You are Scottish, I believe."

Somerset curled his lip. "If I'm not mistaken, your father was Bothwell."

Patrick smiled. "He still *is* the Earl of Bothwell."

Cat lowered her mask and drawled with insolence, "Hal, don't impugn the name of Bothwell; the barbarian Scot carries a knife."

"Lady Catherine knows my secret," Patrick said with a wolfish grin, "but then, I know hers." He watched with satisfaction as the golden fire flashed in her eyes. "Enjoy the play, ladies."

As he made his way back to his ship, Hepburn decided to learn all he could about the handsome courtier with the golden beard.

All he knew at the moment was that Henry Somerset was heir to the earldom of Worcester, but he decided to find out which games of chance he favored and how often he got drunk. Before he was done with foppish Hal, Patrick would know everything, from the names of his favorite whores to the size of his balls.

In the upstairs chamber of the Bull and Bear the two young men were asking pointed questions about the tall, dark Scot. Both courtiers felt threatened by the man's size, confidence and devilish looks. Moreover, he had an overt maleness that both recognized as dangerous, especially where women were concerned.

Arbella was using the encounter to fan Seymour's jealousy. "Patrick Hepburn is a Scottish Border lord. He and I are both related to King James," she explained to the suddenly proprietary Seymour. "There is nothing between us, Will."

"He could be on the prowl for a wealthy English heiress." Fear that the Scot might snatch the marriage prize from him made Seymour's stomach roil.

Cat was furious that Lord Bloody Stewart had caught her where she was not supposed to be. What on earth would she do if he told her mother? "No English lady could stomach the uncivilized brute, let alone give him her hand in marriage."

William Seymour slid a possessive arm about Arbella and whispered, "I love you, Bella."

"Ah, my lord, I warrant you say that to all the ladies."

"Of course I don't, Bella. I've been thinking about buying you a ring." He swallowed hard. "A betrothal ring."

"Will!" Arbella gushed. "Can we go and buy it now?"

Like a rat in a trap he turned helplessly to his friend.

Somerset rushed to his aid. "William, here is that money I owe you." He murmured softly, "Strike while the iron is hot!"

"This is so exciting!" Cat said breathlessly, caught up in the recklessness of the moment. "It will have to be kept secret."

Bella picked up her mask. "Don't wait for me; I shall find my own way back to Whitehall."

"I shall see that Catherine gets safely back to the palace," Somerset said smoothly, "after we enjoy the play."

I shall have to look to my own safety, here alone with you, Hal Somerset. Step over the line and I'll push you from the window!

Arbella Stuart was walking on air. She had waited what seemed like years and years for a proposal of marriage. Her grandmother had tried to arrange a match between her and Henry Percy, the powerful Earl of Northumberland, but he had snubbed her and wed Essex's sister instead. Finally, now that she had given in to Seymour's sexual demands and made him mad with jealousy over Patrick Hepburn, William was going to make her his wife.

Arbella led the way to the Exchange in the Strand with its double gallery of shops that offered everything from Russian furs to Chinese silk. She took her bridegroom's hand and propelled him into the Venetian Jewelers. Seymour, who seemed to be in a daze, allowed her to choose her own wedding ring.

By the time they left the shop, Arbella was in a most generous mood. "I want to buy *you* a present, Will. Oh, just look at those swords. Go inside and look at them, I'm sure there is one that will strike your fancy. I have to pop next door and I'll be right back." Bella hurried to the shop that sold hair products. She needed to buy a saffron wash to brighten her blond tresses.

Liz Widdrington, who had just purchased a pair of tortoise-shell combs, immediately recognized the Stuart girl. "Lady Arbella, how lovely to see you! I am having such a wonderful time today. Your London shops are filled with treasures."

"Lady Widdrington—Liz! Are you shopping for your trousseau?"

"I am indeed. There are so many things a bride needs."

"I, too, will soon be a bride!" She showed off her ring. "It's a secret, Liz. You mustn't tell anyone."

"I wish you every happiness, Bella. Who is the lucky groom?"

"Oh, I can't tell you. It truly is a secret. I must run."

She hurried back to the sword shop and saw that her dearest William had chosen an Italian dagger with a jeweled hilt. She was happy to see that his face had regained most of its color.

"Henry will be pea green with envy when he sees this, Bella!"

•   •   •

When Patrick arrived back at the *Hepburn Rose* he opened an invitation from Robert Carey's sister Kate, who was married to the Admiral of England, Lord Charles Howard. He was invited to dine at Arundel House in the Strand, which was the Howards' official residence. When he arrived the following evening, he saw that the intimate dinner included just six people. His dinner partner was Kate's sister Philadelphia, and the other invited couple was Robert Carey and his bride-to-be, Liz Widdrington.

The dinner was to celebrate the upcoming wedding and give the family's stamp of approval in spite of any objections the aging queen might have. As well as giving Patrick and Charles Howard a chance to meet, it also allowed Patrick and Robert to make plans for a visit to Hertford. Hepburn knew the ride there and back would let them discuss in private their meeting with Cecil.

"Patrick raises horses and has expressed an interest in visiting Hunsdon Grange before he sails back to Scotland. I thought we'd ride up tomorrow since Liz will be busy all day being fitted for her wedding gown."

"I'm looking forward to meeting your brother John."

"You'll like John. He's an avid horseman," Robert declared.

"His wife, Mary, prefers Hertford to the Court," Philadelphia told Patrick. "She's a saint to live with her husband year round."

"If he's a Carey, he cannot be a difficult man," Patrick said.

"True," Philadelphia agreed with amusement, "while my husband, Scrope, has a volatile personality. The only thing we have in common is a weakness for gambling."

"I hear that gambling is a nightly pastime at Court, once the queen has retired." Patrick discerned that Philadelphia would be able to tell him if Henry Somerset had gambling debts. Within minutes he learned that both Somerset and his friend Seymour owed thousands. Philadelphia added, however, that since both courtiers were heirs to wealthy earldoms, their debts were of little consequence.

"Are you pledged in marriage, Patrick?" Philadelphia asked.

"Not yet, my lady. Do you have someone in mind for me?"

"My sister's a determined matchmaker. Watch out," Kate warned.

"Well, I must admit I had young Catherine Spencer in mind,

but the pair of you are like cat and dog with raised hackles. Your physical disparity *is* rather marked, but opposites *do* attract."

"Philadelphia has matched our little Catherine with every titled young man at Court. She does it just to annoy Isobel."

"It amuses me to annoy Isobel. She's so terrified of offending Elizabeth, I swear she'd prefer that Catherine remain unwed."

"I'd wager there's little chance of that," Patrick declared.

"When you visit Hertford tomorrow, take a look at the Spencer estate. Their longhorn cattle are unique," Philadelphia urged. "When Catherine comes of age next March and needs neither Isobel's nor the queen's permission to marry, she'll be snapped up like an iridescent little trout fly. Cat is a man's woman!"

Cat is this man's woman, Hepburn decided, *if the Spencer estate turns out to be as impressive as I've been led to believe.*

On the ride to Hertford, Patrick and Robert thoroughly discussed their meeting with Cecil and declared it a success. "I fully expect him to contact you and entrust you with a letter."

"King James would be pleased if Cecil wrote to him," Robert said. "I think it best if I travel back with Liz in her coach."

"I agree. You can hardly expect your bride to travel alone."

When the pair arrived at Hunsdon Grange, John Carey ran his hand along Valiant's flank as he assessed the horse with the eye of a connoisseur. "You're certain he's not a Thoroughbred?"

Patrick laughed and shook his head. "I bred him myself from my father's Thoroughbred, Valentine, but his dam was a wild mare."

"His bloodlines are magnificent. D'you mind if I put him with a couple of my one-year-old fillies while you're here? Nothing might come of it, but there's always a chance he'll be tempted."

Patrick liked John Carey as much as he liked Robert. He had the same coloring but was shorter and broader than his brother. Patrick envied him Hunsdon Horse Grange and admitted that he'd never seen more lush pastures than in Hertfordshire. The climate produced such a long growing season that the fields yielded two crops of hay each summer, a feat impossible in Scotland.

John's wife, Mary, welcomed them to the noontime meal, which she had cooked herself. She was happy to see her husband's brother Robert, the baby of the family, and overjoyed to learn that he was soon to be married. She had a hundred questions about his bride.

"If Liz and I are half as happy as you and John, I shall consider myself a lucky man, Mary," Robert said sincerely.

As Patrick looked at their handsome, healthy children sitting at the table with them, he too began to long for such a marriage. Later, when he mentioned that he would like to see the Spencer estate, known as Spencer Park, John offered to accompany them.

"Now, there's a landholding! It was a tragedy that John Spencer died without a son to inherit. If I had a son anywhere near old enough to marry, I'd try to make a match for him with the Spencer heiress. Finest two thousand acres in England!"

Spencer Park was only five miles from Hunsdon Grange. When Patrick saw the lush acres with the lovely river Lea running through the property, he experienced a strange sense of destiny, as if he were coming home. John introduced him to Mr. Burke, the head steward, who took great pride in the Spencer longhorns.

"I am familiar with the breed, Mr. Burke. The Earl of Winton, Lady Spencer's father, is a neighbor of mine in Scotland. I just visited him the first week of May. He would envy you your verdant pastures and mild climate."

"I sincerely hope you will give him a good report of Spencer Park, Lord Stewart. We keep up with all the agricultural improvements. Did you know that we supply the Queen's Court with three hundred pounds of freshly churned butter each and every week?" Mr. Burke said proudly. "The home farm across the river is planted with rye and barley. Perhaps next year we will put in hops."

On the ride back to London, Patrick began to anticipate the day when Spencer Park would be his. Add a herd of fine horses and he knew it would be the closest to paradise that he would ever get.

Robert interrupted his musings. "By the way, Liz told me she ran into your kinswoman Arbella in the Strand Exchange on Wednesday. She was showing off a ring and told Liz that though it was a secret, she too was about to become a bride."

Holy God! And I'm willing to bet the little hellcat is up to her whiskers in the forbidden affair!

Chapter Eight

*W*hen Patrick arrived back aboard his ship, he summoned Ian Hepburn, the steward he had brought to buy cargo for the return voyage, and the pair made their way to Whitehall. As Patrick suspected he would, he spotted William Seymour playing primero in one of the crowded gaming rooms. He pointed out the young dandy to Ian.

"Seymour has rooms here at the palace so he'll likely stay put tonight. But if he leaves Whitehall tomorrow, I want you to follow him. His grandfather, the Earl of Hertford, has a mansion in Cannon Row, but my guess is that he will avoid both his father and his grandfather at the moment. The fellow next to him with the clipped beard is his friend Henry Somerset, who may accompany him. They frequent a brothel in Thames Street but that doesn't concern me. Just wait outside, and then resume your pursuit. I need to know everyone Seymour contacts. Report back to me at six tomorrow night aboard the *Hepburn Rose*."

Patrick made his way to the kitchens, which were busy night and day, baking and cooking vast quantities of food for Whitehall's residents. He helped himself to a large meat pie and a jug of ale as he looked over the servants gathered there. Patrick knew that Court pages had ravenous appetites and empty pockets, so he singled out a royal page who looked to be about ten or eleven years old. He offered him a slice of pie and slipped him a gold coin. In return the lad eagerly showed him where Lady Arbella Stuart's chamber was located.

Patrick made his way into the palace gardens, identified Arbella's window and made himself comfortable for the night beneath a flowering hawthorn tree. The next morning he was not surprised to see Arbella emerge from the palace in the company of her dearest friend and conspirator, Catherine Spencer.

Keeping a discreet distance, he followed them as they walked past the cockpit and mingled with a crowd gathered at the archery butts. Both females repeatedly glanced over their shoulders, clearly revealing to Patrick that they felt guilty about what they were plotting. Finally the pair sat down in the empty stands of the tiltyard and bent their heads in whispered conversation.

Though Patrick concealed himself behind one of the six-foot-high tilting barriers, he was tall enough to see over the top. His mind blocked out his surroundings as he focused his whole attention upon the ladies' conversation. Gradually, their words came to him across the distance, indistinct at first, but as he concentrated they became clearer.

"But June is the traditional month for brides," Arbella argued. "The first day of June would be far more romantic!"

"The first of June falls on Saturday. It has to be Wednesday."

"Why does it have to be on a Wednesday?" Bella asked.

"Because it's easier for us to get away on Wednesday afternoon. We had no trouble whatsoever the past few weeks," Cat pointed out.

"Then why don't we arrange it for the following Wednesday?" Arbella counted on her fingers. "That would be June fifth."

"The longer you try to keep a secret, the easier it is for someone to find out, and what if Will changes his mind?"

"You're right as always, Cat. The sooner the better."

They were eventually joined by Henry Somerset, who made a gallant display of kissing their hands. "Good morning, ladies."

"Tell William to make the arrangements for the coming Wednesday afternoon, the twenty-eighth of May," Arbella said quickly.

Somerset bowed to the ladies and strolled off.

Patrick went back to his ship and spent the afternoon in the hold, helping to load his cargo of wine and checking on supplies for the return voyage.

Ian Hepburn returned before six o'clock and made his report. "Seymour didn't retire from the gaming room until almost three in the morning. By that time he was falling-down drunk. This morning he didn't emerge from his rooms. At noon, the other courtier ye pointed out to me visited him. His friend stayed about an hour, then he left. Finally, Seymour, looking a wee bit green about the gills, ventured forth. I followed him down to the Old Palace Water Stairs, where he took a barge."

"Did you take the same water craft, or follow on the next?"

"I took the same one. He doesn't know me and I didn't want to risk losing the weasel once he'd emerged from his hole."

Patrick nodded, agreeing with Ian's reasoning.

"Seymour got off at Queenhithe Landing and I followed him along Thames Street, thinking I knew his destination. But he surprised me when he turned off Thames Street and joined the throng that was crossing London Bridge to Southwark."

"He didn't suspect he was being followed?"

Ian shook his head. "The bridge was crowded with people and carts going both ways. I was able to keep distance between us because his fancy duds made him stand out like a peacock in a flock of starlings. I thought he was going to the Bear Gardens or the newly built Globe Theatre but, believe it or not, the weasel was going to church!"

"St. Mary's Church!" Patrick declared with satisfaction. "Seymour might be sly as a weasel, but he's brainless as a louse."

"He stayed in St. Mary's for some time, then he returned to Whitehall and made no other stops along the way."

"Thanks, Ian; you did well. The cases of wine are stowed, so if all goes well we'll embark for Scotland day after tomorrow."

Patrick went below to his cabin to write a letter to Cecil and one to Gilbert Talbot, Earl of Shrewsbury, who was newly appointed to the Queen's Council. Arbella Stuart was his niece.

On Saturday, Patrick received a note from Robert Carey:

> *You were right. Early this morning I was summoned to S.*
> *We leave today.*

Patrick knew the *S* stood for Savoy. Carey had a letter from Cecil for James Stuart. He and Liz were leaving today.

Hepburn's sixth sense had told him that there would be a letter; it had not told him when. Timing was ever the most important element in any sequence of events. Now that the letter was safely on its way to Scotland, Patrick could give Cecil the information he had gathered.

When Patrick arrived at the Savoy Palace, Robert Cecil did not keep him waiting long. When Patrick was shown into the inner office, he placed the letter he had written before Cecil and remained standing. This time he wanted his height to be imposing.

"Sir Robert, I have discovered a dangerous plot for a secret marriage between two young people at Court. Both parties are in the line of succession to Her Royal Majesty, Queen Elizabeth of England. If two existing claims to the throne are fused together in matrimony, it will strengthen those claims. I don't know how your queen would view this, but I assure you that my king would see it in the worst possible light. If this marriage were allowed to happen, he would suspect double dealing at the English Court and he would never again seek to place his trust in high places."

Cecil read the names in the letter, along with the date and the place of the secret wedding. "A simple inquiry at St. Mary's will confirm if this is more than rumor."

"And if it is, Sir Robert?"

"I shall inform Edward Seymour, Earl of Hertford, of his grandson's mad scheme. In his younger days the earl was imprisoned in the Tower for marrying too close to the throne. He has more good sense than to imperil his life again."

Though Patrick believed Cecil would take action, the other letter he had written would ensure it.

"You need not trouble yourself over my kinswoman Lady Arbella, Sir Robert. I have sent a similar letter informing her uncle, Gilbert Talbot, who will want no trouble now that he has taken his seat on the Queen's Council. He will soon order his niece back to her grandmother's strict supervision in Derbyshire."

Cecil bowed his acknowledgment, and Hepburn knew that he had taken his measure and found it formidable. "When do you leave for Scotland, Lord Stewart?"

Patrick's mouth curved. "I sail tomorrow, Sir Robert."

Maggie opened the chamber door to admit Catherine's friend. "Good afternoon, Lady Arbella. Perhaps ye can distract her. I brought her a lunch tray hours ago but she hasn't stopped sketching long enough to even notice. Perhaps ye can tempt her to eat a bite. I'm way behind . . . it's wash day and these bed linens should have been down to the palace laundry this morning."

Arbella crossed to the window where Catherine sat and looked at her sketch. "A new gown for the queen. What is that motif?"

"It's a Tudor rose that I am entwining around the ragged staff of Dudley. Lord Robert Dudley, Earl of Leicester, was the great love of Elizabeth's life, so I know this design will please her." Cat waited until Maggie left with the great bundle of linen. "Is everything arranged?"

"Yes! Next Wednesday afternoon at St. Mary's Church, across the river in Southwark. Will says it's much safer in Southwark, where they are not likely to recognize us." Arbella helped herself to a mutton pasty. "Don't look for me at the masque, Cat. Hal Somerset has offered us his rooms for the night."

"You're taking a great risk. Judas! I'm supposed to be the impulsive one! Make sure nobody sees you, Bella."

"Tush! From all the gossip I've heard, half the ladies at Court will be sleeping in some man's bed tonight!"

"He must have a very large bed," Cat teased.

"Who?" Arbella asked blankly.

"Never mind. If you're eating in the Privy Chamber tonight, I'll save you a seat. There's always a crush on Saturday night, and Mother will insist we go down early."

"Here comes Maggie, so I'll be off. Save me a seat."

When the waiting woman came in with her arms piled with fresh linen, Cat felt a stab of guilt. "I'll help you make the beds." She relieved Maggie of some of the sheets and bolsters and they went into Isobel's bedchamber. Before they were done, someone knocked. "I'll finish the bed. It's probably Bella again."

Maggie came back carrying a note. "A page delivered this."

Cat was reluctant to open it in front of Maggie until she recognized her mother's writing on the envelope. She tore it open and quickly scanned the lines. "That's strange. I had no idea that Mother was going up to Richmond today. She asks that we both attend her there first thing in the morning."

"I hope it isn't bad news. I saw Lady Howard's serving

woman downstairs and she told me Lord Hunsdon had taken ill." Maggie crossed herself. "When the poor old soul dies, yer aunt Beth will become Lady Hunsdon."

"We'd better pack some things now. There won't be time tonight after the masque. When Mother says 'first thing in the morning,' she means shortly after sunrise."

"I don't think the sun is going to show its face this morning." Maggie opened Catherine's wardrobe. "Ye'll need a warm cloak, my lamb; it will be cool on the river."

Cat put on her gray velvet cape and tucked her curls inside the hood. *If there is sad news, I don't want to look gaudy.*

At this early hour of six, the corridors of Whitehall were empty, and the pair quietly left the palace and made their way to the water stairs. Transportation on the Thames was available day and night, but at daybreak they were the only passengers on the wherry. By the time the watercraft passed the ugly, square-built Syon House, only a mile from Richmond, Catherine was shivering. It was not from cold alone; she was growing apprehensive about what awaited her.

The pair disembarked and Catherine's feet dragged as they walked toward the house. She noticed that all the May blossom petals had fallen from the trees and the lilac blooms had turned brown. Cat told herself that the month of June would bring a profusion of roses and lupins and night-scented stocks but, at the moment, the garden looked rather dismal.

As soon as they stepped into the entrance hall, a servant relieved them of their bags and carried them upstairs. Cat saw that her mother was standing before the entrance to the sitting room, as if she were blocking it from them. Isobel, dressed in black, looked haggard, and Catherine felt an overwhelming impulse to comfort her. "Mother, whatever is amiss?"

"Sit!" Isobel pointed to the hard wooden settle inside the front door and waited until Catherine obeyed her command.

Maggie headed toward the stairs to give them privacy.

"Stay!" Isobel's orders were issued in a tone of voice she would use on a pair of disobedient dogs. "This concerns you."

Maggie moved toward the settle, instinctively closing ranks with her beloved charge.

"I hope and pray that I have been misinformed about your

involvement in a treasonous plot against Her Majesty the queen."

"Of course I haven't plotted against the queen. Mother, how could you think me capable of such wickedness?"

"You are quite capable of wickedness, Catherine. I've known it since you were a child!"

Cat flinched at her mother's words, though she silently acknowledged that she had been a mischievous child.

"It has come to my ears that you have plotted and planned a secret wedding between Arbella Stuart and William Seymour."

Dear God, how on earth did she find out? Cat heard her heartbeat thudding loudly inside her eardrums.

"Is it true? Yes or no?" Isobel demanded.

Much as she wanted to, Catherine could not blatantly lie to her mother. "Bella and Will are in love," she whispered.

Isobel clutched her heart as if her daughter had given her a deathblow. "So you admit you are involved in this conspiracy!"

"We had to keep it secret because marriage always upsets the queen. Please try to understand," Catherine beseeched.

"I fully understand that you are deceitful and incorrigible, but one thing you are not is *stupid,* young madam! You know that Arbella and Seymour are both in the line of succession and a marriage between them would strengthen their claim to the throne!"

"Bella is not conspiring to take the throne; she just wants to get married. She is terrified of becoming an old maid!"

"That's true, my lady," Maggie agreed.

"Shut your mouth, Maggie," Isobel ordered. "I hold you responsible for Catherine's depraved behavior."

"Mother, that is unfair. Please don't blame Maggie for something I've done. I did my utmost to keep it secret from her."

"Unfair? Do you not realize, Catherine, how unfair this is to me? I could lose my position as Mistress of the Wardrobe! The queen might even banish me from Court because of your evil plotting. I am distraught!" Isobel clutched a handful of her faded hair. "Distraught at your vicious willfulness!"

"I'm sorry, Mother," Catherine whispered.

"I too am sorry! Sorry that I ever conceived you!" Isobel vowed. "Go upstairs, both of you, and pack your things. I am sending you away immediately. You are forbidden the Court. You must never be in Arbella Stuart's company again."

But Bella is my friend. In a small voice Cat dared to ask, "How long must I stay at Spencer Park?"

"Hertfordshire isn't far enough from Court for someone who has plotted treason. You must leave the country immediately. I am sending you to your grandfather in Scotland."

Cat jumped to her feet in alarm. "Scotland? I won't go!"

Isobel stepped toward her daughter and slapped her hard across the face. "Don't dare to defy me!"

As Catherine recoiled in horror, a tall figure stepped through the archway from the sitting room. "Lady Spencer, stop!"

Isobel restrained herself with difficulty. "Lord Stewart has generously consented to take you to Scotland aboard his ship. I pray to God that such swift action will keep my good name out of this. I wash my hands of you and Maggie both." Isobel turned on her heel and swept from the hall.

Cat stared at Patrick Hepburn in disbelief. "You! You monster! You have done this terrible thing to me!"

"Lady Catherine, the *Hepburn Rose* sails on the afternoon tide. I must get my horse and my deerhounds aboard. I will send my man for your trunks." Patrick nodded curtly and departed.

Cat was stunned. She looked helplessly at Maggie. "I am so sorry to drag you into this mess."

"It will be all right, lass. It's best ye leave Court for a time until all this blows over. Yer mother is protecting ye from being arrested and mayhap imprisoned. Come on, put a good face on it. We have a deal of packing to do."

"I wish I could send Bella a warning," Cat whispered.

"Dinna even think of it, lassie. There's none here ye could trust to carry a secret note. They'd hand it to yer mother."

"Maggie, I'm beginning to learn that you are the only one in the entire world whom I can trust."

"Then trust me when I tell ye that Scotland isn't a bad place. 'Tis a beautiful country and, though I admit the winters can be cruel, we're going at the best possible time."

When they went upstairs they saw that the servants had already brought down the traveling trunks from the attic. At first, Catherine stood before her wardrobe feeling helpless and at a total loss. The feeling did not last long, however. She soon straightened her shoulders and made a decision. Once she had resolved to take control and pack everything she owned, her spirits lifted a little.

It was the hour of noon before the four trunks sat ready to be taken downstairs. Only one belonged to Maggie, and once again Catherine felt a pang of guilt. She slipped her sketchpads, pencils, charcoal and water paints into a large leather case and fastened it securely. "I'm going to say good-bye to Jasmine."

"Don't be too long. Cook will be sending up lunch. Ye should eat something, my lamb; it'll be a long day."

"I'm not hungry, Maggie." Cat's appetite was small at the best of times. When she was upset, it was nonexistent.

When she arrived at the stable, Cat had to stifle the impulse to saddle Jasmine and gallop away. Upon reflection she realized the only place she could go was Spencer Park, and that was the first place her mother would look. She pressed her cheek into Jasmine's flank and told the small palfrey how much she would miss her. With a lump in her throat Catherine fastened a leading rein to the bridle and led Jasmine to the Hunsdon stables. She handed the rein to the head groom. "I'm going away to Scotland. Would you stable Jasmine here with the other horses, so she won't be lonely?"

"It will be my pleasure, Lady Catherine. How long are you planning to be away?"

"Oh, not long. Not long at all," she said with determination.

It was two o'clock when Ian Hepburn, along with a deckhand from the *Hepburn Rose,* arrived. Cat was amazed when the men hoisted the trunks to their shoulders to carry them downstairs. "Are we going by carriage?" she asked hopefully.

"No, my lady. We are going by river. A water barge will take us from here directly to the ship at the Pool of London."

Cat tried to hide her alarm. The river Thames moved placidly until it neared London Bridge, where watercraft had to shoot the whitecapped rapids. London's Pool, where the ships docked, was at the far east end of the city, past the Tower of London. She made a quick decision to remove her wire farthingale from beneath her skirts. She might look unfashionable, but she would be a good deal more comfortable and probably steadier on her feet without the infernal contraption.

Cat carried her safely bundled sketches as she and Maggie followed the men to the water stairs. "Are all Scotsmen as big and strong as oxen?"

"Nay, lass; I believe the Hepburns are a breed apart."

"Well, they're certainly not human," she said with a shudder.

It took two hours to make the trip from Richmond to the Tower Wharf, because the oarsmen were rowing against the tide. When their watercraft almost made it through the middle arch of London Bridge, the tide carried it backward and they had to do it all again. Maggie turned an alarming shade of green and Cat knew she herself would have certainly lost her lunch, had she eaten one.

As they followed the men along the docks to where the *Hepburn Rose* lay anchored, Lady Catherine drew every eye. Even though she was dressed in subdued gray velvet, men gaped at the exquisite creature as if she were a goddess who'd just descended from Mount Olympus. Cat was unaware of the attention, however, because she was filled with trepidation about the voyage. The only water she had ever sailed upon was the river Thames, and that had just proved a daunting task.

When they arrived at the ship, she watched the men carry the trunks aboard, and then she saw that Patrick Hepburn was standing on deck at the end of the boarding plank to welcome her aboard. Her heart came into her mouth. Cat would rather die than allow the arrogant Scot to see her fear. She indicated that Maggie should go first, then, with her back straight as a ramrod and her chin high in the air, she stepped forward with feigned confidence.

"Watch your step, Maggie." Hepburn lifted the serving woman from the boarding plank to the deck. Then he held out his arms for Catherine.

Cat immediately placed her leather sketch case on his outstretched arms and daintily stepped down to the deck without even looking at him.

"Yer lordship, 'tis a miserable day. Ye don't expect a storm?"

"Surely it takes more than a few squall clouds to intimidate a braw Scots lassie like you, Maggie?" He winked to allay her fear. "Look at Lady Catherine, ready to meet her destiny with courage."

Is the devil mocking me? She glared at him with flashing eyes.

Patrick hid his amusement. "If you will follow me, ladies, I will show you to your cabin." He led them belowdecks and took them to a cabin in the ship's stern. Though it was not yet five o'clock, the light had gone from the day. When he threw open the door the cabin was shrouded in darkness until he lit a lantern.

It was a well-appointed cabin paneled in mahogany with two fairly wide berths, one atop the other, yet to Catherine it seemed unbelievably small, especially with four trunks taking up space.

"I suggest you make yourselves comfortable while we wait for the tide to turn. In less than an hour we'll weigh anchor and be under way. Tonight you may dine with me or I can have trays brought to you here."

"Thank you. Trays would be my overwhelming preference."

He bowed politely. "My cabin is aft. If there is aught you desire, please do not hesitate to come and ask me."

"I assure you, Lord Stewart, that I need nothing from you."

Her tone was sweet yet dripped with disdain.

Patrick had a sudden urge to take her over his knee and tan her arse. It wasn't the first time either. "*Bon voyage, cherie.*"

When he left, Cat looked about in dismay. "This room is so small, we'll be tripping over each other."

"It's roomy for a ship's cabin." Maggie opened a small door beneath a cabinet that held a washbowl and a jug of water. "Here are towels and soap and the chamber pot. That's all we need."

Cat opened a trunk, took out a nightgown and laid it on the upper berth. "I'll sleep up here, Maggie." There was a table and two chairs, so they sat down to wait for the voyage to begin. Finally they heard seamen shouting and the anchor being lifted.

"I should tell ye, my lamb, I'm not a very good sailor."

It was the understatement of the century. As soon as the vessel began to move with the flowing tide, Maggie began to groan with nausea. As the ship rocked slowly, the ship's lantern swung back and forth in the same rolling rhythm as the *Hepburn Rose*. Suddenly, Maggie's stomach erupted and she spewed on the cabin floor. Cat threw off her cloak, grabbed a towel and began to clean it up. Maggie, however, was nowhere near done.

Cat grabbed the chamber pot and held it steady as her companion continued to vomit. "There, are you feeling a bit better?"

Maggie's groans told her the answer was *no*!

"Why on earth didn't I wear a more practical gown for a sea voyage?" As she quickly removed the pale yellow dress and its matching primrose ruff, she answered her own question. "I don't have any practical gowns!" Thankful that she had left her farthingale at home, she brought soap and water and tended Maggie in her petticoat. As soon as Cat washed Maggie's face, the older woman began heaving again.

Catherine picked up the chamber pot and held it once more. It was more than half full before there was a lull in the spewing. "Oh, Maggie, love, you can't go on like this." The sight and smell of the vomit brought on Catherine's nausea and she knew she'd never felt this miserable in her life. She closed her eyes and said a quick prayer for her beloved nurse. "Why don't you lie down and see if that helps?"

Though Maggie lay down, she rolled in agony for a few minutes, then she sat bolt upright and erupted once again.

Catherine knew she had no choice. She could not let Maggie remain in this dreadful state if something could be done for her. Her disdainful words to Hepburn came back to haunt her: *I assure you, Lord Stewart, that I need nothing from you!* Cat cursed her own stupidity. *Now I shall have to swallow my pride and go to Lord Bloody Stewart as a supplicant!* She knew she would never do it for herself, but Maggie was another matter entirely. Cat swallowed her bile, slipped her cloak over her petticoat and hurried along the companionway to Hepburn's cabin.

Chapter Nine

*P*atrick remained on deck until the *Hepburn Rose* reached
the mouth of the river Thames, where it opened into the
North Sea. The threatened downpour arrived and he went below
to his cabin to change into dry clothes. He removed his soaked
shirt and, as he began to towel his shoulders, he heard a knock
upon the door. When he opened it, he was surprised to see
Catherine. "Come in."

She stepped inside, trying not to stare at his naked chest.
Hoping to sound contrite, she said, "I am sorry to bother you,
my lord, but I desperately need something for nausea."

Patrick's brows drew together and his gut knotted. "Are you
with child, Hellcat?"

Catherine gasped. With clenched fists she flew at him and
pummeled his bare chest. "You insolent bastard! Maggie is vi-
olently ill. I need something to stop her seasickness."

Patrick captured her fists and laughed with relief. "Seasick?
Is that all?" He released her, moved to a cupboard built into the
cabin wall and took out a small glass flacon. "This holds about
four ounces of ginger wine laced with laudanum. The ginger
should settle her stomach. The laudanum will make her sleep."
His dark eyes searched her face. "Do you need a dose for yourself, Cat?"

Seething with anger, she spat, "I assure you, Lord Stewart, I
need nothing from you!" She grabbed the flacon and fled.

The moment Catherine opened her cabin door, the sickening
stench of vomit assailed her. She forced herself to swallow rapidly and went inside. Maggie sat on the lower berth with her
arms wrapped around her belly. The chamber pot on the floor
now overflowed with nastiness. "Oh, my poor dear, here is
some ginger wine to calm your stomach. Hepburn swears by it,"

she encouraged. Cat threw off her cloak, sat down beside Maggie and held the flacon to her blue lips. "Sip it slowly."

Maggie obeyed, taking sips between great gulps of air. Though she still retched a few times, nothing came up.

"Oh, thank god, I think it's working. Better drink it all."

Within ten minutes, Maggie had stopped vomiting and her nausea had completely abated. Cat brought water and a fresh towel to cleanse her face and hands. "There, I'm sure you feel much fresher. Now lie down and try to get some rest." Catherine tucked a warm blanket about her companion and within minutes gave thanks that Maggie had fallen asleep.

Cat eyed the overflowing chamber pot with aversion. She knew she had little choice but to get rid of its foul contents. With reluctance she slipped on her cloak and reached for the pot but, before she even touched it, she was convulsed with dry heaves. Cat gripped her stomach to stop the retching and eventually it calmed. She knew if she had eaten anything at all that day, she too would be spewing. *Come on, you can do it!* Catherine held her breath and faced up to the task. Very carefully, she lifted the pot and managed to get as far as the companionway. Creeping along at a snail's pace and balancing her body with the rhythmic sway of the ship, she climbed the steps that led up to the deck.

The sweeping rain was such a surprise that it almost knocked her down, but she steadied herself and, gripping the ship's rail, hurled the contents of the chamber pot into the sea. She was so relieved that she'd managed the difficult feat that suddenly she dropped the slippery pot and it rolled away across the deck. "Damnation!" She had more sense than to go scrambling after it. She was drenched to the skin and shivering so hard that her teeth rattled. As quickly as she could, Cat descended to the cabin. Inside, she shrugged out of her sodden cloak and leaned back against the door to catch her breath. Suddenly, all the fight had gone out of her and she felt weak as a kitten. Cat was freezing and knew she must get out of her wet petticoat and under the warm blanket of the upper berth, but first there was still the mess on the cabin floor to be cleaned. Using her last ounce of strength, she took the towel she had used on Maggie and was about to bend down when suddenly the blood drained from her head and she was overcome by dizziness. She reached out to steady herself, but all she grasped was thin air as she went down in a dead faint.

* * *

Patrick set his wineglass down with a noisy clink. He knew immediately that Catherine was in trouble. He had just finished dinner when the forceful premonition stabbed through him. He was on his feet and running between one heartbeat and the next.

When he opened the cabin door the acrid stink of vomit caught in his throat. Maggie was fast asleep in her berth while Cat lay in a small heap on the floor. When Patrick swept her up in his arms, he felt that she was soaking wet, icy cold and unconscious. He removed her from the cabin and took her along to his. He had no way of knowing if she had been throwing up, but she looked deathly pale. Patrick took a small flacon of ginger wine from the cupboard and proceeded to disrobe her. He had no time to search for undergarment tapes; he simply tore off the wet petticoat. Then he wrapped her naked body in one of his blankets and sat down with her on his knee. He smoothed back her damp hair and tapped her cheek lightly. "Catherine, Cat, wake up; look at me."

Though she didn't know where she was, Cat felt warmer and safer, and all she wanted to do was sleep. She heard the slow beat of a drum in the distance, far away, yet incessant. Gradually it became so loud and so close that her eyes flew open. Dazed, she found herself in Patrick Hepburn's lap, her ear pressed against the slow, steady drumbeat of his heart.

"I want you to drink this, Catherine." He was looking so deeply into her eyes that she felt mesmerized, without a will of her own. Obediently, she opened her mouth and began to sip the potion he held to her lips. The spicy ginger with its bitter undertaste warmed her throat and her belly. *He's rocking me as if I were a babe.* She didn't realize it was the ship that rocked her. Her lips curved. *I like being rocked!* Her eyes wanted to close and finally she stopped fighting the desire. Within five minutes, she was fast in the arms of Morpheus.

With gentle hands, Patrick unwrapped the blanket and gazed down at her delicate beauty. When he had looked his fill, he rolled her so that she lay across his knee, face down. His eyes lit with amusement as they studied the tattoo at the top of her bottom cheek. Patrick simply couldn't resist. He reached out his fingertips to stroke the little black cat until he imagined he could hear it purring. A wave of tenderness rose up in him; she was so small, so vulnerable, and he knew he had never felt this protective about any other female he had ever known.

Patrick carried her to his berth and gently laid her down. Then he stripped off his clothes, turned down the lantern and climbed in next to her, pulling a soft, lamb's wool blanket over them. He eased her onto her side and then curved his long body against her back so that she was lying in his lap. The moment her bare flesh touched his cock he hardened with desire, but a will of iron curbed his passion from flaring out of control.

Patrick tucked her head beneath his chin and slid his powerful arms around her, cupping her breasts in the palms of his hands. It felt so right, so perfect, he knew this was the way he wanted to sleep for the rest of his life. His mouth curved with tender amusement as he imagined her wild reaction if she had known that they were lying naked together in bed. The names she would call him would blister his ears, and all of them would be deserved. He remembered how she had pummeled his chest earlier. If she knew what he was doing to her now, she would use more than her fists. She would likely kick and bite him. His cock throbbed against her bum and Patrick felt totally unrepentant. He wanted Catherine Seton Spencer and he intended to have her. How fortuitous that she came with abundant wealth and estates. *Little Hellcat!*

The sleeping draught that Catherine had taken was inducing strange dreams that were filled with fantasy yet felt amazingly real at the same time:

She was a black feline, not exactly a cat, more like a leopard. She was lying in a cave, curled up safely with her powerful mate, who was twice her size. She felt totally safe as she stretched against him, luxuriating in the warmth and protection his big body provided. She opened her large yellow eyes to gaze at him and he growled deep in his throat as he got to his feet and came over her in a dominant stance. When she rolled into a submissive position beneath him, he bent his great head and began to lick her with his rough tongue. It felt so sensual that she began to purr, deep in her throat.

The dream changed without rhyme or reason, transforming her from a feline into a female:

*Two guards who had come to arrest her in her petticoat
flanked her. "You are charged with a treasonous plot against
Her Majesty the queen."*

"Where are you taking me?"

"To the Tower of London."

"The Tower? I won't go!"

*They stopped before a studded oak door, opened it and
shoved her inside. A tall, dark figure stood awaiting her. Hot
anger erupted. "You! You monster! You have done this thing to
me!"*

*Patrick Hepburn cocked an amused brow and slowly re-
moved his clothes. Then he closed the distance between them
and tore off her petticoat. When she pummeled his bare chest
with clenched fists, he captured her hand, opened her fingers
and placed a big iron key on her palm. "You are free to leave
anytime, Hellcat."*

*She raised her chin high in the air and with the confidence
of a prideful cat walked to the tower window. With great abandon she flung the iron key into space.*

*Patrick came up behind her, slid his arms around her, and
bent to whisper in her ear, "Lady Catherine, you are tempting
as sin. Are you ready to meet your destiny with courage?"*

*She rubbed her bare bottom against his hard length. "I am,
Lord Bloody Stewart!" Cat licked her lips over the bastard.*

Catherine came up through the layers of sleep and lay with
her eyes closed, lulled by a gentle rocking sensation that made
her feel languid. Finally, she summoned enough energy to open
her eyes. She felt slightly disoriented, as if the cabin were the
wrong way about. She sat up slowly and stared at the two huge
hunting hounds sitting with beatific expressions on their faces.
"Satan, Sabbath!" She suddenly knew whose cabin she occupied, and then she realized that she was naked.

The door opened and Patrick Hepburn entered, balancing a
tray. He kept the door open with his foot. "Off you go. Don't
want a cat and dog fight over breakfast."

Her eyes flashed their warning. Her tone was icy, her words
measured. "How did I get here?"

"I drugged you and carried you to my bed."

"I am serious, sir!" she snapped angrily.

"So am I, Catherine." His eyes lingered on her face, then

took in her disheveled cloud of hair with appreciation. Until now she had always been immaculately groomed. "I thought we could eat in bed." He winked. "By the way, I owe you a petticoat."

The look on her face told him that his words had devastated her. He tried to make amends. "Cat, I'm teasing you." Her look of relief mauled his pride. "I'll go and get Maggie so that your cabin can be scrubbed. I think there's enough breakfast here for both of you." He set the tray down and departed.

Cat arose from the berth and wrapped herself in the blanket. Her nose detected his unique male scent. *It must be on the blanket—it couldn't possibly be on my body!*

Later, in the early afternoon, when the sea appeared to be calm, Catherine ventured up on deck. She wanted fresh air, but, more than that, she longed to experience the adventure of being aboard a sailing ship on a voyage at sea. She pulled her blue wool cloak about her and walked slowly with her hand upon the rail. The breeze played merry hell with her black curls, but it felt so exhilarating that for once she didn't care. She filled her lungs with the invigorating salt air and eagerly scanned the horizon. She experienced a sense of total freedom for the first time in her life as she became one with the wind and the sea.

When she turned around to walk back, she spotted the chamber pot resting against a coil of rope. She glanced about quickly to make sure none were watching, then went to retrieve it. As she reached out her hand, the ship's deck tilted slightly and the pot rolled away from her. She quickened her step and pursued it, determined that the obstinate object would not elude her for long. As she grabbed the handle firmly, deep male laughter rolled over her. Her head snapped up and she saw Patrick Hepburn standing directly above her on the quarterdeck. She had no idea how long he had been watching her. She blushed furiously. "What the devil are you laughing at?"

"You." He could not contain his amusement.

Still clutching the handle, she stalked up the steps to confront him on the quarterdeck. "Well?" she demanded.

"The sight of the elegant Lady Catherine brings tears to my eyes as I watch her throw caution to the wind and chase after a—"

"Piss pot?" she shouted, glaring daggers at him. Suddenly, it struck her that the ridiculous situation was rife with humor and she began to laugh. When he joined in, Cat laughed harder. "You are a devil, Hepburn! I get the distinct impression that you have been laughing at me since the moment we met."

"That is an unjust accusation. There have been times when I wanted to tan your arse."

As she set the china pot down, her eyes narrowed. "Your retribution was worse. You found another way to punish me."

"Catherine, if your plan for Arbella to marry Seymour had succeeded, they would have both gone to the Tower. If the queen discovered your part in it, you too could have gone to the Tower."

When he uttered the word *Tower,* it brought back her dream in vivid detail. They had been naked together in the Tower and she had thrown away the key! She recoiled from the memory.

Patrick saw her recoil and was determined to overcome her distaste for him. "Walk with me, Catherine." He put his hands behind his back so that he would not be tempted to help her down the steps that led to the deck. His hounds materialized immediately and bounded ahead of them. He shortened his steps to match hers as they followed the ship's rail. "The match with Seymour was abhorrent for other reasons."

She threw him a challenging look. "What reasons?"

"Arbella is one of the wealthiest heiresses in England. She has already inherited her late parents' money, and when her grandmother dies she will come into a vast share of landholdings."

"You think William Seymour wants to marry her for her money?"

"Of course he wants to wed her for her money, but there is no dishonor in that. The match is abhorrent because Seymour is dissolute. His debts are enormous. He owes thousands of pounds to moneylenders, to tailors, to jewelers, to wine merchants and scores of others. He has squandered a fortune on clothes and drink and women, and he needs Arbella's wealth to tide him over until he inherits from his father and grandfather. On top of everything else, his gambling debts are staggering." Patrick did not tell Catherine that Henry Somerset pissed in the same pot. He hoped her innate intelligence would now make her begin to question Somerset's motives for courting her.

Cat looked disillusioned. "Arbella is in love with him."

"Arbella is in love with the idea of marriage. She is a young woman who fears she will be left on the shelf. She longs for a husband . . . any husband." He made no effort to mask his contempt.

"You cocksure devil! You think you know everything there is to know about women, but you don't. You, sir, are in for a rude awakening!" She turned on her heel and left him.

He called after her, "You forgot your pot, Hellcat!"

Catherine could hear the laughter in his voice. "You can stuff your bloody pot, you insufferable oaf!"

For the remainder of the afternoon, Cat stayed in the cabin she shared with Maggie. Though she would have preferred to be up on deck, she remained stubbornly secluded so that she would not encounter Patrick Hepburn.

"My lovely gray velvet cloak got soaked last night. I'm afraid it's ruined," Cat said with a sigh.

"When it's thoroughly dry, a good brushing might restore it to respectability," Maggie mused. "Seton's not the fashion center of the world. It isn't Court, don't forget."

"I'm not likely to forget, when I'll be in the wilds of Scotland. I warrant the climate won't be suitable for half the clothes I've brought. Will it be warm in June?"

"Not warm like London. We may be lucky and get a few warm days in July or August."

"Good God, I shan't be there that long! I haven't been given a life sentence," Cat said with a shudder.

When a knock sounded on the cabin door, Catherine bristled. "If that's Hepburn, I shan't speak to him!"

Maggie opened the door and took the chamber pot Patrick held out.

"Are you feeling better, Maggie?"

"I'm right as rain, yer lordship, now that I have my sea legs. Won't ye come in?" Cat glared daggers at her, but Maggie pretended not to notice.

"Lady Catherine"—Patrick addressed her back—"since I deprived you of attending a wedding, may I escort you to—"

"You may escort me nowhere, sir!" She kept her back to him.

"As you wish." When he was halfway out the door he murmured, "Robert and Liz will be disappointed."

She spun about. "Wait! Come back! Liz and Robert's wedding?"

"Widdrington is close by, on the coast. The happy couple should have arrived this afternoon, so my instincts tell me they will marry tomorrow. I was going to suggest that the *Hepburn Rose* drop anchor there tonight, but since you don't wish me to escort you, I'll order the captain to press on."

"Don't you dare, you hellhound! I wish to go to Widdrington."

"Then sheathe your claws and ask me nicely, Lady Catherine."

Her face showed dismay. *He means it. He wants me to beg!* Cat had no intention of climbing off her high horse gracefully. "Dearest Lord Stewart, I beseech you to escort me to Widdrington."

"Lady Catherine, you beg so sweetly, you are tempting as sin."

Tempting as sin? He said those words in the Tower last night! Catherine shivered at the evocative memory.

Patrick saw. "Perhaps we can tuck you into a nice warm bed tonight to banish your shivers."

Her senses suddenly became drenched with Hepburn's male scent. *Did the uncivilized bastard sleep with me last night?* The thought was so outrageous, she immediately denied it. When the wicked thought persisted, her eyes narrowed to slits. "Perhaps you were not teasing this morning. Mayhap you *do* owe me a petticoat."

In less than an hour's time, the *Hepburn Rose* lay at anchor in Widdrington, and Liz couldn't believe her eyes when she saw who her visitors were. "Cat, darling, whatever are you doing here with Patrick? Don't tell me you two have beaten us to the altar?"

"Don't even jest about such things; I cannot think of a worse fate. We are deadly enemies—far more so now than when we first met," Catherine declared. "So, you two truly aren't wed yet?"

"No, we just arrived this afternoon and made arrangements to be married tomorrow. How lovely that you will be here."

Catherine stared at Patrick. "How the devil did you know?"

"He's a warlock! Didn't he tell you?" Liz teased.

Though the words were said in jest, Cat could not dismiss the idea lightly. There was too much about the uncanny Scot that defied explanation. "I hope you have room for Maggie and me; we had a dreadful first night aboard ship, coping with *mal de mer.*"

"Of course we have room," Robert declared. "Do you think I would take a wife who didn't own a grand house?"

"You might as well know that Mother has banished me from Court. I am being shipped to my grandfather in Scotland because I got involved in my friend Arbella Stuart's plot to marry William Seymour."

"You are so damned impulsive, Cat; didn't you realize that match would be forbidden by Her Majesty?" Robert asked bluntly.

"The queen's wishes didn't stop you, Rob Carey!"

"The queen doesn't wish us to marry?" Liz asked Robert.

"Elizabeth doesn't wish any of her courtiers to marry." Robert frowned at Cat, hoping she wouldn't pursue the subject.

"She's grown extremely jealous and possessive in her old age. She wants other females to be as unhappy as she is," Maggie said.

"I told you she was jealous of you." Robert slipped his arm about Liz, kissed her temple and hoped she would drop the matter. "I'm taking Liz to Edinburgh for our honeymoon. Though she has always lived close to the Border, she's never been across it."

"You must both come to Crichton for a few days," Patrick invited. "Perhaps Lady Catherine will come and stay too."

Cat knew it would insult Liz if she refused. Also she admitted to herself that she wanted to see Crichton; nevertheless, she bristled at the way Hepburn manipulated her so that she had to comply.

After dinner, Maggie excused herself and went up to bed.

Cat and Liz talked endlessly of weddings and clothes, which gave Patrick and Robert a chance to withdraw to the library for a drink and some private conversation.

"It was a clever idea to travel to Edinburgh for your honeymoon," Patrick said with approval.

"Well, I could hardly get married one day and depart the next, leaving my bride of one day to explain my absence."

Patrick grinned. "Women have a way of complicating matters."

"Obviously! What the hell is Catherine doing in your

clutches? Wouldn't it have made more sense for Isobel to send her to Hertfordshire until the Arbella Stuart matter was dealt with?"

"Not once I got through putting the fear of God into Isobel, or the fear of Elizabeth, which amounts to the same thing. Do you object to my interest in Catherine?"

"I just don't want her to be hurt."

"*Homo homini lupus*—every man is a wolf to every other man."

"The queen would never approve of marrying Lady Catherine to a Scot. Better look elsewhere, Patrick. You saw Spencer Park. Catherine's estate is far too valuable for Her Majesty to give it to any but an English nobleman."

"I did indeed see Spencer Park. But Elizabeth will not reign forever, Robert."

Carey, convinced that Hepburn had second sight, gave him a long, speculative look. "I realize her years are numbered."

"Her *months* are numbered, Robert."

"Patrick"—Carey cleared his throat, anxious to ask a favor—"do you think we could arrange to see King James together? He may be livid that I gave his letter to Cecil rather than Elizabeth, and I would rather have your company when I beard the Lion of Scotland in his den."

"Of course. Once again, a united force of two against one?"

"Precisely! With the wedding, I can't leave tomorrow, but Liz and I can travel the next day. I'll stop at Bewcastle to pay my men and be in Edinburgh by June second."

"If we sail after the wedding, the *Hepburn Rose* should arrive at the Port of Leith tomorrow night. The following day I shall safely deliver Lady Catherine into the hands of the irascible Earl of Winton and join you in Edinburgh on June second. The Castle Rock is a fine inn where the Canongate meets High Street. I'll meet you there and we'll go to Holyrood Palace together."

"Thank you, Patrick. The confidence you exude tends to rub off on me when I am in your company."

My confidence will be a figment of the imagination when Jamie demands that I give him the exact date of Elizabeth's death. Ah well, Hepburn, perhaps you will have an epiphany in the next forty-eight hours. If not, you will simply have to fob him off with some mystical hocus-pocus!

Chapter Ten

*C*atherine Spencer watched raptly as Liz Widdrington was joined in holy wedlock to Robert Carey. The bridal gown that Liz had commissioned in London was pale green velvet embroidered with white Tudor roses, its sleeves slashed with white satin. She had chosen the Tudor colors of green and white to honor her new husband.

George Carey, Warden of the English East March, had ridden in from the Border stronghold of Bewcastle early this morning to be his brother's groomsman. George, Cat's uncle, was married to her aunt Beth, and, as Catherine's glance traveled over the two brothers standing at the altar, she wondered if their marriages were love matches. Robert seemed to love Liz in spite of the remark he'd made about marrying a woman with a big house, but she doubted that her aunt Beth loved George, since they lived apart for most of the year. She had likely wed George because he was Lord Hunsdon's heir and one day soon she'd be Lady Hunsdon.

As the couple pledged their vows, Catherine's thoughts strayed to her own mother. She knew Isobel had married her father to escape Scotland. Then she had used Court to escape her husband. Cat's thoughts moved on to Arbella Stuart and she shuddered. *How horrific it would be to have someone marry you for your wealth.* Catherine closed her eyes and innocently vowed before God that she would never marry, except for love alone.

While most eyes were on the bride this morning, Patrick Hepburn's attention was caught and held by the ethereal beauty of Lady Catherine. She wore blush pink velvet, her bodice and sleeves embroidered with snowdrops, and she had threaded pearls through her dark curls. She was such an exquisite creature that he wondered wryly what she would think when she met her grandfather. Though he was an Earl of the Realm, Geordie Seton was no polished nobleman. He was a rough, blunt Scot who cursed and drank whisky, and Patrick wondered how Cat would cope.

"Forasmuch as Elizabeth and Robert have consented together in holy wedlock, and have witnessed the same before God and this company and thereto have given and pledged their troth either to other, and have declared the same by giving and receiving of a ring, and by joining of hands; I pronounce that they be man and wife together, in the name of the Father, and of the Son, and of the Holy Ghost. Amen." The minister took the newlyweds and their witnesses into the vestry to sign the register, and within minutes Liz came back down the aisle, flushed with happiness, on the arm of her new husband.

All the villagers of Widdrington had gathered to see Liz marry Sir Robert Carey, and they congregated outside the church to throw rice and help celebrate the happy occasion. Though the sun shone brightly, the weather was mild rather than warm. Liz's younger sister, Sarah, who was the bride's maid of honor, slipped her arm through Patrick Hepburn's and gazed up at him with undisguised desire. " 'Tis not fair," she murmured as her eyes slid over his muscled body with hunger. "Liz has had two husbands, while I'm still unwed."

Patrick laughed down at her and squeezed her hand. "But not unwilling nor untried, I warrant."

"There's only one sure way to find out, Lord Stewart."

"Alas, I sail within the hour, my lovely. Perhaps I can be of service at another time, in another place," he offered gallantly.

"Why do females cling to him?" Cat asked Maggie with disgust.

"Wishful thinking. They'd all like a chance to lie with him and mayhap tame him."

"Maggie!" Cat was shocked at her candor.

Maggie winked. "Sorry, my lamb; weddings make me lusty."

Refreshments were being served in the Widdrington House gardens, and Patrick joined the Carey brothers to drink a tankard of ale.

"Any Border trouble while I was gone?" Robert asked.

George rubbed his chin. "Nothing I couldn't handle. Had a visit from a Scots Border warden, Armstrong, making accusations that you'd hanged his brother. He was looking for trouble."

"I'm the one who hanged Armstrong," Patrick stated flatly.

George nodded. "Watch your back, *both* of you. There's a streak of madness in the Armstrongs on either side of the Border."

Before the hour was up, Patrick sought out Catherine. "Say your good-byes, then I advise you to change into something more sensible for the rest of the voyage."

Cat's chin went up. "I do not own any sensible clothes, sir."

"So I've noticed, Hellcat. But you look so lovely in this particular gown, I think you should save it for when you go to meet your grandfather. You will surely be the envy of your Seton cousins if you arrive looking like a lady-in-waiting who has just stepped from the Queen's Court."

Is the devil mocking me or complimenting me? Cat doubted it was the latter and was loath to do his bidding, but since the picture he painted appealed to her, she decided to change.

Wearing a blue woolen dress with a quilted bodice, and wrapped in her blue cloak, Cat stayed on deck for the entire voyage. By the time the *Hepburn Rose* reached the Firth of Forth it was evening. She watched the seamen climb the rigging to take in the sails against a spectacular crimson and purple sunset, which was followed almost immediately by a black night sky. There were few lights on shore until the ship neared Leith. The port was almost an extension of Edinburgh, and since there was no fog tonight the city was all lit up. Maggie joined Cat on deck while the ship sailed up the Forth. "It's been more than twenty-one years since I last saw Edinburgh. I can't believe I'm home!"

Cat took Maggie's hand. "Don't you think of London as home?"

Maggie shook her head. "I'm a Celt to the bone, God help me."

"Ladies." Hepburn's deep voice startled them. "If given the choice of sleeping aboard or spending the night at Netherbow Inn, I am sure you would prefer the latter."

"How perceptive of you," Catherine said sweetly.

"At the inn you'll have all the amenities of home, Maggie. Haggis for supper and a bath in a wooden barrel."

"Och, yer lordship, stop plaguing the child. She'll think the Scots are all wild and uncivilized."

His dark, compelling glance met Catherine's. "When in reality only some of us are wild and uncivilized."

She hated to let him have the last word. As he led them from the ship, she saw that he carried a book in his hand. "I had no idea you could read, Lord Stewart."

He smiled at the taunt. "*Julius Caesar.* I like to read in bed, unless you have something else in mind, Lady Catherine?"

Maggie's words rushed back to her: *A chance to lie with him and mayhap tame him!* Cat lowered her lashes, thankful that the darkness concealed her blushes.

As they walked up Leith Wynd toward the inn, Patrick told them his plans. "I'll hire a carriage to take you to Seton tomorrow. Winton Castle is about a dozen miles from here. There is no need to arise early. I'll call for you about ten." When they got to the inn, he paid for two of their best rooms and also paid to stable his horse. "By the time you have ordered your dinner, your trunks will be here. I hope you'll be comfortable, ladies."

Later, when she heard a knock on the door, Catherine opened it eagerly. As two seamen from the *Hepburn Rose* carried in their trunks, Cat felt a pang of disappointment. A short time later, her spirits lifted when a second knock came. This time it was a buxom maid with their dinner, and again Catherine felt let down. She pinned a smile to her face, refusing to acknowledge that she had hoped it was Hepburn. "It smells good . . . I hope it isn't haggis."

After dinner both she and Maggie had a bath, then she laid out her clothes for morning. She washed some stockings and kept herself busy until bedtime, but once the lights were out, Cat lay with eyes wide-open, feeling homesick, lonely and vulnerable to the lurking fear of the unknown. She listened in the darkness but heard no sounds from the next room. *The dissolute devil is out carousing, no doubt!*

The dissolute devil, however, was lying quietly in bed trying to read *Julius Caesar.* His thoughts kept conjuring the image of the young female in the adjoining room, so he closed his eyes for a few minutes to concentrate on merging his mind with hers. He could feel her loneliness and her vulnerability. He searched for what was causing it and discerned that she was afraid of tomorrow. Patrick breathed deeply, focused his concentration and

allowed his spirit to slip from his physical body. He was aware
of the danger involved in this practice, for sometimes the spirit
had difficulty rejoining the body. Lying immobile in bed lessened the risk.

Patrick took her small hand in his and murmured soothingly,
"Don't be afraid, Catherine; don't be afraid. Your courage will
shine through. Be brave, little Hellcat." His spirit surrounded
her, reassuring her until at last she let go of her fear and slept.
Then he returned to his bed and picked up his book.

Julius Caesar was Patrick's favorite work of Shakespeare,
and he'd read it many times. *"I am constant as the northern
star."* He enjoyed its fire and passion and fury. The qualities of
the characters were so real: the nobility of Caesar, the poisonous envy of Casca and Cassius, the cunning of Marc Antony.
When Patrick read of the prophetic dreams, he knew such
things existed, and he totally identified with the Soothsayer and
his predictions. *"Beware the ides of March."*

As he read, Elizabeth Tudor intruded into his thoughts. He
concentrated on the words to banish her, but as well as visualizing her funeral procession, he could hear the music of a death
march. The volume of the march steadily increased. He could
hear the plodding hooves of the black horses that pulled her bier
and the slow footsteps of her mourners as they marched behind
her coffin. *"Beware the ides of March . . . March . . . March.
The ides of March are come!"*

Suddenly, Patrick knew that his uncanny sixth sense was
foretelling Elizabeth's death. He was gripped with certainty that
the life of England's queen would end in the month of March!
He set the book aside and quickly counted—nine months to the
beginning of March, ten months to the end. From what he had
seen of her with his own eyes, the time rang true. *How can I be
sure?* he asked himself. *I cannot, but I have learned to trust my
instincts. They are constant as the northern star!*

Lady Catherine sat in the carriage dressed in her gray velvet
cloak with its furred hood pulled up over her hair. Beneath it she
was wearing the gown that Patrick Hepburn had suggested. She
clasped her hands tightly and tried not to think about Seton.

Maggie gazed avidly out the carriage window, exclaiming
every few minutes about the various landmarks that she recognized. Every once in a while, Cat too glanced out the window,

but she did not see the sheep-covered hills or the gushing streams. All she saw was Patrick Hepburn astride his big black mount, Valiant. Earlier when she'd asked about the dogs, he'd laughed and told her his steward had taken them to Crichton. "I don't want Satan and Sabbath bringing down one of your grandfather's prized longhorns!"

Catherine thought of her father. Cattle had been his whole existence. The females in his family got little enough attention, and she had no doubt it would be the same with her grandfather.

All too quickly Maggie announced, "We're on Seton land, my lamb." Cat gazed from the carriage and saw that there were miles and miles of it. Soon she began to see grazing herds of cattle and realized they were exactly like the animals at Spencer Park in Hertford. It reassured her a tiny bit. If the cattle were the same, could the people be so very different?

The carriage attracted attention, and soon dozens of men on horseback were riding toward it. Hepburn greeted them but did not slow his pace as he led the way toward Winton Castle. The coach driver pulled his team to a halt in the flagged courtyard, where Hepburn dismounted and handed Valiant's reins to a stableman.

Patrick opened the carriage door and lifted down Maggie. "Plant your feet on your home turf, lass."

Geordie Seton rode into the courtyard at full gallop, reined in and dismounted. "Who the hell ha' ye dragged to Seton, Hepburn?"

Cat's serving woman curtsied with respect. "Lord Winton."

Geordie's bristly brows drew together. "Maggie? Is it ye?"

Patrick did not offer to lift Cat; he held out his hand instead and looked into her eyes. *If you ever need me, just whisper my name.* She heard the words as clearly as if he had spoken them aloud. Then he did speak, "Courage, Hellcat."

She lifted her chin, placed her hand in his and daintily stepped down into the courtyard.

"Lord Winton, may I present Lady Catherine Seton Spencer."

Catherine stared at the wiry male, desperately trying to mask her dismay. *This is the Earl of Winton, my grandfather? This scraggly man lives in a castle?* Nervous hands pushed back her fur hood to reveal her black curls threaded with seed pearls.

Geordie Seton stared back as if he were seeing an apparition. "Catherine? Yer never Isobel's child?"

Cat nodded apprehensively.

"Christ Almighty, yer never tellin' me a carthorse like Isobel produced an exquisite thoroughbred like this?" he asked Maggie.

"Aye, yer lordship. Miracles never cease!"

"My wee sweet bonnie lass, mayhap I wasna' cursed after all!"

He lifted Catherine's small hand and kissed it. "I won't smother ye wi' a hug. Are ye afraid of a rough old bugger like me?"

Suddenly Cat smiled. "I am afraid of neither man nor beast!"

"Wheest, lass, yer the spittin' image of yer old granddad!"

Cat began to laugh at the absurd idea that she was his spitting image. "Yes, Maggie told me the resemblance was uncanny!"

Geordie signaled to one of the mounted men who sat gaping at the scene in the courtyard. "Go and fetch Janet and Jessie. My sisters won't believe their eyes." He looked at Patrick. "Hepburn, I'm in yer debt. Come on inside fer a drink. This calls fer a celebration!" He swept them all into the castle, shouting his orders as soon as he was through the door. "Fetch all the servants to the hall," he told the steward.

As Cat's gaze swept about the Great Hall's vaulted, beamed ceiling hung with Winton banners displaying its winged dragon, she felt pride in her Scottish ancestry for the first time.

When all the servants, from the potboys to the scullery maids, were assembled, Geordie Seton climbed up on a hall bench. "This is a day to celebrate! I want ye all to take a good look at Lady Catherine, my beautiful granddaughter and my heir. This castle and everyone in it will be at her disposal fer as long as she graces us wi' her presence. There's bin none this lovely enter Winton Castle since I brought my bride home forty years ago." He signaled Hepburn. "Patrick, lad, lift her up onto this table, so they can take a gander at what an elegant lady looks like!"

Hepburn's hands removed her gray cloak, then closed about Cat's waist as he hoisted her onto the table. His lips touched her ear. "Geordie already thinks the sun shines out yer arse, and I know how you relish being the center of attention, Hellcat."

As she stood with every eye upon her, adorned in her pink velvet gown embroidered with snowdrops, she could almost kiss the dark, dominant devil for suggesting that she wear it.

"Good! Here's the rest of the family come to greet ye." Seton pointed to his sisters. "Jessie, Janet, this is my wee grand-daughter, Catherine, come to visit. I think ye'll agree she makes up fer my no' havin' sons to brag about."

As the two women, who looked to be in their fifties, gazed in amazement at the delicate doll-like female displayed on the castle table, Cat thought, *My mother looks just like her aunts. Two men, far too young to be their husbands, accompanied the women. They must be their sons!*

One young man shouldered the other aside and boldly stepped forward. He raised proprietary hands and lifted Catherine to the floor. "I'm Malcolm. Welcome to Seton, Catherine."

She smiled up at him. "You must be my second cousin. I am delighted to meet you, Malcolm." She looked over at the other male. "And you are another cousin, I presume?"

Her aunt Janet brought the young man forward. "This is my son, Andrew. I must say, you look nothing like Isobel."

"Fer which we are eternally grateful, amen," Geordie said with irreverence as he jumped down from the bench.

Andrew grinned at Cat and she knew she liked him immediately.

"Whisky fer everybody," Seton ordered his steward.

Everyone, including the servants, received a dram of whisky. When the steward began to pour one for Catherine, she asked tentatively, "Do you have any wine, please?"

"O' course we ha' wine and anythin' else yer heart desires." While it was being brought, Geordie raised his glass. "To Lady Catherine, my granddaughter. The most beautiful lass in Scotland!" His eyes searched the gathered servants. "Where's Cook? There ye are, Peg. Haggis tonight; this is a celebration!"

Cat could not resist glancing at Hepburn. She knew the devil wouldn't be able to hide his amusement. When he came forward to say good-bye, her granddad invited him to stay for dinner.

"Tempting as it sounds, my lord, I'm off to Crichton. In the last five months I've spent only three nights under my own roof."

Catherine's eyes followed the tall figure as he left the hall.

She experienced a small pang of anxiety at the separation, but it melted away as her new family clustered about her.

She and Maggie were given adjoining rooms in one of the turrets, and Cat knew she was going to enjoy living in a Scottish castle. It had a parapet walk and its own dungeons, now used for storing casks of whisky and wine, and tomorrow she intended to explore Winton Castle from top to bottom. At dinner there were so many people, she had difficulty learning everyone's name. Though her aunts Jessie and Janet had passed their looks on to her mother, their personalities were not nearly so austere. As well as sons, they had daughters, all married, and Cat was relieved that none of the females seemed to resent her. They generously complimented both her looks and her clothes and seemed ready to be her friend. She especially loved the fact that both her grandfather and the rest of them took it for granted that Maggie would eat with them.

"Well, what do ye think o' the haggis?" Geordie demanded.

Gingerly, Catherine took a mouthful and decided it wasn't going to make her stomach heave. "It's better than I expected."

Geordie laughed. "There's a brave lass. We let the English think it's all ears and arseholes just to keep the recipe secret."

Cat laughed merrily. Salty language appealed to her and she was willing to bet her granddad wouldn't reprimand her use of it.

She was aware that both Malcolm and Andrew never took their eyes from her during dinner. Though it was easy to see their personalities differed, she hoped they were friends and not rivals. She was surprised to learn that none of them lived in the castle. The Earl of Winton lived alone, and his two nephews each had their own home on the vast Seton acres. Since neither was married, their mothers kept house for them. Cat accepted invitations to dine in their homes and looked forward to meeting her aunts' grandchildren. When they all departed, Cat sighed. She felt blessed the day had gone so much better than she had anticipated.

Cat retired to her turret chamber with its huge feather bed, and as she replayed the day's events in her mind, she drifted into a dream. As usual it was about Hepburn, and her lips curved. *If you ever need me, whisper my name.*

"Patrick." The whisper hung in the air for a moment, then vanished. When nothing happened she got out of bed and went to the open window. "Patrick."

"I'm here." The deep voice behind her floated on the darkness.

She spun around. "What do you want?"

"You summoned me."

"I did not!"

"Don't lie to yourself, Catherine."

"I do not need you," she said emphatically.

"I know you don't need me. You are in no danger. You simply wanted to see what my name felt like on your lips."

"No," she denied, "I wanted to see if I had power over you."

"'Tis I who have the power, Catherine."

His dominant words turned her knees to water and she grasped the stone sill for support. The feel of the rough stone awakened her and for a moment she wondered what she was doing out of bed. Then she remembered. "I was dreaming about Patrick Hepburn," she said aloud. She had never sleepwalked before, had she? "Was I going to meet him?" Somewhere in the shadowy recesses of dreams half-forgotten she suspected it wasn't the first time.

"That is preposterous! I despise the dominant devil. I dislike everything about him."

Don't lie to yourself, Catherine.

Cat admitted that she lied upon occasion, especially when it was expedient, but she seldom lied to herself. As the truth slowly began to dawn upon her, she became horrified. In spite of the fact that she disliked Hepburn and he irritated her beyond reason, was it possible that he appealed to her on a physical level? No, no, that was impossible!

Do not lie to yourself, Catherine.

"Tell the truth and shame the devil. It's more than mere physical appeal. It is far darker. It is sexual attraction." The moment she said the words, she knew they were true, and she felt guilty revulsion with herself.

Cat knew she must put an end to such reckless nonsense before it went farther. And the surest way to do that was to stop fighting . . . it was far too seductive. They must be friends . . . it was far less alluring. She gazed from the window. *A truce, Patrick?*

At Crichton, Hepburn stood at his bedchamber window, his big hands resting on the rough stones. *A truce, Hellcat.*

He turned from the window and began to undress, half wishing he hadn't promised to be in Edinburgh tomorrow. In light of what Jock Elliot had reported, he needed to spend more time at home. *If wishes were horses . . .*

Ordinarily, he'd take in stride a report of reivers descending in the night, since it happened a few times throughout the year. But the fact that his hayricks had been set afire, coupled with the warning George Carey had delivered about Armstrong looking for trouble, alerted his instincts. Tomorrow on his ride to Edinburgh he would protect his back with a half dozen moss-troopers.

Chapter Eleven

*H*epburn and Robert Carey rode up to the stables at Holyrood in mid-afternoon. Patrick had sent a scout to the palace earlier in the day and learned that King James had gone hunting. He indulged in his favorite activity whenever the weather permitted. As they turned their horses over to royal grooms, they heard the horns of the returning hunters and the baying of the king's hounds.

Mounted, James showed at his best; he looked a commanding figure when he was in the saddle. It was when he dismounted and began to shamble about with an uneven gait on spindly legs that he lost all semblance of majesty.

Patrick saw the pair of roe deer James had bagged and knew he would be in a good mood. He intended to keep him that way.

The king spotted Hepburn's great height and his face lit up with expectation. "Man, ye've bin gone near a month!"

"Patience is a virtue, Sire," Patrick quoted in Latin.

"And had better be rewarded," James replied bluntly. "Carey, let us hope ye do not come empty-handed."

Robert successfully masked his apprehension. "I do not, Sire."

The king looked down at his hunting clothes. "I'm all blood an' guts. Come up wi' me while I change."

The king's attendants trailed after the trio as they traversed the corridors of Holyrood to the royal apartment. At the door he dismissed them. "I dinna need ye. Lord Stewart will attend me." Hepburn and Carey followed him into his bedchamber, where he told his body servant he wanted privacy. James stripped off his clothes and Patrick went to his wardrobe, chose the robe that had the least stains on it, and helped him put it on. Patrick knew the thought of bathing would never enter his head, so he poured water from a jug so that James would at least wash his hands. "So, I take it ye were successful?" he asked Robert.

"We met with more success than we hoped," Patrick replied.

"Ye gave Elizabeth my letter?"

"Better than that, we gave it to the power behind the throne. Cecil will present it in the best possible light once he has prepared her to look favorably upon you."

"Cecil has agreed tae deal wi' me?" James asked hopefully.

"Secretly, of course," Patrick confirmed.

Robert produced the heavily sealed letter. "The Secretary of State asked me to deliver this into your hands, Your Majesty."

James took the letter greedily, rubbing his thumbs over the red wax seals with lustful anticipation. "I prefer dealin' wi' a mon; yer cousin Elizabeth treats me like a lackey," he told Carey.

Robert cleared his throat. "I should give you privacy to read your correspondence, Your Majesty."

"Aye," James agreed, "take a walk round the palace an' return in an hour." He looked at Patrick. "Ye can stay put."

The moment they were alone, the king tore open the letter and read the three pages avidly. "He signed it wi' a number!"

"Cecil has an intellect that matches yours, Sire, and, like you, he is cautious. The letters you exchange must be in cipher."

"Aye, so he indicates." James tapped the letter and reread it.

Patrick focused his mind on the pages. The first was a letter from Cecil to James, the second was instructions the king must employ when writing to Elizabeth, and the third laid out the cipher. A list of names and places had each been assigned a specific number, and at the bottom was a warning that the cipher should be shared with none. Patrick saw that Cecil was 10, James was 30 and Elizabeth was 24. His father had taught him the ancient science of numerology. Numbers had their own special power.

"Can I trust Carey, or is he Elizabeth's man?"

"If he ever was Elizabeth's, he is her man no longer. She kept him on his knees for hours. She was so jealous of the woman he had chosen to marry that she forbade her the Court. Robert Carey knew the queen would not be amenable to receiving your letter, so wisely suggested we seek out Cecil. It was a shrewd move, Sire." Hepburn readily gave the credit to his friend Robert.

"Elizabeth is a vindictive old bitch!"

"If you make the new Lady Carey welcome at your Court, Robert will be indebted to you forever."

"Waesucks, he defied Elizabeth and wed the lass?"

"He is aware that the sun is setting on her reign, Sire."

"Now we come tae it. Sit down, Patrick, an' tell me."

Hepburn did not yet know the exact date of Elizabeth's death, but even if he did, he would rather not divulge it immediately. He preferred to draw it out to his advantage. "Her flesh is frail, yet her spirit burns brightly with fire and fury."

"How much longer?" James demanded.

"Less than a year, Sire."

"Ye're canny as a fox, Patrick. Admit it; ye've had a vision."

"I've had many. I even envisioned you signing a document that pledged me *any* English heiress of my choice, plus an earldom."

"Christ Almighty, must ye hold my feet tae the fire?"

"It seems I must, Sire."

James unlocked his desk, shuffled some papers about, then withdrew a document and thrust it at Hepburn.

Patrick scanned it to make sure there were no slipping-out phrases, then raised his eyes. "It needs your signature, Sire."

"Aye, Lord Stewart, and I need a date."

Stalemate!

Patrick felt confident about the month of March. "It will be in the spring, Sire. Early spring."

The king dipped his quill into the inkwell and held it poised above the document.

Patrick had the month, but needed a day. He searched the recesses of his brain. The number 24 was all that came to mind. It was the number that Cecil had assigned to Elizabeth. He reminded himself that there were no coincidences. Numbers had their own mysterious power. The cipher number given to her had sealed Elizabeth's fate. It was the Queen of England's destiny.

"For your ears alone."

The king eagerly nodded his agreement.

"Elizabeth will die on March twenty-fourth, Sire."

James put his signature on the paper with a flourish. "Patrick, lad, ye have just made me the happiest mon in Scotland!"

Hepburn slipped the signed pledge into his doublet. *I pray God and the devil that you have just done the same for me, James.*

When Robert Carey returned, the king thanked him profusely for his services and told him that in due time there would be another letter for him to take to England. He congratulated Robert on his marriage. "Ye must bring Lady Carey tae Court. The queen is plannin' one o' her fancy functions next week an' I know Annie will welcome an English lady. Where are ye stayin'?"

"My bride and I are at the Castle Rock Inn, Your Majesty."

"An inn? Nay, that will never do. Patrick, go an' have a word wi' the Earl of Mar. Johnny has apartments here at Holyrood an' has a town house in the Canongate he seldom uses."

"Thank you, Sire." Carey was taken aback at the generosity.

"Don't thank me; thank Johnny Erskine." The king chuckled.

"Sire, the Earl of Winton's granddaughter is visiting him from England. I'm sure he would like to bring her to Court."

"Haven't seen Geordie in years. See Annie about invitations."

When the pair was safely away from the king's apartments, Robert, vastly relieved, thanked Patrick. "Lord, the audience went so much better than I ever anticipated. Do you think the Earl of Mar will have no objection to our using his town house?"

"John Erskine was James's playmate when they were children. They've been close as brothers all their lives. His mother was a Stewart too—we're all loosely related."

"Liz will be thrilled to death about all this!"

At Seton, Catherine was surprised that her grandfather took breakfast with her, but he explained that he wanted to give her a tour of Winton Castle. "D'ye think ye could call me Geordie? Granddad makes me feel decrepit."

"It would be an honor to call you Geordie."

"Is that all ye can eat, lass?"

"She doesn't like porridge, and unlike ye, she cannot shovel down lashings of kidneys an' eggs." Maggie eyed his plate. "Nor leftover haggis. She likes fresh-baked bread and heather honey."

"I have hollow legs," he jested.

"Is that what's wrong with them?" Maggie teased right back.

A short time later, Geordie's tour started in the dungeons. "These were once well used an' not solely fer our English enemies. Clan feuds generatin' hatred, steeped in blood and ripened by centuries of antagonism linger to this day."

"Did the Setons feud with the Hepburns?" Catherine asked lightly.

"I reckon so, since they often intermarried," he jested.

Next, they stopped in the kitchens, where he introduced her to Peg, the head cook. The place buzzed like a beehive, with potboys and scullery maids preparing food for the cattle herders, but they stopped working to stare after the earl's beautiful granddaughter.

Maggie met up with them again as they left the library and went up to the solar. Though seldom used these days, it held comfortable chairs and pillows set before a stone fireplace.

"Use this fer yer sittin' room, if ye like." Geordie then led the way up to his own two-room Master Tower. His inner chamber had a huge four-poster bed and a massive fireplace that took up an entire wall. A large portrait hung above the mantel.

Cat stopped before it and gazed up, entranced. "Who is she?"

"My beloved Audra, Countess of Winton. Yer grandmother."

"But it could be me!" Catherine was stunned at the likeness. "Mother never once told me about her."

"Aye, well, Isobel was an unnatural daughter. There was always a deal of antipathy between them, to Audra's great sorrow."

As Catherine stared at the elegant, *petite* lady in the painting, with the profusion of black glossy curls, she suddenly realized why Isobel had never loved her. "Every time Mother looks at me, she sees Audra! Maggie, why didn't you ever tell me?"

"Isobel forbade me, my lamb."

Geordie touched Catherine's cheek. "Havin' ye here is like seein' my Audra again." His eye held a tear and he left the room.

Catherine turned to Maggie. "Mother hates me because I look exactly like my grandmother."

"Isobel hated her mother because she was beautiful and did not pass that beauty along to her. It's yer beauty she cannot abide."

"How sad," Catherine said softly. "Yet I don't feel sad when

I look at my grandmother. I feel happy and extremely fortunate!"

"Audra must feel happy too, when she looks down and sees ye."

Geordie came to the door. "Come on, Catherine, we're goin' to the stables so ye can choose a mount. Seton's too vast fer walkin'; ye need to ride."

The first thing she encountered when she walked into the stables was a black cat. "Oh, how lovely. Come, puss!" She bent down to stroke the small feline, and it arched its back in pleasure. She picked it up and it gazed at her with huge golden eyes. "Oh, I think she likes me!"

"Then take it," Geordie said.

"To the castle? You don't mind?"

"Why would I mind ye havin' sommat as gives ye pleasure?"

"Why indeed?" Catherine was beginning to adore this man.

Young stable boys, busy cleaning stalls, stopped their labors to stare as Geordie asked, "See anythin' ye fancy, lass?"

There were no white palfreys like Jasmine but she spotted a glossy black filly that wasn't too tall. "I like this one."

"Good choice. She's a dainty piece, too small fer a mon. Come an' pick a saddle an' we'll put some silver bells on it."

Cat looked at the row of saddles. "Do you have a sidesaddle?"

Geordie laughed. "Most women ride astride in Scotland, lass. Wheesht, ye'll soon get the hang of it. Ye'll be bowlegged as me afore long." He spotted one of his nephews whom Cat had met last night and waved him over. "Andrew, there's a pony cart around somewhere. Find it an' make sure the axles are not rotted." He turned to Catherine. "D'ye think ye could learn to drive a cart?"

"I can learn to do anything," she vowed.

"Andy, lad, she's the spittin' image of me!"

Andrew winked at Catherine. "Then God help her, Geordie."

She smiled at Andrew. "Let me see if I have this right. You are Janet's son. I'm invited to your house for dinner tonight."

"Yes, I'm Janet's son, but ye are going to Malcolm's tonight. He's the elder nephew and Jessie is Geordie's elder sister. There would be merry hell to pay if ye ignored the pecking order."

Damnation, I detest rules and regulations!

•   •   •

Catherine decided to wear her lilac velvet with slashed sleeves that showed the cream satin beneath. Maggie helped put up her hair, then fastened the matching ruff around her neck. "Are you not coming with me tonight?"

"No, I'll stay and have dinner with yer grandfather."

"He's not coming either?" Cat asked, surprised.

"Too many females under one roof fer his liking."

"But Malcolm will be there."

"Aye, he's the head of that household. He was married, but his young wife died. He has no children, but his sisters do, all of them wee lasses. Go and enjoy."

The grand house was a little more than a mile away from the castle, and Catherine was transported there in the earl's carriage. Jessie met her at the door and a servant took her cloak. Cat was immediately surrounded by four little girls between the ages of three and seven who were so excited they danced about her in a circle. The two young women who were their mothers seemed just as thrilled as the children.

Jessie hurried through introductions and Cat quickly memorized their names as they all moved to a big sitting room.

"Are you a princess, Lady Catherine?" the seven-year-old asked.

Cat laughed. "No, I'm not a princess, Jessica."

"You are wearing a princess gown," the child insisted.

"Thank you. Would you like a princess gown?" She looked into the four upturned faces. "Would you all like princess gowns?"

Catherine spoke to their mothers, who were little more than her own age. "Do you have a sewing woman who makes their dresses?"

"We make most of them ourselves," Jessica's mother replied.

"That's quite an undertaking. I only sew a little, but I love to design clothes. Would it be all right if I designed party dresses for your girls?"

They all clustered about Catherine telling her their favorite colors and stroking her velvet and satin with eager fingers.

"Where the devil are yer manners? The lady is our guest! Joan, Judith, control yer unruly bairns," a man's voice ordered.

Cat looked up and saw Malcolm. "It's all right. I love children." She looked into his gray eyes. *God, mayhap I said the wrong thing. He too loves children but sadly has none of his own.* "Malcolm, thank you for inviting me." She held out her hand.

He took it and raised it to his lips. "I just don't want ye to think all Scots are barbarians."

She smiled into his eyes. "Why would I think that?"

He smiled back. "After meeting Lord Stewart and the Earl of Winton, why would ye not?"

Cat laughed, delighted that he had a sense of humor. "Neither could be described as *gentle men,* but surely not barbarians?"

Malcolm signaled his sisters and they bade the children to say their good nights. "They eat in the nursery," Joan explained.

Cat felt a pang of disappointment. "Good night. I will begin designing your princess dresses right away," she promised.

When they sat down to dinner, Malcolm was the only male. "Won't your husbands be joining us?" Cat asked Judith.

"They are busy with the calving tonight," Malcolm answered.

No children allowed at his table and no husbands either, by the looks of it. Another controlling Scot, Cat thought irreverently.

The food was delicious and the atmosphere warm and welcoming. The women asked her about her mother and had dozens of questions about the English Court. She in turn asked questions about Seton. In essence they told her that Malcolm was indispensable to the Earl of Winton's estate and that her grandfather relied on him for everything. They made it sound as if the business success was solely due to Malcolm. Catherine smiled to mask her thoughts. *I don't doubt that Malcolm has heavy responsibilities, but I don't believe Geordie Seton would allow any to control him or Seton.*

When the meal was over, Malcolm poured her a glass of wine. "Come, let me show ye the house, Catherine."

As she walked beside him, she noted that he was not nearly as tall as Patrick. *Do not compare all other men to Hepburn!*

"This is my wing. I enjoy the family but value my privacy."

She noticed that the chambers were not furnished in a starkly masculine style and wondered if that was a result of a wife's influence. He looked to be about thirty, and Cat was curious about how long he had been widowed. She decided it would be impolite to ask and sipped her wine instead. When he led the way up a wide staircase, she followed and, before she knew it, found herself in a spacious master bedchamber with tall windows.

"My house faces the sea, though it's too far off to see it; ye can smell the salt tang." He opened the windows.

"Since Seton land goes all the way to the sea, wouldn't it be a good idea to have its own port?"

"Someday." He asked abruptly, "Catherine, why are ye here?"

She took a deep breath, reluctant to answer. She had been so happy that her grandfather had not asked, and that it had been unnecessary to confess that she'd been banished from Court as a result of her foolish plotting.

Because of her reluctant pause, Malcolm answered the question himself. "Ye are here to survey yer domain, of course. Geordie made you his heir, since yer mother showed no interest. Someday ye will be a wealthy woman."

She raised her eyes to his. "I am already a wealthy woman."

He took a step closer and ran his fingertip along the edge of her ruff. "Wealthy, aye, but perhaps not yet a woman?" He gazed at her mouth. "Are ye betrothed to an English nobleman?"

Catherine almost took a step back but decided against retreat. She lifted her chin and asked her own question. "Why do you ask?"

"It would be hard to stomach an Englishman owning Seton."

Do you dream, Malcolm? Do you dream of becoming master of my domain by seducing me into marriage? "No, I am not betrothed."

He dipped his head and covered her lips with his in a kiss.

Catherine stood perfectly still and did not yield her mouth to him. *You think I've lived at the Queen's Court all my life and not learned to handle seduction?*

Malcolm raised his head, and then looked down at her. "Do ye want to slap me?" he asked huskily.

Catherine knew laughter was as effective as cold water to a male bent on intimacy. "Slap you over something as innocuous as a kiss between cousins? I like a man with a sense of humor." She drained her wine, handed him the glass and strolled from the room. Downstairs again, she made a point of thanking Jessie profusely for her hospitality. "I shall write to Mother and tell her what a lovely welcome you have given me."

When she arrived back at the castle she found her grandfather and Maggie in a small chamber off the great hall, where they had obviously taken supper and were now enjoying a dram of whisky.

"Catherine, my beauty, come an' join us in a drink."

"I will happily join you, but I've already had wine."

"Wine? Ye've sadly neglected her education, Maggie. I'm about to give ye a lesson in how to appreciate Scotch whisky. Are ye game, lass?"

"I've never turned down a challenge in my life."

"We'll cut it with water until ye acquire a head fer it, then we'll gradually make it stronger every night. By the end of summer, ye'll be drinkin' strong men under the table."

"Oh, I won't be—" She hesitated mid-sentence. She had been about to say that she wouldn't be here until the end of summer, but didn't want to say anything that might hurt Geordie. "I won't be able to climb the stairs to my turret, if I'm legless."

"Wheesht, I'll carry ye if that happens." He looked at Maggie and winked. "I'll carry both of ye—one under each arm!"

"Is that by any chance a dice box?" Cat asked with interest.

Geordie laughed. "Shades of the Devil, ye want lessons in gambling too, d'ye, Lady Catherine?"

Cat pulled up a chair. "I do indeed, Lord Winton."

It was two o'clock in the morning before the three dice players attempted the stairs. They finally managed, but only because they threw their arms about each other and climbed in concert.

Chapter Twelve

*E*arly Monday morning, Patrick Hepburn, accompanied by
four of his moss-troopers, rode to Seton. He had invitations from Queen Anne of Scotland for the Earl of Winton and
his granddaughter, Lady Catherine Seton Spencer, to attend the
Court entertainment planned for Saturday night and to join in
the Royal Hunt on Sunday.

Four moss-troopers per week took turns patrolling Seton
land at night to ensure none of the longhorns were stolen by
reivers.

"Have there been any attempts to lift livestock from Seton?"
Patrick asked Keith Hepburn.

"Nay, my lord. We expected it when we had trouble at Crichton an' were ready fer the bastards, but no attempts made so
far."

"Good." *That points the finger at someone with a personal
grudge against me, namely the Armstrongs.*

When the men arrived at Winton Castle, the four moss-
troopers went to relieve the Hepburns who'd just finished their
week's patrol, while Patrick visited at the castle.

Geordie had once again taken breakfast with Catherine in the
small dining room off the great hall, so that he could present her
with a gift that had belonged to her grandmother.

"She wore it always, whether out riding or dancing in the
ballroom. I know Audra would want ye to have it, Catherine."

Cat ran her fingers over the small silver dagger whose
chased handle and sheath were set with precious amethysts.
"It's lovely. I fancy having a weapon of my own! I shall treasure it because it belonged to Audra. Thank you, Geordie!"

"I think we have company, lass—something else to keep me
from my outdoor work. I've neglected it shamefully of late."

Cat followed her grandfather into the hall and her heart skipped a beat when she saw the tall figure of Hepburn.

"Lord Stewart, ye've caught me dawdlin' about this morning."

"Just look at what my grandfather has given me." Cat displayed the knife proudly. "It belonged to my grandmother, Audra."

Patrick grinned. "D'ye think it wise to give a weapon to a lady with such a volatile temper, my lord?"

"I refuse to be baited, Hepburn. In fact I believe a truce is in order between us." She blushed when he looked into her eyes.

Geordie laughed. "Audra had a fierce temper when riled, but she never threatened me wi' her knife more than a dozen times." He winked. "What good is a woman without fire in her belly?"

"I'm here to bring you invitations from Queen Anne to attend a Court entertainment. The king said he hadn't seen you in years."

"That's a splendid idea. Would ye like to go, Catherine? It'll give me a chance to show ye off!"

"I would love the opportunity to visit the Scottish Court!" Cat read her invitation avidly. "Oh, dear, there is to be a hunt the following day. Queen Elizabeth hasn't hunted the last few years. I'm not very experienced . . . could I be excused, do you think?"

"Hunting is James's passion, so he'll think you fainthearted, but Anne and her ladies will understand your timidity, I'm sure."

"I have no *timidity* in me, Hepburn!" Catherine flared.

"I thought you refused to be baited," Patrick teased.

"If you must know the truth, I've only ridden sidesaddle."

"It would be my pleasure to teach you to ride astride."

If her cheeks had blushed before, now they positively glowed. She silently cursed her imagination and lowered her lashes.

"If you know how to handle a horse, there's nothing to it. You'll be able to master it in just a few miles. Crichton is only five miles distance. Come with me now, then I'll escort you back."

"She picked out a nice wee filly fer herself." Geordie turned to Cat. "Go fer a gallop to Crichton; ye'll be safe wi' Hepburn."

Catherine was far too impulsive to refuse. "I'll have to change. Will you wait?"

"If you don't take all day about it," he conceded.

Catherine moved toward the stairs with dainty steps, torn between hurrying and dawdling to annoy the dominant devil. The minute he could no longer see her, however, she began to run.

"Maggie," she cried breathlessly. "I'm riding to Crichton with Patrick. Which of my riding dresses has the widest skirt? I'm going to learn to ride astride. I've been invited to Court!"

Within minutes, Catherine, dressed in her hunter green riding dress, was pulling on black leather riding boots. Then she brushed her hair back and secured it with a pale green ribbon. "I shall wear the knife Geordie gave me. It belonged to Audra."

"Here, let me fasten it to your riding skirt with this silver fan clip so you won't lose it. I remember Audra wearing it."

When Cat descended the stairs she found that the men had gone.

"If he left without me, I'll never forgive him!" But when she arrived at the stables she found that Hepburn had saddled her horse. "Thank you." She led the filly outside to a seldom-used mounting block and saw four rough-looking men garbed in leather ride into the yard. "I don't want an audience," she said softly.

"They are my moss-troopers." He raised his voice, "No need to wait; we'll follow you."

When they rode off, Cat asked, "Which foot do I use?"

"The same one. Put your left foot on the block, bend forward and swing your right leg back over the horse."

Though her skirt was restrictive, she managed to mount with grace and only a small flurry of petticoats. When she thrust her boots into the stirrups she threw him a triumphant glance.

"You'll do better with practice."

She had opened her mouth to deliver a cutting retort when she spotted Malcolm standing outside the stables watching her. His eyes were narrowed and he did not look pleased.

"Seems you have an audience after all," Patrick observed.

"He must be glowering at you. That look of disapproval couldn't possibly be directed at me," she said lightly.

It's a look of hatred, not disapproval. Your cousin's malevolence had better be for me! He mounted Valiant and kept him on a tight rein so that he would not surge forward into a gallop.

"When you ride sidesaddle you use your reins to guide your mount. When you are astride, you can use your knees to give you much more control. She'll respond to the slightest pressure. Try it."

Catherine found it strange to feel the animal between her legs with only her stockings separating her flesh from horseflesh. *My legs have never been this far apart in my life!* When the filly quivered, she felt its rippling hide against her inner thighs and realized that riding astride required a far more intimate relationship with your mount than riding sidesaddle.

Hepburn set a slow pace for the first mile. "You're a fast learner. Is it starting to feel more natural?"

"I am more in control, and being astride makes me feel more free, less constricted. Can we go faster?"

He grinned at her. "Clasp your legs tighter and give her more rein." He watched as her filly moved into a steady canter.

Cat looked at the way the heavy saddle muscles on his thighs gripped his huge mount. Valiant was a hell of a lot of brute animal to control, yet Hepburn held the reins loosely in one hand. Her eyes lingered on that hand. It was big and powerful, like the rest of his physique. She remembered what his hands had felt like on her body when he'd lifted her in the dance, and she shivered.

He saw her quiver and wondered if riding astride was arousing her. He pictured her naked, then he imagined her straddling him, and it was his turn to shudder. "Ready to gallop?"

She nodded eagerly and he fantasized about her responding to all his suggestions with such reckless abandon.

"Damnation! When I gallop, my skirt rides up and entangles my legs. I wish I could wear breeches!"

He imagined her in leather pants, and then cursed under his breath as his cock became unruly. "We'd better go a bit slower." He willed himself to think of less prurient matters. "You seem to get along well with your grandfather. Seton isn't as bad as you imagined."

"I adore Geordie; he indulges my every whim. He even let me have a little black cat I saw in the stables."

"Don't tell me . . . you named her Tattoo."

She stared at him. "How the devil did you know?"

"It just seemed *apropos.*"

"Good God, you know about my tattoo!" *I'll kill Maggie!*

He grinned. "It isn't a catastrophe, though it certainly sets you apart from other females." He waggled his black eyebrows. "Impulsiveness is a curse, Hellcat."

"Then tread carefully. You're not the only one with a knife."

"Keep it sheathed. We're on Hepburn land—Crichton is ahead."

She saw tenant farms with sheep and cattle. They passed numerous pastures where horses grazed and acres of apple orchards.

He saw that the breeze had loosened tendrils of hair about her face and her golden eyes glowed with the joy of being alive. "I officially proclaim that you know how to ride without a sidesaddle."

Suddenly, Cat spotted a girl riding like the wind, her red hair flying behind her like a banner. "No, I don't! That's how I want to ride. It's all or nothing for me!"

His glance was admiring. "At last we've something in common."

Crichton Castle sat on the crest of a hill, and as they rode into the courtyard, Catherine was amazed at its beauty. Built of pinkish sandstone, it had an Italianate façade with an arched colonnade. "Such decorative conceits—I love it!"

"Something else we have in common."

"It looks so modern."

"This part is. The Earl of Bothwell added it seventeen years back. Originally there was only the keep, the tower, and the gatehouse. The new kitchens and living quarters are above the arched colonnade. The decoration is the Hepburn rose."

They entered the stables, where Catherine dismounted gracefully and a Hepburn groom took their horses. "Walk slowly," he teased. "It will feel strange to have your legs back together."

She glanced away shyly and saw the girl with the red hair.

"Jenny, come and meet Lady Catherine Seton Spencer. She envies the way you ride."

Jenny approached them eagerly and swept her a curtsy. "My lady." Her eyes were wide with admiration for the beautiful young female. "I envy yer elegant riding dress!"

"Oh, don't curtsy, and please call me Cat. If you teach me to ride the way you do, I'll design an elegant riding dress for you."

"Truly? But I simply ride like a Hepburn moss-trooper."

"Exactly! That's how I want to ride. Will you come to Seton?"

Trying to contain her excitement, Jenny looked at Patrick.

"We'll see. Tell your mother we have a visitor."

Catherine walked with Patrick beneath the stone arch and up some stone steps, and entered the living quarters. The chamber was spacious and to one side was a straight stairway that led up to a gallery. Its balustrade was lavishly carved with roses, and Cat suddenly experienced *déjà vu* as if she'd been here before . . . almost as if this castle belonged to her.

The housekeeper, Jenny's mother, came forward with a tankard of ale for Patrick. "Would ye prefer wine or ale from our own brewery, Lady Catherine?"

"Wine," Patrick decided.

"Ale," Catherine contradicted, accepting a tankard.

"Ale isn't a lady's drink," he said with a straight face.

"I know. Next time I'll have whisky. Geordie is teaching me how to tolerate such vile stuff."

He looked down at her and murmured quizzically, "Will he teach me how to tolerate such a vile woman?"

He thinks I'm a woman! The thought pleased her inordinately. Suddenly, Cat realized there were a great many females about. Though they kept a respectful distance they were surely taking a good look at her. "Do all these women serve you?"

"Each in her own way, but they are not servants; they are my Hepburn and Stewart clan, with a few Douglases and Elliots thrown in for good measure. Many are my moss-troopers' wives and daughters."

"They are flirting with you," she accused.

"They are Scots lasses; it comes naturally to them."

Maggie's words rushed back to her: *Wishful thinking! They'd all like a chance to lie with him and mayhap tame him.*

"Drink up and I'll show you the ancient part of the castle."

Cat looked at her tankard doubtfully. She had managed about half of the ale but with one more mouthful she would surely burst.

"Let me help you." He took it from her and drained it.

She tried to match his steps as he led the way to the keep.

"This is the Great Hall."

The long, vaulted room with its huge open fireplace at one end was occupied by moss-troopers. The moment Hepburn entered, Sabbath and Satan began to lope toward him. Patrick quickly stepped in front of Catherine so they would not overwhelm her. He rubbed their heads and ordered, "Down! Stay down!"

When Catherine saw them sit obediently, she stepped out from behind Hepburn. "Satan, Sabbath, good boys!"

Both hounds lifted their heads and howled their greeting.

Cat couldn't wipe the grin from her face. "I love animals."

"And animals love you. Sabbath, however, is a bitch."

Her eyes widened. "Really? Then it was Satan who brought me to you—" *That was a dream!* "I mean it was Satan who knocked me down in the woods at Richmond."

Patrick gave her a wolfish grin. "It was Satan both times."

"The hound's name is Satan, but you are the devil, Hepburn!"

"Whatever you say, Hellcat. Come, let me show you the view."

He took her to a large square aperture in the south wall; in effect it was a window without glass. Stretching out below them lay the beautiful Tyne Valley.

"Oh, look, there's a pair of hawks. I love birds too!" A raven flew onto the window ledge and Catherine was enthralled.

"This is Tor, an extremely intelligent bird. He often flies ahead of me when I go hunting."

"A tame raven?" she asked.

"Nothing here is tame, Catherine. He is wise enough to know that when a hunter bags a deer, the animal is gutted on the spot so the venison won't be tainted. He gets a free meal."

"Ah, very intelligent indeed." She refused to shudder.

"Well, my lady, if your posterior will allow it, I shall escort you back to Seton."

"My posterior is no problem, my lord; it is my bloody skirt that prevents me from riding well."

As they walked back to the stables she wondered if he was trying to get rid of her. She decided that he had shrewdly guessed she was about to take her leave and had decided to precipitate her request. It was his way of being in control.

Patrick led their horses from the stables, then he made a stirrup with his hands to aid her to mount.

Impulsively, Catherine unsheathed her knife and slit the skirt of her riding dress almost to the thigh. She was about to slash her petticoat when Patrick held up his hand in supplication.

"I beg you not reveal your limbs if they resemble Geordie's."

"You dare offer me such insult while I have a knife in my hand? I'll cut your tongue out, you reckless devil!" In spite of her best efforts, she could not keep a straight face. Patrick Hepburn had a wicked humor and she realized that it added to his sexual attraction. Catherine looked about for a mounting block, and, seeing none, had no choice but to accept his help. She placed her booted foot in his clasped hands and ordered, "Close your eyes." As he bent down, his face was on a level with hers, and when he lowered his eyelids she examined his face closely. He raised black lashes, looked directly into her eyes and caught her gazing at him. Disconcerted, Cat mounted with haste.

The pair of hounds bounded into the courtyard, determined to accompany their master. "Come on, then," he relented.

As soon as they began to canter past the orchards, Tor flew into a gnarled apple tree and began to caw loudly. Then the raven took wing and followed the dogs.

"Because of the hounds, the raven thinks we are hunting."

Hepburn let her set the pace. When she began to gallop, the wind stole her ribbon and her hair streamed out behind her. Cat knew that she felt more exhilarated than she could ever remember. Suddenly she began to laugh with the pure joy of the moment.

Hepburn kept a wise silence and let her enjoy herself. When they got closer to Seton, Patrick raised his head and scented the wind. For a fleeting moment, as they passed a thick stand of fir trees, he had the feeling they were being watched, but when the hounds bounded into the wooded grove, the impression faded away.

When they arrived at Winton Castle, he ordered his dogs to heel and Catherine remained in the saddle, expecting him to dismount and lift her down. When he remained mounted, she did not know whether she felt relief or disappointment. "Thank you kindly for the riding lesson, my lord."

It is the first of many lessons I will teach you, my beauty!

"You will allow Jenny to visit me at Seton?" she begged.

"I'll see what her father says."

She watched him gallop away until he was out of sight. Cat

dismounted gingerly and rubbed her bottom. Tonight she was dining with Andrew and his mother, Janet. Perhaps if she soaked in a warm bath she'd be able to sit at their table without squirming. First thing tomorrow, she intended to design herself a practical riding dress. Perhaps she and Maggie could go into Edinburgh to buy cloth, and at the same time she could pick out some fancy material for the little girls' princess dresses.

When Maggie drew back the drapes, Catherine sat up in bed.

"How are yer aches and pains, moans and groans, stones and bones, my lamb?"

"My bum is stiff as a board. I was so tired last night, I almost fell asleep at Andrew's table, but he didn't take the least offense. I like him very much, and I like his mother too."

"Geordie's sisters, Jessie and Janet, both married Lindsays, and their clan is northwest of Seton."

"So both Andrew's and Malcolm's last name is Lindsay?"

"That's right. It's hard to keep the names straight at first."

"I get the impression that Malcolm wishes his name was Seton."

"And who wouldn't want to be a Seton, pray tell me if ye can?"

A short time later, when Cat and Maggie went down to breakfast, Geordie announced, "Ye have early visitors, Catherine."

She stepped into the Great Hall and saw the red-haired girl she had met yesterday, accompanied by a brawny man in leathers. "Jenny! Oh, I'm so glad you came." *Thank you, Patrick!*

Jenny bobbed a curtsy. "This is my father, my lady."

Catherine held out her hand. "Mr. Hepburn, thank you for bringing Jenny. She has offered to give me riding lessons. Do you think she could stay for a couple of days, sir?"

"Please, Father?" Jenny implored.

Hepburn finally nodded his consent.

"Thank you, sir. We will escort Jenny safely back to Crichton tomorrow evening," Catherine promised him.

He nodded again, bent an admonitory look upon his daughter and then departed as silently as he'd arrived.

"Come and have breakfast," Cat invited.

"I've had one, but I can manage another," Jenny agreed as she followed Catherine into the small dining room.

"This is my grandfather, Geordie Seton, Earl of Winton. This is my new friend, Jenny Hepburn, who's come to visit."

"I'm honored to meet you, yer lordship."

"Sit down, lass. Help yerself to some breakfast."

"Jenny, this is Maggie." She turned to Geordie. "We would like to go into Edinburgh this morning. I need to buy material."

"Ye need a gown fer Court?" he asked.

"Oh, no, most of my clothes are suitable for Court. It is my riding dresses that are woefully inadequate. Since it's already Tuesday, I have little time to waste."

"Off ye go, then. I'll get Andrew to go along, just to be on the safe side. Tell the shopkeeper to send me the bills."

"Thank you. Jenny, the reason I asked your father if you could stay was so you could come to Edinburgh. Do you mind?"

"Oh, no, my lady, that'd be grand!"

"Please call me Cat. I'll bring my sketchpad and do some designs in the carriage. Are you ready to go, Maggie?"

"Sit! Eat! Or I don't budge, Mistress Impulsive."

"She loves to bully me," Cat told Jenny as she obeyed orders.

When the trio of females emerged from the castle, Andrew sat on his horse, waiting for them beside the carriage.

"Andrew, I'm sorry to take you away from your duties at Seton, but Geordie insists we have another man besides our driver."

"It's my pleasure, Catherine. I never turn down a chance to go into Edinburgh." Andrew's glance strayed to the red-haired girl.

"This is my friend Jenny Hepburn, from Crichton."

"Hello, lass, welcome to Seton." His eyes lingered on her face.

As soon as the carriage began to move, Cat took up her sketchpad and began to design a riding outfit. Nothing seemed right until she got an idea to make the skirt divided. While the wearer was standing or even walking, the split wouldn't be evident if she made the skirt full enough. "What do you think?" When Cat glanced up she saw that Jenny was not looking at her sketch but had her attention riveted upon Andrew as he rode alongside them.

"I think he's very handsome." Jenny sighed.

Cat began to laugh. "Don't you think he's a bit old for you?"

"He's a man. What woman would want a lad?" Jenny asked.

"Andrew can't be more than twenty-eight. He's just a bairn," Maggie argued.

"That's still twice Jenny's age," Catherine pointed out, "but he is handsome." She changed the subject. "What sort of riding dress do you fancy for yourself, Jenny?"

"Exactly like the one you wore to Crichton. I never saw anything so lovely. Green would be a bonnie color for me too."

Cat sketched quickly. "I'll make the bodice the same, but make the skirt wider, like the one you are wearing. Green of course."

Catherine put the pad aside as they entered the city. The carriage turned onto the Canongate and suddenly Edinburgh Castle loomed into view, towering over and dominating the whole city. Cat gazed in fascinated horror. It was a formidable fortress, its history steeped in blood like the Tower of London. The carriage turned down High Street and came to a halt before some shops at the bottom of the hill, where they had a clear view of Holyrood. "No wonder the queen prefers to live at the palace."

Andrew opened the carriage door and lifted down Jenny, who went into his arms eagerly. Next he assisted Maggie, then with a bit more formality held out his hand to aid Catherine.

She smiled at him. "You have made a conquest, Andrew."

"Only one?" he teased. "I fixed up the pony cart. When we get back perhaps ye'd both like to go fer a ride?"

"We'll see," she temporized.

Inside the shop, Cat was amazed at the number of bolts of serviceable cloth in somber hues and wondered who would wear such ugly stuff. She let Jenny pick her own material and laughed when she unerringly found a bolt of hunter green velvet. There were no bright colors, so Cat decided on jet velvet as her imagination conjured a riding outfit in dramatic black and white. She bought some feathers and beads, though there was little to choose from.

Catherine asked if they had any finer material in pastel shades. From the back room the shopkeeper brought yellow taffeta and watered silk in blue and pink, so she bought all three bolts. "When there isn't much choice, at least you don't waste hours deciding which to buy."

"Ladies, I took the liberty of buying us some meat pies."

"Thank you!" Cat winked at Jenny. "Let's eat them in the carriage. I'm sure we can make room for you, Andrew."

Chapter Thirteen

*W*hen Catherine and Jenny got back to Seton, they spent the entire afternoon in the saddle. They found a meadow filled with clover where no longhorns were grazing and, side by side, rode the perimeter, at first cantering, then galloping and eventually riding full out. Cat watched everything Jenny did, and then tried to emulate all her moves. The pair became firm friends as they rode, talked and laughed until they were breathless. The outward contrast between them was marked. Jenny was long-limbed with a fresh-faced attractiveness, while Catherine was small and dainty. Both, however, had an abundance of courage and impulsive energy.

While their horses grazed, they perched atop a rail fence and watched as cattlemen branded some longhorn calves.

"Are you betrothed, Catherine?"

"No, though I have one or two serious admirers at the English Court. I'm in no hurry to wed. I don't come of age until March."

"Have you lost your heart to Lord Stewart?" Jenny asked avidly.

"Lost my heart to Hepburn? Good God, no! We have a difficult time even being civil to one another."

"Then you must be the only woman in Scotland who isn't in love with him. He seems oblivious to admiring glances and treats all the females at Crichton exactly the same, but some lucky lady will be sure to capture his heart." Jenny sighed.

"I'm not sure Hepburn has a heart. If he does, I warrant it's as hard as his head."

"Catherine, you don't know him very well. Patrick is generous and tenderhearted. That's why we love him."

"Really? It has nothing to do with the fact that he is taller, darker and more handsome than the Devil himself?"

"Ah, so you *have* noticed his physical attributes?"

"How could I not, when he's so blatantly . . . male!"

Jenny giggled. "I've found someone new to sigh over."

"Come on, it's time to eat. After dinner, we can work on our new riding dresses, if you like. Do you sew, Jenny?"

"Yes; all the women at Crichton sew. I help my mother make my clothes. I made this riding skirt."

"That's wonderful. I'm good at designing and making patterns and even cutting the cloth to the pattern, but Maggie is much better at the actual sewing than I am. She has lots of patience."

Before the pair went to bed that night, Jenny's green riding dress was designed, cut out and pinned together, ready to be stitched. Catherine had designed her divided skirt and cut the sections from the rich black velvet. Maggie told her she would probably be able to finish the unusual garment by tomorrow night.

"You are so generous with your time, Maggie. I'm glad you came to Scotland with me. I'd be lost without you."

"Go on with ye. Ye're the child I never had."

"I know, Maggie," Cat said softly. "I love you like a mother."

The next morning, the two friends arose early to go riding. Cat knew her skills were rapidly improving, but she doubted she would ever become as accomplished as Jenny Hepburn.

After lunch, Andrew appeared as if by magic and offered to hitch up the pony cart and give them a driving lesson. Cat soon learned the skill of maneuvering the cart and at the same time learned a few tricks about flirtation from Jenny. *Hepburn was right. It seems to come naturally to Scottish lasses.*

"Andrew, I promised Jenny's father that we would see her safely home. Would you escort us, later?" Cat asked innocently.

"It would be my pleasure. Ye should go before gloaming."

"What a lovely, descriptive word. Yes, I agree. If we leave it too late, your father may not let you come again, Jenny."

Catherine took Jenny to the kitchen, where Peg, the cook, fed them slices of cold beef and homemade cheese. Maggie wrapped up the cutout sections of green velvet for Jenny's riding dress and Cat made her a present of green silk hose.

Jenny carefully placed the luxury items in her saddlebags

and bade Maggie good-bye. "Please thank the Earl of Winton for me."

They rode three abreast with Jenny in the middle, on Andrew's right. Catherine felt a growing excitement and was appalled at herself. *Surely it isn't because I'm going to see Hepburn? Perhaps I'm excited to see Crichton again.* An inner voice said, *Crichton and Patrick are the same thing, Cat. Damnation, there are two people inside my head, arguing!*

When they arrived at Crichton's stables, Andrew dismounted in a flash and lifted Jenny from her saddle.

"His lordship gave me my pony. I don't allow the grooms to take care of her; I do it myself," she told Andrew.

"Very commendable. Good-bye, Jenny. I'll see ye again soon."

Catherine suffered a moment of panic thinking she might not see Hepburn, when he emerged from the stables and strode to her side. He was wearing leathers and smelled of horses. Cat felt her breasts tighten and experienced a strange sensation in the pit of her belly. "Thank you for letting Jenny come to Seton."

"Do you ride like a moss-trooper yet?" Patrick teased.

"I ride adequately, but I shall never be as skilled as Jenny."

"You will, Catherine. I'll let you in on a secret. It's not the rider; it's the animal. Jenny has a sure-footed Border pony."

His words pleased her. Then she remembered their escort. "I'm sorry. This is Andrew Lindsay, my grandfather's nephew."

"We've met. Take good care of her, Andrew. You'd best be on your way, Catherine. Once the sun sets, darkness descends rapidly." He grinned. "I'll see you on Saturday, at Court."

When he used her full name, he rolled the *r* in Catherine and the sound never failed to thrill her. She finally realized that the strange sensation she felt in her belly was desire.

Late Saturday afternoon Catherine and Maggie unpacked their clothes and hung them in the antique wardrobe.

"I can't believe we have our own chamber at Holyrood Palace." Maggie was in awe. "I'm glad ye talked me into bringing both my blue dress and my burgundy. I don't want to be outdone."

As Catherine hung up her riding outfit, she was pleased with the way it had turned out. She had decided to pair the black vel-

vet skirt with a tight-fitting white padded doublet, and had
arisen at dawn to embroider it with the black winged dragon
with a bright red fiery tongue that was the Winton device. She
already owned a black-and-white ruff, black riding boots and
soft black riding gloves. A small hat onto which she had sewn a
black ostrich feather completed the outfit. It was so dramatic;
Cat was confident she would stand out.

Catherine had known since the moment she received the invitation which gown she would wear tonight. It was her newest,
made especially for the English Court. The pointed bodice emphasized her tiny waist, then flared into a full skirt. It was made
of white silk tulle, embroidered with golden beads. Her ruff was
delicate gold lace, edged in seed pearls, and she had a matching
fan. Cat recalled when Philadelphia had seen the gown, she'd
declared it looked as delicious as a wedding cake.

Maggie said, "The earl is wearing his Winton dress tartan
tonight, according to Craig, his valet."

"I was stunned when I learned that Geordie had a valet."
Catherine could not help laughing.

"Oh, aye, yer grandfather is quite the dandy on rare occasion. I want ye to rest yer feet for the lively Scottish dancing.
I'm going to have a prowl round, and if I find the kitchens I'll
bring a wee snack to fortify ye."

Within the hour Maggie returned with a tray of traditional
Scottish confections—shortbread, currant cakes, plum tarts and
marzipan comfits. She also brought a bottle of Rhenish wine. As
Cat reached for a piece of marzipan, Maggie smiled knowingly.
"I thought these would tempt yer sweet tooth, my lamb."

"Mmm, just one more; then it's time to do my hair."

Ninety minutes later, when Geordie knocked on the door,
Maggie opened it and was amazed at the earl's transformation.
A frothy white lace jabot topped his formal black jacket, and his
kilt fell below his knees to disguise his bowlegs. He stood gazing with undisguised delight at his granddaughter. "Catherine,
my wee lass, without doubt ye are the most winsome lady to
ever grace this palace. I am so proud of ye. Come, or we'll be
late."

"Thank you, Geordie. We make a handsome couple. At
Court, it is always fashionable to be late and make a grand entrance."

Maggie handed her the gold lace fan, then Cat slipped her

arm through her grandfather's. "I'm ready," she said breath-lessly.

The connecting chambers where tonight's entertainment was being held were ornate and brilliantly lit with myriad candles. They already overflowed with people, and still a small line of royal guests waited at the entrance to be announced. When it was their turn, Geordie gave their names to the chamberlain, who called out, "The Earl of Winton and Lady Catherine Seton Spencer."

Catherine held her head high and stepped forward, sensing that every eye was upon them. The crowd moved aside, allow-ing them to walk down the center of the chamber toward the royal dais where the King and Queen of Scotland were holding Court.

The first thing that Cat noticed was that she was the only one wearing white. Her glance swept the chamber seeking another female gowned as she was. When she saw none, she became nervous.

It was the custom for Elizabeth to surround herself with maidens and for those tender young ladies to wear white at her Court, but it was obvious now to Catherine that such was not the custom in Scotland. She began to hear whispers and realized people were talking about her. She searched desperately for young ladies her own age, but the youngest females she saw were in their late twenties, and most were in their sophisticated thirties. She clutched Geordie's arm tightly as she heard a woman say, "What a beautiful child!"

My gown is all wrong! I'm too short! I shouldn't be wearing white silk tulle! They think I'm a child because I look like a lit-tle girl! Catherine wished the floor would open up and swallow her. She pinned a smile to her face and tried desperately to stretch her neck to make herself appear taller.

"Everyone's starin' at ye," Geordie murmured with delight.

Catherine's lip quivered as she swallowed a sob. Finally, after what seemed like an interminable length of time, they reached the royal couple. Though the queen was sitting on a throne-like chair, Cat could see that Anne was statuesque. She looked about thirty and had an abundance of blond hair. Cat swept down in a graceful curtsy and Queen Anne bade her rise.

"Lady Catherine, what a lovely child you are."

Cat looked into blue eyes and saw that the queen was completely sincere. "I am honored to meet you, Your Majesty."

Beside her, she heard her granddad talking with King James.
"I couldn't wait to present my granddaughter, Lady Catherine."

"A right bonnie bairn, Geordie. Dinna forget the hunt tomorrow, an' in ten days it's ma birthday . . . then we'll really
celebrate!"

Catherine tried not to stare at the man on the throne. *This
cannot be the King of Scotland . . . he drools when he speaks,
and I cannot understand a word he says! My God, is this real,
or is it a nightmare? Any moment, Sabbath will appear and lead
me away.*

Catherine took a deep breath to help her get a grip on reality.
Again her glance flickered over the royal pair and she found
herself suppressing a shudder. How could Anne allow this cari-
cature of a king to touch her, let alone make love to her?

Geordie led her to other nobles he knew and Cat, smiling
bravely, exchanged pleasantries though she was cringing with
self-consciousness over her childlike appearance. He introduced John Erskine, Earl of Mar, and his countess. Cat knew
that beside the mature Lady Erskine she looked woefully unso-
phisticated.

When Queen Anne arose and came down from the dais, she
was immediately surrounded by her ladies. Catherine saw that
though their gowns were not the latest fashion and not nearly as
elaborate as those worn at the English Court, the colors and
styles gave the females a certain enticing allure. The ladies who
had come with Anne from Denmark were tall, fair and rather
voluptuous, three qualities Cat did not possess. The expressions
on their faces, coupled with the familiar gestures they used
when conversing with men, made them appear worldly and experienced.

Cat suddenly caught sight of Robert Carey and his bride,
Liz. Relief swept over her as she walked a direct path to them.

"Catherine, darling, you look like a beautiful doll!"

"Oh, Liz, I don't want to look like a doll; I want to look like
a woman. I'm mortified at this childish white dress I'm wearing." She fanned burning cheeks. "We're invited again for the
king's birthday . . . could I borrow a more sophisticated gown
from you?"

"Of course you may. Don't let it spoil your evening, darling. I warrant you are the envy of many a female here tonight."

Liz is right. If I allow the fact that my gown is inappropriate to ruin the evening for me, I would be as immature as I look.

Lord Stewart paid homage to King James, who wanted to make sure Hepburn would be at tomorrow's hunt. Patrick saw the king's eyes roam over his formal black attire. "Get away from me, mon; ye make me look like such a scrub!"

"Never, Sire," Hepburn dutifully denied, and went to make his bow to Queen Anne.

"I had the pleasure of meeting Lady Carey earlier today. I have been led to believe that English ladies are arrogant, but I like Liz very much, Patrick. She met my children and they liked her too, especially Baby Charles!"

"Queen Elizabeth can be arrogant and her courtiers haughty, but Lady Carey has never spent time at the English Court."

"My ladies are clamoring for your attention, but remember that your queen likes to dance too, Patrick."

He kissed her hand. "You honor me, madam." He turned to find Margretha at his elbow. "You look well, Gretha."

"In spite of your neglect," she said lightly. She did not expect Hepburn to explain himself. He never had and never would.

He smiled. "I am flattered if you missed me, *cherie*."

Christina, a slender Danish redhead, touched Patrick's arm.

"I shall be happy to save the first Scots reel for you, my lord."

Hepburn did not hear a word she said. His searching eyes had finally found Catherine. He stared across the room, entranced. Petite though she was, Cat stood out from every other female in the room. She had an ethereal quality that radiated innocence. She made the queen's ladies, whom he knew so intimately, look jaded, almost shopworn. He caught his breath as she was suddenly swallowed by the crowd, and his feet moved swiftly of their own volition in a mission of search and rescue. As Patrick got closer he caught a glimpse of white silk, then she disappeared again as she quickly stepped behind Robert Carey. Instinctively he realized that Cat was trying to avoid him. Hepburn greeted Robert, shook his hand, then peered over his friend's shoulder.

Fairly caught, she stepped out and lifted her chin.

"Lady Catherine, you look exquisite tonight."

"Don't be facetious, Hepburn, I beg you."

"Begging is not in your nature," he said quizzically.

"You are right. I *demand* that you not be facetious. It's difficult enough for me." Her golden eyes glared at him.

"Elucidate your difficulty, Cat; I am at a loss."

"I look like a damned wedding cake!"

"Sweet and delectable," he said gallantly. Then he ruined it by murmuring suggestively, "I enjoy seeing you stripped down to reveal your . . . vulnerabilities."

"Well, to hell with you! And to hell with everyone! I refuse to allow a trivial thing like a dress spoil my enjoyment. Who'll partner me in this reel?"

Three men bowed before her. "Not a chance," Hepburn informed them, and swept Catherine onto the dance floor.

They formed a set and the gentlemen bowed while the ladies curtsied. As they stepped together in time to the lively music, Patrick bent his head. "Every eye is upon us."

"That's because we are the strangest, mismatched couple in Christendom!" She threw back her head and laughed.

As the tempo of the reel sped up, the men's kilts swung high, revealing more than their brawny thighs. Catherine laughed until she had to wipe away tears, and suddenly she forgot about her appearance and began to thoroughly enjoy herself. When the dance was done she told him breathlessly, "I'm relieved you're not wearing a kilt; I'd never survive the shock."

Patrick grudgingly handed her over to Geordie for the next set and went to claim the queen.

Catherine partnered Robert Carey, and then Sir Robin Carr of Ferniehurst, whose father was a Scots Border warden, claimed her. He was a handsome, well-made youth with ruddy cheeks, and Cat concluded that he assumed she was far younger than she was.

Breathless from the rants and reels, she searched for Patrick. When she found him, encircled by a bevy of attractive, long-limbed females, she could not help comparing them with herself. All looked to have had a good deal of experience with men in general, and with this male in particular. She turned away quickly and plied her fan. *I don't give a fig!*

Nevertheless, a few minutes later, when she felt powerful

hands cup her shoulders, her heart gladdened that he had abandoned his harem to seek her out. She turned and smiled up at
him.

"May I escort you to the supper room, Catherine?"

"Perhaps I should wait for my grandfather."

"You'll be waiting all night. Geordie's retired to an anteroom
with the king and his cronies to cast dice and sip whisky."

"In that case I have no objection to your company, my lord."

The buffet tables lined all four walls of the supper room,
which was crowded with hungry guests. Hepburn's size alone
induced people to step aside and make room for them. There
were huge platters of venison, cold roast mutton, partridge and
other game. Pickled herring, oysters, smoked trout and salmon
filled another table.

Hepburn filled his plate, while Catherine took only a slice of
venison and an almond pastry from the dessert table. Even so,
he finished before she did. She set down her empty plate and
drank a glass of wine, which seemed to go straight to her head.
With him this close she felt breathless. "Can we go outside? It's
stifling hot in here."

He took her hand and led her through the labyrinth of the
palace until they emerged through a heavy door that led outside.

Then he took her through a high stone arch. "These are the
ruins of Holyrood Abbey. They are reputed to be haunted."

She tipped back her head to look up and saw that though
there were walls, there was no roof, and the crescent moon
touched the ancient stone with its silvery light. The dark shadow
of Hepburn towered above her, blotting out the moon, and suddenly she was in his arms and he was kissing her. The feel of his
mouth intoxicated her and made her dizzy. *It's the wine,* she told
herself, but she knew that was a desperate lie. His kiss made her
want to scream with excitement. She wanted him to pick her up
and crush her against his hard body.

He lifted his mouth from hers. "Touched by moonlight you
were irresistible, Hellcat."

She licked her lips. "Take me back." *That isn't what I meant
to say. Kiss me again, Patrick!*

He took her hand and led her through the stone arch, and
then they were back inside the palace. Her mouth was so dry she
could hardly speak. "I . . . I'm so thirsty; I need a cool drink of
water."

"Come with me. I know a place where there is water for you and a drink of cool ale for me."

"Where is that?" she asked breathlessly.

He stopped before a door. "Here. In my chamber."

She gazed up into his black eyes and knew she would do this impulsive, reckless thing.

He held her fast with one hand, while the other turned the knob. The door swung open slowly.

"Patrick, I . . ." The tall female in the silk robe stopped speaking when she saw that Hepburn had a lady with him.

"Gretha, what the hell are you doing here?"

Cat pulled her hand from his as if she had been scalded. "That's obvious, Lord Bloody Stewart!" She turned and fled.

When Catherine awoke the next morning, she thought over last night's events. She acknowledged that Patrick Hepburn was so physically compelling, he attracted females like steel filings to a lodestone and he always would. She suspected that the woman in his chamber was one of the queen's ladies but, whoever she was, Cat knew she had saved her from her own impulsiveness.

Her thoughts moved on to the impression she had made at the Scottish Court, and she concluded that though it hadn't been disastrous, she had left them with the notion that she was extremely youthful and therefore inconsequential. Cat had not made the fashionable mark she had intended and she fervently hoped the riding dress she'd designed was not another fashion *faux pas*.

"Maggie, you're so thoughtful to bring my breakfast."

"Nay, it gave me a chance to explore the palace and see what's going on this morning. The hounds are already baying at the prospect of the hunt; King Jamie too, by what I've heard of him."

"Don't get me started on the subject of the king." Cat rolled her eyes. "I want you to help me put up my hair. It was a mistake to wear it down last night. I looked a positive baby!"

"The day'll come when ye'll want to look young, Miss Impatient."

"Yes, Maggie, but not today!"

When Geordie knocked on her door, Cat had just pinned her

hat onto her upswept curls. She pulled on her riding gloves. "I'm ready, Lord Winton. Lead the way."

There was a crowd milling about in front of the Holyrood stables and some were already mounted. Cat was relieved that when Anne and her ladies saw her wearing the dramatic riding outfit, their attitude toward her changed immediately. She was soon the center of attention, and the queen wanted to know where she had acquired her fashionable yet practical riding skirt.

"I designed it myself, Your Highness. I would be honored to design one for you."

"I shall hold you to your promise, Lady Catherine."

Cat saw Patrick Hepburn coming toward her leading Valiant and a small white palfrey. She tried to pretend the kiss had never happened between them, even though she could still feel the imprint of his lips on hers. Cat assumed he had chosen the mount for her. "How thoughtful of you, my lord." She noticed his frown as he took in her attire. "You don't approve of my riding attire?"

"As if that would make the slightest difference, Hellcat."

"I vow I would weigh your opinion carefully, then do precisely as I pleased." Cat had regained all her confidence this morning.

Hepburn helped her into the saddle, then mounted Valiant.

She saw that Queen Anne and the Scottish noblewomen rode astride, but some of the queen's Danish attendants were using sidesaddles, as was Liz Carey. "Good morning, Liz. I believe the ladies hunt with the queen and the gentlemen hunt separately with the king."

Robert stared at Catherine. "Your mother would have a fit if she saw you riding astride."

Cat smiled. "Yes, indeed. His lordship gave me lessons."

Liz's mount seemed restless with all the staghounds straining against their leashes, so Robert escorted her to the queen.

"I have to join the king's hunt shortly. Come on. Let's have a canter to make sure your palfrey handles well," Patrick suggested.

They rode apart from the others and were soon on a wooded path with Cat showing off her riding skills. Hepburn suddenly lifted his head, sensing danger. Mortal danger!

He had scant warning and no idea what, why or how. He

only knew that it was imminent. In a flash, Patrick dismounted, pulled Catherine to the ground and covered her with his body. He heard a whoosh over their heads and knew it could only be an arrow.

Chapter Fourteen

*C*atherine, flat on her back, glared up at Hepburn in outrage. "What the devil are you doing?"

Patrick indicated the arrow embedded in a tree trunk then regretted it as he saw the blood drain from her face. "It's nothing to be upset about, Catherine," he assured her in a calming voice. "Some of the ladies use bows to hunt. This is just a stray arrow. My fault for taking you away from the safety of the queen's hunting party. No harm done."

Cat masked her fear with anger. "No harm at all, except my hat is gone and my lovely white doublet smeared with dirt!"

"You are still more fashionable than all of them put together, and well you know it. Let me take you back to the queen."

When he had safely delivered her to Queen Anne's hunting party, Patrick circled back to get the arrow. Though he searched diligently, the arrow was gone! For a fleeting moment he wondered if it had just been a vision, then he saw the hole it had made in the tree and knew his enemy had retrieved it.

His suspicion immediately fell on a member of the Armstrong clan, but what perplexed him was that he had had no premonition of being stalked or even watched. His instincts had warned him only of the imminent threat, which was highly unusual, since danger had its own dire foreshadowing. A wry smile touched the corner of his mouth. Catherine was more than a distraction; his thoughts and his senses were filled with her. He must keep his wits about him. Was his enemy in the king's hunting party or an outsider hiding in the woods? Either could take advantage of this gathering to commit murder and have it declared an accident.

Hepburn joined King James, who was literally frothing at the mouth over the delay. "This is the last time Annie an' her lasses hunt the same day as us. Waesucks, but women can be a curse!"

Hepburn kept the incident to himself. James was ever fearful of assassination. Patrick scrutinized the hunters, but saw no bows. Most men hunted as he and James did, with dogs and knives. He allowed the inner eye of his mind to scan and search the nearby forests but could detect no trace of a lurking enemy. Either his foe was long gone, or it was a stray arrow from a careless female. *Aye, perchance pigs can fly!*

At last the king's hunt got under way and Hepburn, deciding that forewarned was forearmed, watched his back during the next hours.

When the king's dogs failed to bring down a large stag, James demanded, "When are ye goin' tae present me wi' a pair of yer fine Scottish deerhounds, Patrick lad?"

When hell freezes! "When Sabbath whelps, Your Majesty."

Catherine was enjoying herself. For the most part the females who hunted with bows consistently missed their targets and had attendants to retrieve their arrows. She learned firsthand that what Liz had told her about the queen was true: Anne loved horses and dogs. She also took a keen interest in fashion, and when she learned that Cat's mother was Mistress of Elizabeth's Wardrobe, the queen plied her with endless questions.

"What do you wear beneath your divided skirt? Obviously not a petticoat," Anne queried.

"But it is a petticoat, Your Highness. I simply slit it up the middle and stitched it into two legs."

"But of course! How simple. I can tell you enjoy creating unique fashions, Lady Catherine. You must design for me."

"It would be my pleasure, ma'am."

Though the ladies did not bag much game, they thoroughly enjoyed their hours in the saddle on such a warm June day. Cat refused to seek out Hepburn before she and Geordie left Holyrood. She shrugged a careless shoulder and told herself that she didn't give a damn that he hadn't come to bid them good-bye.

As Catherine had arranged with Liz, their carriage followed the Careys' to the Earl of Mar's town house so that she could borrow a gown for the king's upcoming birthday fete.

Liz ushered Catherine and Maggie to her bedchamber, and Geordie had a chance to get to know Robert.

"I know that yer father is Lord Hunsdon and you and I are somehow related through my daughter's marriage. Explain it again," Geordie requested.

"It sounds complicated, but it isn't really. My eldest brother wed Beth Spencer and your daughter, Isobel, wed her brother, John."

"Oh aye, it was yer brother's wife, Beth, who introduced Isobel to Elizabeth's Court. My daughter's ambition was insatiable. Tell me, Robert, d'ye think my wee Catherine is happy there?"

"I do, Lord Winton. My sisters Kate and Philadelphia are Ladies of the Bedchamber, and Catherine is a particular favorite of theirs. There are half a dozen women who happily mother her."

Catherine and Liz stood at the open wardrobe surveying an array of dresses and gowns. "I don't want to take one of your favorites, because I will have to make certain alterations. You are much taller than I am, for one thing."

"Choose whichever you fancy, darling, other than my wedding gown. The green with the Tudor roses is Robert's favorite."

"Oh, I love this peacock blue; it's so vivid. If I wore such a shade at the English Court it would cause a scandal!"

"I admit such a dramatic color is more suitable for a widow than a maiden, but you may have it if you like. The waist is so narrow, I don't believe I'll ever get into it again."

Cat looked at Maggie. "Mother would run mad!"

"That's the one, then, Mistress Impulsive."

Liz removed the gown from its hanger and Maggie folded it carefully. "Patrick has invited us to visit him before we go back to England, so we've decided to go to Crichton right after the king's birthday. It would be fun if you'd come too, Catherine."

Cat smiled. "I might if he begs."

"Hepburn strikes me as a man who's never had to beg."

Cat remembered the females who'd fawned on him at Court. *No, damn him to hellfire!*

During the next week Catherine finished designing the little girls' princess dresses and gave the pretty pastel material to the children's mothers. Cat had only been able to purchase yellow, pink and blue, and remembering that Jessica had said her favorite color was lavender, decided that the only solution was to use one of her own dresses of that particular shade. Cat did the cutting and Maggie did the sewing and before Jessica's bedtime they presented the child with the dress of her dreams.

"It seems ye are determined to spoil my nieces." Malcolm came upon the scene unexpectedly.

"Girls love pretty things. The look on their faces is most rewarding." Cat was ready to challenge him.

"Such luxuries are costly. It must be gratifying to have unlimited means that enable ye to be so generous."

Catherine did not tell him that Geordie had paid. She got the impression that would please him even less than if she had paid.

"Did ye enjoy yer visit to Holyrood?"

"It was different from the English Court, but I liked Queen Anne very much."

"Really? Some of her so-called ladies are little better than strumpets. Even the married ones are said to be promiscuous."

"Royal Courts are always rife with gossip," Cat declared.

Maggie piped in, "That is why Queen Elizabeth surrounds herself with young ladies whose reputations are spotless."

"Lady Catherine must have seemed a rose among thorns at the Scottish Court." His glance moved from Maggie back to Cat. "I imagine many eligible nobles paid court to ye."

"None that I am aware of, Malcolm," she assured him.

As Maggie climbed into the pony cart, Cat took up the reins to drive them back to the castle. "He takes a keen interest in my finances as well as any admirers I might have."

"He is most likely smitten with ye, my lamb. Your virtue is obvious, and gossip has it that his late wife was unfaithful."

"Men often become smitten with heiresses." Cat thought of her friend Arbella and the avaricious Will Seymour.

"I believe ye're in danger of becoming cynical," Maggie warned.

"I warrant 'tis better to be cynical than hopelessly naïve!"

The next few days were devoted to the clothes Catherine would take to Court for the king's birthday celebration. This time she fully intended to look sophisticated rather than demure. Since the peacock blue gown was far too long for Cat, she removed almost six inches at the front and where the back formed a train she cut off at least a foot. Then with the material she fashioned a fan-shaped ruff and wired it so that it would stand upright to frame her head from behind. Cat had designed this new fashion for Queen Elizabeth and knew it had never been seen at the Scottish Court.

"Tis beautiful material. Sometimes it looks blue and then it changes to green. The neckline is very revealing, my lamb. Are ye sure you don't want me to raise it a bit?"

"No, no, the whole idea of the fan-shaped ruff is to display jewels upon an expanse of deliciously curved breasts," Cat teased.

"Men have a tendency to taste delicious things."

"Maggie, you shock me to the core," she said demurely.

"Well, it cries out for a necklace. All ye have is pearls."

"I like pearls. They are eminently suitable for a maiden."

"I think I'll remove some of the crystal droplets from one of yer white gowns and sew them on the sleeves to make ye glitter."

"Brilliant idea, Maggie. I'll cut; you stitch."

The next day Catherine was surprised to see Jenny Hepburn riding with Andrew. "Jenny, I'm so glad to see you."

Jenny dismounted and said softly, "Andrew asked my father for permission to take me riding."

Cat glanced up at Andrew and saw that he had a bow and a quiver of arrows slung across his back. "Oh, are there archery butts at Seton? We have them at Whitehall. Elizabeth enjoys the sport."

"No real butts; we just use a hay bale or a tree to practice. I promised to teach Jenny to shoot a bow. Please join us."

Cat cocked an eyebrow at her friend, who nodded with enthusiasm. They waited while she had her mount saddled, then the three rode to a wooded area and dismounted in a clearing.

Using an old tree stump at the far end as a target, Andrew demonstrated his skill with the bow.

"You are an expert archer!" Catherine praised.

"Nay," he said modestly. "I have some skill with the bow, but my cousin Malcolm is the expert. He's a master hunter." He offered the bow to Jenny and handed her an arrow, then he placed his arms about her to show her how it was done.

Amazing! Whether at Whitehall or Seton, men use the same tactics to get their arms about a lady they fancy.

Andrew's bow was as tall as Jenny and she could hardly pull back the string. Cat knew she did not even have as much strength as Jenny, because her arms were shorter. "We cannot manage a man's bow, Andrew. The ladies at Court hunted with smaller bows."

Andrew took his hunting knife and cut some long straight branches from a larch tree, then with twine from his saddlebags he fashioned each of them a four-foot bow. Once again he put his arms about Jenny and nocked one of his arrows for her. It went far of its mark and Cat suspected that Jenny only pretended she needed more instruction.

They enjoyed an hour's practice, and after, Catherine invited them both to join her for dinner at Winton Castle.

"I'm sorry, but we cannot. I promised to have Jenny back at Crichton before the afternoon sun started to sink."

"Of course . . . perhaps another time. May I keep a couple of your arrows so I can practice my marksmanship?" Catherine watched them ride off side by side and wished she were going to Crichton.

That night when Cat went to bed she still felt a wistful longing she was afraid to explore. Once she began to dream, however, her reticence was swept away. She found herself back at Whitehall reliving the time when Henry Somerset had invited her to join him at the archery butts to give her a lesson. This time, though, Jenny, not Arbella, was her companion. Catherine was acutely aware that Patrick Hepburn stood close by, casually leaning on his six-foot bow.

The first thing that Cat noticed was that Hal Somerset's bow was quite small, more suited to a youth.

Jenny gazed at Patrick, then murmured to Cat, "He's a man!" Then she glanced at Henry and said, "What woman would want a lad?"

Patrick stepped forward. "I'll show you how it's done."

"Amazing! Whether at Whitehall or Seton men use the same tactics to get their arms about a lady they fancy," Cat drawled, eyeing his six-foot bow.

Hepburn slid his arms about her and bent his head to whisper wickedly, "I bet Henry's arrow is shorter than mine, too!"

"Cocksure devil!" Catherine teased.

In a flash, Patrick pulled Catherine to the ground and covered her with his body. Cat, flat on her back, glared up at him in pretended outrage. "What the devil are you doing?"

He pointed to an arrow embedded in a tree above them. "Just a stray arrow. No harm done."

She gave him a sideways glance. "No harm at all, except my lovely white gown is smeared with dirt."

He lifted her to her feet with powerful hands and murmured, "I know a place where we can rid you of that."

"The gown or the dirt, you uncivilized brute?" she taunted.

"Mayhap both, Hellcat." He took possession of her hand and led her into the palace.

"Where are we going?" She licked her lips in anticipation.

He stopped before a door. "Here. To my chamber."

She gazed up into his black eyes and knew she would do this impulsive, reckless thing. She watched the door swing open to reveal a tall, attractive female in a silk robe.

"Gretha, what the hell are you doing here?"

She smiled sensuously. "Surely you'd rather spend the night with a woman, than a female who is dressed like a little girl?"

Cat looked down in dismay and saw that she was wearing the same babyish white gown she had worn to Holyrood. The door swung closed in her face, with Patrick and Gretha on the inside.

In the morning Catherine awoke with the same wistful longing she had felt when she went to sleep. As the day wore on it melted away, and it was gone by the time she and Maggie packed their clothes for Holyrood. That evening at dinner, Geordie presented her with a velvet jewel case.

"A wee brid told me ye're in need of a gewgaw."

Cat interpreted "brid" as *bird,* and "gewgaw" as *jewel.* She opened the case and saw diamonds glittering upon the black velvet. "How lovely! Did this belong to my grandmother?"

"Aye, Audra wore it when she had her portrait painted."

Catherine lifted the diamond and crystal necklace with reverent hands. "It matches the crystal drops on my gown."

"It must be magic," Geordie said with a wink.

"It must be *Maggie,* who was cheeky enough to ask you if I could borrow Audra's necklace."

"Borrow, my arse! 'Tis for keeps. Her jewels are better worn by a lady who can do them justice, than hidden away."

His words brought a lump to her throat. "I thank you with all my heart, Granddad. I shall wear them proudly."

The following evening when Geordie escorted Catherine down to Holyrood's reception chambers and the chamberlain announced them, Cat stepped forward with confidence and was delighted when a hush descended. *They are amazed at my transformation!*

The males present realized the Earl of Winton's grand-daughter was a woman full grown, and a sophisticated and wealthy one at that. The females stared with envy at the petite, dazzling creature in vivid peacock blue with the fan-shaped ruff that framed her upswept, shining curls and showed off the diamonds blazing at her throat.

When she curtsied before the king and queen, she saw that James was wearing a kilt of Royal Stewart plaid and for once he did not look melancholy. Tonight he was celebrating his thirty-sixth birthday, and Cat realized for the first time that was not old.

"Lady Catherine, you must design me a ruff like yours," Queen Anne declared as her eyes examined Cat's gown and jewels.

"It would be my pleasure, Your Gracious Majesty." *Queen Elizabeth would imprison me in the Tower and throw away the key! How fortunate she'll not be visiting Scotland in the near future.*

A skirl of bagpipes announced the approach of King James's pipe band. When they marched into the chamber the sound almost raised the rafters. They paraded round the perimeter of the room several times, as they played one rousing Highland military march after another. Words had been written to some of the music and the lusty voices of the guests sang out in unison. When the pipe band marched onto the dais and stood behind the royal couple, everyone present burst into spontaneous applause.

Four bonnie youths with rosy cheeks filed into the chamber, each carrying two shining broadswords. They bowed to the king and queen, then bent and placed the swords crosswise on the floor.

"This is a traditional sword dance, Catherine."

Cat knew it was Patrick behind her. The way he rolled the *r* in her name sent a delicious shiver down her spine. As she glanced at him she saw that he too was wearing the brilliant red Royal Stewart plaid. Her eyes quickly swung back to the dancers because his kilt, slung on his hipbones, was scandalously short. *I can see his muscled thighs! His legs are like young oak trees.*

Cat tried to concentrate on the dancers, but even though their kilts swung to reveal their limbs, her wicked imagination was picturing a naked Patrick Hepburn. Aboard ship, she'd seen his bared chest with its dark pelt of hair and now she'd seen his legs. When she tried to fill in his more intimate parts her imagination failed her, but she recognized the ache growing in the pit of her belly as physical desire. Acute, wanton desire!

Catherine edged away from him until others were directly behind her. She knew that her diminutive height would not block anyone watching the sword dancing.

"Anne is extremely shrewd. She handpicked the male dancers to appeal to James's special tastes." Cat recognized the females conversing as two of the queen's ladies.

"Strapping youths with blond curls . . . what a waste!"

Catherine did not understand their asides. Her glance moved past the dancers to observe King James, whose attention was riveted upon the dancers; he was clearly enjoying himself.

The sword dancing garnered deafening applause as the performers went to kneel before the royal couple. The king, effusive in his thanks, reached out to caress the curls of one young man. Cat suddenly recognized him as Robin Carr, who'd asked her to dance the last time she was here. She wondered if he'd seek her out again.

The musicians who played the music for the country-dances and reels entered the chamber and began to tune their instruments, and the guests began to mingle and converse. The two females who'd been behind Catherine stared at her elegant peacock gown, and then had a murmured exchange about her.

"'Tis said that English ladies at Elizabeth's Court are slaves to fashion, Christina," one of them drawled.

"Rumor also has it English ladies are cold as icicles. Is that true, Lady Catherine?" the other one asked spitefully.

From the corner of her eye Cat saw Hepburn advancing upon her. She looked the queen's lady in the eye and said sweetly, "Look ravishingly available, but be unobtainable. Keeps men coming back for more." She smiled. "Hello, Patrick, are you pursuing me?"

He looked at the three females with amused eyes. "Do you ladies know each other?"

Christina said, "Yes indeed, Lord Stewart, we were just discussing the oddities of English ladies."

His lips curved. "If this is a cat fight, my money's on the wee lass. Which one of you ladies will partner me in the reel?"

Catherine gave him a ravishing smile. "England concedes the honor to Scotland, or would that be Denmark?"

"It would be my pleasure to partner you, my lord, in the dance or in any other way," Christina offered suggestively.

The young Earl of Gowrie bowed before Cat. "Lady Catherine, would ye do me the honor of partnerin' me in the reel?"

"It is you who honor me, my lord." She glanced at Patrick and saw him frown. It pleased her immeasurably. She grew less pleased as the evening progressed and Hepburn did not ask to partner her again. Whenever she caught a glimpse of him dancing, his kilt was swinging so high it made her gasp. "Vain swine!" she muttered beneath her breath.

When the dancing was followed by a fireworks display in honor of the king's birthday, however, Patrick was there to escort her outside and refused to take no for an answer.

In the vivid, elegant gown Catherine had never looked more sophisticated, he thought, yet he honestly preferred the lovely innocence of her white Court gown. "Perhaps you should sheathe your claws when conversing with the queen's ladies. It would be wise to make a friend of Anne, rather than an enemy."

"Some of her ladies may dislike me, but I am already firm friends with Queen Anne. She asked me to design her a gown."

"That's good, Catherine. Anne is the future Queen of England."

Cat stared up at him. "What on earth are you talking about?"

"I'm talking about when James Stuart becomes King of England."

"But Elizabeth will have to die before that can happen. Elizabeth Tudor has no intentions of dying, Patrick. You are speaking about the very distant future. She isn't even ready to name her successor."

"Of course not," he conceded. *Elizabeth is so firmly entrenched in the minds of her courtiers, they think her immortal.*

"Look at that!" He pointed to the sky as a shower of golden rain exploded, followed by a fountain of cascading silver stars.

"You can make a wish on a falling star!" Cat exclaimed.

He gazed down at her and touched a finger to the glittering diamonds at her throat. "My wish is that you'll come and stay at Crichton next week. Robert and Liz are coming."

She swayed toward him. "Perhaps I will . . ." Her voice trailed off in a half promise. "But not until the end of the week."

"Don't cock tease, Hellcat; you'll get your tail singed."

Chapter Fifteen

*I*t was the early hours of the morning when James Stuart left his birthday revels and retired to bed. Before he left he had a quiet word with Patrick Hepburn and Robert Carey asking them to attend him in his Privy Chamber before lunch the next day.

When the two men arrived in the antechamber, Patrick refrained from telling Robert about the psychic episode he'd had when he awoke. He had again envisioned the Carey family genealogical table, clearly showing the date of Lord Hunsdon's death, but made a decision not to speak of it until Robert had seen the king.

Jamie left Carey in the antechamber to cool his heels while he had a private word with Hepburn. "I've carefully crafted a letter tae Elizabeth that I want ye tae read before I give it tae Carey. I believe I've followed Cecil's instructions tae the letter. He warns me against any mention, ever, of the succession. Not even a hint. He advises me to secure the 'heart of the highest' by much praise and by showing no curiosity in her actions." King James handed Patrick the letter.

It was filled with flowery flattery and adulation for Elizabeth, telling her how much James appreciated her friendship and guidance. Sprinkled throughout were classical quotations.

"The Latin phrases are the perfect touch," Hepburn approved.

"I'm sending the letter tae Cecil enclosed inside one I've written tae him." James handed Patrick the second letter.

James had thanked the Secretary of State for his trust and assured him it was reciprocated. He asked Cecil's advice about courting popularity in England and if it was possible to start setting up an English Court for the King of Scotland. Hepburn knew that Cecil would tell him it was not advisable, but decided it would be better if Jamie heard it from the horse's mouth.

The king took back his letters and began to affix his seals. "Let's have Carey in. I want him tae leave today and bring back an answer *posthaste.*"

Within half an hour the two friends left the king's Privy Chamber. "Liz will be extremely disappointed that we cannot come to Crichton, Patrick. Can you think of some plausible excuse I can give her that she will believe?"

"Unfortunately I can, Robert. I had a prophetic vision about your father. I believe he died in his sleep last night. I didn't want to tell you until after you had seen James."

"Dear God, though he's aged and ailing and I've been expecting it, it still comes as a shock."

"By the time you cross the Border and stop at Bewcastle, your brother George should just be receiving the message that he is the new Lord Hunsdon. You'll be able to travel to London together."

When they arrived at Carey's chamber, Liz had already finished packing. "Hello, Patrick. You just missed Catherine. She came to say good-bye, but gave me her word she would come to spend a few days at Crichton this week."

"Liz, my dear, we won't be able to visit Crichton," Robert replied. "I've just received word that Father has died. We must leave today."

"Oh, Robert, that is such sad news. I'm glad that I had the chance to get to know him a little." She put comforting arms about her husband and held him for a moment. "Patrick, if I write a note to Catherine, would you be kind enough to deliver it?"

"I shall give it to her personally, Liz. Your visit to Crichton can wait. My deepest condolences to both of you."

As Hepburn rode home from Edinburgh he was glad that Geordie and Catherine had departed earlier for Seton. He was in no hurry to deliver Liz's letter to Catherine. If she believed that Liz and Robert were at Crichton, she might come. Once she learned otherwise, she definitely would not.

The following day at Seton, Catherine decided she needed some additions to her wardrobe. She went in search of a length of Winton plaid. One of the castle sewing women took her to the solar, where an ornate cedar chest held bolts of cloth. Among the finely woven wool, Cat discovered dark green Winton plaid and Winton hunting plaid, which had a great deal of white woven into the green. She chose the Winton hunting plaid because its two main hues were Tudor colors, though she much preferred the brilliant red of the Royal Stewart that Patrick had worn.

As her hands sorted through the material, Cat touched a piece of cloth that was so soft, she knew she must have it. When she separated it from the rest, she discovered that it was doeskin in its natural shade. She carried the two lengths of material down to Maggie. "I would love a riding skirt made from this doeskin."

"I thought ye were off to Crichton today. Instead, yer planning a new wardrobe," Maggie commented.

"Just because the arrogant Lord Stewart invited me to stay at Crichton for a few days doesn't mean I shall go."

"Oh, aye." Maggie's voice was laced with skepticism.

"Well, I do mean to go, but certainly not today . . . perhaps not even tomorrow. I'm not at Hepburn's beck and call."

Maggie lifted the length of tartan. "I remember Audra wearing a skirt made of this plaid. It was so full, it swirled about when she moved quickly to reveal her trim ankles. Ye want the same?"

"Ankles be damned. I want a kilt," Catherine said lightly.

"Ye mean pleated like a kilt?"

"I mean *short* like a kilt."

"*Above* yer ankles?" Maggie asked, scandalized.

"Above my *knees!*"

"I'll have nothing to do with such a wanton garment."

"Then I'll make the bloody thing myself!" Cat declared. She sought out Geordie's valet and asked if he'd let her have a look at one of her grandfather's kilts to see how it was made.

He explained it was a simple length of cloth, gathered into pleats and held in place by a wide belt. A large pin prevented it from blowing open when caught by the wind. Any excess material was thrown over the shoulder.

She went back downstairs and found a tight-lipped Maggie working on the doeskin riding skirt. Cat decided to sew the tops of the pleats in her kilt to keep them in place, then stitch on a waistband to eliminate the need for a leather belt. She also made a loop through which she could secure her hunting knife.

"Do ye intend to display yer limbs to everyone in general, or one man in particular? As if I didn't know the answer!"

Maggie is right. I want to shatter the indifference Hepburn displays toward me. When he looks at me, I want to wipe out the thought of any other female. Cat remembered deliberately leaning toward him when they were watching the fireworks. If she had done that with any other male of her acquaintance, he would have taken her in his arms and kissed her. Instead, Hepburn had looked down at her in amusement and called her a shocking name. *Cock tease!*

Maggie sighed. "I keep forgetting yer almost a grown woman, Catherine. It's time I let ye spread yer wings. All in all it's been a good thing for ye to be away from Elizabeth's Court, and likely it'll do ye good to be away from me for a few days too. Liz and Robert will act as chaperones while ye visit Crichton."

"Are you sure you dare to let me off my leash?" Cat teased.

"Not sure at all, my lamb. The very thought of it gives me palpitations, but if I don't push ye out from under my wing, ye'll never learn how to fly."

Cat impulsively kissed Maggie's cheek. "I won't be satisfied to simply fly. I intend to soar!"

At Crichton, the hours seemed to pass slowly for Patrick Hepburn. He glanced at his reflection in the mirror. "Patience and wisdom go hand in hand." Patrick knew patience had been a hard-won lesson in his life, but where Catherine was concerned he didn't seem to have any at all.

He disrobed, got into bed and lay with his arms folded behind his head. He breathed slowly, deeply, focusing his full attention upon the object of his desire. Within moments he could see the exquisite features of her face as she lay in slumber. He gazed spellbound upon the delicate arch of her dark brows and her closed eyelids with their thick, black lashes. He stared with longing at her tempting lips, lusting to take possession of her mouth and have her yield it to him. He reached beneath his pillow for her white ribbon and rubbed its satiny softness between finger and thumb. On the verge of compelling her presence, he suddenly stopped. If Catherine didn't come to him of her own volition, there would be no satisfaction, no joy in it. *Does that matter?* He hesitated for long minutes. With a foul oath he thrust the ribbon back beneath his pillow. *It matters!*

The next day, as twilight then darkness fell, Hepburn gave up hope that Catherine Seton Spencer would come. Perhaps she had learned that Liz and Robert were not at Crichton, but for whatever reason he accepted that she was not coming. It was time he put youthful fantasies aside and got on with his responsibilities. He hadn't yet gone north for the wild horses. It was his custom to go each year at the end of April or early May when his Border patrol duty was finished, but this year he'd been in Richmond.

Patrick knew he should have passed the task on to David and one of the other Hepburns, but horses were in his blood. They were his passion, and riding through the Lammermuir Hills and valleys searching for a wild stallion and his mares thrilled him deeply. He had put it off long enough. *I'll leave tomorrow!* As he packed his saddlebags for the solitary ride north, excitement began to course through his veins.

The next morning he arose early. At breakfast he informed his men where he was going and put Jock Elliot and David Hepburn in charge of the castle. He packed oatcakes, smoked venison and cheese in his saddlebags and took them to the stables. Patrick sharpened his hunting knives and made sure he had two lengthy coils of stout rope. He decided against taking Sabbath and Satan; wild horses spooked too easily. As he reached for Valiant's saddle, he heard a carriage in the courtyard. He set the saddle back down and went to investigate.

Patrick saw the Earl of Winton's coach driver jump down and open the door. Lady Catherine stepped out and spoke to the driver as he placed her luggage at her feet. The man nodded and departed. Hepburn let him go. *I'll escort Cat back to Seton.*

His glance traveled from her upswept curls to her elegant morning dress of pale primrose. Her arrival threw him slightly off balance and he began to juggle his plans. Perhaps he could persuade her to stay today. The horses could wait till tomorrow. "You came after all," he said quizzically. *Of your own volition.*

She looked into his eyes and saw surprise in the dark depths. "You thought I wouldn't come."

"Yes—no. Let me take your bags. There's a chamber all prepared for you." He led the way beneath the rose-carved stone arch and up the steps into the castle.

Cat's glance traced the staircase and the chamber's lovely balcony. "Crichton is truly full of grace and beauty."

"It is now, Catherine." His husky voice rolled the *r.*

"A compliment, begod!"

Hepburn's housekeeper stepped forward and he quickly waved her away. *I want her to myself for a while.* He led her up the staircase and took her to a well-appointed bedchamber.

"Is my room close to Liz and Robert's?"

"The chamber prepared for them is just down the hall," he said carefully, trying not to lie. Patrick opened the wardrobe doors, hoping she would start to unpack.

"Maggie didn't come. She said the Careys would chaperone me."

He saw the delicate blush on her cheeks and suddenly felt like an uncouth lout to deceive her in this way.

"I wanted to ride, but Geordie insisted I come by carriage. So you will have to mount me . . ." She suddenly realized what she had said and her cheeks flushed furiously.

"I'll be right back. I have something for you." As Patrick strode to his chamber to get the letter, he cursed himself for a bloody fool. *Why the hell am I being so uncharacteristically gallant?* he asked himself. *Because she looks so vulnerable.*

When he returned, he saw that she had begun to hang her clothes in the wardrobe and he immediately regretted bringing the letter.

Her face was eagerly expectant as she tore open the envelope with her name on it. Patrick watched the joy leave her face as she read Liz's words. She raised her eyes. "She wrote this Sunday."

"They left for England immediately. I expected to see you the next day. You didn't come—I thought you'd changed your mind."

"No, I was looking forward to coming. Poor Robert . . . and Philadelphia and Kate. What a wretch I am to feel such disappointment when they are in mourning."

"Life goes on, Catherine. When you arrived I was on my way to the Lammermuirs for the wild horses."

"Wild horses?" Her golden eyes lit up with fascination.

"Every spring, I ride north into the Lammermuir Hills where

herds of wild horses and ponies roam. I usually bring back a stallion and his mares to increase my own herd."

"How exciting that must be." Her eyes began to glitter as she pictured it in her mind's eye. "Take me with you!"

"Catherine, I cannot."

"Why? Because I'm a female?" she challenged.

"Because you're a lady. It would ruin your good character."

Catherine began to laugh. "I *am* a lady and for that no character is necessary."

He couldn't hide his admiration. "You are brimful of wit and *impulsiveness*. It is my duty to save you from yourself."

"To lowest hell with your duty, Hepburn. Take me with you!"

He hesitated. She saw and pressed him urgently. "Saddle me one of your sure-footed Border ponies and I'll change my clothes."

"The earl would run mad, Hellcat."

"He won't know. He and Maggie think me at Crichton for a week." She clenched her fists and pummeled his chest. "If you deny me, I'll hate you forever, Lord Bloody Stewart!"

It was the first thing she had ever asked of him and, in that moment, he could deny her nothing. "We travel rough; sleep outdoors. You'll have to obey me." He could tell his warning made her more eager. "I'll get you some saddlebags. Pack only serviceable clothes. When you've changed, go to the kitchen and wrap up some food. Choose stuff that won't spoil, like oatcakes."

Cat took off her ruff and with impatient fingers unfastened her dress. Off it came, along with her petticoats and fancy slippers. She put them in the wardrobe, then opened her trunk. Right on top she had put the two arrows and the bow that Andrew had made for her, thinking to show off her marksmanship to Liz. She threw them into the wardrobe and removed from her luggage only the things she intended to take with her—undergarments, hose, padded doublets and a riding skirt. She put on the new doeskin skirt and finally found a long-sleeved bodice of Tudor green to go with it. On impulse she decided to take the kilt. A tablet of soap, her brush and comb and some ribbon went onto the pile.

Patrick strode in without knocking and handed her a set of leather saddlebags. He looked askance at the small stack she had made. "You won't have room for all that rubbish," he warned. "You'll need to take a cloak."

"I won't take much food," she argued.

"Don't expect to eat mine. I'll share my bed, but not my food," he teased.

"I am aware of your insatiable appetite."

"English, you have no idea."

"Damn you, I refuse to blush at every innuendo!"

"*Mea culpa.* I delight in making you blush." His face sobered. "Hurry up! I'll be leaving in five minutes."

Then you'll be leaving without me! Cat thought the words rather than saying them aloud. She knew he would do as he vowed. She quickly crammed her belongings into the saddlebags, then rolled up her cloak and fastened it on the outside. She found them heavy as she struggled to the top of the stairs. Inspiration came to her aid as she put a booted foot to the saddlebags and kicked. As they tumbled down, the housekeeper hurried to see what the racket was all about. "Which way to the kitchen?" Cat pleaded.

The Hepburn housekeeper and the cook helped her choose food and wrapped it in a linen napkin, then directed one of the kitchen boys to carry Lady Catherine's saddlebags to the stables.

She decided to start out on a civil note. "Thank you for waiting for me."

"You were quicker than I expected. I issued the five-minute ultimatum because I'm familiar with the ways of women."

Too familiar, with too many women, Cat thought wistfully.

The pony that Patrick had saddled for her was a ruddy color and the same size as a small horse. He helped her mount, then placed the saddlebags behind her across the pony's back.

"What is my pony's name?"

"Chestnut."

As they cantered through Crichton's orchards and across gorsy meadows, her pony kept pace with Valiant. She spotted Tor and pointed him out to Patrick. The crow stopped following them and circled back. "I know why he stopped. No dogs!"

It pleased him that she took an interest in nature and was able to discern how the creatures about her reasoned.

Cat was thankful that they skirted Seton land and headed in a northwest direction through rolling hills. It was almost July and the weather was perfect. She breathed deeply, inhaling the fragrant scent of heather and ferns. She splashed through streams with abandon, reveling in the sense of freedom it gave her. She had forgotten to wear a hat, but realized she didn't really give a damn what the sun would do to her pale ivory complexion.

They had been in the saddle for two or three hours, and when the sun was directly above them, Patrick drew rein beside a shaded stream and dismounted. Cat followed his lead, grateful to be out of the saddle. He did not tether Valiant but allowed him to wander down to the water for a drink. Cat let go of Chestnut's reins and watched it follow the huge black horse.

Patrick knelt at the stream's edge, dipped in his cupped hand, then drank. He splashed the cool water onto his face and neck, then grinned his approval as he watched Catherine mimic his actions. "Monkey see, monkey do," he teased.

"You're not a monkey; you're a bloody ape." She gave as good as she got. "How far did we travel?"

"A dozen miles, more or less. Are you hungry, my wee lass?"

"Yes, I hunger for adventure!"

He towered above her. "And thirst for new experience—the elixir of life. I know exactly how you feel, Cat."

"How do you know?" she challenged.

"I felt that way myself when I was about twelve," he teased.

"You mocking devil, Hepburn. I'm glad I amuse you."

"So am I." He winked. "Let's eat."

They each took food from their saddlebags and sat down on the grass. Patrick munched on smoked venison and oat cakes, while Catherine ate a russet apple. He marveled at her dainty appetite, and the delicate way she ate was almost feline. When he offered her an oatcake, she wrinkled her nose. "Don't turn your nose up at oats, English; they are what made me such a strapping lad."

"Oats are what you feed a stallion." She went hot, realizing she had just aptly compared him to a stallion.

"You said it; I didn't. I refuse to blush at every innuendo."

She laughed. "You have a wicked humor, Hepburn."

"It's my saving grace."

You're the most attractive male I've ever met, damn you to hellfire. She turned her back to him and removed her riding boots. Then she went behind a tree, removed her stockings and reappeared. She lifted her chin and said defiantly, "I want to wade in the stream."

His eyes crinkled at the corners with amusement. "You don't need my permission to indulge your impulses."

Catherine pulled up the legs of her divided riding skirt and stepped into the water, which came almost to her knees. She screamed. "It's freezing!" She scrambled out quickly. "Cold water is good for drinking, dreadful for wading."

"Cold water is excellent for curbing impulses. Remember it."

Shortly after they remounted, Catherine remarked, "This is lovely country. The hills seem to be getting steeper."

"These are part of the Lammermuir Hills."

"Up ahead look more like mountains than hills. Who owns them?"

"We stopped for lunch on St. Clair land. This here belongs to the Cockburns, and where we are going used to be Hepburn land."

"Used to be?" Cat questioned.

"Bothwell, my father, was charged with treasonable conspiracy against His Majesty and as a result all his lands and castles were forfeit. His real sin was flaunting his power—it made enemies."

"But you still own Crichton."

"Yes, my father agreed to exile on condition that I be allowed to keep Crichton. It was heavily mortgaged, but I finally managed to pay it off. Mortgages are to be avoided like the plague."

"You're free to ride on the Hepburn land that you once owned?"

"Most certainly. King James gave Hailes Castle and its land to the Earl of Lennox, who paid off the mortgages. Lennox seldom visits Hailes; it is too ancient and dilapidated. Robert the Bruce gave it to the Lord of Hailes, who was a Hepburn, almost four hundred years ago. Some of the land has tenant farms, but most of it is wild and untamed."

Like you.

They rode on in companionable silence for more than an hour, over hills and through vales. Finally, it was Patrick who broke the silence. "We are now on the ancient Hepburn lands."

Catherine had a sudden revelation. "You take the wild herds you find here because you feel entitled to them."

He nodded. "Perhaps. I believe the Hepburns centuries ago did it. They were always horsemen. For hundreds of years our emblem has been the horse head."

For another hour they rode over Hepburn land and Catherine was becoming saddle-weary. Sensing it, in the late afternoon Patrick looked for a place to make camp. He stopped beside a stand of Douglas firs, close by the river Tyne. He gestured toward what looked like a mountain. "That yonder is Traprain Law. I believe you've ridden far enough for today. We are not likely to flush out the horses this late in the day."

"Good! My bottom is sore. Does *law* mean mountain?"

He shook his head. "*Law* is Scottish for hill or mound. Hailes Castle lies beyond the law."

"Hailes Castle lies beyond the law. That sounds exciting and provocative. Do you mean literally or figuratively?"

"Both. Certainly when my father was put to the horn." He dismounted, relieved Valiant of both saddle and saddlebags and turned him loose to crop the grass between the trees and river.

Catherine followed suit. *God forbid he thinks I want him to help me, though it would have been gallant if he had offered.*

He pointed to the trees. "If you'll gather wood for a fire, I'll set a snare. Hot food would taste good."

Before she was finished collecting fallen branches, he took the axe that hung from his saddle and chopped a tree trunk into logs. Then he kindled a fire with fir needles. "Don't let it go out," he warned, and then took himself off to the river.

The sky was streaked with a scarlet sunset by the time he returned with a small salmon. Then he went back into the trees and emerged carrying a lifeless coney he had snared. Before she could mourn for the furry creature, his words stopped her.

"Will you clean the fish or skin the rabbit?"

She stared at him, aghast, for a moment. Her heart was bleeding for the little creature. "The fish," she blurted.

Gingerly she unsheathed her knife, secretly appalled to even touch something that smelled *fishy*. Then she caught the glint of amusement in his eyes and steeled herself. She cut off its head and tail, then slit and gutted it. Without a word she went to the river to wash her knife and hands and left him to cook.

When the food was ready, Catherine deigned to eat some of

the salmon but adamantly refused to even taste the coney. Instead she nibbled on some cheese and accepted graciously when he offered her one of his oatcakes. She was amazed when he produced a wine skin and delighted when he showed her how to drink from it.

Patrick tethered their mounts for the night and brought their cloaks to the fire. "The night will get cold, Catherine."

She was excited at the prospect of sleeping outdoors. She'd never done it before. The wine and the close presence of Hepburn heated her blood. The jest he'd made about sharing his bed came back to her, making her pulse race and her heart beat rapidly. Suddenly she felt nervous about liberties he might try to take. She touched her knife to make sure it was there.

Without a glance in her direction, Patrick put a couple of logs on the fire, and then wrapped himself in his cloak and stretched out on the ground. "Good night, Catherine."

She felt highly offended. *Damn the lout; I'll never crack his indifference, let alone shatter it!* "What about wolves?"

"Not in summer—prey is too plentiful."

Cat pulled on her cloak. "Do you mind if I come closer?"

The darkness hid his wolf's grin. "Come and lie next to me, if it makes you feel safer, *cherie.*"

Chapter Sixteen

C atherine was convinced that she would never be able to fall asleep on the hard ground. Some of the excitement of the adventure evaporated as she became aware of the lumpy earth digging into her soft flesh. All her senses seemed alert as she watched the flickering flames, heard the flowing water of the river, smelled the piquant evergreen firs and felt the powerful presence of the man who lay beside her. But finally she slept.

When she awoke in the morning she was alone, but an impression of arms that had enfolded and protected her lingered. She persuaded herself that she had been dreaming.

"Good morning, sleepyhead."

She saw that he was coming from the river and by the look of his wet hair he must have swum. He was wearing the damned sheepskin that left his muscular arms bare and he was unshaven. Cat stood up on stiff legs, and when she staggered a little he reached out to steady her. The moment he touched her, her knees turned to wet linen. Catherine felt shy and tongue-tied.

"Your snores woke me early."

Her shyness fled as her outrage soared. Then she realized he was teasing the devil out of her. "Your humor isn't wicked; it is evil. As penalty, Lord Stewart, you may get my breakfast while I attend to my toilet." She walked off with the hauteur of a queen.

Cat removed the soap, hairbrush and fresh undergarments from her saddlebags, then on impulse pulled out the kilt. *If he can display himself in a bloody sheepskin, I can certainly wear my Winton hunting plaid!*

She removed her boots and stockings and dipped a toe into the water. She pulled it out quickly and shuddered, wondering how on earth Hepburn had submerged himself. She washed herself a little at a time, replaced her doeskin riding skirt with the kilt and leisurely brushed her hair. She couldn't fashion it into the upswept style she had worn yesterday, so plaited it into a thick braid. She gathered her belongings, then hesitated. Before she returned she covered her shocking attire demurely with her cloak.

Patrick handed her a stick with hot meat skewered on it and gave her a cup of wine. Since her belly growled with hunger she found it expedient to ignore her scruples and eat the coney.

He eyed her cloak. "Surely you're not cold? It's a glorious day—even warmer than yesterday."

"Do you think we'll locate the herd today?"

"I'm certain of it. Finish your wine and I'll saddle up."

Cat put her belongings into her saddlebag and took Chestnut's reins from Patrick. He cupped his hands, and when she put her boot into them her cloak fell back to reveal all.

He stared at her in disbelief. "A kilt, begod!"

She swung her leg across, sat in the saddle and lifted her chin. "I don't need your permission to indulge my impulses!"

"You fling my words at me with the same abandon you fling your kilt." He threw back his head and laughed until the corded muscles of his neck stood out.

"You were right, Hepburn. It's a glorious day and I certainly won't need this." She whipped off her cloak, rolled it up and secured it beneath the straps of her saddlebag.

As he mounted Valiant he couldn't keep the grin off his face. She was everything he'd ever called her and more besides: *spoiled little bitch, hellcat and cock tease*. He realized he wouldn't want her any other way.

Their mounts climbed up Traprain Law and the two riders drew rein on its peak. At its foot in the valley below sat the ancient pile of stones known as Hailes Castle. On three sides it was surrounded by a moat, whose water glittered like gold from the reflection of the sun. On the fourth side, the river Tyne lapped at its walls. Catherine glanced quickly at Patrick wondering if he still mourned its loss. In repose his face looked dangerous, then he caught her glance and his amusement returned.

He did not ride down the valley toward Hailes, but led her west toward the river, knowing that horses instinctively ranged within an hour's gallop of water. As they slowly made their way through the hills, Patrick occasionally dismounted to examine horse droppings, touching the piles with the toe of his boot to see how recent they were. He grunted with satisfaction, knowing he was getting closer.

They were in the river valley when he cocked his head and listened. The rumble of hooves grew louder and he shouted, "Catherine!" He closed the distance between them, reached out a powerful arm, swept her from her pony and deposited her before him in the saddle: "Hang on tight!"

Cat only had time to gasp before the herd thundered into the valley on the opposite bank of the Tyne. There were at least thirty horses of all colors and sizes, led by a wild black stallion. Hepburn increased his speed to theirs, keeping pace on this side of the Tyne. She was laughing with the pure exhilaration of the ride as he joyfully shouted an ancient battle cry. Her blood sang with the thrill of the race, her spirit gloried in the untethered freedom of the chase.

"Hold tight!" His lips brushed her ear and his arm tightened about her as he spurred Valiant into the river to cross to the opposite side. The water swirled up about her knees and splashed her face before they gained the far bank. Then the pursuit was on again as they dashed headlong to catch up to the wild horses. Slowly, surely, Valiant closed the distance that stretched between them. Then, unbelievably, they became part of the herd, riding on the wind, galloping in tempo until their hearts beat with the same rhythm as the horses. For one shining moment the same silver thread of exhilarating, primal life connected them all.

As they gained on the black stallion, suddenly Cat could not bear the thought of the magnificent creature being captured. "Patrick, no! He is wild and untamed. Let him go free! Please don't attempt to capture and tame him."

"He's mine!"

"Patrick, please! Let him remain free for another year. Leave him untamed for just one more year!"

He looked down at her and in that moment they were one. He nodded. "Yes!" He grinned. "I will!"

Though Valiant did not seem to slacken his pace, gradually the herd pulled ahead of them. Catherine's hair had come loose from its braid and it flew up to brush against Patrick's throat and his face. She turned her head to look up at him and saw that he was as intoxicated by the incredible adventure as she was. He dipped his head, his black eyes devouring her face, then his mouth took possession of hers in a demanding kiss that ignited her desire.

Her arms slid up about his neck and her mouth arched up to his with fiery intensity. Her fingers threaded into his hair, holding him captive for her mouth's ravishing.

With pressure from his knees, Patrick slowed Valiant to a canter, then a walk. He bound Catherine tightly with one arm and slipped down from the stallion's back. She clung to him fiercely, yielding to his great strength, trusting totally in his ability to shield her from danger. He took her down into the tall grasses of the valley floor, imprisoning her small body atop his to cushion her from the ground.

Cat lay prone on top of him, dizzy with desire, frenzied with arousal, insatiable to kiss him, taste him, lick and bite him. She quivered from the sensations coursing through her body and craved for more and yet more as her need curled tightly, hotly about her vitals. She lifted her mouth from his, panting from her intense, uninhibited gyrations.

He gazed up at her, enthralled. *Holy God, she is a firestorm!*

He brushed the back of his fingers against her cheek. "Hellicate." It was Scots for *hellcat* and meant wild and untamed. "Hellicate fits you perfectly," he whispered. The sensuality he had aroused in her almost enslaved him. He rolled her on her back in the grass, taking the dominant position. His smoldering gaze swept from her disheveled curls to her short kilt. "You look sinful."

"Holy God, Hepburn, have you any idea what you look like . . . a six-and-a-half-foot giant with a savage face and wild hair, blacker than hell?" she panted. Her golden eyes glittered. "You rode like a centaur." She reached up and grabbed his bare arms, squeezing and kneading the bulging muscles, relishing the strength and power he possessed.

"You are so eager, Cat. Can you not wait until we rid ourselves of our soaking wet clothes?" He removed her boots.

She pulled his head down to hers and spoke against his lips. "I had no idea I was wet."

He reached beneath her kilt and drew off her soaking hose and drawers. Her hands began to tear at his sheepskin, trying to rid him of the impediment. He shrugged out of it, then stood to remove his boots. He unbuckled his belt and peeled off his wet leathers, closely watching her exquisite features for a sign of denial.

The look on her face was avid, feral, displaying no fear at the size of his cock and balls as he towered naked before her. He went down on his knees, straddling her bare thighs, then slowly, deliberately, he unfastened her bodice and removed it, rendering her naked save for the tantalizingly short kilt.

Her palms splayed across his broad chest and her fingertips felt the rough texture of the dark furred pelt. He covered her hands with his, then lifted them above her head. "Mistress Impatience, I want to see your breasts," he whispered hoarsely.

With difficulty, she kept her hands from him, as her breasts thrust up impudently and her nipples became ruched. In that moment she wanted to be the most beautiful female he had ever seen, or touched or lain with. She wanted to wipe away forever the memory of all other women.

Patrick gazed his fill, then dipped his head to trail hot kisses along the inner curves, then took a nipple into his mouth and sucked. Alternating between the delicious mounds, he licked and kissed and tasted, mesmerized by the silken smoothness of her delicate flesh. He reveled in the knowledge that she wanted him to do these things as she arched her breasts against his mouth.

Finally, he cupped her breasts with his large palms and moved his lips up to hers, kissing her fiercely.

Her mouth clung to his, kissing him back hungrily, and she parted her lips, welcoming his plundering tongue. It was rough-textured and demanding, and she imitated his thrusts with her own tongue. She threaded her fingers into his thick black hair, holding him captive while she explored the dark cave of his hot mouth. Then she lifted her lashes to look deeply into his eyes.

He could tell she had never been kissed in this way before and it was a revelation to her, one that she gloried in, as she relished the hot, gliding friction that made her crave more. He lifted his mouth and sat back on his haunches to gaze down at her. Very deliberately, an inch at a time, he pulled up her kilt to reveal her soft mons covered by a profusion of black silky curls. Then his fingers unfastened the pin that held the kilt together and he spread out the plaid on each side of her over the grass. *Hunting plaid is most apt. Predator and prey? I am certainly the predator, but she is the most aggressive prey I've ever hunted.* She was also a female who excited him. Cat was extremely petite, exquisitely made and tasting her own sexuality for the first time.

She reached out her hand to stroke him. "Patrick, I want—" She knew not what, only that she wanted it.

"I know what you want, what you need." He moved from astride her hips and stretched his great length beside her. He feathered his fingers through the curls of her mons, teasing, touching, titillating, until she was moist, then he slid a finger into her tight, scalding sheath and watched the pupils of her golden eyes dilate with pleasure. When she began to writhe, he knew she was ready for more and thrust deeper in a rhythmic motion that aroused her low, sensual moans. She came to a hard climax, quickly, which surprised him. It also pleased him that she was capable of such a passionate response when she had so little carnal experience.

Catherine came up from the grass, sliding her arms about his neck, fusing her mouth to his in a savage kiss that greedily took more than it gave. He mastered her mouth, forcing her to submit and yield her softness to him. She was submissively sweet and compliant for the space of ten minutes while she reveled in his dominance, then she turned into a little wildcat, straddling one of his hard, muscled thighs and riding it while she fastened sharp, small teeth into his shoulder.

Each time she surged forward her soft thigh brushed against his marble-hard phallus, making it quiver with anticipation. Patrick's powerful hands encircled her tiny waist and he lifted her off his thigh. He rolled onto his back so that he held her above him in midair, and then he slowly lowered her until his mouth was on a level with her woman's center. He nuzzled her, inhaling the intoxicating female fragrance of flowers and spice and sex. Now it was his turn to become insatiable for the taste and the scent and the feel of her. He laid her back in the grass, wrapped her silken legs about his neck, then began to kiss and lick her pink bud until it unfurled its petals and bloomed like a passionflower. When he thrust his tongue into her sugared sheath, she screamed with excitement and arched into his demanding, beautiful mouth. She built steadily to an unimaginable peak, trying to sustain the exquisite pleasure his pulsing tongue gave, then surrendered in an explosive climax that made her breasts and belly feel as if fire snaked through her veins.

Patrick enfolded her tightly, feathering kisses into the wildly disheveled curls at her temples. He was in an agony of need but controlled himself with an iron will, not daring to unleash the fierce, carnal desire that had been riding him for weeks.

Cat, with her cheek pressed against his chest, could hear the thundering beat of his heart as she inhaled the smell of his man-scented skin. She had been madly curious to know what it was that men did to women, and now she knew some of the secret rituals of sex. What she had learned enthralled her, and now she was ready to experience the intimate act when a male and female joined their bodies in full and total consummation. Her hand slid down to his groin to stroke the phallic object of her desire. "Your mouth was magnificent, but I want you to make love to me with your body."

Patrick groaned. "Catherine, I cannot."

"Why?" she asked, completely baffled.

"Hellicate," he said tenderly, "the disparity in our sizes is too great for a quick roll in the grass. You are a virgin, my sweet. There would be pain and blood; you would receive no pleasure at all. It could make you hate sex forever."

"But there is bound to be pain and blood whenever I lose my virginity. Please, Patrick?"

"No, Catherine. There's a time and a place and this isn't it."

"Damn you, what time and what place?" she demanded.

"I would need a chamber, a bed, and all the long hours of an entire night before I would dream of initiating you. The answer is no!"

She clenched her fists and smote them against his chest. "You shall, you shall make love to me, Patrick Hepburn!" she commanded.

"Why is it so important to you, Catherine?"

"I must get you out of my system, Hepburn! I am spellbound by you. Though I have an intense dislike of you, I have developed such a strong physical attraction, I fear I have become obsessed. I have to obliterate you from my thoughts so that I can go home and marry a tame English noble!"

The look he gave her was intense, but it masked the horror her words evoked in him. *You will never wed a fucking English noble!*

He covered her hands with his and raised them one at a time to his lips. "Softly, Catherine, softly. You must have permission from the queen before you can marry."

"Only until I come of age. I shall be twenty-one in March."
He smiled, but the smile did not reach his eyes. "Since you
desire it so passionately, how can I refuse to make you a
woman?"

She sat back on her heels, ready for whatever was to come,
yet suddenly apprehensive. "When?"

She looked small and delicate and vulnerable, like a sacrifi-
cial lamb. His smile became tender. "Before moonrise." He
watched as she let out a long breath and wondered if it was from
satisfaction at getting her own way, or relief that it would not
happen here and now.

Actually, it was a sigh of relief that he had not rejected her.
Cat knew she had shattered his indifference when he made love
to her with his mouth, but she was convinced it had returned
when he was unwilling to share the ultimate intimacy. Her eyes
lingered on his powerful body as he strode to Valiant and pulled
dry garments from his saddlebags. Then he stalked to the river
and submerged. Cat smiled her secret smile. *Cold water is excellent for curbing impulses! Perhaps his control isn't as iron-
clad as he pretends.*

She rolled up her Winton hunting plaid and gathered up her
wet stockings and undergarments, then suddenly realized that she
had forgotten all about Chestnut since Patrick had plucked her
from its back. A quick scan of the riverbank located her pony,
cropping grass not far away from Valiant. She reached its side
with relief. "Good girl to follow us." She rubbed Chestnut's nose,
then pulled out dry clothes and dressed quickly in the doeskin
skirt. *The mare followed the stallion; it is the way of nature.*

When Patrick returned from the river he too was fully
dressed. "We might as well eat before we depart."

Catherine agreed, and as they sat on the grass where they had
been so intimate, she felt a need to express her feelings. "Riding with the wild herd today filled my heart and soul with joy,
and I want to thank you for allowing me to share the experience.
I now understand why you like to be alone when you do this
every year. It's a solitary ritual where you can feel a oneness
with other living creatures."

"The reason I agreed to bring you is because you have a
deep and abiding love for animals. You too experienced the oneness."

She took a bite of oatcake. "Also, I want to thank you from

the bottom of my heart for agreeing to let the stallion remain wild and untamed for another year. That was a divine gift."

"It was the first time you had experienced a moment of total freedom, something we all lust for. You became so enamored of it, you wanted his freedom to continue."

Not only can he read my thoughts; he discerns my emotions. There is a oneness between us that I must have the strength to sever. I am English, and my place is at Elizabeth's Court.

"Though I will let the stallion remain in the hills, I still intend to take some of his breeding mares and perhaps a couple of yearlings. He'll have to make do with a score of mates."

Is that how many you have had? Catherine wondered. Then she chided herself for the thought. It did not matter a whit to her how many women Hepburn had bedded. Did it?

"Are you ready to ride, Cat? I'd like to find out where the herd is and keep downwind of them if possible. I'd rather he didn't know I was stalking them just yet."

"Yes, I'm ready." She tucked her hairbrush into her saddlebag and waited for Patrick to assist her. She could have mounted herself but could not resist the temptation of his hands upon her.

They rode northeast, roughly following the winding river Tyne. The salty tang of the North Sea filled the air as they neared the coast. The sea breeze kept them safely downwind from the herd, and after a two-hour search, as they crested a hill, Patrick spotted the horses. "He's found a lush, protected haven for his clan. They should stay put for a while."

As Catherine gazed down from the summit, she knew she had never seen anything to compare with the wild beauty of the scene that stretched before her. The rough, craggy rock formations, the lush green valley where the herd grazed and the sparkling sea beyond painted a picture she would never forget. *This is a fateful day in my life, one I will remember forever.*

She watched Patrick's hands as he tightened them on his reins and led Valiant back the way they had come. She followed his path, not knowing where it would lead, but secure in the knowledge that he would fulfill the promise he had made to her. One hill and one dale looked much like another to Catherine, but as the afternoon light began to fade from the sky, she experienced a glimmer of familiarity about her surroundings. It stirred her blood and when she saw the hump of Traprain Law in the gloaming, her pulse began to race. *Hailes! He's taking me to Hailes Castle.*

Chapter Seventeen

*V*aliant and the Border pony increased their pace descending the hill, as if they sensed their destination. As the pair of riders approached the ancient castle, it seemed to obliterate whatever light had been left in the day. The hoofbeats of their mounts made a hollow clatter as they crossed the drawbridge, and after a brief wait the portcullis was raised by someone in the barbican.

They walked their horses through the courtyard and stopped before a studded oaken door set in the nine-foot stone wall. Patrick dismounted and knocked. The portal was opened by a man holding a torch. He raised his arm until the light illuminated the face of the tall figure that sought entrance.

Craggy brows drew together momentarily, then cleared. "Yer lordship, is it ye?"

"Aye, Wat. Sorry to disturb your solitude, but I crave your hospitality." Hepburn jerked his head toward his companion. "The lass slept outdoors last night and I promised her a bed tonight."

"It'd be an honor. Go an' stable yer mounts."

Patrick returned to Catherine and led the two horses to Hailes's stone stable. There was only one groom on duty because the only mounts in the stable belonged to the workforce of castle keepers. His eyes lit up when Hepburn tossed him a gold coin. "I'll give 'em oats and a good rubdown, yer lordship."

Patrick lifted Cat from Chestnut's back, removed the saddlebags from both animals and hoisted one to each shoulder.

"Everyone knows you," she murmured shyly.

"They should—they are Hepburns who served when my father owned Hailes. The Earl of Lennox kept them when he took ownership." He strode through the courtyard and Catherine had to quicken her step to keep up. He kicked the door with his boot and Wat let them in.

Flickering torches set in wall sconces lit the ancient hall. Cat saw Patrick's looming shadow, its shoulders made massive by the saddlebags. It towered menacingly over the slight shadow cast by her body and his words rushed back to her: *The disparity in our sizes is too great.* Apprehension threatened to engulf her. She pushed it away and kept it at bay by sheer bravado.

"No need to show me the way," he told Wat. "We'll use the Master Tower."

"I'll bring ye a jug of whisky, yer lordship."

"It's not necessary to wear your legs out on the tower steps, Wat. I'll come back down for the whisky. I'll take care of all the lass's needs tonight," he said with a wink.

They climbed to the second story of the castle, and then took another stone staircase that led up to the chambers of the tower. There were no windows, only narrow apertures from which arrows could be shot at invaders. Patrick lowered the saddlebags to the floor and went to the stair head for a torch. He lit two torches set in brackets and, as some of the darkness was dispelled, he looked about the chamber with a critical eye.

Cat followed his glance, taking in the red Turkey carpet, the tapestry wall hangings, the fireplace and the wide, curtained bed.

"Just what we need."

She blushed, thinking he referred to the bed. She was wrong.

"Wood for a fire. Nothing like a fire for a seduction."

You hardly need to seduce me—I begged you!

He read her mind and grinned wickedly. "Not me! You're the one doing the seducing, Hellcat."

She lifted her chin. "All this amuses you, doesn't it?"

"Vastly. Go to the other chamber and search for some cushions and candles while I light us a fire."

Though the light spilling into the other room was scant, in the dimness Cat found a branch of candles. She took one and lit it from a torch, then carried it back to light the rest. Immediately the scent of roses filled the air, and she realized that the tapers she had lit were perfumed. Quite obviously this was a woman's chamber, and Cat speculated that the lady must be the Countess of Lennox. The carpet was deep blue, the bed hangings a paler shade, and the cushions were covered in gold brocade. There was an ivory screen and behind it a slipper bath. *The castle might be dilapidated but the furnishings are luxurious.*

Cat spied a full-length mirror. When she stepped before it, she was startled to see how disheveled she looked. Her reflection told her that this was not the Lady Catherine of Elizabeth's Court. That young lady was elegant, always perfectly groomed and dressed in delicate, stylish garments. This young female wore boots and a doeskin riding skirt. Her hair resembled a wild blackberry thicket and her lips were bee-stung from kisses. *I look like a Borderer's wench!* She almost recoiled. Then she stared into the eyes watching from the mirror. They were no longer golden; they were yellow cat eyes. *A Border lord's wench is exactly what you will be tonight!* The thought made her so excited, she wanted to scream.

She returned to the other chamber carrying the branch of scented candles, her arms filled with gold cushions. She dropped the cushions to the floor. In the blue room they had looked decorative, but against the Turkey red carpet they looked decadent. She set the candles on a table and noticed that the fire he had lit bathed the chamber with a flickering amber glow.

Patrick got up from his haunches. "The scent of roses lends romance to the atmosphere, but there is something far more alluring that is tempting me to madness." He waggled his eyebrows suggestively. "I smell food! I'll be right back."

She searched for a fitting retort. "Don't forget the whisky!"

Patrick admired her bravado—all five feet of her exuded it.

He seemed to be gone some time. "The uncouth lout can eat at any time, any place," she declared to the room at large. A silent voice answered her. *He has a man's appetite.* The thought made her breasts and belly go taut. She doubted she could eat a bite.

Patrick returned with an iron pot hung on his arm. One hand carried a basket of fresh-baked bannock biscuits; the other held a stone jug of whisky. He set the pot on the hearth. "Mutton and barley stew," he said with relish. "Ever taste it?"

"I've had lamb," she assured him.

"Lamb!" he said with disgust. "Mutton has a more robust flavor. Most things improve with age," he teased.

"I doubt if you will, Hepburn," she taunted back.

He'd be damned if he'd let her have the last word. "True,"
he agreed. "Tonight I am in my prime."

She willed her lips not to tremble. "I'm counting on it."

Bravado—sheer, bloody bravado. He laughed good-
naturedly. "Touché! The first round goes to you, Hellcat."
From the basket he took two bowls and filled them with the
steaming stew. Cat found the aroma so tantalizing, she suddenly
felt hungry. She watched him carry two chairs to the table, and
they sat down to dine by candlelight. He took a bannock, dipped
it into the stew and devoured it. Cat did the same, breaking her
biscuit into pieces, then dipping it. Before she had finished her
bannock, Patrick was on his second bowl. There was something
compellingly seductive about a man with a healthy appetite.

When he finished eating he poured them both a dram of
whisky. Then, no longer able to keep his hands from her, he
moved around the table and lifted her into his lap. "Let me feed
you."

Obediently, Cat opened her mouth for his offering, licking
her lips after each spoonful. Finally, she shook her head.

He whispered in her ear, "You won't get your reward."

She could feel his hard cock beneath her soft bum cheek. "I
warrant my reward and my punishment are one and the same."

Her words were bravely provocative, yet he suspected that
she was more than half afraid of what was to come, though she
would rather die than admit it. He held the whisky to her lips
and was glad that she took a few sips. Patrick knew that a little
fun and laughter might banish her apprehension. He picked up
a pair of dice. "Will you hazard a few throws with me, lass?"

"What will we play for?"

"Forfeits." His black eyes boldly challenged her and he
knew her pride would not allow her to refuse.

"We play forfeits at Court," she said lightly.

"Aye, for handkerchiefs and ribbons. Our game will be for
higher stakes." He began to shake the dice.

"At Elizabeth's Court it is ladies first."

"First, last and always from what I saw, and I encountered
damn few ladies. At Hailes, Hepburn goes first." He rolled the
dice.

"Eleven! You are cheating!" She jumped from his lap. They
were the same height now that she was standing while he still
sat.

"What are you going to do about it?" He handed her the dice.

"Double six! I beat you," she said with glee.

He threw back his head and laughed. "You know as little about a dice game as you know about the mating game. A throw of two, three or twelve loses. You owe me a forfeit . . . *of my choosing.*"

"Those aren't the rules!" As she became engrossed in arguing some of her apprehension melted away.

"They are now. I'll have your garters and remove them myself."

She darted away. "You'll have to catch me first."

He jumped up from the chair and was after her in a flash. She ran from the room and went into the other chamber, which was filled with shadows. She gasped as she saw a figure loom up in the dark, then laughed with relief when she realized it was only a reflection in the mirror. Her hesitation gave him the chance to grab her.

He carried her to the mirror and held her in front of him. "Watch me closely—I cannot be trusted." He stooped and slid his hand up inside the leg of her riding skirt. He stroked the inside of her thigh before he captured the garter and removed it.

Cat was glad of the shadows; they hid her blushes. "You devil; my stockings will fall down."

"What a calamity." He slid his hand up her other leg, pretended he couldn't locate the garter, but managed to touch everything else beneath her skirt.

Watching what he did to her in the mirror was both titillating and arousing. "This game is too risqué!"

He threaded his fingers into the curls on her mons and brushed her ear with his mouth. "This game is called *foreplay.*"

Her eyes widened as comprehension dawned. "Foreplay," she repeated, liking the feel of the new word on her lips.

He captured the second garter and slid them both onto his forearm. Then he lifted her and slung her, like Viking booty, over his shoulder, and carried her back to their own chamber. He stood her on her feet, sat down and handed her the dice. "Your turn."

Cat rolled a double two.

"Four—the Devil's bedposts."

She glanced at the wide bed. "I suspect the Devil and Hepburn are one and the same."

He rolled a seven. "I do have the Devil's own luck. Mayhap you're right. Now what would the Devil ask for?" He leered. "I'll have the rest of your clothes . . . *and remove them myself!*"

She tried to dart away again, but this time he had anticipated her escape and held a handful of doeskin in his firm grasp. He held her captive while he removed her skirt and the divided petticoat she wore beneath it.

Cat looked down in dismay. She had lost one stocking somewhere, and all she wore below her waist was the other one.

He looked at her critically. "You know, in this light your legs do look a wee bit bowed."

She grabbed his hair and pulled hard. "You monster! You may mock me all you want, but leave Geordie alone."

He captured her about the waist, dug in his fingers and tickled her ribs. She was laughing too much to hang on to his hair. He pulled her between his thighs and unfastened her bodice. When she was naked they both sobered as the sexual tension stretched taut between them. Their eyes were on the same level and slowly he drew her close so that their lips touched. Against her mouth he murmured, "I want to see your black pussycat." He kissed her hungrily then lifted his mouth. "Will you walk about for me?"

A refusal sprang to her lips, but she quickly swallowed it. The idea of showing herself naked to him thrilled her. The tattoo hadn't ruined her body after all; it had made it more alluring. She nodded her assent and pulled away from him. Holding her head high, she walked with feline grace and the pride of a queen toward the fire. She paused and looked at him over her shoulder in the age-old gesture a woman uses when tempting a man to follow.

As Patrick rose to his feet, she raised an imperious hand to stop him. "You cannot come to the fire unless you are naked."

"My very thought." He disrobed in short order, then closed the distance between them. He turned her so that her lovely round bottom was to the fire and the bright flames illuminated the saucy black cat. "If you're a good girl and please me, I'll give puss some cream."

Cat licked her lips. "And if I'm a bad girl?"

Patrick groaned. *Watch out, Hepburn. She'll have you by the balls, and then she'll plunder your heart and soul.*

"Fetch the cushions to the fire, so I can see you walk again."

"Spoken like Lord Bloody Stewart, issuing his orders. I much prefer Hepburn, who can get anything he wants without commands."

He smiled wickedly. "We both intend to have our way with you."

"For such a promise, how can I resist?" She moved toward the gold cushions in a sinuous way, undulating as she put one dainty foot in front of the other. She made sure her bottom was toward him when she bent over to pick them up. When she turned to face him her most intimate parts were covered by cushions.

Patrick stretched his length before the fire. She didn't come back until he crooked his finger.

She walked slowly toward him, until her bare toes touched his bare thigh, then she dropped one of the cushions that covered a breast and posed provocatively like Botticelli's Venus rising from the waves.

She watched the pupils of his eyes dilate with desire before she let the cushion fall from her other breast.

The seconds stretched into minutes, then, finally refusing to wait longer, he plucked the gold cushion that covered her mons. He made love to her with his eyes but with a will of iron made a decision to keep his hands from her. It was a sure way to make her ache with desire and crave his touch.

Cat gazed down at his lithe body, which rippled with powerful, sun-bronzed muscle. Everything about him was big and powerful and hard as granite. He reminded her of a marble Greek statue she had once seen, except he was alive with warm flesh and pulsing blood.

"Satisfy your curiosity. Explore me. Indulge your impulses," he invited, knowing it would rid her of her last traces of fear.

She knelt before him and reached out her fingers to trace along his high cheekbone, then outlined his bold lips with her fingertip. She brushed her hand down his corded throat and along his collarbone, then tested the texture of the black hair on his broad chest between finger and thumb. She touched his flat copper nipples and her mouth curved when they turned into hard little spears. Then, growing more daring, she flicked them with her tongue, tasting then sucking first one, then the other. As she sucked, she felt a pulsation between her legs that was new to her. She glanced up quickly into his dark eyes and saw that he was completely aware of the sensual sensations she was experiencing.

Something compelled her to explore farther, drawing her inexorably to his male center. Her fingers trailed down his hard belly, playfully encircled and dipped into his navel, then moved lower. She ran a tentative fingertip along the shaft of his cock, from its root to its blood-engorged head. Her eyes widened as a diamond drop of clear liquid appeared on its tip. She touched it then impulsively licked her finger.

Patrick's groan set up an insatiable desire in her to make him writhe with need. She feather-stroked his granite thigh lightly, and as her fingers inched higher, they moved to the inside, where his flesh was more sensitive. He arched his body up from the floor and she slipped her hand between his legs and cupped his large sac. She squeezed gently to discern the texture and shape, and then rolled the two spheres together with deft manipulation.

A growl erupted from his throat as he came to a sitting position. She was arousing him to the point where he would lose control, and he decided he must shift the focus. He captured her hand in his and brought it to her face. Then, starting at her cheekbone he traced her own fingers along the same path they had taken on his body. Brushing over her lips and along her throat, her fingertips moved down the curve of her breast to her sensitive nipple. When it became ruched, he took it into his mouth and sucked, just as she had sucked his.

She gasped with pleasure and arched her other breast toward his hot, hungry mouth. She wanted more, but Patrick had other ideas. He lifted his head to watch as he drew her fingers down her belly and slipped them between her legs. He dipped one of her fingertips into her wetness, and when she cried out in protest at the intimate thing he was forcing her to do to herself, he withdrew her fingers and took them into his mouth. It was such a seductive gesture that she melted against him.

At last Patrick took possession of her mouth. His kisses deepened and roughened with his mounting desire until she was weak with longing. His strong fingers splayed through her hair and held her captive for his mouth's ravishing. His lips traced a hot trail, seeking the pulse points on her temple, behind her ear, and at the base of her throat. Her scent filled his nostrils, making them flare with carnal desire, and his insistent hands pushed

her down to the red carpet and slid a gold cushion behind her
head and another beneath her bottom. Heat leaped between
them, arousing a smoldering need that cried out to be quenched.
Cat writhed wantonly as she clawed at his shoulders.
"Please."

"Mmm, you please me very much. Will you promise to be
brave?"

She nodded her head, unable to speak coherently, but sure
she was ready for this cataclysmic mating that would make her
a woman. When he came over her, his knees on either side of
her hips, she was suddenly aware of the enormous contrast between them. His big, powerful body, all muscle and sinew, with
its great strength and raw male virility, reminded her of the wild
black stallion.

As he gazed down at her he was acutely aware of how small
and fragile she looked. His great size emphasized her smallness.
His hardness made her all the softer. Her smooth flesh was ivory
pale, virginal, and her face ethereal, beautiful . . . in his eyes she
was absolute perfection. He reached between her legs and with
thumb and forefinger separated the delicate folds; then he
poised, knowing the flames from the fire would heat her soft
flesh to hot silk. "Wrap your legs about my back, sweetheart."

Slowly, firmly, he rubbed the swollen head of his phallus
against her lips, using the drops of his own clear lubricant to
make her sleek. Then he thrust down into her scalding sheath
and felt her hymen tear at the same moment he heard her cry
out. He held absolutely still. "Are you all right, Cat?"

She let out a slow whispery breath. "Yes." Because he held
himself motionless the pain quickly subsided. She took a deep
breath, then another, and knew she would never experience anything more magnificent than the fullness she felt when Patrick
Hepburn was inside her body. She relaxed her rigid muscles and
he slid in deeper, moaning at the unbelievable pleasure she gave
him.

"Hold on tight." He rolled gently until she was in the dominant position. "When you are on top you can take as little or as
much of me as you wish. When you are ready, move up and
down; ride me. Only do what brings you pleasure, Catherine."

She gazed into his eyes, black with passion, and, tentatively
at first, began to move. Her sheath closed sleekly around him,
and the hot, sliding friction began to build in a tantalizing

rhythm, taking her higher until she was in a frenzy of need. She threw back her head, undulating her body, and cried out urgently at the exquisite sensations she felt as he cupped her breasts.

He felt her shiver and he thrust upward twice, then held still to enjoy her liquid tremors. Only his iron control stopped him from spending until he withdrew. She fell upon him in a wanton sprawl, biting his shoulder to stop her from screaming. His hands stroked down her smooth back and cupped her bottom cheeks possessively as she experienced every last pulsation. For him, magic danced in the air. *Before dawn I'll make love to you again, but I shall be in the dominant position,* he vowed.

They lay entwined without moving or speaking for a long time. Catherine knew she had been changed forever. She had experienced the hymeneal right that transformed her from a maiden to a woman. But she also felt safe and secure locked in his arms. More, she felt invincible, for now she had his great strength to add to her own. In her innocence she thought she had enslaved him.

Holding her tightly, Patrick got to his feet and carried her to the bed. He took a corner of the sheet and gently wiped the smear of blood from her thigh, then he climbed in beside her, enfolded her in his arms and brushed his lips against her temple.

Cat raised her eyes to an aperture in the high stone wall. She smiled her secret smile when she saw that the moon had risen, then luxuriating in the warmth of his big body, she drifted into sleep.

When she awoke the candles were burned away and shafts of sunlight poured through the wall's apertures. She was alone in the bed and her first thought was: *How dare he leave me?*

"Hepburn! Hepburn! Where the devil are you?"

Wat appeared at the door. "I'm here, lass."

She clutched the covers to her breast. "Where's Patrick?"

"His lordship departed at dawn, but he'll be back, lassie. He gave instructions tae have a bath waitin' fer ye when ye awoke." He jerked a thumb in the direction of the other chamber, then left.

When Cat was sure he was gone, she slid her feet to the carpet, pulled the sheet about her and went to the next room. She saw steam rising from behind the ivory screen. Cat looked at herself in the mirror, lifting away the sheet to examine her naked reflection. Her body looked the same, yet not the same, and she realized she was looking at herself through different eyes. She abandoned the cover and slid down into the lovely warm water. A flood of memories washed over her.

The first time she had awakened in the bed, they shared a hundred blissful kisses. He aroused her desire slowly, until she was hot and sweet with passion, and then he mounted her in the primal act of domination and submission and mastered her as she yielded her body and her heart to him. She blushed, remembering. *How innocent and naïve I was to think I could get him out of my system. Last night he became a part of me forever.*

She finished her bath and returned to the other chamber to dress. She put on a demure bodice and full-length riding skirt, blushing when she saw the Winton hunting plaid. *I was shamefully impulsive to wear such a thing!*

Cat was brushing her hair when Patrick returned. "Where have you been?" she asked shyly.

"Getting what I came for . . . my horses. I secured eight mares and a couple of yearlings. The stallion put up a hell of a fight for his females but, as I promised, I let him remain free."

"Thank you, Patrick," she said softly.

His black eyes raked her from head to foot. "Well, Hellcat, did you get me out of your system?"

It was such a callous thing to say, she wanted to fly at him and rake her nails down his dark, arrogant face. "Yes! And a bloody good thing I did. I wouldn't want to put myself through that ordeal again, Hepburn!"

Chapter Eighteen

$\mathcal{A}$s Catherine rode beside Patrick on their journey back to Crichton, she decided that her impulsive words had been cruel. He had kept his word about making love to her because she had insisted she wanted to get him out of her system. Though his remark when he entered the bedchamber this morning had been a shock, she was recovering. *He isn't a lapdog; he's a rough Scots Border lord,* she reminded herself, *and he did call me sweetheart last night.*

She glanced back at the string of mares and yearlings he was leading and told herself that the only reason he had let the stallion remain free was to please her. Cat decided to break the silence between them by using the feminine tactic of getting him to talk about himself. "How did you capture the horses?"

He flashed a quick grin. "It wasn't easy, but I've done this before. Divide and conquer is the only method that works. With Valiant's help I separated the herd into three. The stallion rounded them back up by *snaking,* where he puts his head down in a threatening posture and encircles them, galloping like a demon. The minute he had them back together in one band, I did it again. While he was busy rounding up two small herds, I secured the third one and got myself eight mares and two yearlings." He glanced back at the wild horses with satisfaction. "The mad bugger did come after me, but Valiant deterred him. I'm hoping most of the mares are in foal. Wild horses make good dams . . . mothers."

"You never speak of *your* mother"—Cat's words were deliberately personal—"though you often speak of your father."

Hepburn remained silent, deep in thought. Then he said lightly, "About a month after my father went into exile, she followed him to Italy."

"Weren't you rather young at that time?"

"I was twelve. Old enough and certainly big enough to fend for myself," he said with a dismissive shrug.

She abandoned you! Mine never actually left, but she abandoned me emotionally. Cat said softly, "It must have been a difficult choice for her to make, between her husband and her son."

"It didn't seem to be. It did prove to be an unfortunate choice, however. She died in childbed in less than a year."

I'm sorry. Cat had more good sense than to say it aloud; Hepburn would never tolerate pity.

They stopped once at midday to water the horses and let them graze. He shared food with her that he'd brought from Hailes, but he wanted to press on. "Cat, if you are up to riding until dusk, we can make it back to Crichton tonight."

She assured him she was comfortable in the saddle, relieved that they would not have to sleep together on the ground. At Crichton, she would be Lady Catherine, and all the proprieties would have to be observed.

It was full dark when they arrived. Hepburns appeared immediately from the castle and the stables to take care of the wild horses. "I'll give our mounts a good rubdown. You go and relax. My housekeeper will feed you or prepare you a bath—you won't even need to ask. I'll escort you home tomorrow."

Crichton's housekeeper met her at the door. "Lady Catherine, I know you must be hungry. You may eat now, or have your bath first and mayhap dine with his lordship later?"

"A bath would be paradise. I've been in the saddle all day."

The housekeeper rolled her eyes in despair. "He has no idea! He treats a lady like a wench and wenches like ladies, I warrant."

Cat couldn't wait to rid herself of the disheveled riding clothes. After she bathed, she put on the most elegant gown she had brought from Seton and decided to take the time to fashion her hair into an elaborate upswept style, threaded with pearls.

Patrick encountered Jock in the stables. "Since I captured the horses this morning near Hailes, I've had an uneasy feeling I couldn't shake. I didn't waste any time returning."

"The watch reported riders on Crichton land last night. I rode out with half a dozen moss-troopers but found no one.

Nothing was raided, but I've ordered a double watch for tonight."

Hepburn nodded. "Good man." He gave Valiant and the Border pony a feed of oats and went straight to his chamber, where he rid himself of his heavy boots and rough riding attire and then bathed. Dressed in a fine linen shirt and soft Italian leather shoes he went to seek out his housekeeper about food.

"Your dinner is ready, my lord. Lady Catherine chose to wait and dine with you."

Patrick frowned. He had expected Cat to seek her bed after so many hours in the saddle. He went into the small chamber off the library that he used when he ate alone. He was about to sit down at the table, which had been set for two, when she arrived. She was wearing something so ethereal she looked like a gossamer goddess, and his mouth went dry at the sight of her. He held a chair for her, and with an enchanting smile she took her seat. His hands moved to caress her shoulders just as his housekeeper carried in a large, silver covered dish and a jug of ale, so with difficulty he refrained and took the chair opposite Catherine.

When he lifted the cover, the succulent smell of the beefsteak and vegetables piqued their appetites. Without asking, Patrick served Cat a generous portion and set it before her.

She picked up the jug and filled his tankard. "You enjoy ale from your own brew house." It was a statement, not a question.

"Yes, it quenches my thirst." *I thirst for you, Catherine.*

He began to eat, but his eyes never left her lovely face. She ate daintily, licking her lips with the tip of her pink tongue, and desire rose up in him like a smoldering torment.

Catherine's glance lingered on his powerful hands, moved to his mouth, lifted to meet his dark eyes, then with a hint of a blush she smiled and lowered her lashes. Any seeing their eyes meet would take them for bound lovers, longing to claim each other.

The hot, heavy ache in his groin made Patrick's arousal rampant. He tried in vain to tamp down his desire, telling himself that he could not seduce her under his own roof, but the need remained, crouching like a raptor waiting for an opportunity to strike.

Cat basked in the warmth of his ardent glances. When they were alone together like this, his compelling presence almost overwhelmed her. The sweet, lingering ache in her belly and breasts was like a silken torment stirring the memory of his scent, his taste, his touch.

But even their formal attire was a barrier against intimacy, reminding them they were a lord and a lady, rather than a rough Borderer and his wench.

The candles burned low, and the shadows deepened in the corners of the room; the sweetmeats sat forgotten as his hand covered hers where it lay on the table. She curled her fingers into his palm and heat leaped between them.

The housekeeper appeared in the shadowed doorway. "Excuse me, yer lordship; there's a messenger just arrived."

"Thank you. The meal was just what we needed."

Cat stood up and came around the table.

Patrick took her fingers to his lips. "Please excuse me, Catherine." He could hardly bear to relinquish her. "I'll see you in the morning." He cursed silently as he watched her leave.

Hepburn made his way to the Great Hall, located in the oldest part of Crichton, where he knew the messenger would be taken. He was not surprised to see that the man sitting by the fire and quaffing ale wore the king's livery. He took the letter, slit the royal seal with his thumbnail and read the missive.

James was simply informing him that RC had sent word that he would be back in Edinburgh the day after tomorrow, and the king was asking that Hepburn attend him at Holyrood Palace.

That was fast! Robert must have delivered the king's letter to Cecil and been asked to take the reply to James immediately.

"It's late; you must stay the night. The king won't expect my reply before morning. He knows I will come when summoned, but I'll put it in writing for you." Patrick hailed David Hepburn and asked him to plenish a chamber for the royal messenger.

As Catherine prepared for bed, her glance traveled about the lovely chamber, and again she had a proprietary feeling about Crichton Castle, as if it had belonged to her once upon a time. *There is a way it can belong to you again.* She chided herself for the outrageous thought. *Marrying Hepburn is out of the question!* An inner voice challenged, *Do you want Crichton, or do you want its lord and master?* She had no immediate answer, yet when she fell asleep she had a smile on her face. She fancied that Patrick was in love with her and that, if she chose, she could have them both.

•   •   •

When there was no sign of Catherine at breakfast, a tender smile tugged at Patrick's lips. She was so small, he concluded she was exhausted from their exhilarating adventure, and he left instructions that she was not to be disturbed.

He sent the royal messenger on his way, then went to check on the wild horses. He returned to the castle and packed a few things he would take to Court on the morrow. At mid-morning he saw his housekeeper take a tray to Cat's room and knew that within the hour he must escort her back to Seton, no matter how much he'd like to keep her at Crichton.

He paced about like a caged animal, then, unable to resist the temptation, he went up to her chamber. "Good morning, Catherine. Are you all packed and ready to abandon me?"

She flashed him a smile. "I'm usually up with the sun."

"There is no sun. Rain clouds are moving in from the sea."

She sighed. *My heart aches as if Cupid shot an arrow into it.* "Oh, I almost forgot to pack my arrows!" She retrieved the two arrows from the wardrobe and placed them on top of her clothes.

"Where did you get these?" he asked tersely, alarmed that they were the same as the one that had barely missed him at Court.

"My cousin Andrew gave them to me. Is anything wrong?"

"No," he denied quickly. "They're unusual, that's all—made with crow feathers. Most arrows are made with gray goose feathers." He closed her bags, then held her cloak for her. He cupped her shoulders from behind and dropped a kiss on her dark curls.

Catherine closed her eyes at the thrill of his touch. Then, while she still had the strength to leave, she said, "I'm ready."

The housekeeper came in to retrieve her breakfast tray, and Cat turned and thanked her for her kindness, then moved to the stairs.

Patrick's dark brows drew together and he asked his housekeeper, "Where's Jenny?"

"The lass was up at the crack of dawn and off with her swain."

"Andrew Lindsay from Seton?"

"Aye, him and no other!"

Patrick picked up Catherine's luggage and followed her

downstairs. In the stables he strapped her larger bag onto Valiant's saddle and the smaller one to her pony's.

"How are the wild horses faring?"

"All well and accounted for this morning. I'll leave them together for a time. Horses, like people, prefer to be with their own clan. Strangers often clash at first."

"Like us," Cat acknowledged with a teasing smile.

As they rode north, she noticed that Patrick did not indulge in pleasantries or even small talk, but seemed preoccupied with his own thoughts. *He's reluctant to let me go. Perhaps he's thinking of how much he will miss me. I know I will hunger for him.* She saw him glance at the sky and decided he was concerned about the approaching rain. "Do you get many storms in July?"

"Some. Our summer is short—hot and cold air make violent enemies. Don't fret; I think it will just be rain today."

"I love wild storms!"

"You shouldn't, Catherine. Lightning kills. Ask Geordie how many beasts he loses from lightning strikes. Promise me you will curb any impulse to ride out if a storm threatens?"

She wanted to protest that she was not impulsive, but he knew better. *How protective he is.* "I promise . . . forewarned is forearmed." When Winton Castle came into view, she began to worry about what she would say to her grandfather, and to Maggie, about Liz and Robert not being at Crichton to chaperone her. *For three days I wasn't there either!* She shivered, wondering how she had dared behave in such a way. *Sin now; repent at leisure.* Cat shivered again.

As they rode into the castle courtyard, they encountered two other riders. Jenny Hepburn waved excitedly and spurred her pony forward. "Lady Catherine! I'm so glad to see you."

"Jenny, what a lovely surprise. Hello, Andrew."

Hepburn glared dangerously at Andrew. "We are going to have a downpour. I'll escort you home, Jenny."

"Thank you, my lord, there is no need . . ." Her voice trailed off.

"There is every need," Hepburn said tersely. He helped Cat dismount, then unstrapped her bags and set them before Andrew. "Forgive my haste, Lady Catherine, and please give my regards to the earl."

Cat knew that Patrick had vanished and Lord Stewart had

taken his place. She also knew he was in a dark mood, though she did not know the reason. There would be no tender good-byes between them now. "Jenny, take my cloak; you may be drenched before you reach Crichton."

Jenny donned the gray cloak and tucked her long red tresses inside the hood. "Thank you. I'll take good care of it."

Cat watched the pair canter from the courtyard, and her Border pony with its empty saddle trailed after them.

"Hepburn obviously doesn't approve of my attentions to Jenny."

"I think he's just worried about the storm," Cat excused, but she sensed a different storm was brewing.

Patrick set a hard pace and Jenny kept up with him. His face was dark and closed as he thought about Andrew Lindsay, his brain ferreting out reasons he might be a threat. As they rode past a stand of fir trees, he heard the unmistakable whoosh of an arrow, and as he swerved Valiant to avoid the missile, he heard the sickening thunk as it embedded itself in Jenny's arm.

"Christ's death!" He was out of the saddle in a flash, catching her before she fell to the ground. He raised his head and scented the wind, but he heard and saw nothing. Pursuit would be impossible and, in any case, Jenny was his first priority.

She had tears of pain in her eyes, but she was not unconscious. "Good girl, Jenny. We are closer to Seton, but I'm taking you home to Crichton." With gentle hands he snapped off the arrow and put it in his saddlebag. Then he took her before him on Valiant, spurring the stallion to a full gallop while cradling his young burden in the crook of a powerful arm. "I know the pain is fierce, but you are in no danger, lassie," he assured her.

The arrow was meant for me, but why did I have no premonition of the threat? This is the second time my sixth sense has failed to warn me of approaching danger!

Valiant thundered into Crichton's courtyard just as the heavens opened. Hepburn, with Jenny in his arms, slid down from the stallion's back and ran beneath the stone arch of the castle and up the steps.

His housekeeper, the girl's mother, screamed, "My God! Jenny!"

"She's a brave lass." He gave his housekeeper a stern glance, warning her not to go to pieces before the girl. He carried Jenny to the library, and her mother rallied and went to the kitchen for hot water and some powdered yarrow to staunch the bleeding.

Servants and moss-troopers gathered about the door, and Jenny's father arrived. Hepburn handed him one of his knives. "Hold the tip in the candle flame." He told her mother to fetch whisky.

Once Jenny had obediently swallowed the fiery liquor, Patrick gently removed the cloak and cut the blood-soaked sleeve from her shirt. "This will hurt," he warned. Then deftly he probed her flesh with his dirk and pried out the arrowhead. Blood gushed from the wound, and her mother knelt to wash it then sprinkle it with yarrow. Patrick bandaged it tightly and turned to see his surgeon, who had rushed from the Great Hall, nod his approval.

White-lipped, Jenny said, "Lady Catherine's cloak is ruined!"

All laughed with relief. Jenny's father carried her to her bed, knowing if this were other than accidental, it would be avenged.

Hepburn's temper was savage. He would beat Lindsay to a bloody pulp. He snatched up the gray cloak, angrily questioning why his instincts had failed him. His neck began to prickle. Perhaps he had not been forewarned of the danger because the threat had not been to him. His gut knotted as he realized that Jenny had been mistaken for Cat. *The menace was meant for Catherine!*

As he paced the tiles of the library floor, suspicious thoughts darted with the speed of mercury. Someone wanted Catherine dead. *She,* not he, had been the target of the arrow at Holyrood. If Cat was removed from the line of succession, who would benefit? The answer came swiftly. Geordie Seton's elder sister's son, Malcolm Lindsay, would become the Earl of Winton's heir if Catherine died.

The library caged him. He left, went down the steps and strode beneath the canopy of the colonnade, listening to the pelting rain. It was too confining for his soaring senses and thoughts, so deliberately he stepped out into the downpour, his long strides making short work of the distance from the castle to the river. He wondered if the Lindsay cousins were conspiring. He knew that Andrew had not shot Jenny by mistake, because he had seen Catherine give her the cloak. Hepburn's thoughts focused on Malcolm; he knew little about him except that he'd had a wife who died.

He cursed out loud because he had sent word that he would attend the king tomorrow. He thought briefly of Robert Carey and made his plans accordingly. He would ride to Seton at first light. Soaked to the skin, he shivered. *Cat is in grave danger!*

The sun streaming into Catherine's chamber at Winton Castle woke her early. She stretched sensuously and smiled at Maggie. "I was having such a wonderful dream!"

"Oh, aye? Can I have three guesses who was in it?"

"Yes, and the first two don't count!" Cat teased.

Tattoo uncurled from the bottom of the bed where she'd been lying in the sunlight and jumped to the carpet. The feline rubbed against Maggie's legs because she had brought a tray of food.

"And how are the newlyweds, Liz and Robert, faring?"

Guilt immediately washed over Cat. She broke off a piece of crisp bacon for Tattoo to give her time to compose an answer. "Robert's father, Lord Hunsdon, has passed away, so they had to return to London." *Please don't ask me when they left.*

"God rest his soul. Kate and Philadelphia will be upset, even though his death was expected. Yer aunt Beth will be the new Lady Hunsdon. I wonder how that'll sit with Isobel."

"So long as Mother's position at Elizabeth's Court isn't affected, I don't think she cares who dies. Actually, it will elevate her status, having a countess for sister-in-law."

"All that jostling for positions at Court seems ridiculous here in Seton. I'm glad ye are away from the intrigue."

Cat veiled her eyes with her lashes and smiled a secret smile. *I am up to my neck in intrigue, Maggie, if you but knew it.*

"What will ye wear? That dreadful rain has stopped, the heavy clouds have vanished and the sun is out, heaven be praised."

Cat again stretched sensuously and opened her wardrobe. She felt beautiful and wanted a dress to match her mood. She lifted out a gown that was the color of apricots ripened by the sun. When she put it on, she saw that her eyes glowed amber today. *Falling in love does the most wondrous things for your face as well as your spirit,* she told her reflection. She brushed her hair, threaded a matching ribbon through the loose curls, then threw open the window to inhale the intoxicating scents of nature.

Suddenly, her heart lurched at what she saw. *He's coming! I don't believe it! Patrick cannot bear to be away from me!* Cat ran past Maggie and down the stairs. She had never run toward a man before. Even if she'd been attracted, she had maintained a cool indifference. But with Patrick she knew that was impossible. She hurried through the great hall, breathless with excitement, and stopped dead as he flung open the front door and strode inside.

"You're going home! Get packed!"

Catherine recoiled. Hepburn's face was dark and closed, his jaw clenched like a lump of granite, his hands doubled into fists of iron. The thin veneer of civilization had been stripped to reveal the untamed savage beneath. A finger of fear touched her, yet still she found the courage to question him. "What is amiss?"

"I don't want you in Scotland! I'm sending you back to London."

Catherine stiffened. Hepburn's rejection was unendurable. She saw her grandfather appear and saw the two men exchange brief words, their voices too low to be overheard. Cat turned and blindly made her way back up to her chamber.

"Geordie, I have reason to believe Catherine's life is in danger. She will be much safer at home in England."

The earl's face turned purple; he crashed his fist on his desk. "Who dares threaten her?"

"The question I ask myself is, *Who gains from her death?* The answer is, *Your eldest nephew, Malcolm Lindsay.*"

"Malcolm has threatened her?" Geordie was aghast.

"I was escorting Jenny Hepburn home from here yesterday. Because she was wearing Catherine's cloak, I believe she was mistaken for your granddaughter. She was wounded by this arrow. I am convinced she was shot by Malcolm Lindsay."

Geordie looked at the arrow. "Did ye witness him shoot her?"

"If I had, he'd be a dead man."

"Is it a mortal wound?"

"Nay, the lass caught it in the arm. She will survive."

"I find yer accusations impossible to believe. If it is his arrow, it was a huntin' accident," Geordie said with conviction.

"Mayhap it was meant fer ye. Ye're not without enemies, Hepburn."

"Are you willing to take a chance with Catherine's life?"

"Never! Home she goes, but I'll not have ye accuse my nephew without proof, man. Both Catherine and myself would ha' to be dead before Malcolm would inherit."

"Exactly, Geordie. I advise you to watch your back."

The Earl of Winton's eyes narrowed thoughtfully at the warning. "Do you intend to escort Catherine an' Maggie back to London?"

"No, I'll take them to Edinburgh and put them in the care of Robert Carey, who is returning to England tomorrow."

Geordie nodded. "The sooner she's out of harm's way, the better. I'll just go up and have a word with her."

Geordie knocked on Catherine's door and a grim-faced Maggie let him in. For a moment no one spoke, and then he broke the awkward silence. "I want ye to pack yer things with all speed. There is a possibility that it's not safe fer ye here at Seton. Hepburn will escort ye to Edinburgh and Robert Carey will escort ye to London." He held up his hand when he saw that Cat was about to demand answers. "I can tell ye nothin'; the suspicions are not mine, but I want ye to know how much yer visit has meant to me. I cherish the time we spent together and hope ye will come again in the future when the danger has passed." He hugged Catherine, then he did the same with Maggie. "Take care of each other."

When he left, a furious Cat, with hands on hips, told Maggie, "I don't believe it. He's taking orders from Hepburn! Lord Bloody Stewart wants to be rid of me!"

"He must have a reason, my lamb."

He has a reason, all right. He took what he wanted and thinks the price he'll have to pay is marriage. Well, I wouldn't wed the arrogant Scottish brute if he were the last man on earth!

Chapter Nineteen

*C*atherine dragged out her trunks and began packing with furious speed. Inside, her hot anger slowly turned into an icy carapace around her heart. She would not let the hurt touch her; she would distance herself from the pain of rejection, aye, and keep herself aloof from the cruel monster who inflicted that pain.

When she and Maggie had packed everything they owned, she picked up Tattoo and cuddled her. "I won't take you away from the home you love, but I will think of you every day. Goodbye, puss."

Cat swept down the stairs with her traveling cloak over her arm and Maggie at her heels. Though Hepburn was in the hall with Geordie, she did not address him. Instead she spoke to a servant.

"Kindly inform his lordship that our trunks are upstairs."

The servant approached Patrick, who had obviously heard Lady Catherine's words. Hepburn waved him aside, gave Cat a level look and then took the stairs two at a time. While he was gone, she took the opportunity to put her arms around Geordie.

"Good-bye, Granddad. Thank you for everything. I promise I shall come back to Seton again." To allow Maggie and Geordie to say their good-byes in private, she went outside to await the carriage that was being readied, displaying deliberate indifference about how Hepburn would cope with all their luggage.

When Patrick helped Maggie into the coach, he glanced at Catherine. She was sitting ramrod straight with her eyes fixed on a distant mountain. Hepburn was not in the habit of explaining his decisions to women, but in her case he would have made an exception. He would not tell her about Jenny, because he didn't want to alarm her, nor have her feel guilt. He did want to alert her to danger, however. He saw this was not the moment and clamped his mouth shut. If he spoke, Hellcat would use the opportunity to coldly rebuff him. He mounted Valiant and told the driver to make all haste to Edinburgh.

With each mile, his premonition of trouble grew stronger. Since previously his sixth sense had not warned him of danger to Catherine, he assumed the menace was a threat to him or Crichton. He touched the long dagger and the dirk in his belt as his eyes scanned the horizon. The sunny day and blue sky did not lend themselves to foreboding thoughts, and his mind began to explore why he had not sensed the impending danger to Cat.

If Catherine was a part of me, I should have been aware of her peril. I lusted for her and her lands, but I did not allow myself to love her—not until now. Stop being fanciful, Hepburn— to love someone is to lose them. He glanced at her profile in the carriage window. She was easily the most beautiful, elegant female he'd ever known. *Love or lust, I don't intend to lose her or her lands. This is a temporary separation. The queen won't allow her to wed, so she will be safe until she comes of age in March. By then Elizabeth will be dead and Catherine will be mine!*

When the coach driver pulled into the courtyard at Holyrood Palace, Catherine was mildly surprised. Had Robert truly gone to London and back in just over a week? And more to the point, why was he again visiting the Scottish king? Cat smelled intrigue. She watched Hepburn dismount and approach their driver. She deliberately listened to what he said.

"Look after the ladies' trunks while we are in the palace. It may be some hours before you can transfer them to the other traveling coach." Patrick gave the driver money for his trouble. He opened the carriage door, and since Catherine sat immobile as a rock, he helped Maggie descend.

"Would you tell m'lady that I am taking her to Queen Anne while I conduct my business with His Majesty?"

Catherine alighted daintily from the coach and addressed Maggie. "I would ask you to give m'lord my condolences that he must deal with such a shabby excuse for a monarch in his pigsty of a Court, if the swine did not fit in so well."

He did not take the bait. "This way, ladies."

When they arrived in Anne's spacious rooms, her ladies

squealed and flocked to Hepburn's side. "Patrick, it's been a fortnight!" Another asked coyly, "Will you stay until tomorrow?" A third flattered with a double entendre: "I swear you've grown an inch."

The queen gave him a radiant smile and beckoned them. "How lovely to see you, Lady Catherine. Give your cloak to Margretha and come and sit beside me. I hope you will stay for lunch?"

Cat sank into a graceful curtsy. "You honor me, Your Majesty."

Patrick kissed the queen's fingers and whispered in her ear.

"Take your time, my lord; it will give us a chance to visit."

Hepburn cast a warning glance at Cat before he left, and she raised her chin in icy defiance.

As he made his way to James's Privy Chamber, Patrick could not shake the sense of a threat. He hoped it was not connected to the king or Robert Carey in any way. When he arrived in the anteroom, the man he had been thinking about sat awaiting a second audience. "Good to see you, Robert. I trust your family bore up and got through your father's funeral, which I imagine was well attended?"

"Aye, even though Elizabeth was too tight-fisted to declare an official day of mourning, most of London was there."

"Cecil sent you back immediately, which I shall take as an auspicious sign for our future fortunes. Robert, I need a favor, but it can wait until our business with James is done."

Just then the inner door was opened and Hepburn was told the king wished to see him alone. He shrugged his shoulders at Robert and entered James's sanctum.

"Where the de'il ha' ye bin, Patrick, lad?" James demanded petulantly. "It's no' politic tae keep yer old dad waitin'."

Since the king often referred to himself as *yer old dad* when speaking with his younger courtiers, Patrick didn't blink an eye. "Forgive me, Sire. I won't insult you with an excuse."

"Cecil's letter is most encouragin'. He suggests we take someone we can wholly trust intae our confidence and send him tae England as my ambassador. Right away I thought of my old playmate Johnny Erskine an' would like yer thoughts on my choice."

"The Earl of Mar is an excellent choice, Sire. If one ambassador is good, two might be better. I take it upon myself to suggest a second man of utter dependability. Edward Bruce, the Abbot of Kinross, the judge who is Lord of Sessions, has served you in successful missions in the past and will be invaluable when you become King of England."

"True! Bruce made a good impression because he likes the south and envies the English judiciary their fees and perquisites."

Patrick hid a smile. Royalty always thought in terms of money. An inner voice mocked, *As do you, Hepburn.* Another answered, *Am I not descended from royalty?*

"I'll suggest the two men tae Cecil. Let's ha' Carey in."

Patrick opened the door and beckoned Robert inside.

"I meant tae offer ye my condolences earlier, Carey. Lord Hunsdon was a braw mon tae produce ten offspring, I ken."

"Ten *legitimate* offspring, Your Majesty," Carey replied dryly. As James roared with laughter, spraying spittle in every direction, Robert made a mental note to not amuse James in the future.

"I'll ha' a reply fer Cecil wi'in the hour. Are ye willin' tae start back tae England today, Carey?"

"Perfectly willing, Your Majesty."

"Off ye go, then. Patrick will amuse ye fer an hour."

When they left the king's presence, Patrick quipped, "I'll amuse you if you won't spit on me, Robert."

"James fascinates me. I have to stop myself from staring!" Robert confessed. "What is the favor you need?"

Patrick sobered. "I want you to take Catherine back to England with you. Though I have no proof, I am convinced she is in danger at Seton. I suspect Geordie's nephew is lusting to become the Earl of Winton's heir."

"Good God! Does Catherine know?"

"I have not revealed my suspicions because I don't want her frightened. I've told her only that she will be safer at home. Of course I informed her grandfather of what I suspect. I may not have convinced him, but he agrees that Catherine must go home."

"Thanks for keeping your eye on her and guarding her safety."

"I have an agenda, Robert."

"And how does Catherine feel about you, my friend?"

"Why don't you ask her?"

●　　●　　●

"Patrick Hepburn is an uncivilized brute! I rue the day I ever laid eyes on the savage, uncouth Scot in the woods at Richmond." Cat and Maggie sat across from Robert as his traveling coach set out from Holyrood Palace.

"When we met at the hunt, a fortnight ago, I thought you were enjoying your sojourn in Scotland."

"Oh, Robert, I absolutely adore Scotland. I love my grandfather and wish I'd known him all my life." She opened her cloak to show him her amethyst dagger. "He gave me this. It belonged to Audra, my grandmother. I saw her portrait and was amazed that I look exactly like her. No one ever told me; not even Maggie!"

"And of course you tell me everything, like Lady Carey not being able to chaperone you at Crichton," Maggie said sweetly.

"I'm sorry Liz didn't return with you," Cat said ruefully. "I would have enjoyed her company on such a long journey."

"I left her at Widdrington. She has an estate to run."

Cat pounced immediately. "I was surprised to learn you were again at Holyrood. Is there intrigue you are keeping secret?"

"Nothing so interesting. Just mundane Border warden business, I'm afraid. I was delivering reports from Philadelphia's husband, Lord Scrope, who as you know is Constable of Carlisle Castle."

Cat was about to dig deeper, for even Philadelphia said her husband, Thomas, was crooked as a corkscrew and dabbled in intrigue, when the coach stopped so quickly, she was thrown to the opposite seat. "What on earth has happened?"

Robert reached for the handle and was halfway out the door when it was wrenched from his hand and thrown open to reveal six burly Borderers who were armed to the teeth.

"Back inside," the leader ordered. Robert's driver and his armed guard, who had been trussed with rope, were shoved into the carriage with Carey and the ladies.

Robert had a pretty good idea that they were members of the Armstrong clan and immediately thought of the day that Hepburn had hanged Sim Armstrong. "Do exactly as they say, Catherine. These men would not cavil at harming a woman."

Within minutes the coach began to move. Whoever was in the driver's seat turned the coach around and headed back into the city.

"Dear God, Hepburn warned me that Scotland was too dangerous for me, but I didn't believe him!" Cat's heart was thudding with fear and heightened excitement at the thought of being kidnapped.

"They may not know your identity. It may be me they want. We must all avoid giving them your name," Robert said urgently. He was convinced they would search him and find the king's letter.

The coach stopped in a derelict part of Edinburgh that neither Robert nor Catherine had ever visited. The carriage door was thrown open and its occupants were ushered at knifepoint into a shabby three-storied house with shuttered windows. As soon as they were inside, the women were separated from the men and taken upstairs by an evil-looking brute designated as their guard.

Maggie clamped her mouth shut and glared her outrage, but Catherine demanded, "What do you want with us?"

The man leered. "Yer Hepburn's fancy piece. He'll pay gold tae get ye back, or we'll get our money's worth atween yer legs!" He went over to the shuttered window to make sure it was locked.

The moment his back was turned, Catherine became a wildcat. She palmed her dagger and stabbed him in the shoulder.

The ugly brute cried out in pain. "You bitch!" He plucked the knife from his flesh and backhanded Catherine across the face.

She went down to her knees, holding her cheek, which was quickly turning purple. Maggie knelt beside her. "My lamb!"

The Borderer opened the door and shouted, "I need help!"

Cat retrieved her knife from the floor and sheathed it beneath her cloak as heavy boots thudded up the stairs. "Firkin' hell, can ye no' guard a lass an' an owd woman?" When he saw Catherine's face he roared, "We've orders not tae harm the wench! Christ, Hepburn will cut off yer nuts fer this! Get the hell downstairs."

The second man was as dangerous-looking as the first to Cat. She could hardly tell them apart. She sat on the floor with her back against the wall, trying to ignore the smell of damp mold. She decided to behave from now on, but she was filled with a sense of secret satisfaction for the reckless thing she had done.

•   •   •

Patrick Hepburn could not shake the premonition of impending peril. Each time he closed his eyes he saw Armstrongs, which convinced him that the night riders who'd been seen at Crichton while he was away were members of that clan. As soon as he left the city, he urged Valiant into a full gallop, heading home. One minute his path lay clear; the next, he was surrounded by thugs. Outnumbered by five, he was ready to fight until the leader spoke.

"Come quietly, m'lord. We ha' yer lady and Robert Carey."

The danger I sensed was for Catherine and Robert as well as myself. It was a revelation that gave him little satisfaction, for he'd done nothing to protect them. He was certain that none had followed him and Catherine on their trek for the wild horses, but it was obvious someone had been watching Crichton for his return. They'd seen him go to Seton, then escort Cat to Holyrood. He hoped to God that they'd taken Robert Carey because he was a Border warden involved in the hanging of Sim Armstrong and not because they knew he was a secret courier for King James. He bottled up his fury behind a calm façade. "I'll give you no trouble, gentlemen. Lead on."

The mounted men surrounded him as they rode the two miles back to Edinburgh. Hepburn was familiar with the seedy area they entered near the Grassmarket, where freshly killed cattle were hung; he could smell the piles of offal left by the butchers. They clattered through a narrow wynd and then behind a tall house. Patrick recognized Catherine's trunks piled on the black coach that stood in the yard. The men dismounted and tethered their horses and Hepburn did the same, silently vowing annihilation to every man jack of them if aught befell Valiant.

The front door opened and he walked inside with four of the men close on his heels. The windows were shuttered and the only light came from oil lamps. Patrick's inner eye focused on Catherine. He sensed that she was nearby, either a few stories above him or perhaps in the house next door. He knew that Carey and his driver and guard were being held separately from the women.

The outlaw who was in authority laid out his demands, but Patrick noticed with grim satisfaction that he kept a safe distance between them. The man was not Foss Armstrong, the Border warden, but Hepburn knew it was the warden who'd devised the plot.

"You hung Sim Armstrong."

"I *hanged* him," Hepburn corrected laconically.

"We ha' the English Border warden, Carey, who conspired in Armstrong's murder, an' we also ha' yer Seton woman. We demand ten thousand Scots pounds fer their ransom as compensation, or their lives are forfeit."

Hepburn's mouth set and then he said calmly, "Impossible. You cannot get blood from a stone."

"We can if the stone is Crichton Castle. Eight thousand!"

A mortgage is anathema to me. It took me years to pay off the one my father saddled Crichton with. Hepburn was relieved that they seemed to have no idea Carey was a courier for the king. He thought about Catherine and his gut knotted. "Five thousand."

"Done!" The leader agreed with a nod.

"I'll need a couple of hours to arrange a mortgage."

"An hour! Jed, go wi' him."

Hepburn and his escort rode up High Street to Gordon Herriotts, the king's goldsmith, with whom Patrick and his father had previously done business. Within thirty minutes he had mortgaged Crichton Castle and received a note for five thousand pounds. Over an hour had elapsed by the time Hepburn returned to the house. He handed the note to the thug who had set the ransom demand.

The man's eyes gleamed with victory as he carefully read it, then they lifted to meet Hepburn's. "Ye've not signed it."

"How observant you are," Patrick said quietly.

The man handed back the note. "Sign it!"

"When all your captives have been released and allowed to go freely on their way, I will sign the note."

"Do ye take me fer a bloody fool? How do we know ye'll sign it, once they're freed?"

"You will still have me as your captive. I won't sign it until they are freed." He bared his teeth like a wolf. "If you kill me, you will never get it signed. If you kill them, you will have nothing left with which to bargain."

It took a minute for the outlaw to digest Hepburn's ultimatum. Then he summoned three of his cohorts and told them to take Hepburn and hold him in a back room. In a few minutes Patrick heard someone clear his throat and knew it was Robert Carey. A short time later he heard Catherine's voice.

"You filthy swine, I hope the bloody wound I gave you festers!"

"Keep yer tongue between yer teeth, my lamb."

Hepburn smiled at Maggie's words. Cat was far too impulsive. One of the shutters was broken and he saw the ladies' backs and then Robert's as they entered the coach. A few minutes later it was driven from the yard. Patrick, ignoring his guards, walked from the back room and asked to watch the carriage depart the area. He could tell that the captives were free for the moment and knew he could do nothing for them until he gained his own release. With a flourish he put his signature on the promissory note, opened the door and went outside. He mounted Valiant and, showing no haste, trotted his horse down the street and through the narrow wynd. The minute he was out of sight of the house, he rode hell-for-leather the entire eight miles to Crichton.

He was shouting orders as soon as he neared the stables. By the time he had changed horses, six moss-troopers were saddled and ready to ride south. An hour's hard gallop brought Carey's coach in sight. Lumbering under the weight of passengers and luggage it had covered only a dozen miles. Hepburn was relieved to see the carriage was not being followed. He kept well back until the afternoon light began to fade, then sent Jock ahead to the inn at Peebles to make sure it was safe before the coach arrived.

"Can we not go faster, Robert? We're being followed!"

"Yes, I was alarmed until I realized it was the Border lord."

"Bloody Hepburn! *He's* the reason we were kidnapped, isn't he?" She touched her bruised face and winced.

"Patrick and I are both to blame, I'm afraid, Catherine."

"What did you do?" she asked, wide-eyed.

"It was Border patrol business. You don't want to know."

"He's the reason for all my troubles!"

"He's the reason we were released, Catherine."

"By making a deal with the Devil?" she mocked.

"By paying our ransom—I suppose you could call it a deal with the Devil."

Cat shuddered. "Scotland is peopled with barbarians."

"The village of Peebles is just ahead. We'll stop for the night at the inn there. If we start early tomorrow we should make it across the Border by nightfall."

"Ah, good, no barbarians in England," Maggie said sardonically.

When they arrived at the inn, Robert ordered three rooms. One was for the ladies, one for their driver and guard, and the third for himself. As all their luggage was being hauled upstairs, Maggie told the innkeeper's wife, "My lady will need a bath after supper. She likes her water hot." Then she muttered, "She's never out of hot water."

"I heard that," Cat declared. Then she smiled guiltily. "I know I'm a sore trial to you, Maggie."

"Ach, lambie, I'd have no adventures if it weren't fer ye!"

When Cat and Maggie entered their room, Catherine turned the key in the lock. "If Hepburn comes knocking, you are not to let him in. I would die of mortification if he ever saw my face."

"I warrant he's seen more than yer face."

"If you want the truth, Maggie, he saw more than my face the first night aboard ship when we were ankle-deep in spew."

"Well, if that dinna put him off ye, nothing will!"

"Put *him* off *me*? I can assure you it is the other way about!"

An hour later, Robert sat in the taproom drinking ale with Patrick. "How did you get the money?"

"How do you think?" Hepburn said shortly.

Robert knew Hepburn would not mortgage lightly. "Thank you. I shall find some way to repay you, my lord."

"There is no need for that. The Armstrongs will repay me."

"They'll be long gone by now," Robert pointed out.

Hepburn smiled. "Scotland isn't big enough for them to hide." He drank his ale. "I was afraid they would find James's letter."

"You're a liar, Hepburn. Nothing on earth frightens you."

Upstairs, after Catherine had eaten, a wooden tub was dragged into her room and filled with steaming water. She urged Maggie to bathe first so that she could examine her cheek carefully in the mirror and bathe it with cold water from the jug. Cat then took her bath. As she soaked, she feared that Hepburn would arrive at any moment.

An hour later, dressed in night rail and bed robe, she began to fear that Hepburn would not come. *The least he could do is offer his apology that I was kidnapped, threatened and injured.*

Then she remembered that he was not a gallant courtier. *The untamed lout has likely never apologized for aught in his life!*

The next day, with their moss-trooper escort, they covered the seventy-five miles that took them across the Border to Carlisle Castle, where Carey's brother-in-law, Scrope, was the constable. Catherine was overjoyed to see Philadelphia, who had returned to Carlisle Castle with her husband, Lord Scrope, after her father's funeral.

"Darling, whatever happened to your face?" Philadelphia cried.

Cat poured out the whole story to sympathetic ears. She turned quickly as she recognized the spurred tread of Hepburn's boots.

"Lady Catherine is going home. Seton was unsafe for her. I believe her cousin resents the fact that she is her grandfather's heir. He fancies himself as the next Earl of Winton."

"That is a blatant lie!" Catherine was in a blazing fury. "How dare you claim I am in danger from Malcolm or Andrew? My danger came from my association with *you*, Hepburn. I vow that association is ended today." She turned and swept from the hall.

"The irresistible attraction of opposites is stronger than ever, I see," Philadelphia said dryly. She placed her hand on his arm. "Thank you for delivering them safely, Patrick. I warrant the cost was high. Is there aught I can do to help?"

"Just make sure the little hellcat doesn't elope before she comes of age, Lady Scrope." He grinned and kissed her fingers.

In the pitch-dark night, on the battlements of Carlisle Castle, Patrick Hepburn stared into the void, seeing only Catherine. When he closed his eyes he could feel her soft body yield to him. He could taste her mouth as it clung to his. Most of all, his blood sang as he relived her wild, passionate response to him.

I must put you from my mind, Cat. I have a job to do that will take all my energy and my determination. But rest assured that I will settle the score. Then, watch out. I am coming for you!

Chapter Twenty

*C*atherine, I'm so glad that you are back," Isobel declared.
Cat's heart lifted as her mother welcomed her arrival at their apartment at Whitehall Palace.

"The queen was not best pleased that you had gone to visit your grandfather. Her Majesty needs you to design some new gowns."

Cat's joy was muted. *I might have known!* Her mother was happy about her return only because it would please Elizabeth.

"Maggie and I traveled back with Robert and Philadelphia."

"I'm happy to have you back too, Maggie. I dismissed my last ladies' maid because she preferred gossip to duty. My wardrobe needs attention. I'm surprised Her Majesty hasn't commented on the condition of my garments."

"I'll soon put it to rights, my lady, once I've unpacked."

"I'll help you, Maggie." Cat, astounded that Isobel had not asked about her father, Geordie, was glad to escape.

The next morning she presented herself to Queen Elizabeth.

"Lady Catherine, you are returned from your sojourn in Scotland. What did you think of the barbaric land?"

Cat rose from her deep curtsy. "It was beautiful, in a wild and untamed way, Your Majesty."

"So I've been told. A tad too rugged for those with delicate constitutions like you and me, I warrant."

You have the constitution of a warhorse and, come to think of it, I'm no fragile flower either.

"I want you to design me two new gowns for my summer progress. This year we do not intend to go traipsing across the country. Lord Keeper Egerton has invited us to Harefield Place, Middlesex, for the month of August. It will give us an opportunity to see if his new wife, Lady Alice, proves an entertaining hostess."

"I will create a few designs immediately, Your Majesty." *Your poor sewing women will have to work day and night to get new gowns finished by the first of August. I had better get started.*

Catherine went immediately to the seamstresses, who worked under the direction of her mother. They all put their heads together and came up with ideas that would cut hours from their intricate labor. Then Cat sketched her designs accordingly.

That evening she joined Philadelphia and Kate in the Privy Chamber, where they were making mock curtsies to Cat's aunt Beth, their sister-in-law, who had just become the new Lady Hunsdon.

"The queen informed me we are going to Harefield Place on progress. Poor Lady Alice will be in a pother, I warrant."

"She'll be in her glory, Catherine. She went through the Earl of Derby's fortune like a dose of salts; now she'll make inroads on Egerton's money. It'll be poor Thomas who's in a pother."

Philadelphia lowered her voice. "Absence makes the heart grow fonder, Cat. Here comes your lonely swain, Henry Somerset."

"Lady Catherine, you are even more beauteous than I remember. Would you do me the honor of partnering me in this dance?"

She accepted and, as she danced, wondered why she no longer found Hal attractive. *He looks so young and so pretty. Why did I never notice before?* Her inner voice answered: *You know why,* but she ignored it.

"There's a new Shakespeare play at the Globe. Will you come with me, Cat?" Hal begged.

She gave him a cool look at the liberty he took with her name.

"I'm afraid not, since Lady Arbella isn't here to join us." As the dance finished she started to walk away, but then William Seymour arrived and bowed gallantly.

"May I have the honor of the next dance, Lady Catherine?"

Henry Somerset snapped, "Bog off, Seymour; you're nothing but a damned fortune hunter!"

"There's the pot calling the kettle black!" Will sneered.

Cat had a sudden revelation. They were both after her money! "Hal, why don't you partner Will? You make such a lovely couple and have so much in common that you deserve each other."

Hours later, as she lay in bed, Catherine began a ritual that she would follow for many months. First, she vowed to open a new chapter in her life. She needed to find an attractive, noble suitor who had wealth of his own and no interest in hers. Second, she firmly banished all thoughts of Patrick Hepburn. Then she fell asleep and promptly dreamed about the dangerous devil.

At Crichton, Lord Stewart spoke with his moss-troopers. "I know the summer months, while the crops are harvested, are traditionally the quietest of the year in the Borders, but this year will be different for the Hepburns." He watched the dark faces for signs of objection as he laid out his plan. "I want half of you to remain at Crichton to protect our people, the castle and our land. The other half will ride with me to hunt down the Armstrongs." He held up his hand before any could speak. "I must warn you that we are inviting the king's displeasure, since Foss Armstrong is a Scots Border warden and James has outlawed clan feuds." He let that sink in. "You decide who stays and who rides."

A short time later he sought out Jenny and took a look at her wound. She was healing well and seemed no worse for wear. "You may no longer ride out with Andrew Lindsay to Seton or anywhere else. It is unsafe." He saw the mutinous look on her face. "Jenny, I want your word as a Hepburn that you will obey me."

She hesitated before she nodded. "You have my word, my lord."

"Good girl." Patrick hoped her father would choose to stay behind and safeguard his family.

The next morning Hepburn departed Crichton with two dozen of his most hardened moss-troopers. As he had expected, Jock Elliot rode beside him. Most, but not all, were unwed or widowers. The men who had young children had opted to stay behind on guard duty under the captaincy of David Hepburn, who would have preferred to ride but knew where his first duty lay.

Hepburn rode directly to Winton Castle to assure the earl that though he may be gone for some time, the Hepburns would still guard his cattle from theft. Before Patrick left he wanted to make sure Geordie Seton was all right. Then, alone, without his men, he spoke with another to make sure Geordie stayed that way.

He found Malcolm Lindsay overseeing a dozen men who were harvesting a hay crop and took him aside. "I have been making enquiries about your late wife and have learned that some believe she died under odd circumstances." He towered over Malcolm in a threatening stance and saw the black hatred in his eyes. Then Hepburn's mouth set and he said calmly, "I charge you to watch the earl's back and trust you see no harm befalls Geordie Seton."

Patrick Hepburn and his moss-troopers then set out on their mission. Unbeknownst to them, it would take months before their *hot trod* produced results.

While Whitehall Palace was cleaned and aired, the queen and Court enjoyed the hospitality of Harefield for the entire month of August. Lady Alice strove to outdo all other hostesses with lavish banquets, masques and concerts, where Elizabeth was honored as the Sun Queen.

Isobel, for once, did not criticize Catherine. "How clever of you to design the queen's gown to depict the sun, moon and stars."

"Thank you, Mother." *You have no idea how clever. The sewing women cut out the designs from other material and appliquéd them rather than embroidering for days. Then I wrote to Lady Alice, hinting at how Her Majesty loved being honored as the Sun Queen.*

Before the Court departed, Lord and Lady Egerton held a lottery for their guests and deftly arranged it so that the queen and her ladies won all the prizes. Elizabeth declared her progress a resounding success.

During the first week of September, Cat received a poetic billet-doux from William Herbert, whom she had spent time with at Harefield. She hurried along to Philadelphia's chambers to learn all she could about the attractive young man.

"William is heir to the great earldom of Pembroke, Cat. His mother was Philip Sidney's sister. Apparently he's inherited the family's literary talent and, since his writings cleverly flatter Elizabeth, he has a good chance of becoming a royal favorite."

"So that's why he was invited to Harefield," Cat mused.

A few days later, when Herbert joined her in the gardens, Cat found his conversation exhilarating. He frequented a literary circle of poets and dramatists, which she found fascinating.

"Will Shakespeare is truly a friend of yours?"

"Men in the arts frequently need wealthy patrons. Since my father has been most generous to Shakespeare, he regards me as a friend. I regard him as a master from whom I've learned much."

"My lord, why don't you suggest to the queen that the players from the Globe Theatre perform one of Shakespeare's plays here?"

"Lady Catherine, do you believe Her Majesty would be amenable to such a suggestion?"

"Shall we find out, Will? I'll plant the suggestion in her ear, and then you water it with flattery and we'll see if it produces fruit."

By the end of September, Catherine concluded that she and Will Herbert made a good team. He smoked tobacco, a fashion brought from the New World, which Cat found so fascinating, she tried it herself—in private, of course, with only Maggie as witness.

As she lay abed one night, Cat decided she had found the noble suitor for whom she had been searching. Earlier in the evening they had talked about the estates that they would inherit; hers in Hertford, and his in Wiltshire, near Salisbury, called Wilton House. She had also heard whispers that the queen was about to make Herbert her Master of the Horse. She allowed herself to fantasize about marriage. *I could become the Countess of Pembroke. That should banish the persistent specter of Patrick Hepburn, who lurks about in the dark recesses of my mind!*

When she fell asleep, the man she dreamed about was indeed a Master of the Horse, and Master of Cat too, but he was not the noble, fair-haired William Herbert.

During August and September, Hepburn and his moss-troopers rode from town to town throughout the Scottish dales, searching for the Armstrong reivers connected with the kidnapping-for-ransom plot. At Kinmont, Gilnockie and Mangerton they found Armstrongs from No-Nose Willie to Hob Half-Lugs, but Hepburn knew they were little fish, and none of them had been present in Edinburgh that day. He would not be satisfied until he found the cod's head.

"It should be a simple matter to find Foss Armstrong. A warden of the Marches doesn't just disappear," Jock said in frustration.

"He's fleeing and hiding then fleeing again. We'll run him to earth like the vermin he is. He could be in the English Borders. There are many Armstrongs who live there. We'll cross over tonight."

On the first day of October, William Herbert's father died and he came into the earldom of Pembroke. A few days later, Catherine encountered him in the tiltyard, practicing hard to become the Queen's Champion at the Accession Day Tournament in November.

"My lord earl, I had no idea you were back from Salisbury. I offer my deepest condolences for the loss of your dear father."

"Thank you, Catherine. He had been ailing for some time so it wasn't entirely unexpected. Tiltyard practice keeps melancholy thoughts at bay."

"You must try to remember the happy times you spent with him."

"Yes, that's exactly what I did when my grandfather died. He had rough manners and was happiest when he was egging on his retainers to brawl with the neighboring landowners."

Catherine smiled. "My grandfather also is a rough diamond."

"May I have a favor from you, my lady, to wear in the joust?"

"How very romantic, Lord Pembroke. I would be honored if you wore my favor. I'll bring a scarf to the tiltyard tomorrow."

"Tonight would be more romantic, Catherine. Will you come?"

"Perhaps." She smiled her secret smile.

At dinner that evening Cat took a seat beside Philadelphia, and they chatted as they watched the elaborate ritual of serving the queen's food. A lady-in-waiting and a maid of honor, after graceful genuflections, rubbed the monarch's plates with bread and salt as the Yeomen of the Guard brought the gilt dishes from the kitchen. Then Mary Fitton, Elizabeth's youngest maid of honor, took her tasting knife and gave each yeoman a mouthful of the dish he had carried in as a precaution against poison.

"Our sweet maid of honor enjoys letting gentlemen taste her wares. A little bird told me her affair with Treasurer Knollys is a thing of the past and she's already mistress to another. Everyone is trying to find out who her new lover is."

Cat was shocked. "Lover? She is three years younger than I!"

"And what does age have to do with sex, pray tell? Surely you are not still a virgin, Catherine?"

"I . . . a lady never tells," she murmured, taken off guard.

Philadelphia laughed. "That means you are not, thank heaven. Take it from me—gentlemen always tell!"

Judas! I saw Philadelphia talking to Hepburn at Carlisle. Surely the uncouth devil didn't hint? How I loathe the swine!

"Then obviously they are not gentlemen." She changed the topic, slightly. "The Earl of Pembroke has asked to wear my favor in the tournament next month. I think you'll agree that William Herbert is a gentleman."

"Well, he's certainly a nobleman; I don't know about gentle. That's something you'll have to find out for yourself, darling."

After dinner Cat returned to her chamber and took out the white silk scarf she had spent two hours of the afternoon embroidering. She traced the winged dragon's red tongue with her fingertip as she contemplated whether to go and meet Pembroke. *What the devil do I have to lose?* she asked herself impulsively. *Certainly not your virginity,* a mocking voice replied.

"Catherine, I've waited more than an hour, but I couldn't give up. Thank you for coming. You look so beautiful in the light of the huge harvest moon. Did you bring me your favor to wear?"

"Yes, William. My scarf is emblazoned with the winged Winton dragon, my ancient Scottish emblem." She draped it about his neck playfully. "Its mystic power will make you the champion."

He slid it from his neck, kissed the white silk and inhaled its heady perfume. "My lady fair." He slipped the scarf about her neck and drew her close. "Perhaps it is prophetic that Wilton and Winton are only one letter apart."

"Prophetic?" Cat asked breathlessly, anticipating his kiss.

"It seems perfectly natural that they be joined together." He fused his mouth to hers in a demonstration.

"My lord, you go too fast." She pulled away, but not too far.

He's certainly experienced in gallantry. It was a seductive kiss, but, thank God and all his saints, his touch didn't turn me into a wild woman without control. In fact, with William Herbert I believe I shall be the one in control. "The moonlight is so romantic. Shall we walk down by the river?"

He clasped her hand and took it to his lips. "River? I fear I'm in over my head already, Lady Catherine."

"I warrant you are a most experienced swimmer, Lord Pembroke."

"Even so, I could drown in the golden depths of your eyes."

Oh, Lord, save me from a poet, unless his name be Shakespeare.

"By the way, I hinted to the queen that the ladies of the Court would love to see one of Will Shakespeare's plays performed."

"Thank you, Catherine. The queen asked me only this morning if I could arrange for the Globe Players to come to Whitehall sometime during her Accession celebration. What sort of play would you enjoy most?"

"A romance, of course."

He slipped his arm about her. "Then a romance you shall have, Catherine Seton Spencer."

Patience was not Hepburn's long suit, but his determination turned dogged as he and his posse scoured the English Borders, going from one lead to another. Early October even took them to the Highlands, but once again the rumor turned out to be false.

As the Hepburns sat around their campfire contemplating their next move, Patrick stared into the blaze, mesmerized by the blue and orange flames. It came to him that he would find Foss Armstrong back on his own midden. In mid-October the marches needed patrolling as cattle reiving became rampant again, after the quiet summer months.

When Patrick stood up the men looked at him with expectant eyes, awaiting his decision. He bit out one word: "Hermitage!"

Two days later, after a hard ride, Hepburn's instincts had proven infallible. He had Foss Armstrong imprisoned inside the grim fortalice along with eight of his men. Only the warden was trussed, the rest were free to go if they dared take the chance.

"I want my five thousand back, plus a thousand for my trouble."

"I don't know what ye're talkin' about," Foss growled.

"Armstrongs are fond of nicknames. Let's see, there's No-Nose Willie—how would you like to be known as No-Nuts Foss?"

Armstrong's swarthy face actually blanched.

Hepburn smiled. "No, even I couldn't be that cruel—yet. As nicknames go, I prefer Fingerless Foss. I'll chop one off every day until I get my money." He picked up his axe.

Armstrong struggled against his ropes. "Ride tae the king!" he ordered his first lieutenant. "Tell him his top Border warden is being assaulted! Tell him I'm layin' charges against Hepburn!"

Calmly, Hepburn placed Armstrong's hand on the table and brought down his blade swiftly, severing the little finger.

Armstrong's second in command bolted from the castle to ride to Edinburgh. No one stopped him.

As Foss stared at his bloody hand in horror, Hepburn said, "You know, Jamie has a tendency to be ponderous when making a decision. If he only takes a week to act on your behalf, that's seven days. By that time, you'll have only thumbs left." Hepburn nodded to Jock. "Cauterize that so he can think straight."

When Jock stuck an iron poker in the fire, Armstrong cried out, "Go an' get the money! Be back before this time tomorrow!"

"You know, Fingerless, I'm easy. I'll take the six thousand in gold," Hepburn said expansively. He looked at the seven Armstrongs who were ready for flight. "Off you go, lads."

Catherine felt the bodice of her gown being unbuttoned and gave Herbert's wandering hand a sharp slap. "My lord, I do not permit such liberties to any man."

"Not even one who wishes to make you his wife, Catherine?"

She took a deep breath as she digested his words. She had watched him practice jousting earlier in the afternoon and been impressed with his performance. This was a joust of another sort. In the space of a fortnight they had gone from acquaintance to courtship. *Is the Earl of Pembroke hinting at betrothal?* "Her Majesty frowns upon her courtiers marrying, William."

"My cousin Edward Somerset wed Lady Anne Russell a couple of months back, and Elizabeth, far from objecting, attended the festivities at Cobham's house in Blackfriars."

"Ah, but Anne was the widow of Ambrose Dudley, Lord

Warwick. Any with a Dudley connection can do no wrong in the queen's eyes."

"Some say I am Queen Elizabeth's new favorite." He dipped his head and kissed her. "Methinks I can do no wrong either."

"Are you proposing marriage, William?" she asked outright.

"And if I am, what would your answer be, Lady Fair and Chaste?"

"My answer would be *perhaps,* my Lord Favorite. You may propose the day you become my champion in the tournament."

Before the end of October, chatter had spread through the palace about the courtship. Philadelphia was the first person to repeat the rumors she had heard. "Is there any truth to it, Catherine?"

"That I have been asked to become the Countess of Pembroke?" she asked coyly. "You must admit, it is rather tempting."

"He has a reputation as a womanizer. Be sure it's marriage he's proposing. Are you in love with him?" she asked bluntly.

"Don't be silly. I'm wise enough to let my head rule my heart."

"Good! Promise me you won't do anything foolish like eloping. If he wants you badly enough, he will wait until you come of age."

Catherine began to notice all the looks of envy that the other ladies cast her way. She knew it would not be long before Maggie heard the gossip, but she hoped her mother didn't get wind of it.

The next day, Maggie cornered her. "All the palace servants are repeating the rumor that ye and William Herbert have an understanding. Are they true or false, my lamb?"

"The Earl of Pembroke and I *do* have an understanding, Maggie. When he proposes marriage, he understands that I will answer him."

"And I understand that ye are speaking in riddles!"

"That's because I haven't made up my mind yet."

"Good. Ye are far too impulsive. Think long and hard. He's a courtier. His ambition and his life are centered on Elizabeth."

"That's a point in his favor as far as I'm concerned. We both wish to remain at Court, rather than be buried in the country."

Maggie pressed her lips together in disapproval.

The next day Isobel received an invitation for herself and her daughter to dine with the Earl and Countess of Worcester at their house in Charing Cross, which was conveniently close to Whitehall.

"This is quite a coup, Catherine. The invitation is from Anne Russell, who was the Countess of Warwick before she wed Worcester. Anne is the queen's favorite lady, after Kate Howard and Philadelphia Scrope."

Worcester is Pembroke's cousin. William is behind this invitation. If we dine with them, Mother will find out! "You don't really wish to go to Charing Cross, do you?"

"Of course we shall go. To refuse would be a slap in the face to the countess and thus to Her Majesty," Isobel declared firmly.

I cannot believe that only a few months ago I allowed Worcester's son Hal to escort me to London plays. How could I have been attracted to such a boy? Once again her damnable inner voice answered: *That was before you met a real man!* Cat cursed herself. Hadn't she vowed to never even think of Hepburn?

The day after the dinner party, Isobel Spencer consulted with her sister-in-law Beth, and Philadelphia and Kate. "The Earl of Pembroke asked my permission to pay court to Catherine. Since he is reputed to be Her Majesty's new favorite, I thought it best not to refuse him. I told him that they must be chaperoned at all times since the queen insists her unmarried ladies be virgin. Do you think I did the right thing?"

Kate patted Isobel's hand. "Catherine will be twenty-one soon."

But Philadelphia warned, "Elizabeth has never been generous enough to share her favorites with other females."

"Oh, dear. The last thing in the world I want is her wrath!"

The moment Isobel left, Philadelphia penned a note to Hepburn.

My Dear Lord Stewart:
I extend an invitation for you to stay again at Richmond, and Kate offers the hospitality of Arundel House in the Strand, if you plan to come to London for the Accession Tournament.
Lady Catherine is being wooed by William Herbert, who has recently come into his Earldom of Pembroke.

Best always,
Philadelphia Scrope

When Patrick Hepburn read the missive from Lady Scrope, he cursed soundly and immediately set up practice lists at Crichton. If Herbert thought he was going to be Hellcat's champion, he was going to have a rude awakening.

The frosts of November had covered the ground before Patrick defeated every Hepburn, Stewart and Elliot who lived at Crichton. Scores of splintered lances had to be chopped into firewood. Then he took himself off to visit King James.

"Where've ye bin, mon? Ye neglect our Court fer months on end an' turn up when it suits yer own purpose!" Jamie complained.

"I've been practicing for the tournament, Sire."

"What tournament?" the king asked truculently.

"Elizabeth's Accession Day Tournament, November seventeenth, Sire."

"God's toenails, the woman ha' ruled England fer forty-four years. 'Tis unnatural! I warrant she made a pact wi' the Devil! 'Tis high time she slipped this mortal coil and made room fer her successor."

"Do not begrudge her the festivities of her last winter, Sire."

"It had better be her last hurrah!" He bent a threatening glance on Hepburn. "There's no news that she's even ailing!" Jamie complained petulantly.

"Sire," he lied smoothly, "the primary reason for my visit to Whitehall is to bring you details of Elizabeth's physical and mental condition."

"Oh, aye; I ken it has naught tae do wi' scoutin' a wealthy English heiress fer yersen," Jamie said shrewdly.

Hepburn managed to look offended. "You wrong me, Sire."

"I will if the Crown doesna' come tae me on the date ye prophesied, Patrick, mon."

"Trust me, Sire."

Chapter Twenty-one

*T*rust me, Catherine."

"Males can never be fully trusted, William. If the queen desires you to wear her favor in the tournament, how can I be sure you will wear my scarf tucked against your heart?" Cat teased.

"It's there now—feel," he urged huskily.

"Let the queen feel you," she mocked.

"I do," he said outrageously. "That's why I'm her favorite."

"And here's me thinking it was your dactyl pentameter that held her in thrall." Cat often indulged in racy badinage with Pembroke; banter kept him at arm's length. She moved away and changed the subject. "Which play are the Globe Players presenting after the tournament?"

"*Love's Labour's Lost.* I think you'll enjoy it."

"Ah, but it isn't me you have to please; it's Elizabeth."

"Do I please you, Catherine?"

"What an odd thing to say. I wouldn't have given you my favor otherwise, my lord."

"And will you favor me with a *yes* when I pop the question?"

"I might be persuaded to bestow my hand and my affection upon the Champion of the Tourney. Such a man would be hard to resist."

During the week before the Accession celebrations, nobles and their retinues descended upon Whitehall, attracted by the tournament. Percy, Earl of Northumberland, and Clifford, Earl of Cumberland, strutted about the Court issuing challenges for the joust. Meanwhile, the ladies of the Court were busy planning their splendid attire, which would be showcased in the stands, where the best seats were being sold for a shilling apiece.

Catherine had designed a gown for herself that would make her stand out in the crowd. Since Elizabeth forbade the maidens of her Court from wearing brilliant colors, Cat chose angelic white velvet. Because the November weather was extremely cold this year, she and Maggie had devised a matching velvet shoulder cape and hood, trimmed with ethereal white swansdown. A white fur muff completed the outfit. When it was finished and she tried it on, Cat knew she looked like the Snow Queen from a fairy tale.

When the *Hepburn Rose* docked in the Pool of London, Patrick noticed there were chunks of ice floating in the water. This time he had brought his cousin David Hepburn to act as his squire in the jousting. The tall young captain with auburn hair cut a gallant figure. "If the ship traffic was not so busy, the river Thames would have frozen over."

David's eyes widened. "This is my first visit to London—I never dreamt the city would be this big, my lord."

"A word to the wise, David. Don't let the Court or its occupants intimidate you. You have better blood than all the courtiers rolled together. Your natural swagger will carry you through any situation. Just shout, *'Make way fer a Borderer!'*"

David started to laugh, then saw that Hepburn was serious.

"We'll leave everything aboard while I acquaint you with Whitehall. The first thing you must do is speak with the Master of Ordnance, who'll assign a place for my horse, armor and lances." *The first thing I shall do is take the measure of Pembroke!*

At Whitehall, Sir Henry Lee, Master of Ordnance, took Patrick and David into the royal stables and assigned a stall for Hepburn's horse, which wasn't Valiant, but another tall black he had used in jousting practice. The stables were busy and Hepburn thanked Lee and said casually, "I was told to take a look at Pembroke's mount—a fancy piece of horseflesh, I understand."

"The white gelding, yonder. Her Majesty is partial to white horses. If there's aught you need, just ask a groom, m'lord."

Patrick wandered over to the large stall. He was looking for something that belonged to William Herbert. He'd always had great success at divination from holding an object in his hand.

Possessions often revealed hidden knowledge about their owners. He spotted a small tobacco pipe and palmed it immediately.

Inside the palace, a silver coin tossed to a servant furnished
him with the location of Pembroke's chambers. Patrick pointed
David in the direction of a dining hall, then went to the kitchens
for his own food. The fewer people who knew he was here, the
better. He found an alcove that was shunned because of its
drafty window and, as evening descended, he held the bowl of
Pembroke's pipe in the palm of his hand and concentrated. He
immediately discerned that William Herbert had put out the
pipe when he entered the stables because it was a fire hazard.
Then, after he had tended the horse, he had forgotten the pipe.

Hepburn's sixth sense explored for some essence of the man
left behind on the object. The moment he discerned something,
his inner eye focused intently. He smiled slowly. *Pembroke has
a secret he wishes to conceal. He also has a quest—no, two
quests that are linked. The first quest is simple to discern. He
wishes to become Elizabeth's champion in the tournament. I
sense a trinity—Elizabeth, Catherine and another. Could it be
Isobel? I also sense a trinity of emotions—ambition, affection
and animosity. His second quest is matrimony with Catherine.
The ambition is connected to Elizabeth and the affection is
linked to Catherine. Animosity is for the third female—possibly
Isobel, if she refuses her consent.* Hepburn's grip tightened on
the bowl of the pipe, but he received no further impressions. He
finished his ale, made his way to the vicinity of Pembroke's
chambers and waited for him to appear.

Hepburn concealed himself for over an hour before Herbert
left his rooms. The earl wore a dark cloak, and Patrick, sensing
that he was on his way to an assignation, followed the tall, fair
man. Pembroke left Whitehall and made his way to Canon Row,
nearby. Patrick saw him meet a youth also garbed in a long,
dark cloak. The two spoke and seemed to have an altercation.
Hepburn suddenly sensed that the black-haired youth was a female dressed as a male.

"Hellcat!" he muttered. "Dressing as a boy is just the sort of
impulsive behavior the little bitch would indulge!"

Hepburn perceived that things were not going well between
the pair as Pembroke strode away, back toward the palace, and
the small dark female stood looking forlorn before she turned
away. Hepburn crushed the urge to stick his dirk between the

courtier's ribs and, instead, strode across the street. His long legs soon closed the distance between himself and the girl. He reached out a powerful hand, gripped her shoulder and spun her to face him. The female was pretty, but she was not Catherine.

The small young woman stared up at the dark giant who had accosted her and almost fainted from fright.

She was not any more shocked than Hepburn, however. "I humbly beg your pardon, mistress! I thought you were an acquaintance of mine. Please don't be afraid; I mean you no harm."

He cursed under his breath as she hurried away. Fury at Catherine had blinded him to all reason. Since the moment he met her she'd had the ability to affect his dreams, his thoughts, his moods and his actions. Hepburn was unused to anyone else's influence; it chafed him like a burr beneath a horse's saddle. Irritated beyond normal, Patrick went back to Whitehall and found David, and the pair went back to the ship to sleep aboard.

The following day, Hepburn issued a challenge to Pembroke, in the name of the Black Leopard, which was the device that decorated his breastplate and shield. Pembroke was jousting as the Golden Flame. Many jousters used this custom, and before the day was out Patrick had also challenged the Raven's Wing and the Crimson Dragon.

November 17 dawned crisp and sunny. Old Whitehall Palace had a festive air about it today; banners flew everywhere, emblazoned with ELIZABETH REGINA and pronouncing that it was Accession Day.

As Catherine took her seat beside Philadelphia in the tiltyard stands, her outfit drew gasps from many of the other ladies of the Court. Cat was in her glory being the center of attention.

"This is rather exciting, don't you think? Men poking each other with huge phallic symbols should prove entertaining."

Catherine laughed. "It's definitely a cockfight!"

"Poor Kate has been chosen to sit with Her Majesty, whom I warrant is in a demanding mood. Ah, well, better her than me, darling. Oh, look, the parade is starting."

Fifty Yeomen of the Guard in full pomp were followed by dozens of trumpeters and drummers. Then those taking part in the joust rode by on curveting mounts caparisoned in brilliant silks.

"The Crimson Dragon is Cumberland! See the queen's glove on his helmet? He wears the damn thing as a symbol of chivalry," Philadelphia declared.

By the time the first pair of combatants entered the lists, the crowd was cheering and stamping its feet, partly to keep warm. Cat recognized that the Golden Flame was the Earl of Pembroke. As he couched his lance and started to gallop, she stood up and began to shout encouragement. When he unseated the Raven's Wing, Cat's cheers were drowned out by everyone else's.

The next two jousts were both declared draws, and Philadelphia bought herself and Cat cups of spiced hippocras to warm their blood. A frown marred Cat's brow as she studied the Black Leopard. Garbed in sable armor, he wore black from plume to spurs. In the recesses of her mind, a memory stirred. He defeated his opponent with ease, but Cat reminded herself that Pembroke had already unseated the same opponent in an earlier joust.

"The Black Leopard's a dangerous-looking devil." Philadelphia licked her lips. "Big with it, too!"

Cat remembered at Crichton she had sat in a chair whose wooden arms were carved leopards. *Hepburn leopards,* Patrick had told her. A frisson of excitement rippled through her. The thought danced away from her as the Golden Flame took on the Crimson Dragon and defeated him. Cat sat basking in reflected glory, since many at Court were aware that Pembroke was pursuing her.

One by one the challengers were defeated, and in the early afternoon only two champions remained for the final joust: the Golden Flame and the Black Leopard.

"Darling, you won't be too disappointed if Pembroke goes down in defeat, will you?" Philadelphia teased.

"He won't be defeated! He's the Queen's Champion."

"Well, my money's on the big fellow. Their lances may be the same length," she said bawdily, "but I wager the Black Leopard wields his great weapon with more staying power."

Cat watched the pair of combatants as they entered the lists.

It was like a contest between good and evil, light and darkness. The Golden Flame, mounted upon his milk white steed, saluted Elizabeth while the crowd roared. The Black Leopard, astride the huge black stallion, dropped his visor and couched his lance.

The baton fell and clods of earth flew into the air. Hepburn visualized his lance point striking the hostile shield with such force his challenger was flung from the saddle. A split second later it happened exactly as he had envisioned.

The white steed galloped from the lists. The Golden Flame lay prone, unmoving. A woman screamed. Pembroke's squire ran onto the field. Catherine jumped to her feet, nimbly ran down the steps of the tiered stands and rushed to the wooden barrier. The Black Leopard, still mounted, blocked her view.

Hepburn looked down through the slit in his visor and saw Catherine. His breath caught in his throat at the exquisite beauty arrayed in white velvet, her delicate face framed in white swansdown, her golden eyes glittering with apprehension. He raised his visor so that she could see his eyes.

Cat looked up into the black eyes and recoiled. "You!" Her gaze swept over the crumpled heap of the Golden Flame. "You've murdered him!" she accused.

"Nay, I've only muddied him and laid his pride in the dust."

My pride too, you arrogant Scots swine, and not the first time.

Pembroke's squire helped him struggle to his feet, and a great cheer went up from the stands. Cat raised her chin and went back to Philadelphia, valiantly trying to not feel humiliated. When she sat down, Philadelphia took her hand.

"It's Hepburn," Cat said in a tight voice.

"Yes, I rather thought it might be." *He lost no time in coming to place his brand on his possession.* She squeezed Cat's hand.

Elizabeth raised her royal hand and beckoned the two jousters. A hush fell over the crowd. The Black Leopard dismounted and gave his horse and his lance to his squire. Then he walked over to where Pembroke's shattered lance lay in the dust. He picked up the queen's favor, bowed gallantly to his vanquished opponent and handed him the fluttering silk banner. The crowd cheered wildly.

The two men approached Elizabeth and knelt. She told them to rise and then said something that none but the two combatants heard. The man in sable armor bent his head and spoke words for her ears alone.

Her Majesty the queen stood and raised both arms for silence. "The Black Leopard graciously disqualifies himself on the grounds that he is not an Englishman. We therefore declare that the Golden Flame is Queen's Champion of the Tourney. However, I invite both champions to present their shields so that they may be displayed in the Shield Gallery." The crowd, thoroughly enjoying the spectacle, gave them a standing ovation.

"Gracious?" Cat hissed. "Hepburn has never acted graciously in his life!"

"Grace is better suited to a woman . . . Hepburn is all man."

Cat flushed, remembering. "I'm freezing, Philadelphia," she lied. "I really must go in now. I shall see you this evening."

Catherine always took great care with her coiffure, but for tonight's festivities she took special pains fashioning an upswept style with loose curls about her face. Maggie helped her thread a string of crystal droplets that resembled tiny icicles through her tresses. Her white velvet gown, with the shoulder cape and hood removed, was severely plain, except for its deep-cut décolletage. When the white satin sleeves encrusted with crystal beads were attached, however, the gown became spectacular.

Maggie fastened the delicate ruff around her neck. "I hear Lord Stewart put on quite a show at the joust today."

"Yes, he did make a spectacle of himself." Cat looked at her reflection in the mirror. *I'll show him!* She licked her lips and pinched her cheeks. *I'll show him what a prize he has lost!*

Isobel came into her bedchamber carrying a small posy of white Tudor roses. "This just arrived for you, Catherine. I believe it is from your devoted admirer," she said coyly.

"Oh, how lovely! They must have been grown in the royal hothouse." She lifted them, breathed in their fragrant scent and sighed. "An Elizabethan courtier is the epitome of gallantry."

Cat arrived in the Privy Chamber, where the play was to be presented early, followed by the banquet. She spotted Kate and Philadelphia and joined them.

"Catherine, you look absolutely divine," Kate said. "Elizabeth will likely be late tonight. She's in one of her fussy moods. She kept poor Mary Fitton on the run all day fetching wine, then rosewater to dilute it, then glowing coals for her hand warmer, then hot bricks for her feet. I hope she didn't catch cold."

"Or we'll all suffer," Philadelphia said dryly.

"The Globe Players have arrived. I understand we have William Herbert to thank for arranging the play," Kate said.

"Yes, Shakespeare is a personal friend of his," Cat confirmed.

"It's Pembroke's shining hour, first as the Golden Flame and now as Elizabeth's golden-haired patron of drama."

"It's a romance," Cat told Philadelphia. "*Love's Labour's Lost.*"

"Some romances are full of drama . . . if you're lucky, darling."

Catherine saw her aunt Beth across the chamber and used her as an excuse to move away from Philadelphia before she made any more innuendos about Patrick Hepburn. *Hellfire! I must have conjured him.* Cat knew she would never reach Beth before Hepburn's long strides overtook her, so she stopped and, raising her chin, struck a challenging pose as the black-clad devil bore down upon her.

She dazzled his eyes. It was as if her white gown drew all the light and held it. *Mine!* He felt completely possessive of her. His mouth curved in a sensual smile as he looked down at her. "I'm glad you like my flowers, Catherine."

"*Your* flowers?" Her hands clutched the posy desperately as she searched for a cutting remark. Heat sliced to her belly because of his closeness, and her eyes lowered to the roses. With dismay she saw that he had made her crush the delicate flowers. "They are lovely; allow me to share them with you." Impulsively, she raised her hands high and showered his shoulders with crushed rose petals.

She tried to walk away but was horrified to feel his powerful fingers clamped about her wrist, holding her captive. Her eyes blazed with fury. "My lord, you are hurting me . . . again."

Hepburn brushed a petal from his shoulder. His gaze was a promise and a threat. "You can look at the bruise in bed tonight."

When he was ready, and not before, he released her.

By the time Cat reached Beth's side, an amused Philadelphia was there before her. "Love's labor's lost, indeed!" she murmured.

Her Majesty arrived with six of her ladies in attendance, and when she was seated it was the signal for the play to begin. Catherine tried to focus on the story unfolding before her, but her attention kept wandering. She constantly exchanged smiles with Pembroke, who was seated near the queen, but her thoughts were filled with another, whose presence was far too compelling. She could still feel his touch, and her traitorous body seemed to yearn for it, even though it had been cruel.

With difficulty she forced her mind away from Hepburn and tried to concentrate on the black-eyed Rosaline. When she'd seen the play in the theatre where the stage was far away, the fact that the actors were all male hadn't been noticeable. This close, however, it was most distracting to watch the falsetto-voiced Rosaline deliver his lines with exaggerated female gestures. Cat's glance searched the audience until she caught a glimpse of Hepburn. He was making no effort to mask contemptuous amusement at the ridiculous males who were pretending to be the opposite sex. Cat looked away quickly. *A pox on the patronizing devil!*

When the play was over the courtiers moved to the banqueting hall and milled about, exchanging pleasantries and gossip until the queen and her ladies arrived and were seated.

The Earl of Pembroke made his bow and Elizabeth invited him to sit on her right, at the table of honor. Her penetrating glance scanned the hall, missing little. She soon found the man she was seeking because of his great height and beckoned Hepburn with a regal hand. He too was invited to join her at the table of honor and given a seat on Her Majesty's far left.

The moment Patrick sat down he sensed a familiar presence. He looked down into the face of the female beside him and saw the young woman he had encountered last night, who had been garbed in male attire. He felt her panic as she recognized him. He had lost no time learning the identity of the lady who'd rendezvoused with Pembroke. "Do not be afraid, Mary," he said softly.

She clutched his arm. "Pray, m'lord, do not betray me."

He allowed his senses to enfold her as she touched him, and through tactile sensory perception he knew that a man was betraying her. Her fear was palpable, as was the fact that she was with child. He covered her hand with his. "I do not betray."

His strength infused her, and she knew she could trust him.

"I understand your plight." He held her gaze with his. "Do not protect him. Do not shoulder this burden alone. Name him."

Her lashes came down and, strangely, she felt imbued with courage. She lifted her hand from his sleeve. "Thank you, m'lord."

After the banquet, there was dancing in the Privy Chamber, but Elizabeth summoned Kate, her favorite Lady of the Bedchamber. "I fear I have a cold coming upon me. You know how I loathe anyone knowing that I feel ill. Put me to bed quietly, Kate."

Pembroke, emboldened by the absence of Elizabeth's gimlet eye, asked to partner Lady Catherine in the dance, not once but again and again. He wore a flame-colored doublet whose sleeves were slashed with gold and which played counterpoint to Catherine's glittering snow-white gown, and the pair drew every eye in the chamber and guaranteed that they were the center of attention.

Cat caught her mother's stare, which showed her disapproval of the number of times she had allowed Pembroke to partner her; it made her feel defiant. She looked up at William and gave him a radiant smile.

Emboldened by Catherine's receptive mood, he bent to whisper in her ear. "Are you ready for the question, my sweet?"

Cat fought back a tremor of panic. Then Hepburn strolled by with Mary Fitton on his arm. *He spent the entire meal absorbed in that promiscuous little baggage, who is only seventeen years old!* Cat gave William a coy glance. "Are you ready for the answer?"

"Lady Catherine, will you become my Countess of Pembroke?"

She answered impulsively, giving herself no time to change her mind. "It would be my great honor, William."

Cat could not resist going down to the royal dining hall for breakfast. She knew she would be the focus of every conversation. Rumors and whispers spread like the conflagration of wildfire, and she wanted to bask in the warmth of the spotlight. She might not love William, but she loved being the envy of every lady at Court.

Elizabeth arrived with the same ladies who had attended her

the evening before. Cat's heart went out to Kate, who looked as if she'd had an exhausting night.

As was the custom, the queen's dishes were tasted then presented to her. Her Majesty took a small portion of eggs and began to eat. She suddenly threw down her napkin and pushed the gold plate away, her black eyes glittering with fury. "Fitton, taste the food in every dish. I find these eggs unpalatable!"

A look of horror came over the white face of Mary Fitton as she lifted her tasting knife and slowly began with the first dish. Bravely she managed to swallow the rich food from six dishes before she began to vomit. It splashed upon the queen's tablecloth and then the plush carpet as she spewed her heart up.

Elizabeth jumped to her feet, livid at the spectacle and her suspicions of what had caused the explosive eruption. "Yesterday you were dizzy and almost fainted, Mistress Fitton. Today you have morning sickness. I warrant you are with child!"

The lady-in-waiting was sobbing as the ever-kind Kate brought a linen napkin dipped in rosewater and gently wiped her mouth.

"Stand back, Kate! The disgraceful strumpet does not deserve your ministrations. Who is the father? Name him immediately!"

Mary Fitton sank to her knees before the wrathful Elizabeth and bent her head, too afraid to lift her eyes to her sovereign. "The father is William Herbert, Your Majesty," Mary whispered.

"The Earl of Pembroke?" Elizabeth shrilled. "Guards, arrest Pembroke and lodge him in the Tower of London. Take this woman to the Tower also. Remove her from my sight!"

As Kate rushed to Elizabeth's side and began to beseech her in a low voice, Catherine sat stunned, questioning if she had heard aright, almost believing she was dreaming. *This cannot be happening. It is a nightmare from which I must awaken.*

For a full two minutes she denied the reality of what was happening, then a wave of humiliation, embarrassment and shame washed over her. Cat knew she could not leave before the queen left the chamber. She sat still as death, trying to seem invisible, as the pieces of her life at Court shattered and fell about her in tiny, jagged shards.

Chapter Twenty-two

I sobel Spencer paced the floor in agitation as a case of the vapors overwhelmed her. "The queen's wrath knows no bounds! Her courtiers are wicked to the bone, licentious to the core, male and female alike! If she learns Pembroke has been openly courting you, we will both be *persona non grata*," she fretted.

Catherine sat on her bed wishing with all her heart that she had not encouraged William Herbert. She had acted impulsively in the face of Hepburn's cruel rejection, needing to prove to herself and the world that she could attract a wealthy noble. *If only I had not flaunted Pembroke's open courtship of me before everyone. The Court will never stop laughing at me!* She glanced at Maggie, who hovered in the doorway, and saw the pity in her eyes. Cat recoiled; she could survive laughter, though it would maul her pride, but pitying glances from other females would destroy her.

A tap on the door turned out to be from Philadelphia. She came into Catherine's bedchamber to impart the latest news. "Kate begged Her Majesty to show pity for Mary. The Tower is no place for a frightened young girl who is carrying a child. Once some of the queen's vitriolic fury abated, she put the girl in the care of Lady Hawkins. She has ordered the Earl of Pembroke be imprisoned in the Fleet until he agrees to marry her lady-in-waiting."

"The strumpet does not deserve kindness!" Isobel hissed.

Catherine, able to put herself in the frightened Mary's place, did not agree. "Mother, she will need care if she is *enceinte*."

Philadelphia spoke directly to Cat. "What will you do?"

"I shall go to Hertfordshire," Cat said decisively, as it

dawned on her that she had nowhere else she could go. Hertford, she thanked God, was her solution and her salvation.

"Spencer Park is perfect!" Philadelphia declared. "You should spend more time at your country estate. A steady diet of Court life is unhealthy. Poor Kate has already caught the queen's cold and should be abed herself instead of cosseting Elizabeth."

"Oh, dear. Please give her my love. Tell her I shall write to her when Maggie and I get settled in Hertford."

"And I shall write to you, darling. I know you will want to be kept abreast of all the titillating details of the *cause célèbre*."

By the time Philadelphia left, Maggie had already dragged out the traveling trunks. Cat, suddenly imbued with energy, did most of her own packing, while Isobel fell into a chair, weak with relief that a solution to her devastating dilemma had been found.

Patrick Hepburn had slept in Robert Carey's empty chamber at Whitehall, which was next to the suite of rooms belonging to Robert's sisters Kate and Philadelphia. When one of their servants arrived with a late breakfast, the man could not wait to impart details of the shocking scandal that was sweeping the palace.

Once the servant left, Patrick consumed his food, deep in thought. After the tournament, when Elizabeth had beckoned him and he had removed his helmet, he had studied her intently. In the few months since he had last seen her, she had aged markedly. He had been struck by the fact that nobody mentioned it or even seemed to notice. Apparently to her courtiers the queen was a permanent fixture. *The finger of Death has already touched her.*

The Carey servant had told him Kate had caught the queen's cold. *Elizabeth is ill and it exacerbated her temper so that she lashed out at Mary Fitton.* He had known matters would come to a head, but he had not expected it to happen immediately. Apparently the young maid of honor had taken his advice to heart and named the man. Since the man was Pembroke, it fit into his plans perfectly.

Hepburn locked the door to Robert's chamber and knocked on Kate's door. When Philadelphia opened it, he thanked her for the breakfast and pressed the key into her hand. "Please advise Kate to put her own health before Elizabeth's." When she nodded her agreement, he asked a question. "Hertfordshire, I assume?"

Philadelphia smiled. "You assume correctly, Lord Stewart."

As the coach swept along on its twenty-mile journey to Hertford, with both Catherine and Maggie wrapped in warm traveling rugs and their feet propped on a brass foot warmer filled with hot coals, Maggie took a deep breath and broached the sensitive topic. "I am sorry you are heartbroken, my lamb."

"Heartbroken?" Catherine gave a short, brittle laugh. "There is no need to waste your pity, Maggie. I am humiliated and embarrassed, but, thank God, my heart was never involved. Men are such profligate, callous swine, willing to rut with any female foolish enough to lift her skirts. I have had a merciful escape." She clenched her fists inside her muff. "Two of them, in fact!"

A master hunter does not allow his prey to escape. Maggie decided to keep her thoughts about her fellow Scotsman to herself.

When the coach arrived at its destination, Mr. Burke, the steward who ran Spencer Park, tried to hide his surprise. "Lady Catherine, this is an unexpected pleasure." He directed the servants to attend to their luggage. "I shall have all the fires lit and your beds aired immediately. May I convey any special orders to Cook?"

"Thank you, Mr. Burke. No special orders for dinner tonight. Any hot food will be welcome to both of us."

Maggie gave Burke a speaking look, and he knew she would fill him in on all the details of what had brought his young mistress to her country estate at the beginning of winter.

By the time Catherine and Maggie had unpacked, the afternoon light was fading from the sky. Cat looked from the window at the frozen landscape and felt as if she had been exiled. Thinking of the lonely weeks that stretched before her made her feel almost bereft. She knew she needed something to banish the blue devils. "Do you suppose Mr. Burke has a deck of playing cards and, dare I hope, any whisky hidden away?"

"I shall go and find out. The man is so efficient, I warrant he'll be able to produce whatever ye seek."

Maggie found the steward coming from the kitchens, where he had no doubt given very specific orders to the staff regarding the needs of the young mistress of the house. "Mr. Burke, ye are no doubt in a quandary as to why we have suddenly descended upon ye."

"I assume something untoward happened at Court."

"Have ye any whisky, Mr. Burke?"

He crooked his finger, led her into the library and poured them each a dram. Then he held her chair and they sat by the fire.

"Lady Catherine is being courted by William Herbert, who has recently come into his earldom of Pembroke." When Burke made no comment, favorable or unfavorable, Maggie continued. "The wicked devil has gotten a maid of honor of Elizabeth's into trouble, and the queen has imprisoned him."

"He was a professional courtier, as I understand it, with little interest in his estate of Wilton."

Maggie marveled that Mr. Burke knew so much about the nobility. "His days at Court are finished, along with his hopes of wedding Lady Catherine. We will not speak of him again."

"Is she desperately unhappy, Maggie?"

"Not a bit of it! Shamefaced at the scandal and outraged that any man could look at another while courting her, but the wee lass will survive. Don't forget her Scots blood."

"She's a Celt through and through, like you and me, Maggie."

"Aye, and in a day or two we can expect a visit from another Celt, unless I miss my guess. Only this one has more tenacity, backbone and staying power than the rest of the pack." Maggie closed one eyelid. "I'm saying no more. A wink's as good as a nod to a blind horse." She finished her drink and spotted a deck of playing cards on the desk. "I'll take these along to her, and ye can take her a decanter of this fine malt whisky, but fer God's sake don't give it to her until she's had dinner, or Mistress Impulsive will drink herself into a stupor within the hour."

"Thank you for confiding in me, Maggie."

Due to Mr. Burke's meticulous instructions in the kitchen, dinner was most successful. When his young mistress repaired to the sitting room he brought a decanter of whisky and discreetly placed it on a side table. He left and instructed a servant to plenish a guest room, inspected the chamber afterward, and then went to the stables to direct one of the grooms to select a palfrey for Lady Catherine's use while she was in residence at Spencer Park. "My compliments on the cleanliness of the stables. Another arrival is expected soon, so you had best ready a stall." Burke raised his head as he heard the clop of horse hooves. "Sooner than anticipated, by the sound of things."

Hepburn dismounted from Valiant just as the steward emerged from the stables. "Mr. Burke, do you perhaps remember me?" He held out his hand. "Patrick Hepburn—I had the privilege of visiting Spencer Park a few months back with the Carey brothers."

"I do indeed remember you, Lord Stewart. Your Scottish lands adjoin the Earl of Winton's, if I recall correctly. Spencer Park is honored to welcome you once again."

"The honor is mine, Mr. Burke. I've brought Lady Catherine's palfrey from Richmond and also brought a gift, as any guest worth his salt should. These yearling colts are horses I captured from a wild Scottish herd. Their blood will strengthen your herd."

"They are indeed fine specimens. A groom is preparing a stall for your personal mount, so I'll instruct him to ready a few more."

"That is most thoughtful. Tomorrow, I shall come and put them out to pasture for the daylight hours. They are hardened to more severe cold temperatures than you have here in Hertfordshire."

Hepburn unstrapped his luggage from the animals before he turned them over to Spencer grooms.

As Burke walked to the house with Hepburn, each carrying bags, he said, "A guest room has already been prepared." He hesitated, then plunged in. "Are we to expect fireworks, my lord?"

Hepburn grinned. "I hope not, Mr. Burke. A flash of lightning from Lady Catherine, followed by a loud clap of thunder from me, will most likely put an end to the threatening storm."

"Very good, my lord. I will take your bags up to your room."

Patrick followed the light silently, then stood at the threshold of the sitting room. "Drowning your sorrows, Hellcat?"

Catherine spilled the whisky she was sipping onto her playing cards. She jumped up, her eyes flashing with anger. "How dare you intrude here?" She raised her voice. "Mr. Burke! Mr. Burke!"

"He can't hear you. He's taken my luggage upstairs."

"Maggie!" But Cat saw that Maggie's chair was empty. She

had laid her cards on the table and quietly disappeared. Cat glared daggers at Hepburn. "The only *sorrow* I'd like to drown is you!"

"I'm thrilled you still have such passionate feelings for me."

"It's called *loathing*! You rejected my passion, you brute!"

"Damn it, Catherine, I did no such thing!" he roared. "You were in mortal danger. I sent you home where you would be safe."

"Safe? The moment you rid yourself of me, I was kidnapped!"

"Aye, and I mortgaged Crichton to ransom you. I'd do that for no other soul on earth. But what thanks do I get? The moment you are back at Court you fall into the arms of the first wealthy noble who stiffens at the sight of you."

"There is no need to be offensive, Lord Stewart."

"How the devil can you say that with a straight face? You love and adore anything offensive—almost as much as I do."

She was unable to hide her amusement, her mouth curved in a smile.

"That's better." He strode toward her. "Now I want to hear you purr." His arms captured her and his mouth took possession.

His body was so powerful, it made her go weak in the knees, but it also turned her blood to wine—intoxicating, deep red wine. Cat opened her mouth to his insistent tongue and dug her nails into his arms, moaning softly at the pure pleasure he gave her.

"You taste of whisky—a flavor irresistible to a Scot."

"You devil! One minute I want to scratch out your eyes and the next I want to be stroked like a spoiled tabby cat."

He picked her up, walked to the fire and sat down with her in his lap. His teeth nipped her ear. "I like my Cat to have claws."

"*Your* Cat?" she challenged, rubbing her bum against his cock.

He cupped her face with his palms and gazed at her. "At the joust, when I saw you in white velvet and fur, you looked like a prized Persian cat. Your beauty stopped the breath in my throat."

His words melted her icy heart. "Flattery means naught to me."

"Lying little bitch. You thrive on it. You love being told you have the most fashionable gowns, glorious hair, smallest waist, prettiest legs, lush titties, and the sauciest tattoo."

She wound her arms about his neck. "My lover has told you all my secrets." She touched the tip of her tongue to his lips, knowing it would tempt him to devour her mouth.

He kissed her senseless, then set her on her feet so that he could get them some whisky. When he drew close he saw her mouth and her breasts quiver for his touch. "I'm jealous of the firelight that spills over your delicate curves, touching you everywhere, warming you, mesmerizing your gaze."

"You do that, Patrick, not the firelight."

He drew her down upon the couch and proceeded to prove her right. He kissed and tasted and whispered and touched for hours, until the candles guttered and the logs on the fire dropped to ash. Then he picked her up in his arms, held her high against his heart and carried her upstairs.

Though the physical toll he paid was high, Hepburn was too shrewd and calculating to give her what she needed. He set her on her feet and dropped a kiss on her shiny black curls. "Good night, Catherine. Sleep well."

Cat swayed, dizzy from his closeness. She had forgotten how big he was, forgotten how wild her response was to this untamed male she desired above all others. She heard a door close, and when she opened her eyes found herself standing alone. *"Peste!"* she swore.

"Slug a bed."

Catherine's eyes flew open as she felt the covers lifted off her. The man she had been dreaming about had hold of her ankles and was rudely pulling her from her bed.

"It snowed last night. Hurry and get dressed. I want a tour of Spencer Park."

"In the snow?" she asked in disbelief, thinking it would be much cozier if Patrick joined her in the warm bed, rather than her joining him in the cold snow.

"Yes, it's beautiful out there. Wear that white furry thing."

She stared at her chamber door after he disappeared. "He's elusive as bloody mercury!" Yet she knew he was more like a lodestone, irresistibly attracting and luring her to follow him.

The door opened again, and her face fell when she saw it was Maggie.

"Have this warm drink and a bite of food before ye go rushing off to see the surprise his lordship has planned."

Catherine's eyes sparkled. "A surprise? For me?"

"No, fer the scullery maid . . . of course it's fer ye, my lamb."

Cat, her mouth crammed full of bread and honey, said, "Hewantsmetowearthewhitevelvet."

"I understand . . . thousands wouldn't." Maggie produced the gown.

Cat, hastily rinsing the soap from her face, blew a bubble into the air as she instructed, "Fur cape, too."

Maggie rolled her eyes. "Slow down, lass. Make him wait."

"That's what I've always done with gentlemen before, but Hepburn is not like other men."

"Well, for one thing he's no gentleman, but therein lies the fatal attraction," Maggie said knowingly.

When Catherine was dressed, she pushed her feet into fur-lined boots, picked up her muff and ran downstairs. She paused deliberately to catch her breath, and then with a feigned casual gesture slowly opened the front door. Her languid posture vanished immediately and her face turned radiant as she saw Hepburn awaiting her, holding the reins of a two-horse sleigh.

"Patrick, a sleigh-ride will be so exciting!"

He leered suggestively. "English, you have no idea." He watched as her cheeks turned a delicate pink, and his heart turned over in his breast at her exquisite beauty.

As she climbed in beside him, she saw that he had piled in cushions and traveling rugs that he must have gotten from Maggie. He tucked the rug about her, then flicked the reins for their ride through the winter wonderland of Spencer Park.

In reality it was Hepburn who showed off the property to Cat.

Hundreds of shaggy-coated, longhorn cattle roamed about the snow-covered pastures, and he explained that they were bred to withstand cold weather. "Did you know these cows of yours supply the Court with all the butter it uses? No, I didn't think you knew."

Since the river Lea was frozen, the horses took the sleigh across the ice to where the fields of the home farm lay fallow beneath their blanket of snow. "Did you know your main crops are rye and barley and, come spring, Mr. Burke is considering hops? No? You are such an ignorant little wench."

She laughed up at him saucily. "You are a marvelous tutor. I enjoy your lessons and especially your initiations."

"Good. My tutelage has only just begun." He stopped the sleigh on the summit of a hill where the vista of Spencer Park stretched out before them. *Mine!* Then he looked down at the beautiful female beside him and the word repeated in his brain. *Mine! All I have to do is reach out and take it.*

He reached out and enfolded her in his warm embrace. In truth he could wait no longer to taste her. He placed firm fingers beneath her chin, gazed into her radiant, eager face, then took possession of her mouth. Heat leaped between them as their desire ignited, and she turned hot and sweet with passion.

"Catherine, I want you to marry me." He saw her pupils dilate and knew he would get his way. "I know you need permission from both your mother and the queen, so I am willing to wait until you come of age. I want you to pledge yourself to me in a secret betrothal. Your birthday is March thirty-first. Before April dawns, I will come and wed you. I give you my sacred promise, Catherine."

"I hereby plight thee my troth!" Cat cried impulsively.

He took the leopard signet ring from his little finger and slipped it onto her left hand. Though he had a wedding and a betrothal ring, he used one of his own so that his proposal would seem spontaneous rather than premeditated.

The ring was too large for her small finger, but she clenched her hand so it wouldn't fall off. "A Hepburn leopard," she said happily. "Wild and untamed." She lifted her lips to seal their promise with a heart-stopping kiss.

He pulled her hard against his side with one powerful arm and picked up the reins with his other hand. He stopped the sleigh at the back door of the hall and, on cue, Mr. Burke came out with hot mulled cider. Patrick winked at her over the rim of his cup. "I'm not done with you yet."

Fortified with the hot, spicy drink, they drove to the stables. He reined in the horses, turned them over to a groom, pulled aside her traveling rug, then jumped from the sleigh. "Come on."

Cat took his hand and went inside with him. "Oh, Patrick."

Tears flooded her eyes when she saw Jasmine in one of the stalls. "How did you know I longed to have my palfrey here?" "I have second sight. Had you forgotten?" he said lightly.

Catherine's heart overflowed with gratitude and love as she stroked Jasmine's nose. "My beautiful girl . . . how I've missed you."

She watched with growing excitement as he saddled the white mare and his own Valiant. Then he lifted her with powerful hands and kissed her before sitting her in the saddle.

As they walked their horses toward a long pasture, he said, "I brought you a gift."

Cat saw the pair of colts immediately and sadness flickered in her eyes, at war with the happiness bubbling inside her. "These are from the wild herd we rode with on the happiest day of my life. But, Patrick, mayhap it would have been kinder if you had left them with their herd to run untamed."

"They are young males—bachelors. By spring the herd stallion would not tolerate them near his mares. He would kill them rather than let them mate with his females."

"That seems so savage and cruel."

"It's the nature of the beast. Most males feel that way toward their chosen mate." He looked at her possessively. "I know I do."

Cat smiled. She rather liked the idea that he'd kill for her.

"Come on," he urged, "let's gallop with them again."

The pair of wild colts took off like lightning before Patrick and Cat could reach them. When they got to the end of the long pasture, they circled back. Valiant soon caught up with them, but Jasmine was on the third gallop around the field before she came level with the other three horses. Catherine's blood was up, and excitement rushed through her veins, making her feel more alive than she had since they'd ridden with the wild herd in Scotland. *How many hours before dark, so we can go to bed and make love?* She threw back her head and laughed with pure joy.

Patrick laughed too. "In a few days I'll have them eating out of your hand. They'll love it here in the south of England."

When they tired of riding with the wild colts, Patrick took Cat to Hunsdon Grange to visit John Carey and his wife, Mary.

John picked up Catherine and swung her about. "Heavens! I

haven't seen you since you were a little girl . . . well, you are still a little girl, except you are older."

"Catherine, what a beauty you have turned into," Mary enthused.

"Promise you'll come and visit every week that you are here in Hertford? If I promise not to let the children put their sticky fingers on your lovely white velvet, will you stay for lunch?"

"Of course we will, and they can put their sticky fingers anywhere they please. Lord Stewart is mad about children!"

The afternoon light had faded from the sky as they rode back, their stirrups almost touching, both of them counting the moments until they could go upstairs and shut out the world.

Back at Spencer Park, they had a light supper together. Cat hadn't the faintest notion what she was eating. She couldn't take her eyes off Patrick as the longing inside her became unbearable. She was all ashiver with anticipation for what was yet to come, and the minutes dragged by so slowly, she wanted to scream.

"You go up first," he murmured softly. "Make sure the adjoining door is unlocked." Hepburn was at the end of his endurance.

"Maggie, I think I'll go up to bed. The fresh winter air has made me so tired." She stood up and yawned.

Maggie followed her upstairs, closed her curtains and turned down her bed. "It's very early. Are ye all right, my lamb?"

"I feel fabulous. Maggie, where's the key to this door?"

"Ye don't need a key. The door is locked."

"I would feel much better if I had the key. Where is it?"

"It's in my pocket."

Catherine's eyes glittered with stubborn determination as she held out her hand for the key.

"Ye seem to have gotten over Will in the blink of an eye."

"Will who?" Catherine asked blankly.

"Did Lord Stewart ask ye to wed him?"

"That's none of your business!"

"It is if ye want the key. Did he ask ye to wed him?"

"Oh, yes, yes, Maggie, but it's a secret!"

"A secret betrothal?"

Cat nodded and showed her Hepburn's ring. "Promise you won't breathe a word of this to anyone?"

"My lips are sealed." Maggie handed her the key and rolled her eyes. "As if a locked door would stop him."

Cat hugged her tightly. "Thank you. Hurry! Hurry!"

Maggie went back downstairs in time to hear Patrick bid good night to Mr. Burke. She waited until she was alone with the steward, then she lowered her voice to a confidential murmur. "They are secretly betrothed!"

Mr. Burke did not let on that Hepburn had already confided in him. "Thank you for placing your trust in me, Maggie."

Chapter Twenty-three

*P*atrick crossed her chamber in three strides and lifted her high against his heart. "I thought the bloody day would never end!"

"It hasn't ended . . . it's only just begun." She traced the outline of his lips with a fingertip, then kissed him deeply.

He set her feet to the carpet and turned her about so that he could undo her gown. "Hold still so I can undress you. My hands are big and clumsy on these tiny buttons."

"I hardly believe I'm the first female you've disrobed."

His teeth worried her ear. "My previous conquests have always managed to disrobe themselves."

"Cocksure devil!" She rubbed her bum across his hard thighs. "Damn, I'm not even tall enough to reach your naughty parts."

"I like you small." He opened the gown and slid his hands inside to cup her breasts. "You're small everywhere but here." He kissed the nape of her neck and had her naked in a trice. When he sat her on the bed to remove her hose and garters, she teased the bulge between his legs with her toes. He grabbed her foot to tickle it and she rolled onto her knees and tried to scamper away. In a flash he was on top of her, holding her fast.

She couldn't stop laughing. "You brute! How much ransom did you pay for me?"

He dropped a kiss on her bare bottom, right above her saucy tattoo. "Five." Patrick removed his doublet and his shirt.

She sat up on the bed and said ruefully, "Poor Patrick, I'm sorry you had put a five-hundred-pound mortgage on Crichton."

"It was five thousand," he said, amused.

"You paid five *thousand* for me?"

"Yes, so consider yourself bought and paid for, Catherine."

"I love the way you roll the *r* in Catherine. It sends shivers up my spine." She watched intently as he unfastened his belt. "Since my services are paid for, Lord Bloody Stewart, which would you like me to perform first?"

With a straight face, he said, "How about removing my boots?"

"You devil!" She stood up on the bed, grabbed his hair and pulled. He tumbled her down beside him, crying out in mock pain. Then he removed his boots and breeches and lifted her on top of his hard body, holding her captive for his loving.

Hepburn's dark face hardened. "My beautiful little Hellcat. I've never had such intense feelings for anyone before."

"Of course you haven't! I don't want you to merely *love* me. I want you to adore me, to worship me and dote on me." Her hair cascaded down against his throat. "I want you to *treasure* me."

Her words caught him off guard. Cat took it for granted that he loved her, though he had been careful never to declare such a thing in his life. Then all rational thoughts fled as he rolled her to the submissive position and made passionate love to her. Though they drew it out for more than an hour, sharing countless kisses, it was not nearly enough to satisfy them. As soon as she was able to catch her breath, Catherine came over him in the dominant position and they began to make love all over again.

Cat awoke before sunup, when the bed began to feel cool. She sat up and saw that she was alone. Hepburn and his clothes had disappeared through the connecting door, for appearance's sake. Her lips curved in a wicked smile. The only trace he'd left behind was on her sheets. She padded, naked, to the window, threw back the curtains and then climbed back into bed to watch the pale winter sun rise. She hugged her knees and knew she had never been happier in her entire life. A slight shadow clouded her thoughts: *He will only stay until the end of November. How will I bear it when he goes back to Scotland?*

Later in the day, she sat on the pasture fence, watching Patrick work with the wild colts. To Catherine he had never seemed to be a patient man, but when it came to horses, he was patience personified. He stood watching them for the better part of an hour, waiting until they came to him. When they made the first move and came closer, he spoke in a quiet, soothing voice, murmuring and whispering magic words that lured them to him.

Finally, the dominant one of the pair nudged his leather jac. Then, and only then, did he give it the apple he carried.

After another hour had passed and gray clouds began to gather, Patrick lifted Catherine from her perch. "Tomorrow, they will come to you. Have you decided on names for them?"

"I thought of Slate and Shale for the color of their coats, and because I want them strong and indestructible . . . like you."

"Flattery will get you anything you desire, my beauty."

She laughed up at him. "I desire *you* and *you* and *you* again."

"It's too cold out here to be naked"—he waggled black brows—"but we could use a hay-filled stall in the stables."

She punched him. "Too many grooms and horsemen in there."

He snapped his fingers. "I know! We'll go to the library."

"You cunning devil! You're too experienced at this."

"Not guilty! The library simply seems an appropriate setting for a tutor to give his pupil some private lessons."

"Pure logic. It's time that desk was put to good use."

On their way to the library, they passed Maggie. "It looks like rain, so we've decided to read," Cat declared.

"I'll order ye a fire lit in there."

"No need, Maggie, I'll do it," Patrick assured her.

Cat winked at Maggie. "He's good at lighting fires."

The serving woman's glance swept over him. "Aye, carries his own poker, I warrant. Makes me warm just looking at him."

They shut the library door and collapsed against it, laughing. "'Tis no wonder you're a saucy wench, with a tart-tongued Scotswoman like Maggie for a nursemaid."

"Growing up with her as my nurse prepared me for the rigors of having a rough Scots devil like you for a husband." She brushed against his arousal and danced away. "It's a lovely room. If you teach me something that elevates my mind, we can come again tomorrow."

On the morrow, as it turned out, they had a visitor who prevented them from dalliance in the library.

"Robert! How did you know we were here?" Cat puzzled.

"Philadelphia, of course. Here's a letter for you." As Cat opened the envelope, he grinned at Hepburn. "You lost no time getting your feet under the table."

"We need to talk," Patrick said to Robert in a low voice.

Then to Catherine, he said, "I'm taking Robert to see the colts.
Tell Cook to make something special for dinner."
As soon as the men left, Cat read her letter.

> *Dearest Catherine:*
> *The scandal is horrendous. Pembroke absolutely*
> *refuses to marry Mary Fitton. He excuses himself in a*
> *poem that is circulating the Court:*
>
> > *Then this advice, fair creature, take from me*
> > *Let none pluck fruit, unless he pluck the tree.*
> > *For if with one, with thousands thoul't turn whore.*
> > *Break ice in one place and it cracks the more.*
>
> *Kate's cold finally got the better of her and she went*
> *to bed. I've taken her place at the queen's bedside.*
> *Elizabeth is demanding at the best of times but*
> *impossible when ill.*
> *You did the right thing when you removed to*
> *Hertford. I have heard not the slightest whisper of your*
> *name in connection with Pembroke, most likely because*
> *the Court is engrossed with the Mary Fitton scandal. I*
> *shall keep you posted, darling.*
> *Love, Philadelphia*

Catherine read the letter to Maggie. "I feel so badly for poor
Mary Fitton. Pembroke is not only ungallant; he's being vicious. He's as much to blame as Mary—*more* to blame, since
she is so young! I can't believe I let him pay court to me."

"The woman always gets the mucky end of the stick in these
affairs, my lamb. Mary will have an illegitimate child, and Pembroke will be set free to go his lecherous way, I warrant."

"Maggie, I feel so guilty that Mary is disgraced and devastated, while I'm deliriously happy."

"Ye reap what ye sow in this world, lass."

Well, Mary will surely reap what Pembroke has sown! "I
must reply to Philadelphia's letter and write one to Kate too."

Patrick and Robert, their arms resting on the top rail of the
fence where the colts were pastured, had a private conversation.
"You are the one who will take James the news of Eliza-

beth's demise. Since it must be done with all speed, I advise you to start laying your plans now, Robert."

"She's ill with a cold. Do you think her death is imminent?"

"Nay. She will pass just after the spring equinox."

Robert stared at Patrick, fascinated with his prescience. "Four months . . . yes, I should make plans, lay out the shortest route, decide on stops to change the post-horses."

Patrick nodded. "You will have to carry an object taken from her person and deliver it to James so he can trust with certainty that the news you carry is gospel truth. The Stuart does not trust lightly."

"My sisters tend the queen. When Elizabeth is ill, she prefers to have Kate at her bedside. It should not prove impossible for my sisters to pass a personal object to me. But what if she refuses to name James her successor?"

"Cecil will be there. He will see to that, Robert." Hepburn placed a trusting hand on his friend's shoulder. "Come, we'll find a map and plan out your route."

They went inside and found Catherine busy writing letters. "Do you go to London from here, Robert, or north to your wife?"

"I return to London tomorrow, and then I travel north."

"I'm sorry you can spend only one night with us, but will you take these letters to your sisters? And please give Kate my wishes for her speedy recovery. She is far too selfless."

"It would be my pleasure, Catherine."

"Now that I'm in a writing mood, I shall pen a note to Liz. I hope she is well?"

"She is indeed. Married life suits us both. I recommend it." Robert was careful not to mention that Queen Anne had invited Liz for the Christmas festivities at the Scottish Court. It would prompt a hundred questions from Cat, and he must not even hint that he was working secretly for King James.

After dinner that evening the two men withdrew to the library to map out different routes from London to the Border. Catherine took the opportunity to go upstairs early so that she could lock the adjoining door between her chamber and Patrick's. Under no circumstances would she allow Hepburn to spend the night in her bed when Robert was under the same roof.

Around midnight she heard the doorknob rattle, followed by

loud scratching on the wood. Cat jumped from her bed and ran barefoot to the wide double doors. She put her lips to the keyhole and whispered, "Stop! You cannot come in, Patrick."

"Why the devil not?"

"Don't shout! Robert would call you out if he knew you had seduced me. I don't want you to have a duel!"

Patrick chuckled. Her imagination was so dramatic. "The wound you're inflicting is worse than any Robert could give me."

"Robert would lose a sword fight with you, you savage brute. Go away; go to bed!"

"There you are, Robert. Help me break down this door so I can go and ravish the little hellcat."

"You devil! He'll hear you and you don't give a damn."

"How well you know me." He finally relented. "I'm only teasing, sweetheart. Good night."

Cat went to sleep, thrilled that he'd called her sweetheart.

The next morning it was Robert who perched on the rail as he watched Patrick and Catherine lure the wild colts to their side. "When John sees these horses, he'll be green with envy."

"I'll bring your brother a wild stallion when I return."

"Before I leave today I should visit John and his family."

"I'll come with you." Cat wanted to know Robert's feelings about Hepburn's suitability for marriage.

As the pair rode together to Hunsdon Grange, Catherine asked Robert, "Do you think Hepburn would make a good husband?"

"With the right woman," he said carefully.

Cat raised her brows. "Could you explain what you mean?"

"He would be the master of his own household. Liz can wrap me around her little finger. I doubt if such feminine tactics would work on Hepburn; he's far too dominant to be manipulated. He doesn't have money to squander on luxuries that a wife might think of as necessities, especially if she were spoiled. He'd likely forbid his wife from wasting her life at Court. He'd be a powerful protector of his wife and family, though."

"This isn't the first you've thought about him as a husband."

"No. Hepburn made it plain to me that he wanted you."

Her insides melted. She did not focus on the fact that he would be dominant, or consider her spoiled. All she could think of was the fact that he wanted her and would stop at nothing to get his way. It made her blood sing with excitement.

On their ride back to Spencer Park after their visit, Cat was starry-eyed over Mary and John's happy marriage. "Their union was made in heaven. They never exchange an angry word."

"Such wedded bliss is the exception rather than the rule, Cat. Marriage with Hepburn would be nothing like that. You are extremely impulsive, and if you did something that truly angered him, I've no doubt he'd put you over his knee and tan your arse."

Patrick would never do that. He's head over heels in love with me, she thought smugly.

Before Robert left, he and Patrick closeted themselves in the library once again, while Cat regaled Maggie with the details of her visit to Hunsdon Grange. "They are such a happy, loving couple. Mary is having another baby!"

"That's the inevitable outcome of loving. Take heed."

Dear God, what if I'm having a child? I'd be in the same terrible predicament as Mary Fitton. Well, not the same, because Patrick wouldn't refuse to marry me, but Mother would die of shame and the gossip would blacken my name. Cat ran upstairs and examined her reflection in the mirror. No, she was sure she wasn't with child. Her eyes fell on Philadelphia's letter, with its accusation that Mary Fitton was a *whore.* She glanced at the connecting door and decided to leave it locked.

Robert insisted on departing before dinner, so Cat and Patrick ate alone in the big dining room. "Too bad we have to observe decorum. I'd much prefer to eat in bed," Patrick teased.

Catherine threw him a repressive look that he found hilarious. He choked on his wine. "You look pious as a nun!"

"And you look irreverent."

His grin was lecherous. "For what we are about to receive, may the Lord make us truly thankful, amen."

"Irreverent and blasphemous!"

"You sound like you've been eating pickled Bibles." His grin turned into a leer. "I promise you a religious experience!"

Though she tried not to laugh, she found it impossible. "You have a wicked humor, Hepburn."

"It's my saving grace."

"You said that before."

"It bears repeating."

She recalled other words he'd said on that fateful ride north for the wild horses: *Cold water is excellent for curbing impulses. Remember it!* She very much regretted that before the night was over, they would both need cold water. She reached for the wine decanter and then changed her mind. Her blood was on fire now; the last thing she needed was an intoxicant that would heighten her desire and make her insatiable.

As per their arrangement of two nights ago, Catherine went upstairs first, and, as usual, Maggie followed. Cat checked the adjoining door to assure herself that it was still locked, then on impulse took the key and handed it to Maggie. "You'd better take charge of this . . . I don't trust myself."

"An ounce of prevention is worth a pound of cure."

"You have a homily for everything," Cat accused.

"I'm a Celt . . . it's my nature." She drew the curtains. "There's a full moon tonight; be careful, my lamb."

"I am being careful. Good night, Maggie."

"Not only a full moon, but November twenty-fifth is St. Catherine's Day, known to the Celts as Women's Merrymaking Day."

"Enough portents. Good night."

Catherine, knowing she would find sleep elusive, decided to read. She lit another branch of candles and began to undress. She put on her night rail, slipped into bed and picked up her sketch pad. Soon, though, she was interrupted.

"Cat, the bloody door is locked!"

She caught her breath and didn't answer. Inside her eardrums she could hear her heart thudding. Or was he knocking?

"Are you there, my lovely lady?"

"Hush, Patrick . . . everyone will hear you!"

"Everyone but you, it seems. Unlock the door, Catherine."

"I . . . I don't have the key." She hesitated. "Maggie took it."

"Then I shall go and relieve her of it," he said shortly.

"No! You mustn't. Patrick, this is wrong. I forbid you—"

"Forbid?" His voice through the door was ominous.

"I'm sorry, Patrick. I'll explain in the morning."

The silence was shattered by a loud crash as Hepburn battered the double door and broke the lock. He towered before her like an avenging warrior. "You'll explain now, Hellcat."

"How dare you? How *dare* you break into my chamber like a mad bull on a rampage?"

He grabbed her by the shoulders and shook her roughly. "Never lock a door against me again!"

Anger, frustration and desire flooded her eyes with tears. She went limp beneath his hands. "Patrick, I'm afraid."

"Stop lying, you little spitfire. You're afraid of neither man nor beast!"

Cat flung away from him and grabbed the letter from Philadelphia. "Read that. They're calling Mary Fitton a *whore*! That's what I am to you . . . I'm your *whore*!"

He took her by the shoulders once more and shook her till her teeth rattled. "Never, *ever,* say that again, Catherine. You are my betrothed, my future wife. You were virgin until I made love to you." His arms enfolded her. "You are my sweetheart."

Held against his powerful body, she felt a raging lust and took a shuddering breath. "I . . . I'm afraid. Mary Fitton is having a baby, and today at the Grange I found out that Mary Carey is with child . . . I don't want us to make a baby until we're married."

"Is that what this is all about?" Patrick sounded relieved. "You can put your trust in me. I promise not to be careless."

"The queen takes it as a personal assault on her character when a lady of the Court brings disgrace upon herself. Her Majesty metes out a terrible punishment." Cat bit her lip. "Mother would die of shame if it happened to me."

His arms tightened protectively. She was so young and so vulnerable. "There are other ways, sweetheart. I promise not to do anything to put you at risk. Will that make you happy?"

She nodded solemnly and allowed him to pick her up and carry her to the bed. Already she knew that he had more control over himself than she would ever have. Once he began to kiss her and touch her intimately, her passion took over and obliterated all caution. She had an impulsive and reckless nature that seized control like a whirlwind, sweeping up everything in its path.

Patrick undressed her slowly, kissing every inch of silken skin that he exposed. By the time she was naked, he had her writhing beneath his knowing hands and his seductive mouth.

"Now you," she insisted, undoing the buttons of his shirt with impatient fingers. "I love to slide my hands over your bulging muscles and smell your man-scented skin."

When he was naked he pushed her back onto the high bed so

that her legs were draped over the edge. Then he went down on his knees, brushed aside the tiny tendrils on her plump mons and tasted her with the tip of his tongue. He slipped his hands beneath her bottom cheeks and thrilled as she arched up into his mouth without hesitation or reservation. He kissed the insides of her soft thighs until she was moaning with need, then plunged his tongue into her hot, sugared sheath.

Catherine wrapped her legs about his neck, undulating her body with the sensual rhythm of his tongue, yielding everything to his demanding mouth. Cat gloried in the freedom he had given her to be wanton, with his promise that he'd not impregnate her. She cried out at the pleasurable sensations he aroused with his powerful, wicked mouth, which took her higher and higher, until she almost reached a peak. When he deliberately withdrew, she became frenzied.

Patrick moved up over her and took possession of her lips. When she tasted herself on his mouth, she went wild. She thrashed and rolled until she gained the dominant position, then she trailed her hair from his throat to his groin, teasing, tempting, taunting him, longing to make him lose control as she had. Needing him to moan and writhe in his passion, she could resist the temptation of his phallus no longer. On impulse she took the head of his cock into her mouth and stroked him with her tongue. Her black curtain of hair concealed the sexual things she did to him, and suddenly, amazingly, she climaxed.

Chapter Twenty-four

*A*s Catherine came up through layers of heavy sleep, she knew something awaited her that she didn't want to face. She lifted her lashes and remembered. Today was December 1, and Patrick was leaving. The last week had gone by at a strangely uneven pace. The days had gone slowly, since Patrick spent many hours with Mr. Burke, learning about cattle, deciding on spring crops, going over the accounts and all the myriad things connected with a huge estate like Spencer Park. In contrast, however, the nights sped by, hurtling toward the last one they would spend together.

Catherine blushed as she remembered the intimacy of last night. Patrick had taken her fingers and showed her how to touch and stroke her own body to bring it pleasure. "I could never bring myself to do such a thing!" she had protested. "You will, Cat. There will be nights when you ache so much you won't be able to sleep without release." She pressed her hands to her hot cheeks and suddenly became aware that she was wearing earrings.

She threw back the covers and padded to her mirror. To her delight she was wearing a pair of dangling emerald earbobs. The corners of her mouth lifted. She had been so languid from his loving that she had never even felt him thread the gold wire through her earlobes. *A Borderer always gifts his wench with a bauble.* Cat shook her head to watch the emeralds swing. With her wildly disheveled hair, she looked exactly like a Borderer's wench.

Not bothering with a robe, she ran to the connecting door and turned the broken knob. Before the door swung open a feeling of dread assailed her. His bedchamber was empty, and she suddenly knew that he had not only left the room but left

Spencer Park too. He had deliberately gone while she was sleeping. "No! Patrick!" She threw open the wardrobe, knowing she would find it empty. She picked up a shirt from where he had let it fall in his haste to pack and pressed it against her face, inhaling his unmistakable male scent. *It's the only thing I'll have of him for four months.* "That's not true!" she said aloud. "I have his ring, I have the wild horses and I have his love." She smiled, remembering.

During the week that followed, she nearly went mad from loneliness. The days were spent riding Jasmine and tending the wild colts. To keep busy she spoke to Mr. Burke about building a brew house and began to sketch some plans along the lines of the brew house at Crichton. Each night after she undressed, she put on Patrick's shirt, but the ache his scent evoked was almost unendurable. The impulse to follow him to Scotland grew so strong, Catherine began to pack her clothes. Isobel's unexpected arrival thwarted her plans.

Cat gasped and thrust her left hand behind her back as her mother strode into the library with an out-of-breath Maggie following on her heels. Her serving woman shot Cat a look of apology that she hadn't been swift enough to warn her of the impending danger. "Mother! I am surprised you braved the snowy roads to come and visit me. How thoughtful of you."

"Nonsense! I wouldn't waste my time visiting. My journey is one of necessity. Her Majesty is recovered from her cold and has accepted invitations for the Christmas festivities. Cecil has invited her to stay at Theobalds, and the Earl and Countess of Nottingham will entertain her at Arundel House over the New Year. The queen has a fancy for new gowns and is annoyed that you are gone off to the country when she needs your services, Catherine."

"Oh, Mother, I couldn't return to Court so soon after—"

"Rubbish! That's the reason I had to go to the trouble of coming in person. I knew you'd disobey any letter I sent asking you to return. I guessed I'd have to drag you back by the ear!"

"I know the scandal hasn't abated," Catherine murmured.

"Mary Fitton was just delivered of a dead child. A fitting punishment, I would say, for her wanton behavior."

Dear God, you have a heart of ice. Poor Mary was likely in love with Will Herbert. "And what of Pembroke?"

"He has petitioned Cecil to release him from the Fleet

Prison, but Her Majesty is adamant that she will not have him at Court."

Catherine felt relief. Though she had no feelings for Pembroke other than scorn, she had no wish to come face to face with him.

"Don't sit there with your sketching pad. Go and pack immediately. Maggie, I don't know how I've managed without you these last weeks. My burden will be immeasurably lighter when you return to Whitehall. Young maids do not have good work ethics."

Catherine arose from the desk and went upstairs. She closed her bedchamber door and opened her jewel casket, searching for a gold chain. She untangled one from a pearl necklet and threaded it through the Hepburn leopard ring Patrick had given her. She fastened it around her neck and before she concealed it beneath her clothes, set her lips to it gently in a reverent kiss.

At Whitehall, the moment Catherine had unpacked, she made her way to Philadelphia and Kate's rooms. "I'm back, under protest."

Philadelphia kissed her. "When did protest ever sway Isobel?"

"Mother told me of Mary Fitton's child. It's heartbreaking."

"It is, darling, but in the long run perhaps it happened for the best. The child would have borne the stigma of illegitimacy. Oh, I know that sounds like the pot calling the kettle black, when our father was the bastard of King Henry Tudor, but kings can do no wrong. Nor queens," she added acerbically.

"What has Elizabeth done now?" Cat asked anxiously.

"Her *Gracious* Majesty has invited herself to Arundel House for the New Year's Celebration, though Kate isn't anywhere near up to it. She's still coughing from what she refers to as coryza, but which was far closer to pneumonia. That's where she is now, cleaning and decorating and planning and ordering endless supplies to fete the entire Court. I'm doing double duty with the queen for the next few days, so I must run. But before I go, I must know if you had a certain attractive visitor at Spencer Park?"

Cat smiled her secret smile. "I did."

"And?" Philadelphia prompted impatiently.

"And the rest won't be revealed until I celebrate my birthday."

"Celebration indeed, if I know aught of the untamed rogue."

Cat placed her finger to her lips, showed Philadelphia the ring, and then quickly hid it again.

"Why, darling, Elizabeth wears a locket ring on a chain, hidden beneath her clothes. Inside is a miniature of her mother."

"Really? She never, ever speaks of Anne, yet she keeps her close to her heart. That's so touching. Come, we'll go down together. I have orders to present myself to Her Majesty."

Three hours later Catherine was back in her chamber, furiously sketching designs for Elizabeth's new gowns. Because the queen had complained that she was feeling the cold these days, Cat had suggested some quilted skirts and padded bodices of lightweight wool and velvet in brilliant hues. She had been secretly appalled to see that Elizabeth was thin to the point of emaciation and began to design garments that would disguise her skeletal frame.

That night, when Isobel came off duty, Cat offered her mother some suggestions. "Her Majesty is feeling the cold, so I think you should pull some of her fur cloaks from storage. Perhaps we could line one of them with a matching color from the gown I'm designing for her to wear on Christmas Eve. Of course, Theobalds isn't nearly as draughty as Whitehall, but I think you should pack her fur-lined slippers and some muffs."

Catherine was kept busy late into the evenings, and she also helped her mother and her Queen's Wardrobe staff choose and pack Elizabeth's garments, jewels and wigs for Christmas at Theobalds. They also had to plan Her Majesty's wardrobe for the celebrations at Arundel House, since there would hardly be time between the twelve days of Christmas and the New Year. The days flew past; the nights were another matter. At midnight, when Cat climbed into bed, she yearned for Patrick. Her skin became so sensitive that even the feel of her night rail aroused her. She could not fall asleep until she donned his shirt. Then, when she eventually slept, her dreams were so explicitly sexual she was shocked.

She wrote him many letters, pouring out her heart on paper, but because she had no one she could trust to carry them and her words were so impulsively incautious and erotic, Cat destroyed them.

All too soon the twelve-day sojourn at the Secretary of State's mansion in Hertfordshire drew nigh. Catherine, Isobel and Maggie were not too cramped on the carriage ride to Theobalds, but once they arrived and were assigned a small chamber, they were on top of each other. Mother and daughter had to share a bed, while Maggie made do on a trundle.

" 'Tis too bad we are not at Cecil's Burghley House in Stamford. The large chambers have beautifully painted ceilings and silver fireplaces, but of course Her Majesty could not be expected to travel all the way to Lincolnshire in winter," Isobel lamented.

"You will spend most of your hours in the queen's dressing room. I hope they have given you adequate space for her wardrobe."

"Oh, yes, Her Majesty's chambers and dressing rooms are spacious. This is Queen Elizabeth's thirteenth visit here."

Maggie threw Cat a look of alarm, then quickly crossed herself.

"Stop that! I won't tolerate your Celtic superstitious nonsense. Catherine, you will come and help me with the wardrobe."

Isobel had only one other of the Ladies of the Queen's Wardrobe to help her, so Cat assembled the outfits that Elizabeth would wear throughout the Christmas festivities. Each gown was paired with two separate sets of sleeves and jewelry. The bodices and skirts were also interchangeable, and Cat made a chart that color-coordinated the garments. Then she matched each gown with a fur cloak and wigs of varying shades of red. An orange tawny wig was married to gray velvet and fox fur, while Tudor green was paired with white velvet and swansdown as well as gold velvet, sable fur and an auburn wig.

When Catherine was finished, she asked Philadelphia, who had been chosen as First Lady of the Bedchamber, to view her work.

"Your taste in fashion is impeccable, darling." She lowered her voice. "These padded gowns will make her look almost human. Show me the new one that you designed for Christmas Eve."

Cat lifted the lid of a huge box and pulled aside the tissue and muslin. "I chose scarlet velvet embroidered with gold crowns, lions and unicorns. Her ermine cape has been relined with the same scarlet. Her wig will clash, but I've designed an

ornamental headpiece of black and white ostrich plumes that
will conceal it."

"Isobel, your daughter is a genius. I congratulate you."

"Philadelphia, such flattery will turn Catherine's head."

"Then we shan't know if she's coming or going."

Cat bit back a laugh at Philadelphia's jest, but her mother's
face was stiff with disapproval. "I must inventory the jewels."

Philadelphia winked at Cat. "I shan't steal them, Isobel."

The Secretary of State had organized a hunt for the gentlemen and of course provided gaming rooms for the courtiers addicted to games of chance, but he left it up to the queen's
younger gentlemen to entertain Elizabeth and her ladies. Since
the weather kept them inside, games of blindman's bluff, hide
the thimble, and forfeits became the order of the afternoons and
evenings. The men took liberal advantage of the mistletoe.

William Seymour sauntered up to Cat and made her a leg.
"Lady Catherine, have you by chance been corresponding with
Arbella?"

"I did write to her, Will, but I received no reply, I'm afraid."

Seymour looked downcast. "She doesn't reply to my letters
either. I apologized profusely for being the author of her difficulties, but I don't suppose she will ever forgive me."

Cat, to her utter amazement, felt sorry for him. "Perhaps her
grandmother, the Countess of Shrewsbury, seizes her letters before she can see them. That would explain why Arbella has
replied to neither one of us. She was extremely fond of you,
Will."

He looked carefree again as he went off to join Hal Somerset, who was blindfolding Lady Bridget Manners and spinning
her about until she was dizzy. *How immature they look and act*,
Cat thought as she stood observing the childish antics of all the
males present. *I cannot believe I ever considered them as suit-
ors!* Her fingers sought the ring beneath her bodice, and she felt
her heartbeat quicken at just the thought of Patrick. How lucky
their chance meeting had been. That Hepburn found her attractive and had asked her to marry him was more than luck; it was
a miracle, she decided. Catherine smiled her secret smile.

The Spencer ladies were kept so busy at Theobalds that
Christmas was quickly over and done and they found themselves on the way to Arundel House in the Strand, where Kate

and her husband, Lord Admiral Charles Howard, were hosting the queen and Court for New Year's. When they began to unpack, Isobel panicked because she could not find the costly gift she intended to present to Her Majesty. Maggie located it at the bottom of a trunk, and a relieved Isobel went off to see to the Royal Wardrobe.

"Elizabeth needs another jeweled prayer book as much as she needs another set of gold plates," Maggie said dourly.

"Gold plates are what Mother gave her for Christmas . . . oh, I see; that is your point! She does tend to overdo it. She worships the ground the queen walks upon. Elizabeth is her life."

"You could build your brew house for what she's spent on Her Majesty's gifts, and the queen won't give them a second glance!"

"The expense of being a courtier is exorbitant. Imagine what it is costing Kate and Charles to host this New Year's visit. Not just in money, either. It is at great cost to Kate's health."

For the first time, Catherine was beginning to see that life at Court was rather shallow, as Maggie had always contended. It was both exciting and entertaining to spend time at Elizabeth's Court, but a steady diet of Court life, all year round, was to have no meaningful life of your own. Isobel should never have deserted her husband for a permanent appointment at Court. *I never really knew my father, and that was wrong!* Cat vowed that she would never sacrifice her children's relationship with their father. The thought took her breath away: *Patrick Hepburn will be the father of my children!*

Catherine sighed happily and went to help her mother. The gown she had designed for Elizabeth to wear on New Year's Eve was quilted cream wool. Each square was embroidered with a pink rose, a purple thistle and a sprig of green shamrock, to represent her kingdom of England, Scotland and Ireland. Its sleeves were slashed with rose velvet, and her sable cape was lined with royal purple velvet embossed with two green dragons to represent Wales.

Kate had planned finer entertainment for the queen and her courtiers than Cecil had arranged. She provided them with London's greatest musicians, and minstrels playing viols and lutes strolled about amongst the guests. In every chamber on the first floor were performers presenting living tableaux from Greek mythology, and poets created a verse for each lady present before gifting her with a favor that consisted of a tiny silver basket that held a bauble and comfits.

"Have you seen Kate?" the Earl of Nottingham asked Catherine. "I'm worried to death about her. She was in bed less than two hours last night. I have my hands full trying to keep the male courtiers entertained so they don't become falling-down drunk."

"I'll look for her, Uncle Charles, and urge her to rest a bit." Cat searched every room from the top of Arundel House down. She finally found Kate in the kitchens, surrounded by crates of produce, game and shellfish, amid a bevy of tearful scullery maids.

"Oh, Catherine, I'm at my wits end. The chef hit the head cook with his ladle and walked out. Cook says he knocked her addled and she can't handle these young kitchen helpers. I've been on my feet since midnight, and by the look of things tonight's banquet will be nonexistent." Kate's face was pale as death.

"I'll get Maggie. She'll soon shift them round. Her favored weapon is a wooden spoon, but if that doesn't work she'll threaten them with a red hot poker and a Celtic curse."

Cat ran upstairs and soon brought Maggie to the kitchens. "We'll take over here, Kate. I promised Uncle Charles that I would make you go up and rest."

"I thank you both with all my heart. I shall go upstairs, but only to bathe and change. When it is your turn to entertain the queen, my dear, you will realize that resting is an impossibility!"

The following day was New Year's Eve, and disaster was averted only because Beth Carey brought her entire kitchen staff over from the Hunsdon mansion in Blackfriars. Following the evening banquet, Elizabeth, sitting in a throne-like carved and padded chair, accepted costly gifts from everyone present.

When it was Isobel's turn to approach the queen, she curtsied low and set the jewel-inlaid prayer book at her monarch's feet.

Philadelphia, standing at Elizabeth's right hand, said dryly, "She's been asleep for the past hour. Sorry, Isobel."

As midnight approached, the queen was roused so that she could welcome in the New Year of 1603, which would prove a fateful year indeed. Precisely at midnight, the Earl of Nottingham lit the first firework of a magnificent display he had arranged in the Arundel House gardens, where they sloped down to the river Thames.

Catherine retired to her bed around one in the morning. *This is the year that will change my entire life! January has finally arrived. In March I will celebrate my twenty-first birthday and become the wife of Patrick Hepburn!* Cat hugged herself. *What if he doesn't come?* The thought was fleeting. *Of course he will come! Patrick loves me. I trust him with all my heart and soul.*

It was an exhausted Court that returned to Whitehall after all the holiday festivities, and it took the courtiers a few days to settle back into their routines. Philadelphia was still filling in for Kate, who stayed behind at Arundel House to put all back to rights after the invasion that left the place depleted as if a plague of locusts had descended.

"Isobel, you must help me. The queen has angrily rejected every gown I have suggested this morning. She's complaining of the cold, and I fear she's about to work herself into a tirade."

"Philadelphia, I haven't even finished unpacking and refurbishing the garments she wore over Christmas and New Year's. I'll get Catherine. She must think of something."

A page brought an urgent summons to Cat, who spoke with her mother in the Wardrobe Department then sought Philadelphia in the Queen's Bedchamber. She was just in time to witness the tirade.

"Finally!" Elizabeth screeched. "Finally, someone who knows something about gowns. What's your name, girl?" she demanded.

How could she have forgotten my name? "Lady Catherine, ma'am."

"Get that warm gown I wore at Theobalds and be quick about it!"

Cat was hard-pressed to know which she meant, for during the twelve-day sojourn the queen had worn twenty-four gowns. She curtsied, rushed to the Wardrobe Department, took out the warmest quilted velvet she could find and hurried back.

Philadelphia, with the help of two tiring ladies, changed the queen's gown and fastened a ruff around her neck. Her Gracious Majesty immediately plucked it off and threw it to the carpet. "Piss on the lot of you! Where's Kate? I want Kate to attend me! She has gentle hands." The queen boxed a startled Philadelphia's ear. Offended, Philadelphia immediately withdrew. Cat followed her.

"Kate has far gentler hands than that old bitch," Philadelphia declared, "and a hell of a lot more patience than I!"

"I wanted to tell her that Kate was cleaning up after her Court visit and needs a well-earned rest, but I didn't have the courage."

"No, the virago is rather formidable, and she's getting worse by the day. Nothing pleases her, and she accuses all of conspiring against her. Her language has always been blue, and that certainly doesn't bother me, but when she resorts to blows, I've had enough."

By nightfall, the long-suffering and gentle Kate returned to Whitehall, but even that didn't stop the royal complaints. "I hate Whitehall! The bloody place is as cold as a tomb! I want to be warm like I was at your Arundel House. Even sprawling Theobalds is cozy compared to this draughty mausoleum! That's it; we shall move the Court to Richmond Palace. It has ever been our favorite dwelling place. Pack everything! My Ladies of the Wardrobe and Bedchamber are a gaggle of lazy strumpets. I want the move accomplished today. *Today!* Do you understand?"

"Yes, Your Majesty. Would you like me to brew you some herb tea?" Kate did her utmost to soothe her irate monarch, though she felt poorly herself.

Though Isobel had the gargantuan task of packing Elizabeth's entire wardrobe and commandeering Catherine and Maggie to help her, she would utter no criticism of the queen.

"Once we've managed the move, I prefer Richmond myself," Cat told Maggie. "Maybe we'll be able to spend time at our own house."

By the beginning of the third week of January, Kate collapsed and was put to bed with pneumonia. By the end of the third week, Kate was dead.

Chapter Twenty-five

"Y" ou cannot be serious." But Catherine had the sinking feeling that a distraught Philadelphia was indeed telling the truth.

"Charles and I sat at Kate's bedside all night as she struggled for breath. The doctor could do nothing. She died just before dawn. Nottingham is beside himself with sorrow." Tears streamed down Philadelphia's face.

Catherine felt numb as she watched Maggie cross herself.

Isobel's first thought was of Elizabeth. "Her Majesty will be devastated. Who will dare to tell her such news?"

"That job will fall to me," Philadelphia declared. "I sincerely hope she *is* devastated. The queen caused Kate's death!"

"What a wicked thing to say. You are not in your right mind."

"No, I am mad with grief."

Cat feared that any moment her mother and Philadelphia would come to blows. "Let me help you. There are so many you must notify. I'll come with you now." *I want to say good-bye to Kate.*

They found Charles with his head down on the bed, still holding his wife's hand. Cat took Kate's other hand and silently thanked her for acting like a mother to her, then she bade her farewell. She and Philadelphia put their arms about the Earl of Nottingham and urged him to allow Kate's women to wash her, tend the body and change the bed linen before anyone else came.

"Philadelphia, you must put on a black dress, and I will redo your hair before you take the sad news to the queen."

When Philadelphia left to inform Elizabeth, Catherine summoned a page and handed him a note she had scribbled to Cecil.

She returned to the writing desk and penned short notices to all of Kate and Philadelphia's siblings. Then, crying, she wrote a letter to Patrick Hepburn, which she would send north with Lord Scrope's letter. She missed him so much. Her heart overflowed with sadness, but sharing her thoughts about Kate somehow eased her grief.

Queen Elizabeth fell into a state of melancholy when she was given the news that Lady Nottingham, the most long serving of her ladies, had died. The queen summoned her Lord Admiral, Kate's husband, and kept him with her for long hours each day. She even forbade him to leave Richmond Palace.

The Carey family began to gather. Philadelphia's husband, Lord Thomas Scrope, traveled from Carlisle Castle; George Carey, the new Lord Hunsdon, came from the Border stronghold of Bewcastle; John Carey and his wife, Mary, came up from their farm in Hertford; and Robert Carey and Liz journeyed to the Richmond house immediately.

"Elizabeth is convinced her grief is greater than any of ours. She even expects poor Charles to console her when it should be the other way about. It's our fault, I suppose. We've convinced her that she is the center of the universe and that the sun and the moon rise and set upon her," Philadelphia declared.

Robert waited until Isobel left the room, then handed Catherine the letter he had brought from Patrick Hepburn. Cat went out into the winter-ravaged garden to read it.

> *My darling Catherine:*
> *I kiss the dried teardrops upon your letter. Though I cannot be there physically to comfort you in this time of sadness, my thoughts and my spirit are with you. The loss of Kate is tragic, but after you have mourned her passing, I urge you to remember the happy times you shared together to celebrate her name. Talk to her often to relieve your pain.*
> *I had business with your grandfather Seton last week and have reason to believe that he approves our match. By the time you read this, it will be less than sixty days before I come to claim you. To me that seems an eternity, yet it will pass. Winter will end and spring will inevitably follow.*

*I am entrusting this letter to Robert but advise you to
burn it once you have read it. You have all my heart.*
    Patrick

Catherine slipped the letter into the bodice of her black
gown, where it rested against Hepburn's betrothal ring. She
wiped the tears from her cheeks and glanced down at her feet.
There, among some dead leaves, a tiny snowdrop had raised its
head. *Patrick is right! Winter will end and spring will inevitably
follow.* She bent down and picked the delicate flower, then
pressed it between the folds of his letter. Cat knew she must destroy the note, but not quite yet. *Tonight I will sleep with it beneath my pillow.*

Patrick Hepburn was once again riding to Winton. Though
he had told Cat that he had reason to believe her grandfather approved their match, it was more of a feeling than a fact. He had
said nothing to Geordie Seton about betrothing Catherine.
    Hepburn had fallen into the habit of riding to Seton every
week because of his suspicions that Malcolm Lindsay wanted to
be the next Earl of Winton. But since Geordie adamantly refused to believe such a base accusation against his nephew,
Hepburn never broached the matter again.
    "Hello, Lord Winton. You're looking well these days."
    "Dinna *Lord* me—call me Geordie. I hope we have a mild
spell o' weather soon so we can turn the beasties out to pasture."
    "February arrives tomorrow—we'll likely have a thaw be-
fore another blizzard in March. If it turns mild, I'll start some of
my moss-troopers on their guard duty again."
    "Good lad, Patrick. Bloody English Border reivers will be at
it again as soon as the weather lets up!"
    "I received sad news. Your daughter's sister-in-law Kate
Howard has died at the Court in Richmond. She was the queen's
principal lady."
    "Elizabeth will outlive us all!" Seton said with disgust.
    "Nay, Geordie, that is a fallacy. I believe her days are num-
bered, and losing Kate will put another nail in her coffin."
    "So ye think Jamie will achieve his ambition soon, d'ye?"
    "Yes, I do. I predict that this is the year James will become
King of England as well as Scotland. When that happens the

Border will disappear and James will set up his Court in London."

Geordie laughed. "God Ahmighty, the English will shit theirselves when a horde o' untamed Scots flock to London an' swallow up all the best appointments and landholdin's!"

"The only English who will thrive are those with Scottish connections. Would you be interested in a merger that would benefit the Setons, the Spencers and the Hepburns?"

"A merger?" Geordie puzzled.

"How would you feel about a match between your granddaughter, Lady Catherine, and myself?"

The puzzled frown disappeared as all became clear to the Earl of Winton. He looked Hepburn up and down. "'Tis no' a question of how I feel, but of how Catherine feels in this matter."

Patrick grinned. "I have reason to believe Lady Catherine favors a match with me. When she comes of age in March I shall ask her to marry me. I wanted to apprise you of my intention."

Geordie thought it over and concluded, "I'd rather see my Seton lands and prize cattle go to ye than a bloody Englishman, but"—he assessed Patrick's size one last time—"make my wee Catherine unhappy an' yer a dead mon, Hepburn. Come inside an' we'll drink a dram o' good Scotch whisky on the merger."

As Patrick Hepburn left Seton he sensed that he was being followed. He stopped and waited for the rider to catch up with him. Hard black eyes stared into the blue eyes of Andrew Lindsay.

"Lord Stewart, ye have forbidden Jenny Hepburn from ridin' out wi' me, and I ask that ye reconsider the matter."

Patrick stared long and hard at the well-built youth, using his sixth sense to guide him. "Have you been seeing Jenny on the sly, Lindsay?" he demanded.

"Nay, but if ye persist in yer refusal to let me court her, I shall try to see her behind yer back."

In the face of such an honest admission, Hepburn was tempted to relent. "I'll speak with Jenny and her father. She's been hurt once, and I won't allow her to be hurt again."

"Fair enough, my lord."

"Tell me true; do you think it was your cousin's arrow?"

"I don't know, Lord Stewart."

"Do you think him capable of such a thing?" Hepburn persisted.

Andrew remained silent, and then slowly he nodded.

On a bleak February morning, Kate Howard, Countess of Nottingham, was laid to rest. Her cousin, Elizabeth Tudor, flanked by Charles Howard, Earl of Nottingham, and Robert Cecil, Principal Secretary, swayed dangerously at the graveside. The two men immediately steadied their monarch and escorted her aboard her royal barge, which took her back to Richmond Palace.

Most of the nobility attended the funeral, not only because Kate was the wife of the Lord Admiral, but also because the queen held her in such high esteem. After the public funeral, Kate's family gathered privately at their Richmond house.

Philadelphia took Catherine, Isobel and Beth aside. "I know that Kate would want each of you to have a token of jewels from her collection." She gave her sister-in-law Beth a string of precious pearls, and she gave Isobel a large topaz broach. "You always admired her ruby and diamond earrings, Catherine. So here they are. Wear them in good health." The three ladies were touched by the generous gesture.

Maggie, who was serving tea, made a dire prediction. "Death comes in three. First was Mary Fitton's babe, now our dearest Kate. There'll be another yet; mark my words."

"Don't you dare to include a child begotten in sin with the honorable Countess of Nottingham," Isobel hissed.

"Death plays no favorites, my lady. It thumbs its nose at rank and wealth and even crowns," Maggie said ominously.

"How dare you? Take your Celtic gibberish and go back to the house. Catherine will take over for you and serve the tea."

Maggie withdrew as bidden, but Catherine and Philadelphia exchanged a glance indicating they believed in the rule of three.

"Isobel, death and superstition go hand in hand. Maggie didn't invent it," Philadelphia chided.

"Her veiled hint was directed at Her Gracious Majesty. I will not have my servants mouthing treason." Isobel's face was grim.

"Maggie is not your servant, Mother; she is my woman," Catherine admonished quietly. "In any case, I am sure she was not referring to Her Majesty. We all know the queen is invincible."

Philadelphia murmured to her brother Robert, "I'm afraid Cat is deluding herself, and of course Isobel is terrified for her position at Court."

Robert agreed, "You are right, but least said, soonest mended."

"Yes, emotions run rampant when a beloved dies. Will you be staying, Robert, or going back north with my husband, Scrope?"

"Since Liz is forbidden the Court, I shall take her back north." *Then I will apprise King James of the queen's condition.*

"The queen has come down with a sore throat because she insisted on using the royal barge rather than taking a closed carriage to Kate's funeral. The wind on the river Thames was bitter that day, but she wouldn't listen to advice," Philadelphia told Catherine in the dining hall at Richmond Palace.

"Has she gone to bed?" Catherine asked.

"No. She banished Lady Throckmorton for suggesting it." She bit her lip. "Elizabeth called me Kate three times today. I don't know if it's just a slip of the tongue, or if the queen is confused and truly thinks I am Kate. She's very demanding."

Catherine touched Philadelphia's hand. "I don't want you to get sick. If she dismisses her other ladies, you will be overburdened. I know Mother is at the moment. She's had to clean and put away all Elizabeth's garments that have any trace of color and take all the black clothing out of storage and refurbish it."

Philadelphia looked about the hall. "The entire Court, men and women alike, is in mourning. I know it shows respect for Kate, but it drapes the entire palace with a suffocating air of melancholy. I not only feel drab, I look drab too!"

"You need a new gown to cheer you. Black can be elegant in the extreme. I have nothing to design at the moment; the queen has an abundance of mourning garments."

"Thank you, darling; that will be lovely. I'd better get back to Elizabeth. Cecil has an audience with her this evening, and she will want everything to be just right before he arrives."

Philadelphia entered the Queen's Bedchamber and found her with her eyes closed. Elizabeth lifted her scant sandy lashes and a look of relief came over her face. "Kate, I dreamt something awful happened to you. What time is it?"

"It's almost seven, Your Majesty. Lord Cecil is coming."

"I remember. Help me to my desk; it lends me authority."

When Philadelphia ushered Robert Cecil into the chamber, he saw Elizabeth propped like a death's-head behind her desk. He set his portfolio of papers on the chair and approached her. He bowed solemnly and waited for her to speak.

"We see you are well."

"Very well, Your Majesty." He coughed. "I come about Ireland."

"It's always about Ireland!"

"I have dispatches from Mountjoy. He confirms that Tyrone has taken refuge in the wilds of Ulster, where it is nigh impossible to run him to ground. The Lord Deputy and myself are in favor of permitting Tyrone to make a formal submission, Your Majesty."

"I refuse! To show favor to him now would allow the world to impute weakness to us. We will hunt him down!"

"Your Majesty, the Council as well as Mountjoy and myself advocate extending mercy to Tyrone. War in Ireland is costing three hundred thousand pounds a year and too much bloodshed."

"I shall take the matter out of your hands and give it to your father. Burghley is absolute and will never back down."

Robert Cecil immediately realized that Elizabeth was not in full command of her faculties. His father had been dead for almost five years. He bowed. "As you wish, Your Majesty."

As he left, Cecil signaled to Philadelphia that he wished to speak with her in private. "Does Her Majesty seem confused?"

"Since my sister's funeral she confuses me with Kate, my lord."

"Keep this matter confidential, Lady Scrope. Allow only those in whom you put complete trust to have access to the queen's person. Her Majesty may well improve."

Cecil did not believe for one moment Elizabeth would improve. He returned to his office and sent a dispatch to Mountjoy, Lord Deputy of Ireland, informing him that Her Majesty authorized him to accept Tyrone's offer of submission, and accord the rebel life, liberty and pardon to avoid any further bloodshed.

Cecil then penned a letter, in cipher, to King James Stuart of Scotland.

After meeting with the king and Robert Carey at Holyrood Palace, Patrick Hepburn was returning to Crichton late. Having heard Robert's report on Elizabeth's deteriorating condition, James was now convinced that Patrick's prediction of March 24 for the Queen of England's death could be relied upon. The King of Scotland would put his affairs in order so that he would be ready to depart for London the moment Carey brought him the official news. Robert was returning to Elizabeth's Court on a deathwatch.

During the eight-mile ride on the moonless night, Hepburn's thoughts were filled with Catherine. Not only could he see her image, he experienced her sadness over Kate's death and he could feel her loneliness. Moreover, he knew more sadness would follow.

When he arrived at Crichton, he went upstairs, took Cat's white ribbon from his bedside table and climbed into bed. He focused his full attention on the object of his desire, and gradually her image came before him. She, too, was abed, and he saw that one delicate hand was tucked beneath her pillow. It rested upon his letter, which he'd advised her to burn. The corner of his mouth lifted. *Impulsive little wench.*

Since she was touching something that came from him and he held an object that belonged to her, it would be easier to make the distance between them disappear. "Come to me, Cat."

Catherine stirred restlessly in her sleep. The slight breeze that touched her face and ruffled her hair made her lift her lashes. She was not really flying, but floating, and decided it must be a dream. Then she saw Tor, the raven, at her side and knew exactly where the black bird was leading her.

"Patrick!" She stood just inside the door of his chamber.

He held out his arms. "Cat, why do you hesitate?"

"Your arms are like a circle of fire. Once I step into them, the flames spiral high about me, the heat leaps between us, and I lose complete control of my senses."

He grinned. "Come, feel the fire."

She tossed her hair about her shoulders in feline abandon and ran to his waiting arms.

Catherine awoke to find herself back at Richmond Palace.

The hand on her shoulder was not Patrick's, but Maggie's. She blushed at her disheveled hair and kiss-swollen lips.

"Yer mother is ill, my lamb. She's come down with a bad cough and a cold. I've persuaded her to stay in bed but only because she fears infecting Her Majesty. She asks that ye take her place in the Queen's Wardrobe today."

"Of course I will." Cat dressed quickly and entered Isobel's chamber. "Mother, I cannot hope to fill your shoes, but I will do my best. Promise me that you will stay abed and let Maggie look after you today?"

Catherine told Isobel's assistants that her mother was ill and that she was taking over her duties. She quickly unpacked two large boxes of mourning garments that had been sent upriver from Whitehall and selected a black velvet gown. She chose white silk undergarments for next to Elizabeth's body, a black farthingale and black shoes and stockings. She unlocked one of the queen's jewel cases and took out a set of jet beads as well as pearls.

Cat picked out a small, unadorned red wig and carried everything to Philadelphia in the Queen's Bedchamber. "I thought I'd save you the trip to the Wardrobe Department," she murmured.

Philadelphia rolled her eyes, indicating that perhaps it wasn't a good idea that Catherine had invaded the inner sanctum.

Cat brought the garments to the bed and stared in disbelief at the frail figure wearing a damp night rail who'd just been sponge bathed by two ladies who were now removing the hipbath. Without magnificent royal garments, and without wig and makeup, the shriveled and emaciated female sitting on the edge of the bed was reduced to a pathetic old woman. England's monarch was almost bald, with a few patches of short gray hair and no eyebrows.

Black beady eyes examined Catherine with uncertainty. "Mother?" A thin, blue-veined hand went to her throat, which hurt when she spoke. A smile that looked more like a grimace came over her face. "I wear your picture in my locket ring," she croaked.

Philadelphia whispered in Cat's ear, "Because of your beauty and your shining black hair, she thinks you are her mother."

She thinks I'm Anne Boleyn!

"This is Cat, Your Majesty. She designs your lovely gowns."

"Kat? Kat Ashley? My Mistress of the Robes and my dear old friend! Where have you been? My throat's sore; please make me some barley water, Ashcat?"

Cat curtsied. "I shall make some immediately, Your Majesty."

She hurried to the kitchens and told the head cook that the queen had asked for barley water. Then she sat on a stool to wait. For the first time it dawned on her that the queen was a mortal woman. The façade her ladies created, dressing her in clothes and wigs and makeup, and then propping her up like a doll, was completely false. *Her body wasted away long ago; now her health and her mind are deteriorating too. Only the spirit seems willing, but the flesh is frail.* Catherine sat, stunned. *We are living a lie! This is all a fantasy. Queen Elizabeth is going to die.*

By the time Cat returned with the barley water, Elizabeth was dressed in the black gown Cat had chosen. Wearing wig and makeup seemed to have helped clear the queen's mind somewhat, for she was issuing croaking orders to Lady Huntingdon and Lady Radcliffe.

Philadelphia heaved a huge sigh of relief. "We've managed to hold it together for one more day . . . one more month, actually. It's March tomorrow." She passed Cat a hand mirror. "Take this away."

When Catherine returned to her own rooms, she took Maggie aside. "You were right about Death coming in three. This morning I saw Her Majesty in her night rail."

"Don't say aught to yer mother, or she'll become the third one."

"I won't say a word. She would run mad at the thought of the queen's death. She has no other life but here at Court."

Robert Cecil, Secretary of State, decided that the time had come. Bearding the lioness in her den, or more precisely her bedchamber, he broached the delicate subject matter-of-factly. "Your Gracious Majesty, it is my duty to put the question to you. Will you have the King of Scots to succeed you in your kingdom?"

Black eyes narrowed. "We will not speak of it, little man!"

Cecil bowed, withdrew and had a private word with

Philadelphia. "Keep me informed on her condition. I shall return tomorrow."

"She has stopped sleeping. Her physician comes each day, but she refuses all medication for her swollen glands. She eats less than a bird, though she has developed an incessant thirst."

Cecil nodded. "Keep her clean and comfortable."

Later that day, one of the queen's godsons, Sir John Harrington, came to read some of his fashionable verses to her. Elizabeth took no interest. "When you feel creeping Time at your gate, these fooleries will please you less."

The following day, Robert Carey arrived, and Philadelphia brought him to Elizabeth to see if he could cheer her. She had stopped eating, and all she drank were sips of rosewater.

"Robin, *I am not well.*"

That night Elizabeth refused to undress and go to bed. In the morning, her ladies realized that she had stopped speaking. When darkness fell, the queen lay on the floor. Philadelphia, with the help of Lady Huntingdon and Mary Radcliffe, forcefully undressed her and lifted her into her royal bed. Catherine took away the queen's soiled garments, which she had worn for fifty hours.

The next morning, Cecil paid his usual visit. With Philadelphia at his side, he again asked Elizabeth, "Will you have the King of Scots to succeed you in your kingdom?"

After a moment's silence he looked into Philadelphia's eyes. "The queen nodded her assent."

When Philadelphia Scrope did not demur, Cecil withdrew.

From that moment on, Cecil, Philadelphia and Robert Carey were on a deathwatch. The Queen's Council filed in to see her, and after that she saw only her physician and Archbishop Whitgift. Her Ladies of the Bedchamber professed that they could not bear to see her in such a pitiable state. Philadelphia alone sat vigil.

Two hours past midnight, Thursday, March 24, Elizabeth Tudor drew her last breath and died. At last she slept the long sleep.

Philadelphia stepped into the antechamber and shook her brother awake. Without a word she handed Robert the beautifully wrought locket ring that Elizabeth had always worn next to her heart.

He gazed down at it, almost in disbelief, then he kissed his sister and swiftly departed for Scotland.

Within the hour Cecil arrived and insisted that no one else leave Richmond Palace without written authority. At 7 A.M. the councilors rode to Whitehall for a formal meeting to draft the Accession Proclamation making James Stuart King of England.

Chapter Twenty-six

$\mathcal{A}$t the same time the councilors were meeting, Maggie hurried into the rooms the Spencers occupied at Richmond Palace, and before she set the breakfast tray down on the table, the words came rushing out. "Her Majesty the queen is dead!"

Catherine's face paled. "Sit down, Maggie. You learned this in the kitchens? Don't tell Mother yet; she'll be devastated."

"She'll know soon enough, my lamb. She intends to go back to work this morning, now that she's recovered from her cold."

Her emotions in turmoil, Cat greeted her mother when she emerged from her room. "You must eat a good breakfast to give you stamina for all your duties today."

Isobel sat down at the table. "I can only imagine the chaos I shall have to face in the Wardrobe Department. Thank Heaven my health is improved. I sincerely hope Her Majesty is in like case."

Cat and Maggie exchanged a significant glance and kept their tongues between their teeth. After Isobel left, however, Cat broke their silence. "I feel so guilty! Inside, I've tried to contain a growing excitement about my birthday a week from today and Patrick's promise that he would come. Now this has happened, and my first thought was that Elizabeth has spoiled it for me. Oh, Maggie, how can I be so selfish?"

"Yer no' selfish, my lamb. Life is fer the living. Elizabeth had a spectacular life. Death brings her peace and ends her suffering. In the kitchens, all the talk is of the new king and what changes James will make, and if they'll keep their jobs."

"Truly? Perhaps the servitors; but the courtiers will mourn her deeply and perhaps not wish to give their loyalty to James."

"Wheest, lassie; human nature being what it is, Elizabeth's

courtiers will fall o'er theirselves to be first in line to bow and scrape before the new King of England."

"But, Maggie, they are used to having a magnificent royal personage. James Stuart doesn't even look like a king."

"Och, he'll descend on London with all the trappings. He's been waiting fer this day fer decades; mark my words."

The apartment door opened and Isobel walked in looking as if she had seen Elizabeth's corpse. Clearly, she was in a state of shock. "The Court is in mourning. I cannot cope, Catherine."

"Make her some chamomile tea, Maggie. I shall go down to the Wardrobe Department and do whatever is necessary, Mother."

When Catherine encountered Philadelphia, they hugged each other. "Your long vigil is over. Why don't you go and rest?"

"I could sleep for a month, darling, but there is much to do. If I let down my guard I shall come to a standstill."

"Mother is in a state of shock, as if this is the end, but Maggie says life is for the living and already the Court's focus has turned to King James."

"Maggie is right. This isn't the end; it is a new beginning. Queen Anne and her ladies are barely in their thirties. The new king and queen have young children. You'll see. The Court will come to life in a brand new golden era."

At 10:00 A.M. Cecil delivered the first reading of the Proclamation at Whitehall Palace naming James Stuart sovereign.

By nightfall there were bonfires and bell ringing to celebrate the accession of the new king, and as Philadelphia had predicted, a certain excitement began to manifest at the dawn of a new age.

Elizabeth's body was wrapped in cerecloth, according to her wishes, and at midnight was placed on the royal barge and taken to Whitehall to lie in state while funeral arrangements were made.

Philadelphia visited Isobel the next day. "I think it would be a wonderful gesture if each of Elizabeth's ladies had the choice of one of her gowns. I believe the queen would want that."

"How can you suggest such a thing?" Isobel was shocked and offended. "It would be desecration!"

"No, Isobel. It is a practical way of thanking her Ladies of the Bedchamber, her ladies-in-waiting, her maids of honor, and her Ladies of the Wardrobe for their devoted service. Once the new queen arrives, you do realize that all will belong to her?"

Isobel's eyes widened. "I hadn't thought of it. Your idea has merit, but many of Her Majesty's gowns are sewn with jewels."

"Only semiprecious jewels, Mother," Cat interjected, "like crystals, jet, garnets and carnelians. There are no diamonds, rubies, emeralds or real pearls."

"Courtiers are already thinking ahead about garments for King James's coronation. The gift of a royal gown would save her ladies much expense, Isobel," Philadelphia pointed out.

"Coronation?" Isobel was horrified. "Her Majesty is not yet buried. How can people be so heartless? The Court is in mourning. I shall be in mourning for the rest of my life."

Philadelphia glanced at Cat with pity but hung on to her patience. "There is much to do. We have to move the Court from Richmond Palace back to Whitehall. Thank you, Isobel, for agreeing to gift the queen's ladies with her gowns. Elizabeth is smiling down upon you."

"Elizabeth, are you venting your fury upon me?" Robert Carey, on his headlong dash north, had made careful arrangements to have ready the best horses at stages all along the road from London to Edinburgh, but not all was going according to plan.

With every mile north the weather deteriorated, and just before he reached the inn where a fresh horse awaited him, his mount slipped on the icy road and he was thrown from the saddle. He got gingerly to his feet and examined his rapidly swelling leg. "I pray it's not broken," he muttered as he groped in the darkness for the reins of his horse. He slid a hand over its forelegs. "Thank God, you don't seem any worse for wear, old man."

He limped into the inn's stable and told the hostler that of necessity his plans had changed. "I will need a carriage, a stout team of horses and a driver."

"Ye need a doctor to look at yer leg, sir."

"No time for that, I'm afraid." He gave the man gold. "While you ready a carriage, I shall go inside and get some warm food."

Through the night as the coach hurtled northward, Robert got little sleep until the whisky he had procured dulled his pain. Midday on March 25 his team of horses was changed and the posting inn provided another driver and another hot meal. He did not take the time to bathe or change his clothes. He simply propped his aching leg on the opposite seat and pressed on.

He reached Carlisle Castle early on March 26 and gave the news to Philadelphia's husband, Lord Scrope, who knew he was on his way to take the momentous news to England's new king. Robert asked for a messenger and scribbled a note to be taken to his wife, Liz, asking her to meet him at Holyrood Palace.

"Why don't you bed down for a few hours? You're exhausted."

"Nay, Thomas, if I leave now I may be able to reach James before he retires to bed tonight."

As it turned out, Robert missed his goal by one hour. It was almost midnight when he hurried through Holyrood's passageways with a King's Guard at his side. At the bedchamber door he told those guarding it that James had given orders to deliver the news he brought, day or night. After a few moments' delay, they ushered Robert Carey into the presence of James Stuart.

Carey, disheveled and travel-stained, had difficulty going down on one knee. "The queen is dead; long live the king!"

"Eh, laddie, ye speak true?" James tugged at his sparse beard.

"My cousin Elizabeth died two hours past midnight on March 24, Sire. I salute you by your rightful title of King of England, Scotland, France and Ireland." He placed Elizabeth's locket-ring in James Stuart's hand.

James's Gentlemen of the Bedchamber busied themselves bringing the king a bed robe and lighting the candles. James took the ring over to the light and gazed down upon it as it lay in his palm. " 'Tis the bonniest thing I've ever seen." The large gold ring was lined on the inside with mother of pearl and ringed on the outside by a circle of rubies. The ring was opened by pressing on a big pearl that lifted her hinged initial, *E,* made from huge square diamonds.

James's fingers fumbled and shook as he opened the locket. "Look at this," he bade Robert. " 'Tis a miniature paintin' of herself an' one o' Anne Boleyn, the mother she spent her reign disownin'. Blood is thicker than water. Our mothers are always wi' us, deny them how we will." James lifted his eyes and gazed at Robert as a thought struck him. "The laddie was right. Hepburn foretold the day I would become King o' England!"

•   •   •

Patrick Hepburn had spent the last two days preparing his people of Crichton for his departure. He put Jock Elliot, the captain of his moss-troopers, in complete charge. He asked David Hepburn if he wanted to travel to London with him as his attendant, and that young man readily agreed. David packed their trunks; Patrick locked his important documents and gold in a strongbox, and they selected a pair of packhorses.

Hepburn, booted and spurred, broke his fast in the Great Hall, with all his people present, early on the morning of March 27. When he was finished eating, he climbed onto a trestle table and waited for silence. "King James will shortly travel to London to be crowned King of England. I will be one of the nobles going with him. I may be away for as long as six months, and when I return I shall be bringing a bride home with me."

The people in the hall erupted in cheers and shouts of approval, which were accompanied by the deafening clatter of pewter tankards banging on the tabletops. On his way out, Patrick winked at Jenny Hepburn. "Don't do aught I wouldn't do, lass."

The women of his clan clustered round him, kissing him, touching him and wishing him Godspeed. All at Crichton knew, as he did, that his time had come. In the stables, the two men mounted, and each led a packhorse into the courtyard. Jock Elliot held Sabbath and Satan on stout leashes so they would not follow their master. Patrick saluted Jock. "Look after the dogs for me."

On the ride to Edinburgh, Hepburn felt confident that all he had seen in his visions had come to pass. He had known the very moment that Elizabeth had drawn her last faint breath, and he'd "seen" Philadelphia pass the locket ring to Robert Carey. Last night he had even envisioned the moment Jamie learned that the queen was dead and heard him say, *"The laddie was right. Hepburn foretold the day I would become King o' England."*

March 28 was a bleak, cold day, with clouds that threatened London with rain. Catherine and Maggie flanked Isobel as they stood on the Strand outside Arundel House. Philadelphia had taken them by carriage to Kate's house because the walk from Whitehall to Westminster Abbey, where Elizabeth was to be interred, would prove too far for Isobel in her melancholy state.

The funeral procession was headed by more than two hundred poor women, followed by the packed ranks of royal servants and household officers. "The Lord Admiral and Treasurer Stanhope made all the arrangements, though Kate's husband isn't yet over his own loss," Catherine told her mother.

As Elizabeth's leaden coffin on its bier, drawn by four black horses with black plumes, drew abreast, Isobel began to sob. When Catherine spotted the admiral and the treasurer following in the coffin's wake, she took her mother's arm. "Here come the wives and daughters of the nobility. We can join the procession here. Walk on her other side, Maggie, just in case."

Every noble lady present wore a black gown, black cloak and black veil. The Yeomen of the Guard brought up the rear, with their halberds trailing downward as a mark of respect. After the service at Westminster Abbey, Elizabeth was interred in the crypt beside her grandfather Henry VII.

As they left the abbey for their return to Whitehall, the rain that had threatened all day began to fall. "Even the angels are weeping!" Isobel cried melodramatically. When they arrived back at their chambers, Catherine and Maggie put Isobel to bed. But even the next day, she did not rally; she sat in a rocking chair wreathed in black, looking stunned as a bird flown into a wall.

Cat, glad to escape, went down to the Wardrobe Department and began the task of putting all the late queen's garments into storage. Whitehall Palace began to empty as more and more noble courtiers made hasty preparations to ride north so that they could greet the king as he journeyed from Scotland.

"I shall go too," Philadelphia informed Cat. "I will not allow the ambitious flatterers and arse-lickers to be before me, darling. And in any case, I expect my husband, Scrope, joined James's party when it reached Carlisle Castle."

Only two more days until my birthday! Cat hugged the thought to herself. *Will Patrick come?* Her thoughts flashed about like mercury, her emotions roiling like the sea in a storm. *Of course he'll come! Patrick is in love with me and can't wait to marry me.* Her excitement grew to such a pitch, she became breathless with anticipation. Her mood was so mercurial, she was suddenly overcome with doubts. *Of course Hepburn won't come. You are such a foolish female. Hepburn told you he'd wed*

*you by April first just to pacify you. Now that James is king, all
will have changed for Lord Bloody Stewart!*

When she was certain he would come, Cat felt dizzy with
joy. When she convinced herself that he would not come, she
was in the depths of despair. She couldn't eat, she couldn't
sleep, and she feared that by the time her birthday arrived, she
wouldn't be able to breathe. *If he doesn't come, I'll kill myself!*
She swore. *That's ridiculous. If Hepburn doesn't come, I shall
kill HIM!*

Patrick Hepburn rode in the king's cavalcade beside Robert
Carey as they departed Carlisle Castle. "Congratulations on
your appointment as Gentleman of the King's Bedchamber. I
predict you will go far, Robert. Jamie considers you his most
stalwart English supporter, and I doubt you can do any wrong in
his eyes."

"I am extremely happy for my wife. Queen Anne has welcomed her wholeheartedly and declared that Liz is her first English friend. The queen has given her charge of Baby Charles,
who is only three. Liz is over the moon."

"Liz has great maternal instincts." Patrick grinned. "Thank
God we are traveling with James and not Anne. It will take the
Queen's Court at least a month to get organized for the jour-
ney."

"My conscience plagues me a bit because Elizabeth was my
cousin and I did what was expedient for once."

"I *always* do what's expedient; my conscience *never* plagues
me."

"That's because you don't have one," Robert jested.

Hepburn grinned. "Guilty as charged."

Robert's brother, the new Lord Hunsdon, and his brother-in-
law Scrope rode up, ready to rag the youngest Carey. "By God,
Thomas, who would have thought the runt of the litter shrewd
and calculating enough to raise our status to such dizzying
heights?"

Scrope traced an arched eyebrow in a feminine gesture that
looked ludicrous on such a rough-hewn man. "A king's favorite."

"Damn you both! Don't you dare insinuate that Jamie is bug-
gering me," Robert protested.

His two relatives and Hepburn roared with laughter. Then,

like a good brother should, George rubbed salt in the wound they'd just inflicted. "Always thought you were too pretty to piss!"

Robert laughed with them, as he realized it was their crude male way of saying they were proud of him.

To give Valiant some exercise, Hepburn galloped back along the cavalcade for a couple of miles and then returned for a word with King James, who was in the vanguard. "Sire, there's no end to the procession of Scots rushing to England in hope of spoils."

Jamie winked. "Like me, ye've already got yers picked out."

Hepburn grinned his acknowledgment, then added, "The English too, I notice, are joining the throng."

"Guid! The more the merrier. Naught beats a cockfight fer bloody, savage entertainment."

"There's so many traveling coaches back there, it looks like a Roman chariot race," Hepburn commented dryly.

"Veni, vidi, vici," James declared with a rare flash of wit.

Hepburn raised his arm in a mock salute. "Hail, Caesar!"

At Leeds Castle, Henry Percy, Earl of Northumberland, and George Clifford, Earl of Cumberland, joined the king's party. Patrick remarked to Robert, "I see Clifford has removed Elizabeth's glove from his hat. Perhaps we could slip him a pair of James's on the sly."

Carey's face lit with laughter. "James wears gloves?"

At Leicester, where the king's party was preparing to stay the night, Patrick was surprised to see Arbella Stuart arrive, with a maid in attendance and her carriage piled high with luggage. Hepburn rode up to her coach and gallantly kissed her hand.

"Lord Stewart, I'm delighted to see you. Take me to *our* cousin James, so that I may make my obeisance to the new King of England."

"You have managed to escape from your grandmother, Bess."

"Oh, no," Arbella said ingenuously. "My grandmother urged me to come with all speed. Now that the hateful, vindictive bitch Elizabeth is dead, I shall never be banished from Court again."

Hepburn masked his amusement. "Never speak ill of the dead."

"Oh, dear, it's supposed to bring ill luck, isn't it? I've had enough bad luck to last me a lifetime."

"I'm sure Lady Catherine will be happy to see you, Arbella."

"Cat was one of the few ladies who befriended me. But since I am related to the new monarch, everyone will wish to be my friend."

Hepburn's mouth twitched. He dismounted, turned Valiant over to David for stabling and helped Arbella from her carriage. "Come, we shall elbow our way to James."

The next morning Jamie was booted and spurred and in the saddle before dawn broke. "Curse these laggards! Ha' they no notion how fain I am tae see my capital?" It seemed the closer he got to London, the faster he wanted to reach it.

"I too am anxious to get to Whitehall, Sire. I'm ready to ride if you are," Hepburn assured him.

"My King's Guard will shit theirselves if I ride off wi'out 'em. They can never keep up on a hunt, and 'tis the same now when I'm on the greatest quest o' my life. Let's ride, laddie, while they're strugglin' intae their britches."

It wasn't until the small riding party arrived at Northampton and stopped to water their horses that the full regiment of guards caught up with James. He was in too high a mood to rebuke them. The first English nobles, who had ridden north to meet him from the Court of Whitehall, began to arrive. James was pleased that they saw him in the saddle, where he always looked his best.

"They obviously lost no time, Your Majesty. Only two days past these same courtiers walked in Elizabeth's funeral procession."

"They're no' thinkin' o' the funeral now; they're thinkin' o' the *coronation o' James the First o' England!*"

Or, more to the point, what they can get out of you, Patrick thought. *Don't hold them in contempt, Hepburn; they are merely being expedient.* Now that he was less than a hundred miles from the capital, Patrick had a decision to make. Tomorrow was Catherine's birthday, and he'd promised Cat he'd be in London by April 1. Then again, he lusted to see Spencer Park, the estate in Hertford that would soon be his. Hepburn weighed his options. If he spent March 31 in Hertford he'd still be able to keep his word. He smiled. *It never hurts to keep a female waiting.*

•   •   •

Catherine awoke early. *I'm twenty-one today* was her first thought. *Patrick WILL come* was her second. She slipped quietly from bed and lifted the heavy curtain to look outside. *Spring is here! The trees are budded and the birds are busy building.* She opened the window and smiled as a light breeze ruffled her hair. *Everything looks green and fresh and promising!* She inhaled the soft spring air. *Spencer Park is legally mine today.* She pictured her magnificent country estate and smiled. *This will be the happiest year of my life!*

"Happy birthday, my lamb." Maggie handed her a small parcel.

Excited as a child, Cat opened it quickly. "Oh, Maggie, it's beautiful!" She held up the delicate shell-pink nightgown embroidered with love knots and blushed at its transparency. *If he doesn't come, I'll remain a spinster and no one will ever see this!* Cat banished the disquieting thought immediately.

"Until this last year, I wished ye'd remain a child forever. But now I'm glad yer a woman at last, ready to drain life's cup."

Catherine put her arms about Maggie and hugged her close. "I love you, Maggie. You understand me well and accept me as I am."

"I don't like black. Too bad ye have to wear it on yer birthday, but ye look lovely in any color. What would ye like fer yer breakfast?"

"I'll dress and do my hair, then I shall go down myself. The dining hall will be almost empty." *I'm too excited to eat.*

Catherine paid extra-special attention to her hair, fashioning it in an elegant upswept style that gave her a sophisticated look. Then she put on the emerald earrings Patrick had placed in her ears the last time they'd slept together. She gazed into the mirror and decided they made her eyes look more green than gold. She fastened a small white ruff about her neck to relieve the somber black and emerged from her bedchamber.

"We are in mourning. Replace those earbobs with jet."

"No, Mother. I've quite made up my mind to wear these today." She opened the door and fled. *If Mother knew they were a gift from Hepburn, she'd have a fit. She's so obsessed with the death of Elizabeth, she's forgotten it's my birthday today. I wish she could get on with her life.* Cat immediately felt guilty. *I only wish that so I can get on with mine.*

As she passed through the Great Hall and the Presence Chamber, she saw no one of interest. She stepped into the Privy

Chamber, turned about and left. *I'm already looking for him. I must stop!*

For the next three hours she walked through the corridors of Whitehall, and then she visited the chapel. At lunchtime she went to the kitchens and filched a quince tart. It eased the ache inside her slightly, though she knew it was not caused by hunger.

Catherine went outside into the pale afternoon sunshine. She walked through the gardens, which were just springing to life, spent an hour at the stables, and then, keeping her inner panic at bay, she went down to the river and decided to go into the Shield Gallery. She searched for Patrick's shield, and when she saw it, emblazoned with the Hepburn leopards, her heart began to hammer.

Impulsively, she reached for the fine gold chain about her neck, unfastened it and slipped the leopard ring Hepburn had given her in lieu of a betrothal ring onto her finger. She stayed there for a long time, not wanting to leave. Here, at least, she felt some connection with him.

As the shadows grew long, she stood up reluctantly and walked from the Shield Gallery. She stood watching the traffic on the river and gradually the ache in her heart told her she must face facts. Hepburn was not coming today. Perhaps tomorrow, perhaps never. Wanting and wishing did not make it happen. She fought the lump in her throat. The hours had gone by so slowly, time had seemed to stand still. With lagging steps she entered the palace and climbed the stairs. When she arrived at their rooms she couldn't go in. Instead she climbed to White-hall's ramparts to watch the sun begin its descent upon the city of London.

She blinked as she caught sight of a lone figure riding into the courtyard. Surely only one man could be that tall! She picked up her skirts and started to run. She met him striding from the stables. Ignoring everyone abroad, she cried his name.

"Patrick! Patrick! You came!"

Suddenly, he was there, his black eyes meeting hers with an intimate look that stole her breath and her senses. Hepburn picked her up and swung her round. "Did you doubt me for one moment, Hellcat?"

Chapter Twenty-seven

$\mathcal{A}$s Patrick kissed her, Cat clung to him so fervently, he realized that she had indeed been uncertain of him. *I made the right decision to ride here first, with all speed, rather than go to Hertford.* "Happy birthday, sweetheart."

She gazed up at him in wonder. "You must have ridden hell-for-leather to get here before April."

"I left King James to eat my dust. He's most anxious to gain his capital and will be here tomorrow at the latest, but that simply wasn't fast enough for me." He touched one of the earrings he'd given her and grinned. "I knew you'd be wearing them."

"Cocksure devil," she said happily and raised her hand to show him that she was also wearing his leopard ring. He immediately removed it and slipped it back onto his own little finger. Before she could protest he kissed her quickly and kept one possessive arm about her. "Come on."

She allowed him to lead her inside the palace, but when he started to climb the stairs, she pulled back. "We cannot go to my chambers. Mother doesn't know about us—"

He hugged her to his side. "I'm taking you to Philadelphia's rooms. She won't be back tonight; she's busy flirting with Jamie."

Cat shuddered at the thought. "You lie!"

"Frequently."

The female servant who opened Philadelphia's door made a great fuss of Hepburn, then discreetly disappeared.

"You devil. All you have to do is raise an eyebrow to have a woman eating out of your hand."

"Nothing so overt. If I raised an eyebrow at a woman, she'd jump into bed," he teased.

"Oh, God, I'd forgotten how big you are and how compelling." Cat ran her hands over the hard muscles in his broad chest.

"And I'd forgotten how small and delicate you are, though I remember your impulsiveness and your *passion*."

"Hepburn," she said breathlessly, "please don't start making love to me." Cat hovered on the brink of surrender.

He hid his amusement. "I have no such intent. Custom demands that the bride and groom sleep apart until they are wed. We've waited this long; I'm sure we can manage one more night."

She looked up into his dark face. "Tomorrow?" She hesitated, then plunged in quickly. "Patrick, Mother will be outraged!"

"Cat, you are twenty-one. You don't need her consent."

"That's true, isn't it? But, Patrick, I would like her approval. If only there were some way I could—"

"Catherine, you can safely leave Isobel to me."

She looked at him with uncertainty. "She is obsessed about mourning Elizabeth. The thought of King James taking the queen's place is anathema to her. She isn't like other women. She's cold and distant . . . she doesn't respond to men."

"Does she not?" This time he couldn't hide his amusement. "Now, I'm starving. Let us go and dine. Sometime tomorrow, David Hepburn and my luggage should catch up with me. I shall speak with Isobel, and when King James arrives he can marry us."

He says everything with such certainty. He must be a wizard or a warlock. "You are my magic man."

He reached into his doublet and took out a small box. He opened it and removed a magnificent emerald and diamond ring. "This is the betrothal ring I chose for you." He put it on her finger.

Her eyes shone with happiness. "Patrick, I love you so much!"

He kissed her thoroughly. "You had better, my little Hell-cat!"

When Catherine opened her eyes the next morning, happiness flooded through her like a tidal wave. Last night, by the time she returned, her mother had retired to her chamber. "He's here!" Cat had whispered to Maggie as she showed her the emerald betrothal ring.

"Ye intend to wed him?" Maggie whispered back.

With a furtive glance at Isobel's closed door, Cat nodded. She went to bed and enjoyed her first good night's sleep in weeks.

Maggie drew back the curtains, and the April sun spilled into the room. She took an elegant black silk gown from the wardrobe and when Cat was bathed and dressed, helped her fashion her hair.

Catherine left before her mother emerged from her bedchamber. She had a good idea where she would find Patrick. He had a man's healthy appetite and would be seeking food at this early hour. When she spotted his tall figure in the Great Hall, her heart did a somersault and she wondered if it would always be so. He was talking with the Lord Chamberlain, who usually displayed a haughty manner because of his supreme power in allocating lodgings at Court. Today, however, his manner was ingratiating toward Hepburn. She watched Patrick nod and the Lord Chamberlain bow deeply.

"Good morning, sweetheart." He took her hand to his lips and smiled intimately into her golden eyes. "I have just been offered one of the most commodious apartments in the palace."

"That's amazing. The chamberlain is not known to be generous."

"Not amazing." He grinned. "He is aware I am cousin to the king and is bribing me to put in a good word for him with James."

Her eyes widened. "All will now depend on James's pleasure. Everyone at Court will be filled with hope and fear and uncertainty about the offices they hold, and even their palace accommodation. Nothing will remain the same."

"Many of the English nobles are wondering if they will be ousted by favorites from Scotland." He led her to a seat and immediately servers rushed up to offer them breakfast. He gazed about the Great Hall, where the courtiers dined and which opened into the Presence Chamber. "Once the king arrives, this place will be like a circus. There will be the equivalent of performing dogs, clowns, trick ponies, tumblers and even fireeaters, all juggling for position."

She slanted him a sly glance. "And which will you be?"

He winked at her. "I shall be the magician, of course."

Cat nibbled her bread and honey and sipped some rose water, and then she simply sat and gazed at him. "I love to watch you eat."

"You'll have the rest of your life to watch me. If you are finished eating, I want you to go upstairs and change. Today is not a day of mourning; it is a day of celebration. James won't take kindly to those subjects wearing black. You have such beautiful clothes, Cat. I don't want you looking like a nun on our wedding day. I would feel as if I were robbing a convent."

She drew in a swift breath, "Mother—"

"Ah, yes. Mother. She is the next item on my agenda."

Patrick escorted Catherine to her chambers. He remained at the door. "Tell your mother I would like a word with her."

Isobel, draped in black, came listlessly to the door.

"Lady Spencer, would you do me the honor of walking with me? No one is more familiar with Whitehall, and I would appreciate your help in learning the layout of the palace." He offered his arm.

"Why, of course, Lord Stewart." She was mildly surprised yet flattered at his request. She looked with approval at his black doublet, took his arm and walked at his side. "I am in deepest mourning, and my heart is heavy with sorrow. The loss of my queen fills me with a melancholy I cannot shake. I know not what will become of me now that my position at Court has been lost."

He covered her fingers that lay on his arm with his own large hand. "My dear Lady Spencer, whatever makes you think your position has been lost? You are a Scot. With all your dedication and experience as head of the Wardrobe Department, who better to take charge of Queen Anne's wardrobe? She is a young, attractive woman with a keen interest in clothes. She will need a knowing hand to guide her in matters pertaining to a wardrobe that is fitting for a Queen of England. One door has been closed, but another threshold beckons you to step into a new golden era."

"But . . . but I have never even met Queen Anne . . ."

"My dear Lady Spencer, that is easily remedied. I myself will present you and sing your praises. I have an idea!" he declared as if it had just occurred to him. He led her out into the gardens. "The queen and her household, her children and ladies, will have to travel in short stages with many stops along the way. Why don't you and Lady Catherine offer them the hospitality of Spencer Park? Hertfordshire could be their last stop before they arrive in the capital. I know that planning for a royal visit would take a great deal of skill and know-how, but for a lady with your ability it could be a triumph."

Isobel gave him her full attention. "You think she'd accept?"

"Not only would Queen Anne accept, she would be eternally grateful for your generous hospitality. She has already asked Liz Carey to take charge of her youngest son, Prince Charles."

"Really? Since you are second cousin to King James, I imagine you have a great deal of influence with the royal family."

"A certain influence," he admitted modestly.

"Spencer Park belongs to Catherine, but I'm sure I can persuade her to invite Queen Anne and her Court." Her face was animated.

"With my voice added to yours, I am *sure* we can persuade her. I have asked Lady Catherine to be my wife, Isobel."

She looked stunned. "You wish to marry my daughter?"

"I do," he said firmly. "Your father, Lord Winton, as well as King James have approved the match. Do we have your blessing?"

She blinked rapidly as her mind quickly grasped the advantages of uniting her family with a Stewart. "I think it a splendid match, my lord. Catherine will need a firm hand if she is to become a worthy Lady Stewart. She is impulsive and willful."

"I appreciate your advice, Isobel," Hepburn said solemnly. "I expect the king to arrive this afternoon. I'm sure you will want to change your gown before you greet His Majesty. I believe blue is your special color, Lady Spencer. It's Anne's favorite too."

She threw him a coy look. "I believe you can maneuver your way about the Court of Whitehall extremely well, without any help from me, your lordship."

The woman who returned to the apartment bore little resemblance to the Isobel Spencer who had left with Patrick Hepburn. Gone was the air of tragedy that had made her seem as if she were in a trance. Vanished was the melancholy mood that made her droop like a wilted flower. In their place was an air of purpose and resolve.

"Maggie, is my blue gown here or at Richmond Palace?"

"Ye have two or three; I'm sure there's one in yer wardrobe."

"Good! We must put away our mourning and prepare ourselves to welcome James Stuart, our new King of England. There is no time to waste. He's coming this afternoon. He could be here now!"

Surprised but pleased at Isobel's attitude, Maggie searched the back of the wardrobe until she found a blue dress.

"Catherine!" Isobel took the gown from Maggie and gestured toward Cat's chamber. "Tell her she must change out of black."

Maggie opened the door, slipped inside and found Catherine standing before her mirror fastening a lavender-colored ruff about her neck. It set off her cream silk gown embroidered with tiny purple thistles. "I'll get yer amethyst combs for yer hair and Audra's jeweled knife." She unlocked the jewel casket. "I don't know what's come o'er yer mother. She's actually changing into a blue gown to meet the new king, begod!"

Catherine's eyes sparkled. "Patrick Hepburn has come over her. He's a magician!"

"Well, he's certainly waved his magic wand over Isobel!"

Cat couldn't suppress her laughter. "That sounds risqué."

"I warrant his lordship's wand is a formidable tool that no woman can resist."

Fortunately, I don't have to. Cat blushed at her own thoughts.

"Maggie, I need help with my hair." Isobel opened the door and stopped on the threshold. "What a clever minx you are to choose a gown with a Scottish emblem. Lord Stewart told me he had asked you to become his wife and that you had accepted him."

Catherine was hesitant. *Is it possible that she isn't going to make a scene?* "I did accept, Mother." She held out her hand. "This is my betrothal ring."

Isobel took her hand and gaped at the large emerald surrounded by diamonds. "Do you know, I believe you are like me, after all, Catherine. How very shrewd of you to snare a husband who will have power at Court. This marriage will elevate not only you but your family as well. We must make wedding plans. Who would have thought the Seton name would carry more weight than Spencer?"

Catherine was so relieved that her mother was not furious

about her pledge to Hepburn that she decided it would be politic to agree with everything Isobel said. "Do I hear someone knocking?"

Maggie opened the door and held it wide.

"Surprise!" Arbella entered with a flourish and did a little pirouette to show off her traveling outfit. "No more ghastly white dresses for me. Oh, Cat, I'm deliriously happy to be back!"

"Arbella! Everything at Court is changing so quickly."

"I am now extremely high in the pecking order. How fortuitous that my dear father and King James's father were brothers."

"I, too, am Scottish, Lady Arbella," Isobel said importantly.

Cat and Maggie rolled their eyes at each other.

"The chamberlain has given me new rooms. I'm no longer confined to the ladies' quarters under the hateful eye of that dragon, Throckmorton. I intend to find myself a husband."

"My daughter, Catherine, is to be married to Lord Stewart."

"You're to marry Hepburn?" Arbella's lips tightened with chagrin. "I met him at Leicester, and the devious devil never gave me a hint! When is the wedding to be?"

"Arbella, why don't you show me your new chambers?" Catherine changed the subject quickly. Hepburn had his own ideas about when they would be wed, and it was Patrick who would make the decision.

"My maid is unpacking for me. Come and help me choose a gown and we can go down and welcome my cousin Jamie together."

"Where on earth can she be?" Patrick didn't expect Robert Carey to know; he was simply voicing his frustration. James Stuart had arrived at Whitehall accompanied by Cecil, his Secretary of State, more than an hour ago. Dozens of noble Scots, as well as the multitude of English courtiers who had ridden out to welcome their new king, were arriving by the minute.

"Take it from a man with a wife and sisters; females take an inordinate amount of time dressing and primping so they will look lovely in our eyes when there is a special occasion."

Hepburn laughed. "Don't delude yourself. Women dress for other women. They love to outdo one another."

"You are a cynical devil, Patrick."

"Mea culpa!" He was too cynical to believe in love, and yet the feelings that Catherine stirred in him were profound. He was highly attracted to everything about her . . . her beauty, her elegance, her wit, her impulsiveness and her deep passion for life. He felt both possessive and protective of her and admitted to a towering pride that the exquisite lady was his and his alone. He wanted her on his arm so that he could show off his great marriage prize to this throng that composed the Court of King James.

"The Great Hall, Guard Chamber and Presence Chamber have never been this crowded. I think James is enjoying the attention."

"I went to the kitchens for food before daybreak and found it a hive of activity with preparations for special dishes for tonight's reception. I warrant there could be no better time for a wedding."

It took Carey a moment to comprehend Hepburn's meaning. "You intend to wed Catherine this afternoon?"

Patrick nodded. "If the lady in question ever deigns to put in an appearance."

Robert frowned. "Cat has agreed? She wishes to marry you?" *Only a short time ago, this marriage would have been out of the question. Both the queen and Isobel would have forbidden it. Now Hepburn is in a position to take whatever he desires.*

His grin was wolfish. "Lady Catherine wants what I want."

"Patrick! It's a good thing you are so tall or I would never have found you in this crowd." Cat reached out to touch him.

Hepburn took possession of her hands and drew them to his lips. His dark eyes devoured her. "My sweetheart, the wait was worth it."

Robert saw the intimate look they exchanged and knew that any witnessing it would recognize they were bound lovers. *When was it that Catherine stopped being a child and became a woman?* He answered his own question. *When she laid eyes on Hepburn.*

"Oh, hello, Robert, I didn't see you," she said breathlessly and gave him a radiant smile. "Is Liz here with you?"

"No, she will be traveling with Queen Anne."

Patrick took Cat's arm possessively. "Come, I will tell you about Liz's royal appointment as we walk."

Arbella looked at Robert. "Hepburn has swept her off her

feet." She watched the crowd part for them. He was wearing a deep purple doublet, the same shade as the thistles embroidered on Catherine's cream-colored silk. "They look like actors on a stage."

Robert agreed. *Catherine has given him her heart. I pray Hepburn is not merely playing a part.*

"Queen Anne put Liz in charge of three-year-old Prince Charles and his household as a reward for Robert's services to the Crown."

"What services?" Cat asked Hepburn.

"It's not for me to say. You'll have to ask Robert. Anne is clever. By this appointment she demonstrates that she places complete confidence in an English lady, which will endear her to her new subjects."

"You suggest the queen did it for political expedience."

"Don't look down your beautiful nose at expedience, Cat. It is a powerful motivator. I suggested to your mother that if she wants to be in charge of Queen Anne's Wardrobe, she must get your permission to offer the hospitality of Spencer Park to the queen and her entourage on their long trek to London. Isobel instantly saw it was expedient and miraculously cast off her mourning."

So, Mother was not mourning Elizabeth; she was mourning her position at Court. "You found her weakness and manipulated her!"

He covered her hand. "We all have an Achilles' heel."

She slanted an amused glance at him. "I shall have to discover yours, my lord."

He dipped his head and brushed his lips against her ear. "You are my weakness, Hellcat."

She laughed up at him. Whether it was true or not, he always knew exactly the right thing to say.

"Catherine, you remember John Erskine, Earl of Mar?"

"I do indeed. Welcome to Whitehall, my lord."

"Lady Catherine and I are about to be wed, Johnny."

"Congratulations! Trust a canny Scot tae wed a Seton." He winked at Cat. "Put a ring through his nose, lass."

Patrick placed her hand on John's arm. "Look after her for a moment, while I have a word with James." He easily elbowed aside the men about the king and bent to murmur in His Majesty's ear.

Catherine watched Hepburn breathlessly as he spoke with the new King of England. She saw James smile, then laugh, then nod his head in agreement. *Is he manipulating the king?*

"Bruce! Where are ye, mon?" the king shouted. "We're aboot tae celebrate our first weddin'." When Edward Bruce, Abbot of Kinross, stepped forward, James said, "Ye can perform the nuptials, an' I shall give the bonnie bride away."

Catherine's hand flew to her mouth and her cheeks flushed a delicate pink. "Patrick said the king would marry us today, but I scarce believed him." She glanced at the people surrounding her and found they were all part of her extended family.

Philadelphia kissed her cheek. "You are the most beautiful bride I have ever seen, darling."

Her aunt Beth beamed as her husband, George, the new Lord Hunsdon, slapped Hepburn on the back and congratulated him.

Robert Carey ushered Isobel and Maggie to the front of the crowd milling about the king, and Catherine saw the expression on her mother's face change from astonishment to smug satisfaction.

Arbella spoke up importantly. "I shall be your maid of honor."

Catherine's smile was tremulous. "Thank you, Arbella." She felt Patrick tug on her hand and, following his lead, knelt before the king and the abbot. Edward Bruce's accent was almost as broad as Jamie's, and she couldn't decipher his words. Patrick, however, must have understood.

"I will." Hepburn's voice was so deep it rumbled.

The abbot addressed Catherine and she had to concentrate to understand. When he paused expectantly, she said, "I will."

"Who gi'eth this woman tae be wed tae this mon?"

"I, James Stuart, King o' England an' Scotland, gi'e this woman tae be joined in holy matrimony tae this mon."

When Patrick firmly took her right hand in his, the contrast in size was so marked, it looked incongruous and she almost laughed. Then Patrick was repeating words that Bruce spoke, but to Cat's ear they sounded totally different.

"I, Patrick, take thee, Catherine, to my wedded wife, to have and to hold from this day forward, for better for worse, for richer for poorer, in sickness and in health, to love and to cherish till death us do part."

Without waiting for the abbot's prompting, Catherine repeated what Hepburn had said. Bruce bent a stern eye upon her. "And to *obey*," he admonished.

She nodded quickly. "Yes, love, cherish and obey." She saw Robert spread his palms to show that they were empty, then she saw Patrick smile, reach into his doublet and bring out a gold wedding band.

His large hands were slightly clumsy as they found her third finger and managed to slip on the tiny gold circle. "With this ring I thee wed, with my body I thee honor, and with all my worldly goods I thee endow."

He's endowing me with Crichton. Somehow I always knew it would be mine. All I have to give him in return is Spencer Park.

"I pronounce that they be mon an' wife taegether."

King James motioned for them to rise. "It is my great pleasure tae present Patrick and Catherine Hepburn, Lord and Lady Stewart."

Without any prompting, Patrick lifted his bride in his arms and planted a kiss on her beautiful lips as a symbol of his possession. The throng cheered wildly, and when he set her down a loving cup of wine was pressed into the bridegroom's hands.

As he held the cup to her lips, Catherine gazed up into his dark eyes, and the king, the Court and the entire world receded from her consciousness. Hepburn was her husband, her lord, her mate and her entire universe. Her heart overflowed with joy.

The next hour was taken up with people congratulating the newlyweds, but finally they managed to slip away from the crowds for a few private moments. "Tell Maggie to pack your things and take them to Spencer Park. David Hepburn will accompany her." He brushed the backs of his calloused fingers across her delicate cheek. "We'll only go as far as Richmond tonight, but don't tell anyone that. Come on, we'll have to put in a show at Jamie's reception banquet, but eat quickly because I intend to spirit you away at the first opportunity."

Within half an hour of the food and wine being served, the lovers made their escape from the banquet hall. Hands clasped, they went upstairs to Cat's chambers, where Maggie had a small bag waiting that held only toilet articles and the new nightgown.

Catherine covered her cream silk gown with a warm cloak, and as they were about to leave, Isobel opened the door.

Hepburn lifted her by the elbows and kissed her on both cheeks.

"Isobel, I charge you to give us at least a week alone before you descend on us in Hertford to make plans for the queen's visit."

Isobel simpered. "You have my word, Lord Stewart."

"Good-bye Mother," Catherine said breathlessly.

As the pair made their way to the stables, Cat remembered, "I have no horse, Patrick. Jasmine is at Richmond."

"I will take you up before me. It won't be the first time Valiant has carried us both. I have no intention of letting you out of my arms for the next twenty-four hours."

Chapter Twenty-eight

*V*aliant settled into an even, rhythmic, slow gallop as he followed the winding river road that led from Whitehall to Richmond. Catherine, filled with excitement, leaned forward eagerly, impatient to reach their destination. The lights and sounds from the Thames were the only things to penetrate the velvet darkness, and as she began to relax she realized that this night ride was deliciously romantic. Held fast in the powerful arms of Hepburn, she knew she had never felt this safe and secure before. She leaned back against his hard body, closed her eyes and inhaled deeply. The air was fragrant with lilac and the tang of the sea. The smell, mingled with the scent of leather and horse, became a potent aphrodisiac. Catherine shuddered at the intensity of the emotions that swept through her.

"Are you cold, my sweetheart?" Patrick's arm tightened about her, drawing her closer to his body. His lips brushed her ear. "Slip your arms about me and share my heat."

She turned so that she was facing him and slid her arms about his hard, muscled torso. Beneath her ear she could feel the steady thud of his heart, which she fancied was filled to overflowing with his love for her, and she went weak with longing.

As Cat snuggled against his body, Patrick became aware of how small and delicate she was. Desire pulsed at his groin with a sweet, almost unendurable ache. She lay softly between his thighs, and her breasts swelled against him, filling his arms and his lap with her loveliness. He wanted her in the bed like this, both of them naked. The heat from his body now mingled with hers, and the scent of her perfumed flesh intoxicated him. When a strand of her silken hair brushed across his cheek it aroused him so much that he became marble hard, in an agony of need, and he doubted that he'd ever grow soft again in her presence.

Slowly he became aware of how precious a prize she was. He realized that he was the luckiest man on earth to have found her, wooed her and won her. She was that rarest of treasures, a wealthy heiress who was not only a great Court beauty but also a maid who was innocent and had known no other man save him. Feelings of possessiveness and protectiveness rose up strongly. He dropped a kiss on the top of her head and knew he would rather be here in the saddle with this woman between his thighs than anywhere else on earth tonight.

When they arrived at the Richmond stables, Patrick slid from the saddle and held up his arms. His bride came down to him in a flurry of petticoats, clinging to him sweetly, eagerly, and he held her imprisoned against his body for long minutes as his demanding mouth claimed hers in a dozen rapturous kisses. He took her small bag and turned Valiant over to a groom who had been told to expect them. When Cat heard Jasmine whinny a welcome, she hurried to her stall. "My lovely girl . . . how I have missed you."

Patrick waited, concealing his impatience. Finally he took her hand. "You can visit with Jasmine tomorrow. I need you tonight."

She laughed up into his dark, demanding eyes, thrilled at the blazing desire she saw burning there. He wrapped a possessive arm about her, and as they reached the steps of the Richmond house, he swept her up against his heart and carried her over the threshold. He set her on her feet before the gathered servants.

"Lord and Lady Stewart, welcome to Richmond." The housekeeper bobbed a curtsy and the others followed suit.

"How did you know we were married?" Cat asked in amazement.

"I sent them a note days ago to expect us," Patrick declared.

She looked up at the man towering at her side. "But I didn't know days ago," she protested.

"I did." Once again he swept her into his arms and carried her up the stairs. His teeth gently bit her earlobe. "I am your destiny, Hellcat. Surely you knew from the moment we met?"

Catherine looked at him in wonder. She did have a strange, heady feeling that their union was predestined.

Once they were safely inside her bedchamber, he kicked the door closed and set her feet to the carpet. "My own precious Cat, though I knew this day would come, I don't know how I endured the endless wait. I never want us to be separated again."

Her eyes flooded with tears at his touching declaration.

"Don't you dare let those tears fall, my beauty. I'm a brute to make you cry." He kissed her eyelids. "I want to make you delirious with happiness." His fingertips wiped away her tears.

"Patrick, I've never been this happy in my life. You are my very own brute, and I love you just the way you are."

He removed her cloak, then sat her down on the high bed and went down on his knees. "I kneel in awe at your delicate beauty, Cat. I vow to protect you always and swear you will never be sorry that you chose me for your husband." He removed her shoes, then lifted her gown to peel off her stockings and garters. "My hands are so rough and clumsy, how can you bear me to touch you?"

"Your hands are big and powerful, and I crave your touch."

"Will you allow me to undress you if I promise to be gentle?"

Her eyes filled with wonder. "You know how to be gentle?"

"I can try, sweetheart," he promised earnestly.

The corners of her mouth lifted. "Try some other time, I beg you, my love. I wed a Border lord and tonight I want to be treated like your wench, Hepburn!"

He threw back his head and laughed until the cords of his throat looked like cables. He got off his knees, then lifted her so that she stood on the bed, and he reached up her skirt to pull off her drawers and petticoat. As his fingers fumbled to unfasten the tiny buttons on her gown, she inched up her skirt until her bare thighs were on a level with his face, then taunted him by lowering it to her ankles and beginning again. This time she lifted it even higher to reveal the black curls on her plump mons.

"You wicked little witch, hold still or I'll ruin your gown."

"Do you want me to be a decorous little bride, or do you want me to be a cock tease? You decide."

He deftly managed the buttons and stripped her naked. "Let me undress, and I'll do some cock teasing of my own!" He removed his clothes with the speed of a man who knew what he was about. He grabbed her ankles and toppled her to the bed, then launched himself on top of her, imprisoning her beneath his big hard body. He captured her lips, traced their outline with the tip of his tongue, then plunged inside with a ravishing kiss that plundered her mouth. He trailed his erection along her soft thighs, deliberately avoided her mons and rubbed it across her belly. When his cock touched her breasts, it began to buck and throb with the feel of her warm, silken flesh.

Cat reached up, slid her fingers around his hard length, squeezed gently and heard his groan of pleasure. She teased him until he was at the end of his endurance, cupping his large sac with her other hand until his entire groin was rigid and swollen with rampant need. Then she opened her legs and arched beneath him in wanton invitation, yielding wildly, generously, with a passion she could no longer control.

The mating was cataclysmic. The lovers had been apart far too long, and now their bodies couldn't get enough of each other. When their climax came, it was strong, and their shudders went on and on as if they would never end.

Patrick gathered her in his arms and took her with him as he rolled his back onto the bed, enfolding her softness against him with her luscious breasts upon his muscled chest and her belly against his. He opened his thighs so that she lay between his long legs with her woman's center resting on his groin—no longer rigid but still tumescent. He dipped his head to feather kisses into the curls at her temples and kissed her eyelids as she sighed with languorous pleasure at the great release he had given her.

His whispered love words mesmerized her, as his warm breath swept her neck and his lips touched her ear. At first his murmurs lulled her, sounding like the purr of a huge cat, and she stretched against him luxuriously. Gradually she became aware of the things he was saying and listened intently.

"Until now we have only shared hot, driving sex. Tonight, Catherine, I am going to show you how to make love."

She lifted her head and stared into his dark, fathomless eyes. She caught her breath as she realized she was about to embark upon a journey with him from which there might be no return. She sensed it was a place where only a few dared to go. It was a destination that demanded the surrender of not only your heart, but your immortal soul as well.

He took possession of her fingers and bestowed lingering kisses upon each one, his lips savoring her loveliness, his eyes worshipping the delicate beauty that was hers alone. He dropped magical kisses into her palm, then closed her fingers over them to keep them from escaping. His mouth lavished her wrist and the tender flesh of her inner arm. His lips and his fingers anointed her shoulder until Catherine was floating in a sea of mystical sensuality. His tongue traced over her flesh, tasting, licking, cherishing, every inch of silken skin, making her feel like the most beautiful woman who'd ever lived or been loved by a man.

His possessive fingers followed where his mouth had led, stroking and caressing and evoking an anticipation that was so intense she wanted to scream. As his mouth and fingers cherished her breasts and nipples she writhed with deep pleasure, longing for more and knowing he would give her more.

It took him more than an hour to reach the insides of her thighs. By now she was reeling from his touch and the male scent of his body. Heat and chills chased through her, and a myriad of sensations she'd never dreamed of danced over her sensitive skin, evoked by the slow hot glide of his lips and his provocative tongue, seeking out all her secret female pleasure points.

He rose up above her, making love to her with his eyes until she was panting with need. He towered over her, choosing the moment when she was luscious and ripe and smoldering with dark, erotic fire. He thrust into her slowly, inch by delicious inch, until his shaft was seated to the hilt. Then he held still, allowing his cock to throb and pulse against her unbelievably tight honeyed sheath. He felt her close sleekly around him, and both enjoyed every quiver and vibration of the achingly perfect consummation.

He dipped his head and slipped his tongue into the hot, dark cave of her mouth. Then, moving his cock and his tongue in unison with long, slow thrusts, he brought her to a peak of ecstasy. He stopped then, wanting to draw out her rapture. He was in no hurry to bring such an exquisite mating to a climax. Three times he brought her to the brink of fulfillment, and finally, it was her love cries that made him lose control. His white-hot seed flooded into her, at last bringing her to orgasm, and he thrilled as her shattering cry of bliss poured out into the still, dark night.

He gathered her to him in a tender embrace that was heart-scalding. She clung to him, knowing that what they had shared was a rare gift from the gods of love. He had made the age-old act of domination and submission absolutely perfect. Her body softened in his arms as she drifted to the edge of sleep. *I will never be alone again. Patrick Hepburn will keep me safe forever.*

In the morning, when Cat lifted her lashes, she found Patrick's arms still about her, his dark eyes gazing into hers. She smiled shyly. "What a lovely way to awaken." She reached out and traced the arch of a black eyebrow with her fingertips.

He kissed her nose. "Mrs. Dobson brought us breakfast."

Cat gasped. "She didn't see us in bed together?"

"She did indeed and stared long enough to satisfy her female curiosity. She must have decided you were in good hands . . . it will take a week to get the grin off her face."

Cat blushed prettily as he arose and brought the tray to the bed. He piled up their pillows, got back into bed, lifted her so that she sat between his legs and proceeded to tempt her with food and caresses. She opened her mouth for his delicious offerings then licked her lips. "It tastes better when shared with a naked husband. Aren't you hungry?"

"Ravenous."

She felt his erection stir against her soft bottom cheeks and knew he did not refer to the food. "Are you always in that rampant condition, my lord?"

"Of course not," he denied. "It only comes upon me at morning and at night and a dozen times in between."

She turned in his arms and yielded her mouth to him. "Let me slake your appetite for me so that you can think about food."

An hour's love play satisfied them for a time. Later, when the bathing tub was filled with water, they bathed together, with Cat again reclining between his legs. "I love being held this way."

Her glance fell on the small traveling bag she had brought. "Oh, I never wore the lovely nightgown Maggie sewed special for me."

"She didn't intend you to wear it on your wedding night. Maggie knows better. She made it for you to wear this morning. Surely you don't think I'm going to let you get dressed?" He squeezed the large sponge and the water cascaded over her breasts, making her quiver, and she realized that Patrick intended to keep her in a state of arousal all day. She sighed with happiness.

The afternoon shadows were lengthening before they could bear to leave their idyll. Patrick saddled Valiant and Jasmine, then lifted his bride into the saddle, and they cantered stirrup to stirrup, oblivious of everything except each other. They rode contentedly side by side, talking and laughing until dusk began to fall, then Patrick, realizing they were still five miles from Spencer Park, issued his challenge.

Before the word *race* was out of his mouth, Cat was galloping like the wind, her laughter and her lovely hair streaming out into the soft air of the April evening. Both of them knew he could easily overtake her, but he had no desire to pass her. Instead, he kept apace, his glance filled with admiration for her impulsive courage and her *joie de vivre*. Simply being in her company and watching her filled him with happiness.

When they arrived at Spencer Park, everything was in readiness for them. Mr. Burke led them to the library, where he performed the ceremony of turning over the keys to Lady Stewart. The deeds to the mansion, the tenant farms and the vast acreage were laid out on the desk along with a strongbox and the account books. Catherine smiled gratefully at Mr. Burke and the head servants he had gathered to welcome them.

"I deeply appreciate the years of dedication, loyalty and hard work you have put into making Spencer Park not only a magnificent country estate but also a profitable enterprise. I proudly accept the keys as chatelaine and turn the deeds and all else over to my husband, Patrick Hepburn, Lord Stewart, who will henceforth be master of this household."

"I too thank you for your years of loyal service until my wife became old enough to claim her inheritance. Mr. Burke, I value your stewardship, which I shall be hard-pressed to improve upon, and assure you that I will seek your guidance in many things."

The newlyweds hurried through the dinner that awaited them in the vast formal dining room and escaped upstairs at the first opportunity. David Hepburn and Maggie, who had arrived the day before with a coach filled with luggage, had transformed Catherine's bedchamber and the room adjoining it into a master suite. The double door between had been removed, and deep, comfortable chairs placed before the fireplace had turned the other chamber into a sitting room. It also held a small table where they could sit and share an intimate meal.

Cat threw open her wardrobe. "Maggie, you managed to bring all my favorite gowns. How on earth would I manage without you?"

Patrick came up behind Cat and slipped his arms about her waist. "You spoil her to death, Maggie. Where the devil will all my stuff go?" he asked in mock dismay.

"David filled the wardrobe in the other room with yer clothes, my lord, and he put yer strongbox on top of the tall chest fer safekeeping." She handed Cat a small key. "Yer jewel case is on yer dressing table. David brought up a jug of ale and some wine and assured me the only other thing ye'd insist upon is privacy."

"I bow to his intuitive power and thank you for everything, Maggie, my love." Patrick held open the door. "Don't think I'm pushing you out, but I would like to be alone with my blushing bride."

Maggie's amused glance swept over the tall Scot and lingered at his groin. "Well it's obvious ye've no intention of hiding yer impatience, or anything else fer that matter. I bid ye good night."

Hours later, as his beautiful wife lay asleep in his arms, a feeling of contentment stole over Hepburn. Not long ago he had assumed the married state would suffocate him because he had always ranged alone, but the anticipation of sharing his life with Catherine now brought him deep pleasure.

After they had made love, they lay curled together and talked for hours. He told her some of his plans for Spencer Park. Patrick wanted to breed horses as well as cattle, and Cat agreed wholeheartedly. He suggested that they enclose some commons and wasteland adjacent to their property and even increase the number of their tenant farms.

She told him of the plans she had sketched for a brew house, patterned after the one at Crichton.

"Did you know that England's most profitable export is wool?"

"You think we should breed sheep here at Spencer Park?"

"No, sheep and cattle can't graze on the same land. Sheep grow thicker coats in the Borders. I'd like to take some of

Spencer Park's profits and buy a herd of ewes for Crichton." His arms tightened. "We will have to divide our time between England and Scotland. There won't be much time for Court life," he warned, expecting her to protest.

She lifted her mouth to his. "I don't want Court life; I want *our* life. I don't wish to be at the beck and call of a queen and do her bidding; I only hunger to do your bidding."

His eyes filled with amusement. "Little Hellcat, that will last only until the honeymoon is over."

She set her lips to his throat. "Our honeymoon will never be over. I'm mad in love with you, Patrick. Let me show you."

Now, as he gazed down at her lovely sleeping face, he grinned into the darkness. No wonder he felt contented. Her sexual appetite was almost a match for his.

During their first week at Spencer Park, Patrick and Catherine spent every day and night together. It gave him deep pleasure to educate his wife about the magnificent country estate she had brought him in marriage. They rode out over the two thousand acres, visiting all their tenant farms, and met the families who lived and worked on their land.

She listened proudly as Hepburn eased the fears of their people by assuring them that there would be no drastic changes in their lives because Lady Catherine had married a Scot. He promised to answer any questions they had and to address their grievances. He encouraged them to speak freely and pledged to work with them to solve any difficulties that might arise and were inevitable on such a large estate.

As they rode side by side, Catherine's eyes glowed with admiration. "You have them eating out of your hand. How do you manage to earn their loyalty so quickly?"

"When they speak, I listen. I show respect for the hard labor involved in working the land and tending the herds. They see my calloused hands and know I am no stranger to manual labor. When I urge them to voice their grievances, I am not being magnanimous; I am using common sense. People are happier and more productive if they have some measure of control over their lives."

It was the height of calving season and Catherine watched, enthralled, as the cows on every farm began to give birth. She learned that a newborn calf did not have long horns, but devel-

oped them over its first year of life. Patrick explained that a
healthy cow that had previously given birth had no difficulty
delivering her calf, but a heifer that went into labor for the first
time sometimes needed help. This was graphically demonstrated when one of the young longhorn's loud mooing and
frantic struggles alerted Catherine that she was in trouble. Cat
was out of the saddle in a flash, but Hepburn was quicker. She
stood by, holding her breath, as Patrick and a cowherd helped
the animal to deliver not one but two calves. Cat heaved a deep
sigh of relief as both the newborns struggled to their feet. Her
eyes sparkled with joy. "Oh, twins. It's a miracle!"

"I'm thrilled that you are developing a keen interest in the
working of the estate. I know that watching the milking and
learning the process of butter and cheese making has brought
you satisfaction this week, but I believe it will also help you to
become a good businesswoman."

Her husband's praise flattered her more than compliments
about her beauty. "I remember that you once told me Spencer
Park supplied butter to Elizabeth's Court. With your connections to England's new king, do you think you could increase
the things we supply to include milk and cheese?"

"You have been reading my mind. I'm supposed to be the
one with occult powers," he teased.

"Perhaps it's catching!"

He lifted her into the saddle. "Perhaps it is. Tell me what I
am thinking this very moment."

She laughed seductively and bent to whisper in his ear.

He grinned wickedly. "You are cheating, Hellcat. When I lift
you into the saddle you know I turn hard as marble."

When they returned to the manor they went upstairs immediately. Patrick lit them a fire and then they bathed together.
Since they planned to dine in the privacy of their chamber, Cat
donned a pretty night rail, but only when Maggie brought up
their food did Patrick shrug into a robe.

They laughed and made love, and finally, as she lay in his
arms in front of the fire, Catherine admitted she'd never had
such intense feelings before. She didn't merely love this man.
She adored him, worshipped him and doted on him. She
threaded her fingers into his black hair. "Patrick Hepburn, I
treasure you."

"You are my treasure." He lifted her and carried her to bed.

Chapter *Twenty-nine*

*T*en blissful days of privacy came to an end when Isobel and her sister-in-law, Beth, descended upon Spencer Park.

"Catherine, I have persuaded your aunt to help plan for Queen Anne's stay. Lady Hunsdon has far more experience entertaining the nobility than either of us and she has generously offered her staff of servants, if we need them. I hope you don't mind?"

"I welcome you both with all my heart. Accommodating royalty would surely overwhelm me if I tried to do it alone. Fortunately, Patrick is a font of information regarding the queen's household. He spent the entire day with me yesterday, calming my jitters as we inspected every chamber and decided where to put everyone."

"On top of the mundane problems of feeding and housing her entourage, there is the issue of providing suitable royal entertainment." Isobel stood wringing her hands.

"Patrick assures me this will not be a prolonged visit. At most it will be a two-night rest before the queen travels on to London. Don't forget—Queen Anne has young children, and her Court is not nearly as formal as Elizabeth's was. Liz Carey has been put in charge of Baby Charles, and Prince Henry, who is nine, and Princess Elizabeth, who's seven, each have their own household of servants. I've decided to put all the children in the east wing."

Catherine's words stirred Beth's memory. "That's the nursery wing, which gets the morning sun. Your father and I had our rooms there when we were children."

"But the nurseries are no longer furnished. There won't be enough beds," Isobel fretted.

"Royalty travels with its own featherbeds, Mother. That's

why the entourage is moving south at a snail's pace. The servants have to set up and then dismantle all the furnishings."

"Where will you put Queen Anne and her ladies?"

"Come, I'll show you. I've decided to give them the entire second floor of the west wing overlooking the river."

As they walked through the rooms, Isobel's critical eyes inspected the carpets and window drapes. "But the view is better from the top floor, and the chambers up there are far more splendid, don't you think, Catherine?"

"Indeed they are, but Hepburn refuses to give them up, even for royalty. Lord Stewart is undisputed master of his own household."

"Do I hear my name being taken in vain?"

As Cat watched Patrick kiss the ladies' hands, she hid her amusement at the way they simpered. It was obvious that females of every age were susceptible to his virile charm.

"Beth has offered us her servants, if we need them."

"That is most generous, Lady Hunsdon. Anne will have her ladies to serve her and the royal children will have servants aplenty, but our kitchen staff will need extra hands to prepare the meals. Food itself will be no problem, since we have our own beef, poultry, eggs, butter and cheese. The river is filled with trout and, thanks to your late husband, Isobel, Spencer Park has its own gristmill for flour to bake our own bread and pies."

"I shall send to Blackfriars for the Hunsdon kitchen staff. Have you any idea how many will be traveling with the queen?"

"I plan to send David Hepburn north to find out how many and exactly which day we can expect them. The Earl and Countess of Bedford have offered Anne's entourage the hospitality of Woburn Abbey, a distance of approximately twenty miles from here. If she and her ladies ride, they could arrive here by midday, but the baggage carts lumber along much more slowly and won't be here until evening."

"Catherine, how fortunate you are in your choice of husbands. He seems to have everything under control," Beth declared.

Patrick exchanged an intimate glance with his bride. "Nay, I am the fortunate one, Lady Hunsdon."

"We must post guards at the gate to ensure that the hordes of riffraff that are streaming down to the capital don't follow the queen's entourage onto Spencer property."

Patrick cocked an eyebrow. "Would that be Scottish riffraff or English, Isobel?"

She colored slightly, but held her ground. "I mean no disrespect, Lord Stewart. Since I'm Scottish myself I feel justified in voicing my criticism. It seems that hundreds of slum dwellers from both Glasgow and Edinburgh are flocking south."

Beth nodded. "The Lord Mayor is considering closing the gates of London to these indigents because of their vast number."

"That won't solve the problem. The impoverished masses will never turn around and go home. They see England as a land flowing with milk and honey, compared with the harsh conditions they have endured in Scotland. They will simply live in hovels outside the city walls, begging and stealing alongside the English slum dwellers," Patrick predicted.

Catherine felt sudden compassion for these unfortunate masses. "You cannot blame people for wanting to improve their lives."

"That is exactly what King James has done." *And you, yourself, Hepburn,* he admitted silently. "You are too tenderhearted, Cat. Marriage to me will soon cure you of that," he jested.

The ladies laughed. It was obvious that he doted on his bride.

It was the end of April before Queen Anne, accompanied by five of her ladies-in-waiting, rode into the courtyard of Spencer Park. A dozen well-armed grooms known as the Queen's Guard accompanied them. Lord and Lady Stewart were waiting outside to greet her.

Patrick Hepburn stepped forward to lift Anne from the saddle, and a groom led her horse away. "Welcome to Spencer Park, Your Majesty. It is my great pleasure to present my wife, Catherine."

Cat, smiling radiantly, curtsied to the queen.

Anne exchanged a knowing glance with Hepburn and murmured, "You lost no time securing the prize, Patrick." Then she stepped forward, took Catherine's hand and raised her. "I congratulate you on having the good sense to marry a Scot, Lady Stewart. I could not resist riding on such a glorious day. I must confess that I have fallen in love with England. With every mile the countryside becomes lovelier, the weather warmer and the flowers prettier. I thank you with all my heart for your hospitality."

"Your Majesty, it is our great honor to have you. In May, every hedgerow will be abloom with wild roses, and the orchards will be a profusion of blossoms. You couldn't have chosen a more perfect time of year to see England at her best."

From the tail of his eye, Patrick saw the guards lift the queen's ladies from their saddles. Margretha, however, remained mounted, as if she were awaiting his assistance. He knew it must have come as a surprise to her that he had taken a wife since the last time they had seen each other, but he took it for granted that she would have the good sense to accept his *fait accompli* with grace. *She has no choice,* he thought bluntly, dismissing the lady-in-waiting from his thoughts as he and Cat led Anne into the house.

Isobel and Beth stood in the entrance hall awaiting Queen Anne. Cat presented her mother to Her Royal Highness, and Isobel swept into a deep curtsy. "Your Gracious Majesty."

"Lady Spencer, you are the Earl of Winton's daughter, I believe. Geordie attended the king's birthday at Holyrood Palace and brought your beautiful daughter to our Court."

Patrick said smoothly, "Isobel held the post of Mistress of the Queen's Wardrobe. Elizabeth held her in the highest esteem in spite of the fact that she is Scottish. The late queen, who prided herself on having the most magnificent wardrobe in Christendom, insisted all the credit belonged to Lady Spencer."

Anne took the bait immediately. "Catherine must get her gift of fashion design from you, Isobel. How fortuitous that we have met. As the new Queen of England, I believe your advice about my wardrobe could prove invaluable to me."

"You honor me, Your Majesty." Isobel immediately transferred the deep reverence and loyalty she had always reserved for Elizabeth to the new, young, statuesque Queen of England.

"May I also present Lady Hunsdon? Beth is married to Robert Carey's eldest brother," Patrick explained.

Queen Anne raised Beth from her curtsy. "Robert has earned the eternal gratitude of King James. His wife, Liz, was my first English friend. She will be arriving shortly with Baby Charles, who absolutely adores her. I am delighted to meet you, Beth."

Catherine saw that Queen Anne's female attendants had

caught up with her. "If you will follow me, Your Majesty, I will show you to the chambers we have prepared." Cat led the way to the west wing. "This second floor is entirely yours. The bathing chamber is at the end of the hall. The moment your baggage arrives, I will see that it is sent up. Lord Stewart and I occupy the chambers directly above. If there is aught whatsoever you need, please do not hesitate to ask. We are all here to serve you."

Anne and her attendants exclaimed over the spacious, elegant chambers of Spencer Park, which were in stark contrast to the dark, gloomy rooms of Holyrood. All except Margretha, who looked at Catherine through narrowed, malevolent eyes.

Poor Lady Gretha. Not only does she covet my husband; she envies me my home as well. Cat could not help pitying her. She hurried back downstairs to signal Beth that her staff could now take up refreshments and offer hot water for bathing. She was in time to hear her mother offering Hepburn her gratitude.

"My lord, I cannot thank you enough for singing my praises to Her Majesty. Because of you, I feel confident that Anne will appoint me her Mistress of the Queen's Wardrobe."

His possessive glance swept over Catherine as she descended the stairs. "Isobel, you gave me my heart's desire. I am simply trying to return the favor." He cocked his head. "I hear a carriage—perhaps some of the royal children have arrived. I'm confident that Mr. Burke has all under control in the courtyard and stables, but I'm sure he'll welcome my help. Don't be surprised if Robert rides in from London so he can be with Liz."

Because of the detailed plans they had made for Queen Anne's stay at Spencer Park, all seemed to go reasonably smoothly the rest of the day. The baggage wagons arrived before the royal children, and their trunks were taken to the east wing and their beds set up in readiness for them.

"Liz, how lovely to see you. Let me help you." Cat took Baby Charles from her arms. "What a beautiful boy you are. The nursery is all set up for you, Liz."

"Thank you, Catherine. I just saw Hepburn outside. I can't believe that you two are married!"

"He rode like a madman and arrived on my birthday. The next day the king married us. Patrick swept me off my feet."

"You sly devils, pretending to be enemies. Yet I always suspected a smoldering attraction between you."

"Congratulations on your royal appointment. Queen Anne could not have chosen a lovelier lady to be in charge of her baby's household, but isn't a prince a heavy responsibility?"

"Not really. Babies just need love. I have two nursemaids at my beck and call, and Queen Anne is a devoted mother."

Patrick and Robert walked into the nursery, and Liz flew to her husband's side. "Darling, how is your leg?"

"In grave need of a wife's attention," he teased.

Patrick's gaze swept over his own wife holding the baby. "I too am getting lusty ideas. Such a fine nursery cries out for a Hepburn heir."

Catherine's heartbeat quickened at the thought of giving Patrick a son. Reluctantly she handed Baby Charles back to Liz.

"I have planned dinner for eight o'clock so there will be ample time to feed the children early and get them to bed. Liz, I am counting on you and Robert to engage the queen in conversation in case I become totally tongue-tied when we sit down to eat."

Patrick slipped his arm about her for a reassuring hug. "This queen is not a formidable tyrant, nor does she insist on rigid formality. Believe it or not, she is almost human," he teased.

Thanks to a concerted effort on the part of everyone involved in planning, cooking and serving the dinner, it was a success. Everything on the table was provided by the estate, from the fragrant day lilies to the oxtail soup, trout, pheasant and roast beef. The strawberries served with thick clotted cream proved an outstanding favorite with the queen and her ladies.

Catherine had seated Anne next to Hepburn at the head of the table and was amazed at the ease of their conversation. Every guest contributed an amusing anecdote, and it was evident that the queen had a delightful sense of humor. When she tasted the pheasant and admitted she preferred it to Scottish grouse, it prompted Cat to tell the amusing story of how she had gone into the woods at Richmond to release the tiny ruffed grouse and had been accosted by an uncivilized brute wearing a sheepskin.

"He obviously made a lasting impression," Anne said, laughing.

"It was my deerhounds that stole her heart," Patrick insisted.

After dinner, they were entertained by a piper. Hepburn had spotted one of the queen's guards carrying a set of bagpipes and had recruited him to play some lively reels. A party atmosphere prevailed as everyone laughed, sang and sipped golden Rhenish wine. Anne did not retire to her west wing until midnight, stamping the evening with the royal seal of success.

Catherine kissed her mother and her aunt Beth and thanked them for their help and moral support. "I couldn't have done it without you." Then she went into the kitchens to thank both the Spencer staff and those who had come from the Hunsdon household in Blackfriars. "The food was delicious and the service superb. Everything was truly fit for a queen. If tomorrow turns out to be as successful as today, I shall be forever in your debt."

When she came from the kitchens she saw her husband heading toward the front door. "Everything went like clockwork, Patrick. Thank you for being my magic man."

His arms went around her and he dropped a kiss onto her silken curls. "Nay, the lion's share of the credit is yours, sweetheart. It was a resounding triumph, especially for a little wench who's only goal used to be wearing the most elegant gown."

She stood on tiptoe and lifted her mouth to his. "I'm still wearing the most elegant gown. Where are you going?"

"I asked David Hepburn to organize a guard patrol while the queen is here. I just want to be sure that all is well. I won't be long. Are you going up now?"

"I was on my way to the servants' wing to see if there is anything they need. They've worked so hard today."

He lifted her chin and looked into her eyes. "Mr. Burke will see to all that. You need to rest for tomorrow. Promise me you'll be in bed by the time I return?"

She nodded, blissfully happy to be surrounded by his love.

Patrick checked on all the horses in the stables, then spoke with David. The young Hepburn had captained Crichton's garrison, and Patrick put complete trust in him. When he saw that David had everything under control he returned to the house.

A female slipped from the shadows in the entrance hall and whispered his name. "Patrick. I've been waiting for you."

Even in the dark, he knew the tall Danish woman was Gretha. Hepburn was experienced in fending off unwanted overtures from the opposite sex. "You should not be here." His tone was forbidding.

"Is there somewhere we can be alone tonight?" she cajoled.

Patrick hung on to his patience. "That is impossible." His reply was blunt and to the point. "Good night." He dismissed her and put her from his thoughts. Then he took the stairs two at a time, eager to join Catherine in the privacy of their bedchamber.

The first day of May dawned gloriously. Patrick and Catherine accompanied Queen Anne, her ladies and her two eldest children as they rode over the lush acres of Spencer Park. In the small hamlet of Spencer, the village children captivated them as they danced around the Maypole in their annual May Day festival.

Seven-year-old Princess Elizabeth was drawn to Catherine, not only by her beauty and pretty clothes, but also because of the attention Patrick's bride gave her, answering all her questions. Prince Henry attached himself to Hepburn until Margretha rode up and told him that a prince's rightful place was at the side of his mother, the new Queen of England.

"That was a callous dismissal," Patrick said curtly.

"Rather like yours last night, my lord."

He gathered his patience. "Gretha, I have a wife."

"All the more reason you will need the diversion of a mistress," she murmured seductively.

Hepburn, who had never considered her his mistress but only a casual lay, knew he must make things clear once and for all time. He looked into her eyes. "It was finished between us more than a year ago. Gretha, you should aspire to be more than a mistress. Take advantage of your position at Court. A lady with your ample charm could easily marry into the wealthy English nobility."

"As you have done!" Her eyes narrowed to slits, then she dug her spurs into her mount to catch up with the queen.

That night, after a leisurely dinner, Queen Anne and her courtiers withdrew early in preparation for their departure the next morning. Isobel was in her glory as she took over the packing of the queen's wardrobe and instructed her ladies-in-waiting how to wrap the fine garments in tissue paper and muslin to avoid crushing the delicate material.

At dawn the trunks were carried to the waiting wagons and the beds were dismantled and loaded with the myriad of royal furnishings accompanying the queen's household to London. Cat had made arrangements for a large buffet breakfast to be set up so that the guests could help themselves before setting off on the last leg of their long journey to the capital.

Queen Anne made certain that her children and their attendants were safely on their way before she herself departed. A courier from the king had brought word that James and his nobles would ride out from Whitehall to meet the queen at Westminster and formally escort her into London. Courtesy prompted her host, Lord Stewart, to accompany Anne and give her safe escort until she was symbolically delivered into the hands of the king.

Catherine urged Isobel and Beth to return to London with the queen's party, insisting that Mr. Burke and his staff would soon help her restore order to Spencer Park once the influx of guests had departed. When the pair climbed into their carriage, Cat thanked them profusely and bade them good-bye.

Though the courtyard was crowded with horses, grooms, attendants and Queen's Guards, Catherine easily spotted her husband's dark head above the throng and made her way to his side.

"If I don't make a decisive move, this lot will take root."

Cat smiled up at him. "Try not to let your impatience show."

"You know me so well." He grinned. "No matter how much Jamie induces me to carry on to Whitehall, I shall refuse. I am coming home today, and that's a promise. At last, here comes Anne. If I can get her out of here, the stragglers will soon follow."

Catherine watched Patrick lift the queen into the saddle of her white palfrey, then he mounted Valiant and signaled her guards.

Queen Anne gathered her reins and smiled down at Catherine. "Thank you for your gracious hospitality, Lady Stewart. I shall look forward to your joining our Court. I welcome your ideas for a coronation gown. Your own clothes are truly exquisite."

Cat swept into a graceful curtsy. "Thank you, Your Majesty."

She hoped it was an invitation and not a royal command. She stood watching as Hepburn's powerful hand reached for Anne's bridle. Cat waved until the queen's attendants fell in behind her and obscured her view. With a sigh of relief, she picked up her skirts and returned to the house, remembering that she hadn't taken time for breakfast. In the reception hall she came face to face with Margretha, the queen's lady-in-waiting.

"Queen Anne left five minutes ago. My husband was impatient to get started . . . I'm so sorry that they have left without you."

"It is more discreet if Patrick and I do not ride together."

Cat stiffened. "What do you mean?"

"Come, Lady Stewart, let's not pretend. You must know I am Hepburn's mistress. Surely you didn't think that marriage would put an end to our liaison? On the contrary, his having a wife can only strengthen our intimate relationship."

Catherine fought the impulse to snatch the riding crop from Margretha's hand and lay it about her skinny hips. The woman was obviously green with jealousy that Hepburn had taken a wife.

"When I learned a few days before I arrived that Hepburn had wed you, I confess I was surprised and at a total loss. However, once I saw how vast and magnificent Spencer Park was, I suddenly understood the compelling attraction."

Catherine laughed in her face. "You are deceiving yourself. You cannot bear the thought that Patrick is in love with me!"

"Love?" Gretha's face was wreathed with amused pity. "You are the one who has been deceived. Hepburn had the king draw up a signed and sealed contract, granting him any English heiress of his choice. James told Anne, who divulged the secret to me."

"You lying bitch! Get your aging carcass out of my house before I knock you on your bony arse!"

Margretha hurried to the door and delivered her parting shot. "Don't expect your devoted husband to return tonight."

Catherine was seized with a furious anger that almost blinded her. She closed her eyes and saw crimson behind her lids. The red turned to purple and then to black. She opened her eyes quickly, fearing that she might faint, and reached for the banister.

"Ye've had no breakfast," Maggie chided as she came from the dining room. "Go up and rest and I'll bring ye a tray."

"No! Food would choke me at the moment. I need to be alone."

Chapter Thirty

*H*ow dare that bitch make such foul accusations? She is
nothing but a jealous strumpet, determined to destroy my
happiness!" Cat spoke aloud as she paced across her bedchamber, where only a few short hours ago her heart had been filled
with joy. "I must not let her filthy lies touch me. Patrick Hepburn loves me. He is not capable of such deceit and cold calcu-
lation."

Cat recalled the horror she had felt when she learned that
Henry Somerset's interest in her had been prompted by her fortune and she remembered the vow she had made to marry only
for love. "I kept that vow. I married Patrick because I love him!"

Yes, but does Hepburn love you?

"Of course he loves me!" Catherine felt a rising panic that
she desperately tried to quell. "He kept his promise that he
would come on my birthday and that we would be married."

*He waited until you turned twenty-one and had legally in-
herited Spencer Park.*

"Nay, he had to wait. Neither my mother nor Elizabeth
would have given consent for me to marry a Scot. Everything
changed for Patrick when a Scot became King of England."

*Everything changed for you too. They are both Scots and
both Stewarts. A pact between them is not inconceivable.*

"Don't do this to yourself! Do not doubt Patrick . . . do not
doubt his love for you."

Are you afraid of the truth, Catherine?

"Yes! Desperately afraid! If I learned that he did not truly
love me, and had married me for my wealth, I would be devastated. It would crush me, destroy me. I could not endure such
betrayal."

Then pretend you never heard Margretha's lies.

"But what if they are not lies? More than likely she is telling the truth when she claims that she and Hepburn were intimate. Is she telling the truth about a signed agreement?"

Catherine lifted her chin. "I shall confront him when he returns and ask—nay, demand—that he answer such accusations."

Hepburn will deny it!

She paced to the window and looked out with unseeing eyes. Feeling caged, she hurried into the adjoining room. Needing to be comforted, she threw open his wardrobe and clutched the sleeve of the purple doublet he'd worn the day they were married. His scent lingered on the velvet. "Patrick . . . please."

Are you pleading for love? Truth? Denial?

As she turned away from the wardrobe, her glance fell upon the tall chest of drawers that held his belongings. Of their own volition her eyes lifted to Hepburn's strongbox. Though she knew it was a breach of trust, Cat was far too impulsive to leave the box untouched. She carried a footstool to the bureau, climbed on it and lifted down the heavy metal strongbox. When she took it to the table and tried to open it, she realized that it was locked tight. Without hesitation she went to her jewel case and took out the small dagger that had belonged to Audra.

Her heart hammered as she deliberately pried open the lock on her husband's strongbox. She lifted the lid slowly, afraid of what she would find, yet determined to examine every item. Hepburn's store of gold coins did not interest her. It was the papers and documents she focused upon. Her mouth went dry as she lifted a document with royal seals. When she unfolded it and read the words, she caught her breath.

"This is a pardon from King James to Francis Hepburn, Earl of Bothwell, in return for his voluntary exile." A lump came unbidden into her throat, provoked by the poignancy of the yellowed parchment. *These papers are private.* The thought, however, did not deter her from her search.

She found the deed to Crichton Castle as well as the mortgage papers signed by Patrick's father more than fifteen years ago. Then she read another document certifying that Patrick had repaid the mortgage in full and that Crichton was free and clear of debt. It was dated only five years ago, and Catherine realized that it had taken him ten long years to pay off what his father had borrowed. What he had endured touched her heart, yet it also clearly showed her that he had a driving need for money.

She had too much integrity to read the two personal letters from his father in Italy, and a wave of guilt washed over her as she set them aside along with his parents' marriage certificate and his own baptismal paper from St. Giles Cathedral in Edinburgh.

The next document she read was a contract drawn up between Patrick and her grandfather. Geordie was paying Hepburn to guard the Winton longhorn cattle against reivers and rustlers. The contract had been renewed six months ago. *If they do business together, the earl must trust him.*

Or fear him.

Catherine picked up another document with a royal seal. She scanned the words quickly. Her heart stopped and she turned icy cold as she reread it slowly. Six condemning words leapt out at her: *Any English heiress of your choice.*

Cat's heart constricted. A tear splashed onto the parchment. Impatiently her hand lifted to wipe away the wetness that trailed down her cheek. *Damn you, Hepburn. Damn you to hellfire!*

She read the words again and saw that the document also promised Hepburn an earldom. It was immediately obvious to Catherine that the earldom he intended to have was Winton. She raised her eyes from the paper. "Through his marriage to me, Hepburn *will* become Earl of Winton when Geordie dies."

Dear God, he did not lust for me. He lusted for what marriage to me would bring him—the landholdings of Spencer and Seton, and the earldom of Winton.

She sat, stunned. "How could I have been so blind? How could I have been so besotted? Hepburn controlled and manipulated me from the moment he learned who I was. Mayhap even before he met me!" Her mind rapidly wove together the strands that would condemn him.

Seton land is close to Crichton. In his dealings with Geordie he must have learned that my grandfather had made me his legal heir.

"He came to England with one purpose in mind—marriage with the wealthy heiress Catherine Seton Spencer!"

Cat desperately clung to her outrage. It was her armor, her protection against the unbearable pain that hovered, searching for a chink in her carapace so that it could sink its fangs into her heart and deliver its deathblow.

Her hands were trembling as she set the incriminating document aside and put all the other papers back into the strongbox. Then she returned the strongbox to the top of the tall chest and removed the footstool. She took the paper and her dagger back to her bedchamber and set them on her dressing table. Cat looked into the mirror and examined her reflection dispassionately.

How strange that I look exactly the same on the outside, when inside I am completely changed. Then she looked into the eyes that stared back at her. *No, I don't look the same, after all.* Gone was the shining, naïve innocence. In its place glittered the age-old wisdom of Eve.

Catherine called for a bath. She poured herself a goblet of wine and sipped it slowly as she lay in the warm, perfumed water. An hour later, she opened her wardrobe and deliberately selected her most flattering gown, a pale peach velvet, whose sleeves were slashed with vibrant emerald green. She sat down at her dressing table to fashion her freshly washed hair into a cascade of shining black curls, held in place by a peach-colored ribbon. Then she adorned herself with the emerald earrings Hepburn had given her.

She heard the echo of Margretha's words: *Don't expect your devoted husband to return tonight.* Catherine smiled knowingly into the mirror. The enticement of the slim, seductive lady-in-waiting paled into insignificance when measured against the irresistible lure that awaited him here. Spencer Park was the object of Hepburn's undying passion. Gretha didn't stand a chance of keeping him in London.

Twilight was deepening into darkness by the time Patrick arrived home. He stabled Valiant and praised the grooms for the excellent job they'd done cleaning the stalls used by the royal party. His irritation at the slow pace of the day's travel dropped away from him as he walked toward the house. The lit windows of the stately mansion welcomed him, and a sense of well-being filled his soul. Hepburn marveled at his good fortune. Spencer Park was like a gift from the gods.

Though he was hungry, he curbed his impulse to go to the kitchens, hoping that Catherine was awaiting his return so that they could eat dinner together. The nightly ritual in the privacy of their bedchamber had become such a pleasurable interlude that his anticipation mounted with every step as he climbed the stairs.

He walked into the room and paused at the vision before him. His wife, bathed in candlelight, was the loveliest female he had ever seen. "Cat, your beauty takes my breath away."

"I hope so," she murmured softly.

He threw off his doublet and crossed the room with the intention of taking her in his arms. Instead, he took the tankard of ale she thrust into his hands. He grinned as his glance slid over the bed with its covers turned down so invitingly. "You fulfill all my needs. I hope you didn't eat yet. I'm ravenous."

"You have a rapacious appetite for all things—not just food."

"You know me so well," he said with a wicked leer.

"I thought I did, but my curiosity about you is insatiable. I have many unanswered questions."

"My greatest desire is to satisfy you. Ask away, my beauty."

"Did Margretha manage to catch up with you this morning?"

Her question took him off guard for a moment, but it awakened his natural instinct to be wary. "Margretha?"

"She deliberately stayed behind so she could have the pleasure of taunting me about you."

"Sweetheart, Gretha means nothing to me!" he vowed.

Cat laughed prettily. "Oh, I know that compared with what you have now, she means less than nothing. And Gretha knows it too."

"Exactly. Why else would she try to hurt you with her desperate lies? What did she tell you?" he demanded.

"She couldn't tell me anything about your relationship that I hadn't already guessed. In spite of her claiming to be your mistress, I know it was a casual affair. You simply took what she so freely offered. Then you met me and it was all over."

"It was over long before we met, Catherine."

She saw him reach out to touch her cheek and stepped back. "She deliberately intended to hurt me with the things she said. I wanted to show her that her words could not wound me, so I told her she was deceiving herself; that you were in love with me."

"Sweetheart—"

Catherine held up her hand to stop his words. "She told me

that I was the one who had been deceived. Margretha claimed you did not marry me for love, but for money."

"Cat, you know that is untrue!"

"She said that Anne told her King James had pledged to give you your choice of any English heiress you desired."

"That's a damned lie!" he growled.

Her eyes glittered triumphantly. "I knew you would deny such a foul accusation, Patrick."

He stepped forward to take her in his arms, but with a feline movement she eluded him. Silently, she picked up the document from her dressing table and handed it to him.

He saw the royal seals and immediately knew what it was. An obscenity fell from his lips. He silently cursed himself for not burning the evidence once they were safely married. Yet he knew full well why he hadn't. The agreement promised him an earldom that hadn't yet materialized. Hepburn took the offensive; he knew no other way to fight a battle. He flung down the document. "You opened my strongbox!" he accused. "You went through my private papers!" He grabbed her by the shoulders and shook her. "You broke a sacred trust."

Cat snatched up her dagger and plunged it into his hand, which gripped her shoulder so powerfully.

Stunned that she would do such a thing, he released her instantly and stared down at the blood that flowed from his hand. "You stabbed me," he said with disbelief.

"That wound is nothing beside the one you have inflicted upon me, Hepburn," she snarled through bared teeth. "To learn, *from your whore,* that your towering passion was for Spencer Park and not me was such a cruel blow, it shattered my heart."

He snatched up a bed pillow, ripped off the pillowcase and tore it into linen strips. He bound his hand tightly and tied the bandage with his teeth. Then he grabbed the dagger from her hand and flung it across the room. It embedded itself in the doorframe that opened into the adjoining chamber.

"You are uncivilized!"

"That makes two of us, Hellcat."

She snatched up the incriminating paper and waved it in his face. "You made a deal with the Devil. Nay, I'm wrong. It was Jamie Stuart who made a deal with the Devil! What did you promise him in return? The document is purposely worded vaguely: *for services rendered to the king's satisfaction.* What were those services, Hepburn? Something unholy connected to his obtaining the throne of England, I suspect!"

"Your suspicions are wrong, Catherine," he lied smoothly. "The service I rendered was finding a man whom James could trust to carry private letters to Elizabeth. That man was Robert Carey."

Her eyes widened as another piece of the puzzle fell into place. "You lured him with promises of gain. Robert and Liz's royal appointments are rewards *for services rendered.* And Spencer Park is your reward. How bloody naïve I was!"

Patrick heard the bitter regret in her voice and tried to dispel it. "I understand how this document condemns me in your eyes, but don't you see that the words *any English heiress of your choice* should absolve me? Catherine, I chose *you!* I had my choice of *any* and I chose *you.*"

"I see quite clearly. You chose me, an heiress to vast land-holdings in both England and Scotland, because I was tailor-made for your devious scheme." Her eyes glittered with contempt. "Jamie also promises you an earldom. Can you deny that the earldom you have in mind is Winton?"

Hepburn's jaw set. "You are my wife, Catherine, and nothing you can say or do can alter the fact."

"Oh, I am painfully aware of all the legalities of this unholy union. A wife's property becomes her husband's once the marriage is consummated, and you certainly made sure that it was well consummated. Spencer Park is yours, and there is naught I can do about it. But I'll be double damned if I will let you have your cake and eat it too. I wish you joy of your ill-gotten gains, but you'll enjoy them alone. I will never again live with you as your wife, Hepburn."

The words she threw at him challenged his manhood. The need to bend her to his will rose up in him. In her raging fury, with her eyes glittering like golden fire and her luscious breasts rising and falling with every breath, she had never been more sexually alluring. Anger and desire mingled, driving him nearly to madness. He wanted to throw her on the bed, mount her and ride her until she yielded everything to him and admitted that she loved him with every fiber of her being. He took a threatening step toward her.

You've hanged men for committing rape, Hepburn.

The thought did not deter him. It was pride that stopped him.

His towering pride would not allow him to be intimate with a woman who was not eager for his passion.

"Geordie will have to die before you become the Earl of Winton," she spat. "Are you plotting his early demise?"

Hepburn clenched his fists, fighting to master the violence her accusation provoked. "If any other man or woman dared to utter such words to me, I would knock them down."

"Such control," she mocked. Then her anger dropped away and was replaced by an attitude of cool indifference. Slowly, deliberately, she removed the emerald earrings. "I once said that I wanted to get you out of my system." She slipped his rings from her finger. "With your help, I have finally achieved my goal." She laid the jewelry on top of the royal document. "In the morning I shall pack my things and leave you alone with your beloved, Spencer Park. I bid you good night, Lord Stewart."

Cat made her way to Maggie's chamber and slipped inside without knocking. "I'm sorry to disturb you. May I sleep here tonight?"

"I heard ye shouting at each other and kept my distance. What is amiss between ye, my lamb?"

"Nothing!" Cat shook her head. "Everything! You are the only one who ever loved me, Maggie."

"What nonsense. Yer husband loves ye to distraction."

"You are confusing love with lust, just as I did. Patrick Hepburn only married me for the landholdings I would bring him."

Maggie knew better than to argue. Catherine was too impetuous for her own good. In the morning, she was sure that the newlyweds would regret their lovers' quarrel and all would be forgiven. "Let me help ye with yer gown. Then I'll give ye a glass of whisky to comfort ye and drown yer sorrows."

It was Patrick's turn to pace the bedchamber. He stormed back and forth like a caged beast, trying to control the urge to drag his wife back to their room, throw her over his knee and tan her arse until she came to her senses. He caught a glimpse of his dark furious face in the mirror and realized that he must not lay a hand on her until his temper had cooled. Catherine was right, he acknowledged; at the moment he *was* uncivilized. He strode into the adjoining chamber and lifted down his strongbox from the tall chest. He ignored the throbbing in his hand as he opened the lid and stared down at the papers he'd put there for safekeeping.

"The bitch! I'd like to wring her neck." He was not speaking of Catherine, of course. He was speaking of Margretha and wondered what it was that prompted one female to poison another with such deadly venom.

Hepburn cursed James Stuart. *Why the hell did he have to blab our agreement to Anne? Surely Jamie knows a woman is incapable of keeping a secret. Once the queen knew I'd been promised an heiress, she couldn't wait to share the amusing gossip with her ladies. Women love to see men shackled in wedlock!* He booted the footstool across the chamber and carried his strongbox into the other room.

Patrick sorted through the papers and saw the contract he and Geordie Seton had drawn up. *That was the day I had my first vision of Catherine. She enchanted me before I even knew who she was. Then, when I finally met her in Richmond, I knew I wanted her for my wife that first day.*

You decided to marry her when you learned her name was Catherine Seton Spencer.

"I was attracted to her long before I knew she was an heiress. Then, in Scotland, the day we rode with the wild horses, I showed her how much I loved her."

That was lust, not love, Hepburn.

"I proposed marriage to her last November," he insisted righteously, as he stabbed his fingers through his hair.

You waited until she turned twenty-one and legally inherited Spencer Park before you went through with the ceremony. Expedience is your motto, Hepburn.

"What the devil is wrong with marrying a woman of property so long as I treat her well and make her a decent husband?"

You want to have your cake and eat it too.

He strode to her dressing table to retrieve the damnable document that had caused such horrendous trouble between them. Her emerald earrings and betrothal ring lay on top of the folded parchment. He picked them up and weighed them in his hand before reluctantly putting them in the strongbox along with the accursed agreement. He stared at himself in the mirror for long moments.

"Well, Hepburn, the honeymoon is over." He laughed without mirth. *Catherine is convinced that my desire for her land-*

holdings is greater than my desire for her, and at the moment nothing will convince her otherwise.

Patrick knew it was impossible for him to remain at Spencer Park. His pride was too great to allow his wife to pack and leave her own property. He had no intention of relinquishing his ownership, of course, to either his property or his woman. He would return to Scotland. Catherine would soon mourn his absence. He was in her blood. He was convinced that she could not exist long without him. When she begged him to return, he would do so.

Hepburn packed his bags, then he sat down and wrote a letter to Mr. Burke, reaffirming him as head steward. He set out clear instructions regarding various business matters he had put in motion and informed him that he had appointed David Hepburn to the position of steward with authority to proceed on the contracts that had been arranged between Spencer Park and the Crown.

He stood up, and his dark glance swept slowly about the chamber as if he were committing every detail to memory. Then he looked at the bed. "Good-bye, Hellcat."

Chapter Thirty-one

*C*atherine opened her eyes and for a moment was startled to see Maggie in bed beside her. Then she remembered all that had happened yesterday and her spirits plummeted. She ignored the ache in her head that the whisky had induced, but it was impossible to ignore the far greater pain in her heart.

Maggie threw back the covers. "Ye need some food. I don't believe ye ate one morsel yesterday."

Cat was about to protest that on top of last night's whisky, food would make her queasy, when she thought better of it. She would need breakfast to fortify her in case she again had to do battle with Hepburn this morning. Her resolve was firm. She intended to pack and leave no matter how much he protested. *My mind is made up. I shall refuse to remain under the same roof even if he gets down on bended knee and begs me to stay!*

An hour later, Catherine, an elegant vision in peach velvet, tapped lightly on the bedchamber door. When she got no response, she sighed with relief and stepped inside. "Hepburn's an early riser. Perhaps we can get everything packed while the insufferable lord of the manor is out." She saw that the bed had not been slept in and hoped he had paced the floor all night.

She threw open her wardrobe doors, lifted out an armful of gowns and laid them on the bed. Maggie followed suit, and when all the garments had been removed, they started on the shoes, slippers and riding boots. Cat could not find her favorite cloak and remembered with a blush that the last time she and Patrick had returned from riding, they'd been in such haste to undress that they'd flung their clothes into his wardrobe. She walked into the adjoining chamber, noticed immediately that his strongbox was missing and felt a thrill of guilty satisfaction that she'd broken the lock and he'd had to take it for repair.

Cat opened his wardrobe and gasped. All his clothes were gone except the outfit he had worn when they were married. That he had left his wedding doublet behind was an insult in itself. She ran across the room to the tall chest of drawers and found it empty also. "He's gone! The whoreson has beat me to it. Lord Bloody Stewart has left me before I could leave him!"

Maggie came to the adjoining doorway in disbelief. She saw the empty wardrobe and then she glanced up at Catherine's knife, embedded in the doorframe.

"What went on here last night?"

"I stabbed him!"

Maggie's face paled. "Ye stabbed the Border lord?"

Cat dug her fists into her hips defiantly. "I stabbed him and I'm glad I stabbed him! I'd stab him again if he were still here!" She stood on tiptoe and after a long struggle managed to dislodge the dagger. She carried it to her dressing table and returned it to its lovely amethyst-encased sheath.

Cat noticed that he had taken the abominable document as well as the jewels he had given her. Her eyes searched for a letter or a note that he might have left her, but there was nothing. Then she saw her gold wedding band. "The swine took my emerald betrothal ring but left my wedding ring!" She snatched it up and flung it across the room. When she saw Maggie bend down to retrieve it, she cried, "Leave it! Hepburn will be the one who must pick it up, or it will lie there forever!"

Catherine went downstairs and summoned Mr. Burke. "What time did Lord Stewart leave?"

"It was around one o'clock, my lady. He had injured his hand and I insisted on cleansing it before he left."

Her conscience began to prick. "Did he leave me a message?"

"No, ma'am. He gave me a letter instructing me about Spencer Park business, then he spoke with David Hepburn."

"May I see the letter, Mr. Burke?"

"Of course. It's on the library desk, ma'am."

"Thank you." Cat wanted to ask if he knew where Hepburn had gone and if he'd said when he might return, but she didn't want Mr. Burke to know that her husband had not confided in her.

She went directly to the library, sat down at the desk and picked up the first page. Her fingers trembled slightly as she noticed a bloodstain beside his bold handwriting. Hepburn was reconfirming Burke as head steward of Spencer Park. *This must mean he'll be gone some time.* She read through the pages of instructions, surprised at their detail. He'd promised to loan John Carey one of the wild colts for stud. In return, Spencer Park was to get a filly from one of the mares the colt covered.

Hepburn laid down what crops were to be planted in which fields. Some were to be left fallow for hay and others were to be used for grazing their longhorns. *He obviously intends to rule Spencer Park, even in his absence.*

She read on, skimming over the various repairs and improvements that were to be made to the tenant farms, but the next words gave her pause: "Before I leave for Scotland, I intend to finalize contracts to supply the Crown with milk, cheese and beef. I have appointed David Hepburn as steward to oversee this lucrative business for Spencer Park." *I assumed he'd gone to London, but the infuriating devil is returning to Scotland!*

"Finally, after much consideration, I have decided not to use our English profits to pay for the sheep I am buying for Scotland. Crichton will bear the expense so that Spencer Park's coffers will not be drained in the event that the enterprise fails."

Damn him! He's going to mortgage Crichton! She looked up, sensing Mr. Burke's presence. "Why did he change his mind about using money from Spencer Park?"

"Something to do with pride, I believe," Burke said quietly.

Insufferable arrogance! Unbending pride! Towering insolence! I accused him of marrying me for my wealth, so now he won't condescend to use my money. Her fist clenched. *I swear before God to bring him low.*

Catherine went back upstairs and found Maggie wrapping her gowns in tissue paper. "I've changed my mind about leaving. Hepburn has gone back to Scotland, and good riddance. It will give me a chance to enjoy living at Spencer Park on my own. How refreshing to be able to do whatever I wish without the lord and bloody master issuing his orders!"

Without a word, Maggie began to hang Catherine's gowns back in the wardrobe.

"I'll take care of all this. You go and have some lunch." Cat bit her lip. "Listen to the servants' gossip and see what they are saying about him in the kitchens."

• • •

Patrick Hepburn had little trouble gaining audience with the new King of England in spite of the fact that there was a long waiting list of petitioners cooling their heels at Whitehall.

James had approved the contracts with Spencer Park that guaranteed the Royal Court be supplied with beef at a cost lower than that offered by any other bidder. "Ye have a shrewd head fer business, laddie. What new scheme have ye devised fer our mutual benefit?"

"Now that you are king of both England and Scotland, in theory the dividing line between the two countries has disappeared. You and I know in reality that is wishful thinking. Since your determination to unify our two countries is paramount, you will need a strong force to keep law and order in the Borders."

"The lion and the unicorn *shall* lie down taegether, even if it means beating them intae submission," James vowed. "Clifford, Earl of Cumberland, and Percy, Earl of Northumberland, have both pledged allegiance tae me and will enforce my laws in the north."

"Percy and Clifford are Englishmen. Do you believe for one minute the Scots will obey them and lie down in submission? It cannot be one-sided if you are to achieve true cooperation. You will also need a strong Scottish force with an iron hand to achieve peace and quiet in the Borders—Scots with guts enough to hang Englishmen when necessary. I offer my Hepburn moss-troopers, Your Majesty, providing we can agree on a price, of course."

"Wheesht, mon, ye couldna' wait tae get here and now ye can no' wait tae get back. Ye'll miss my coronation!"

"I think you can manage without me, Sire," he said dryly.

When Patrick left the king, he was pleased with himself. Jamie Stuart loved to haggle, but he could no longer cry poverty now that he was monarch of the wealthiest realm in Christendom, and he'd finally agreed to pay Hepburn a hefty price for his services. Moreover, James had signed a draft on the exchequer so Hepburn could draw the money as needed. Hepburn's mouth curved with satisfaction. It would no longer be necessary to mortgage Crichton to buy the sheep he wanted.

Before Patrick left Court he sought out Philadelphia to tell her that he was returning to Scotland on business for the king.

She saw his bandaged hand. "Don't tell me; let me guess.

You and your beautiful bride are fighting like cat and dog
again?"

Hepburn grinned. "A certain queen's lady could not wait to
taunt Catherine about a past indiscretion. But my wife has a
sensible head on her shoulders. If left in solitude, she will soon
get over her pique. When she gets lonely, she will likely come
to Court. Will you keep an eye on her for me, Lady Scrope?"

She gave him a sideways glance. "You want me to keep her
from taking a lover, I warrant. Do you trust me, Lord Stewart?"

"Of course I don't, Philadelphia. It is Catherine I trust."

"Cocksure devil!"

"I'm a Borderer—it's the nature of the beast."

When Hepburn left Whitehall, he made his way to the Pool
of London, where more than a dozen Scottish ships lined the
wharves. He booked passage for himself, Valiant and his packhorse to Berwick, the port closest to the Cheviot Hills, where
they bred the heavy-fleeced Cheviot longwool sheep he wanted
for Crichton.

At Spencer Park, Catherine enjoyed her newfound freedom
for the first few days. Then loneliness crept up and crouched
close by, waiting to pounce the moment she let her guard down.

She decided to accompany the groom who was taking the
wild colt to John Carey's horse farm. When Slate recognized
her, he approached warily as if he were still ready to flee at the
least sign of danger. As she slipped on the bridle, she rubbed his
nose and whispered, "I'm glad there's a small part of you that
will always remain untamed." Memories came flooding back,
reminding her of the first time she'd seen the wild herd. *If only
I could turn back the clock and relive that day!*

When Cat arrived at Hunsdon Grange, she saw that Mary
Carey was now swollen with the child she carried. "Oh, Mary,
you look so beautiful. When is the baby due?"

"I know I look as if I'll drop it any day, but I've still two
more months to go. How about you? Any sign yet?"

"Mary, I've only been married six weeks."

"That's long enough. I've seen the way Patrick looks at
you."

Catherine could not bring herself to tell Mary that Hepburn
had deserted her; it was too painful, too humiliating, too devastating. She made up an excuse and left as soon as she could.

As one day slowly merged into another, Catherine found that everything at Spencer Park reminded her of Hepburn. She took her meals downstairs with Maggie, in an attempt to keep at bay memories of the intimate dinners she'd shared with Patrick in their bedchamber.

Cat retired later and later each night because her rooms were haunted by his compelling presence. She began to dread the night and shun the dark. She lit the fire to keep off the darklings but could not dispel the cold and the loneliness. Each night as she lay in bed, aching with need, she repeated the same words, over and over, like a litany: "I hate, loathe and detest him!"

Hepburn bought a large flock of Cheviot longwool sheep. Over half of the five hundred ewes were in lamb. He paid for the services of two shepherds and their dogs to deliver the flock to Crichton. Patrick sent a message to Jock Elliot, telling him of the purchase and asking him to meet him in Kelso with a dozen moss-troopers. Though it was a distance of only twenty miles, he would take no chances with the valuable animals. The Borders were still inhabited by English reivers who were ready to steal the Scots blind, and vice versa, despite the fact that James Stuart now ruled both countries.

As always, the inhabitants of Crichton came out to welcome home their laird. When he entered the castle, the women greeted him with eager smiles, unable to conceal their curiosity. Finally his housekeeper put into words what all of them were thinking.

"I thought ye planned to bring a bride back to Crichton."

Hepburn gave her a level look. "You were mistaken," he said curtly. His tone clearly told them the subject was closed. The women naturally concluded that he was still unwed.

That night at the evening meal in Crichton's Great Hall, he told his moss-troopers about the arrangement he had made with the king to keep the Borders peaceful. "Percy and Clifford have pledged their allegiance to patrol and disarm the English shires and we'll do the same in the Scottish dales. The old warden system and march laws will be abolished. The Border inhabitants will be subject to the same laws as the rest of the kingdom. If they refuse to disarm and keep the peace they will be hanged."

Jock scratched his head. "How is this different from the Border patrol we've done fer years?"

Patrick grinned. "The difference is the new King of England

is paying us three times as much for our services." His expression sobered. "I've invested the money in sheep. Next year when we export the wool, using our own Hepburn ships, we'll share the lucrative profits. Any who don't wish to be included can have their money now." He was relieved when none opted for their pay.

"We'll split the moss-troopers. Half will guard Crichton lands; the other half will patrol the Borders. We'll switch about every month. All in favor?"

A chorus of *ayes* was followed by the clink of pewter tankards.

Hepburn's first days home were occupied by the necessity of establishing a range where the sheep could graze. Tyne Water formed a natural barrier along the western and northern boundaries of Crichton's landholdings, but stone walls needed to be built in the south to prevent the valuable animals from wandering into the Moorfoot Hills, where they could be lost to wolves or human predators. Despite hours in the saddle, and the backbreaking tasks of collecting and piling stone, Patrick was restless. For the first time since he was a boy, he had difficulty sleeping, and as a result the hours of the night seemed endless.

Sometimes he arose at four in the morning and went hunting, with Sabbath and Satan his only companions. On the third successive morning of watching the sunrise over the Lammermuirs, he sat astride Valiant and addressed his deerhounds. "She's ruined it for me, you know. I used to relish being alone. I loved nothing better than ranging on my own. Now, all the joy, all the pleasure, has gone out of it." It took him a few more days before he admitted to himself that he was suffering from loneliness.

When Patrick saw newborn lambs, his first thought was of Catherine and how thrilled she would be if she could see them. He forced her from his thoughts, but she returned unbidden, and a gnawing ache grew inside of him that he found difficult, then impossible, to ignore.

Eating alone killed his appetite. He began taking all his meals with his moss-troopers, yet his food remained tasteless and unappetizing. His temper grew short; his usually wicked humor deserted him. Finally, Jock confronted him. "Ye're like a bear with a sore arse. 'Tis obvious ye did not get yer hands on the English estate ye coveted."

Though Hepburn was not given to brooding introspection, he lapsed into it now. Perhaps it was not the English estate he missed and longed for; perhaps it was the Englishwoman who owned it. *Is it Catherine I want, or Spencer Park?* He forced himself to be truthful. *I want them both!* Moreover, he was stubbornly convinced there was no reason on God's earth why he couldn't have them both. All he had to do was bring the little hellcat to heel.

"I'll take the first Border patrol," he told Jock, trying to make amends for his accursed temper.

"Nay, yer needed here at Crichton. I'll patrol the Borders fer the month of June, and ye take over in July."

At Spencer Park, Catherine grew wan and listless. She had stopped riding out on Jasmine because the solitary exercise brought too many memories of the glorious rides she and Patrick had enjoyed every day. She stopped going into the library for books, because it reminded her of times they had stolen into the room for an intimate hour when they could not wait until night.

To fill her hours, she sat with a sketchbook, but now that Queen Elizabeth was gone, there was no reason to design the fantastic garments the aging monarch had demanded. Cat often caught herself drawing the leopard and horse-head symbols of Hepburn, and one day she looked down to see that she had sketched Crichton Castle.

There were times that she longed for Scotland, for her grandfather and for Tattoo, her little black cat. With horror, she began to suspect that what she really longed for was Patrick, and then she would deny it with every fiber of her being.

She and Maggie began to sew tiny garments for Mary Carey's child, but the ache inside her for a baby of her own became intense and then unbearable, and Cat began to fear for her sanity. What saved her was the letters that David Hepburn brought her when he returned from one of his journeys to London.

"Maggie, I have two letters: one from Philadelphia and one from Queen Anne herself!"

Maggie offered up a silent prayer of thanks. It was the first time she had seen delight on Catherine's face for a long time.

Impulsively, Cat slit the wax seal on the envelope from Queen Anne first, saving the best for last. "It is an announcement of the coronation in July." She passed the official card to Maggie and then read aloud the brief note enclosed.

> *Lady Stewart:*
> *Please don't wait until the coronation. I need your services now. Though I am only Queen Consort of England, my royal lord insists that we be crowned together at Westminster Abbey.*
> *HRH Anna Stuart*

Suddenly the Royal Court with all its trappings of pomp and splendor, along with its courtiers vying for attention, seemed far preferable to her lonely days and endless nights at Spencer Park.

With eager anticipation Cat read aloud from Philadelphia's letter. The second paragraph was most gratifying.

> *Queen Anne complimented me on a gown I wore yesterday, and when I told her that you had designed it, she asked me to persuade you to return. Her Majesty shows no desire to surround herself with virginal maids of honor, preferring married ladies instead. She is also careful not to show marked favor to her Danish ladies-in-waiting and seems determined to appoint English ladies. Both Liz Carey and your mother have given her their devotion, and I warrant Anne is far less demanding than her predecessor.*
> *There is only one of the queen's ladies that I do not care for. Her name is Margretha, and I have been matchmaking in the hope that some English noble will wed her and remove her from Court. My efforts seem to be bearing fruit. I introduced her to Sir Mortimer Chesham, who saw in her an opportunity to curry favor with England's new monarchs. Margretha of course sees herself as Lady Chesham, in spite of the fact that he is neither handsome nor in his first prime. Darling,*

you see the devious devices I've had to employ, just to amuse myself?

Do come for a visit, and don't wait until July. Lord Stewart's chambers at Whitehall are far more splendid than my own and it seems an utter waste to leave them unoccupied. Your friend Arbella is enjoying herself immensely now that she is high in the Stuart pecking order.

Summer has arrived early in London, which will give both of us a chance to show off our lovely silk and finespun gowns. The coronation is less than a month away, and time is fleeting.

Fondest love,
Philadelphia Scrope

Catherine raised her eyes from the letter. The picture Philadelphia's words had painted was too enticing for Cat's impetuous nature to resist. "Maggie, we are going to London for the coronation. I shall pack all my finest spring and summer gowns. Come, there isn't a moment to lose!"

Chapter Thirty-two

"*W*hat on earth is happening?" Catherine's voice showed traces of fear as she looked at the milling crowd of filthy beggars who had stopped their carriage outside the city gates.

"Dear God, the slums have become overrun with the dregs of Scotland. Like rats, they've deserted Edinburgh and Glasgow and will soon turn London into a cesspool," Maggie declared.

David Hepburn, who was sitting beside their driver, picked up the coachman's whip and laid it about the backs of the more aggressive thieves who had climbed onto the carriage. The mob fell back long enough for the Spencer coach to get through the Aldergate. Inside the city, though the streets seemed packed with people, the crowds were not unruly.

"It's stifling hot in here. I need some air," Cat said.

"Dinna open the window! Overcrowded slums breed contagion."

"You may be right, Maggie." Cat shuddered and plied her fan.

By the time they arrived at Whitehall, it seemed like they were in another world, and Catherine heaved a sigh of relief. She thanked David for keeping them safe. She didn't approve of his brutal tactics yet admitted they had been necessary.

"I'm sorry ye were subjected to danger, Lady Stewart. If ye confine yerself to the Court, ye will be safe." He unloaded the luggage, lifted a trunk to his shoulder and picked up another. His great height and strength reminded Cat of another Scot. *He's ordering me to confine myself to the Court. All Hepburns are insufferably arrogant!* She led the way to her husband's chambers. The well-appointed rooms were comfortably spacious but, since they hadn't been used for some time, seemed airless. Cat threw open all the windows, and David went to get the rest of the luggage.

"I'll order ye some bathwater, then ye can change into a lighter dress. If June is this hot, what will July be like?"

"If I unpack immediately, my gowns won't be creased too badly."

"Let's see if we can do it before yer water arrives."

That evening, when Catherine and Philadelphia strolled into the Great Dining Hall, adjacent to the Privy Chamber, they were immediately surrounded by ladies of the Court who were envious of their lightweight gowns. The Scottish females for the most part wore woolen garments whose colors tended to be deep and dark. Their clothes were designed to keep them warm in their drafty, cold castles. As the chamber filled up, the courtiers became overheated. Some gentlemen opened their doublets and the necks of their linen shirts, but the ladies were not so fortunate.

It wasn't long before Queen Anne sent Christina, one of her ladies, to summon Catherine to the dais.

As Cat went down in a graceful curtsy, the queen beckoned her to come up onto the dais. "Lady Stewart, I am delighted you came."

"Thank you for inviting me, Your Highness."

"Christina will give you her seat so we may talk. I am sweltering to death. How do you appear so cool and elegant?"

"I'm wearing a summer dress of silk organza, Your Highness."

"Are the summers always this hot in England, Lady Stewart?"

"Please call me Catherine. It's not usually this hot until late July or August, but I think summer is here to stay, ma'am."

"In that case I am in urgent need of a wardrobe like yours."

"I shall confer with my mother tonight, and I promise we will devise a new wardrobe suited to this stifling hot weather."

Philadelphia and Cat found Isobel with the sewing women. Many were English ladies who'd worked with her for years, but others were from Holyrood, and had previously sewn Anne's garments.

"Catherine! This is a surprise."

Cat braced herself for rejection. Her mother's tone indicated it was not a *pleasant* surprise. "The queen invited me.

She saw my gown tonight and voiced a desire for something similar. I promised you'd devise garments more suited to this hot weather."

"That *I* would devise, or *you* would devise, Catherine?"

Philadelphia jumped in. "For pity's sake, Isobel, your daughter isn't trying to undermine your authority. We must all put our heads together and come up with a solution. Tonight! Anne and her ladies are roasting alive in their woolens."

Isobel changed her tune. "Her Majesty's comfort is paramount."

"Mother, I know there is a vast array of materials packed away in storage. We must go through it and sort out all the lightweight cloth. We will need finespun lawn for undergarments and silk, sarcenet, cambric, lace, faille, organzine or taffeta for day dresses and gowns. I think Queen Anne would look especially elegant in taffeta."

"Like the one I'm wearing. It rustles deliciously," Philadelphia pointed out.

"I know that Elizabeth had well over a hundred fans. They need to be brought out of storage and put to good use," Cat advised.

"I shall lead the way. Follow me, ladies," Isobel directed.

Catherine began to sketch some designs that would flatter Anne's statuesque figure, and within the hour the sewing women began work on a gown that the queen could wear the next day.

It was midnight before Cat retired, and as she lay abed feeling pleased with all she had accomplished tonight, Patrick's words came floating back to her. *The lion's share of the credit is yours, sweetheart. It was a resounding triumph, especially for a little wench who's only goal used to be wearing the most elegant gown.* Suddenly, she felt that life at Court was shallow. She turned over and thumped her pillow, vehemently denying that she missed him. *Damn you Hepburn, you've spoiled everything for me!*

Throughout the month of June, Catherine, Isobel and the ladies of the Queen's Wardrobe worked diligently creating garments for both Queen Anne and her ladies. Before work could begin on Anne's coronation robes, a design and a color had to be decided upon.

"Green is a Tudor color, and I don't care for purple," the queen told Catherine. "White doesn't flatter me, and cloth of gold or silver would likely put James in the shade. Though it's never been used for a coronation, I wish I could wear plain blue."

"Your Highness, as Queen of England it is your right to set the fashion, rather than follow it. Why not wear blue? Not plain blue, of course; we will have to give it a more splendid name."

Cat took out her colored chalks and experimented on the sketches she'd drawn. "This deep shade of blue is so vibrant and would be a glorious contrast to your blond hair. I know! Why don't we call it royal blue, Your Highness?"

"Royal blue? I like that! You are so inventive, Catherine."

"And the ladies who attend you in Westminster Abbey could all have matching gowns in soft powder blue."

The only dissenting voice was Margretha's, and when Anne overruled her, Catherine tried not to look smugly triumphant, though she certainly felt it.

Anne saw some of her ladies from Scotland whispering in a corner and, thinking to stem some petty rivalry, she demanded to know what the problem was.

Lady Erskine stepped forward. "Your Highness, I don't wish to cause alarm, but there is talk of *plague* in London."

Philadelphia spoke up quickly. "That is a common occurrence in London. Every summer there are a few cases of plague reported."

Isobel added, "It only occurs among the lower classes in the slums. The Royal Court is never endangered by the contagion."

Later that day, conversing with James, the queen realized that the king was greatly alarmed at the reports of plague. In an effort to calm him, she repeated what Isobel had said about it not endangering the Royal Court.

"Oh, aye, that's why Elizabeth deserted London every summer on her endless *progresses* tae her nobles' country estates!"

"When the coronation is over, perhaps we should remove the Court to the castle at Windsor. I don't much care for Whitehall. It's such a ramshackle old palace, and far too close to the rabble." As an added incentive, she said, "The hunting in Windsor's forests is reputed to be unsurpassed."

The following week, Arbella Stuart flounced into Catherine's chambers to voice her frustration. "I'm so vexed, I could scream! Will Seymour invited me to attend a play at the Globe Theatre next Wednesday, but now I hear that by order of the king all the playhouses have been closed!"

"It's to stop the spread of plague. Robert Cecil is ordering that the city gates be closed today to keep out the 'unruly infected.' Did you not see this notice?" Cat handed her a pamphlet. "King James has ordered that these be distributed, advising everyone of the best medical cures."

"Too bad the masses canno' read," Maggie said dryly.

Arbella waved her pomander. "I cannot be infected. I carry rue and wormwood at all times. Closing the city is preposterous!"

"The king and Cecil intend keeping the city free from contagion for the coronation. Hundreds of English and Scottish nobles are in London for the celebration. It's a wise precaution, Arbella."

Catherine did not tell her friend that one of her aunt Beth's servants at Hunsdon House in Blackfriars had died of the plague and that they'd had to bury her in secret. Such tidings must be kept from the ears of the Royal Court, or panic would ensue and ruin the king and queen's coronation. Cat had promised Philadelphia that she would keep her mouth shut, but as a result her conscience began to prick her sorely.

At Crichton, in spite of the fact that Patrick was kept busy from dawn till dusk and beyond, his thoughts began to nettle him. Hepburn, never, ever, bothered by conscience, denied that he even had one. But Catherine was constantly in his thoughts, and sometimes she evoked the feeling that he was in the wrong.

It opened a tiny crack in his façade and as loneliness assailed him in the long hours of the night, he acknowledged that he missed her. Sleeping alone was like torture. The feel of the sheets against his flesh provoked such raw lust for his wife's body that he was in a constant state of arousal. Finally, though, Hepburn was forced to admit that this wasn't the heart of the matter. Over and above the sex and the passion, the thing that he missed the most, the thing that he yearned for, was the warm intimacy he and Catherine shared.

He quit the bed though the first glimmer of dawn was still hours away, and began to pack his saddlebags. It was July; Jock Elliot would be returning from Border patrol today, and Patrick had grown so restless that he was glad it was his turn to ride with his moss-troopers. He knew he must train Ian Hepburn as a captain to lead the men during the times that he would be absent in England. Patrick was eager to ride the dales to see firsthand how the Border residents of both countries were adjusting to one king, one law, for all. He was realistic enough to know that bitter feuds among the riding families that had gone on for centuries could not be brought to a peaceful resolution overnight. It would take an iron hand, fair and even justice, coupled with patience and perseverance, to attain neutrality, let alone harmony.

Hepburn and his moss-troopers found Midlothian trouble free, as Jock Elliot had reported. Its inhabitants were educated, and because of its close proximity to the capital of Edinburgh, the Scots there were knowledgeable about the king's longstanding ambition to unite the two countries.

Patrick warned his men, "Many in Teviotdale, Eskdale and Liddesdale are only vaguely aware that there will be inevitable, sweeping changes, and most are ignorant of English law. It will be our job to educate them."

Whenever they saw posses of men riding the dales, Hepburn stopped and engaged them in conversation. He explained that it would no longer be tolerated if they rode into England for plunder. "King James has appointed Percy and Clifford to enforce peace. Their men have authority to hang on the spot any caught thieving, looting, burning or reiving anywhere in the Borderlands.

"As a Scot, I'll do all I can to stop injustice and atrocity. Past crimes will be overlooked if you start fresh today. You must take responsibility, disarm and abide by the laws of the land."

Some Borderers listened, despite the dark surly looks on their faces, but others were ready to fight, determined to kill the messenger. In these cases Hepburn and his moss-troopers were quick to break a few bones or set a stern example with an occasional hanging. Hepburn hammered home the same message throughout the dales. "Those who resist the king's law will have to go, either by exile or by the gallows. The choice is yours."

Long hours in the saddle and nights by campfires, lying on the hard ground, gave Patrick Hepburn's mind the freedom to roam. His thoughts were consumed more and more by Catherine. He knew that by now she would have returned to Court. His mouth curved into a cynical smile. *The little hellcat won't be thinking of me. Her only thought will be which gown to wear for the royal coronation!*

He threw a heavy log onto the campfire, then stretched his long limbs on the ground and stared up at the star-filled July sky. Patrick knew he could conjure her image if he wanted. Until now he had resisted the temptation. Tonight, however, the desire to see her was irresistible. *Just a glimpse,* he promised himself.

The sound of the horses tethered to the nearby trees faded away along with the murmured laughter and curses of the moss-troopers who sat dicing in the firelight. Gradually, he envisioned a room and recognized it as his own chambers at Whitehall. He focused on the polished silver mirror, knowing Cat could not long resist her own image. A voice, faint at first, came to him from afar. He sensed it was Catherine's, long before the words became audible.

"I know I swore off white, but the heat is so oppressive, I cannot bring myself to wear anything else tomorrow."

A vision in white silk, with white roses entwined in her shining black hair, materialized in the mirror. Her stunning beauty and elegance robbed him of breath. He stared, mesmerized, at her delicate loveliness. She was luminescent, as if lit from within, as Maggie made a last-minute alteration with her needle. Cat's voice, breathless with excitement, sent a frisson of pleasure curling about his innards. She struck a pose and asked Maggie, "What do you think?"

"I think I'm in love," Patrick whispered.

The vision of Catherine faded, but his words hung in the air, suspended like an echo in the night. He jumped up and strode away from his men and the firelight into the darkness, ostensibly to check on the horses, but in reality to resurrect the shield that guarded his vulnerability.

After a short period of seclusion, he began to examine the words he had uttered aloud. *What prompted me to say such a thing?*

Her beauty, of course.

That's a glib answer—a shallow answer. He allowed his mind to delve below the surface, warily penetrating the layers of protection he had built up over the years. Then he forced it deeper, to where his emotions lay hidden.

Hepburn's head had always been at war with his heart, and each battle fought and won reinforced his tough façade, submerging his more tender feelings. Now, for the first time, he realized that if he could not acknowledge the truth, at least to himself, he was not demonstrating his strength; he was revealing his weakness.

His head had always insisted that love was a useless emotion indulged only by women and fools. Love was also dangerous; his mother had died because of it. But now he realized that love might not be something you chose. Perhaps love was so powerful that it did the choosing. Though he had resisted, he finally admitted that love had conquered. For a man who always had to be in control, it was a humbling revelation.

I love Cat! I lost my heart the day I had my first vision of her. Without her, my life would be bleak and barren. Without Catherine, Spencer Park means nothing. In any choice between my wife and her wealth and property, Hellcat wins—hands down!

Hepburn walked back into the firelight, wondering why it had taken so long for him to accept the truth. He looked down at the scar on his hand and chuckled. *Like a terrier, Catherine bites above her weight. She is special. She has that rare quality of being vulnerable and also being strong—it's like a fragile crust.*

He looked down at his large boots and his long limbs encased in soiled scuffed leather. He rubbed his hand over the rough stubble of his unshaven chin and marveled that such an uncouth brute had managed to wed a delicate lady whose ethereal beauty and elegance made other females seem plain and dowdy. And whose fire and passion had captured his heart and soul.

Hepburn decided on the spot that at the end of the month, when his Border patrol was done, he would return to England. He had no idea how he would do it, but he knew he must convince Catherine that he loved her. *Nay, more, I must show her that I adore and worship her. She is my treasure!*

In Westminster Abbey, Catherine sat between her mother and Philadelphia. Liz Carey was not present. Because of the threat of plague, the queen had ordered that her children take up residence at Windsor Castle, a safe twenty miles from London.

Only by craning her neck could Catherine catch glimpses of the ancient and historic crowning ceremony of the new King and Queen of England. The pageantry, if not James himself, was spectacular. The royal couple had ridden to the abbey in a gilt coach, and the sweating throngs of Londoners who lined the streets jostled and gaped as the parade of monarchs and mounted nobles passed, though few cheered until the Yeomen of the Guard, plodding along in the stifling heat, came into view.

Inside the abbey, the pulpit was arrayed with cushions and cloths of gold silk where James and Anne were now kneeling. As the Archbishop of Canterbury said the orison over the king, Philadelphia yawned. Isobel, fanning herself frantically, cast her a glance of pointed disapproval, but before the archbishop droned to a close, she was yawning herself.

With the aid of the Abbot of Westminster, James and Anne were anointed, and then the Archbishop of Canterbury put the Crown of St. Edward on James Stuart's head and took his oath. The Consort's Crown was then placed on Anne's head. Catherine thought of the queens who had worn this crown before Anne. They had been the wives of Henry VIII, and in spite of the heat Cat shivered.

King James took the rod and scepter from the archbishop, and then Anglican mass was celebrated. A few fainted in the hot, close atmosphere, but most simply nodded off from the soporific heat. During the sacrament, however, something happened to jolt the congregation awake. Queen Anne refused the offering of bread and wine. There was a commotion when Jamie ordered his wife to take the sacrament. Anne adamantly refused, and England's new monarch went red in the face. The archbishop moved on to serve the nobles, and shocked whispers spread throughout the pews.

Back at Whitehall, Cat stripped off her dress and told Maggie what had happened as she took a cool sponge bath.

"That's an omen!"

"Philadelphia said it was a good sign. Anne showed that women don't have to blindly obey their husbands. And I agree!"

"In the kitchens, the English servants are blaming this plague on James. They say he has incurred the wrath of God by taking the throne. But the Scots are saying that God is making England atone for the sins committed by the previous reign. Either way, the coronation celebrations will be short-lived."

"I think you're right Maggie. They didn't want people to panic before the coronation could take place, but Lord Scrope says that tomorrow Cecil will issue new orders. The infected must be isolated. Anyone found on the streets with a plague sore will be whipped from the city. Any who willfully pollute the air and infect others can be condemned as murderers and hanged. Searchers are being sent out to keep the infected out of the city."

"I was talking to Rose, one of the cooks. She said farmers have stopped bringing in produce. She was sent into London to buy food and saw scores of red crosses over doorways and heard the death knell ringing constantly. 'Tis already in the city, my lamb."

Arbella knocked on the door and Maggie let her in.

"Aren't you ready yet, Cat? The banquet will be over before you are even dressed!"

"We were discussing the dreaded bubonic plague. It's already spread into the city. The contagion could come to White-hall."

"What nonsense! Plague is the poor-man's disease. It only infects unemployed, dirty beggars. It will get rid of a lot of filthy, unwanted wretches. It's God's punishment!"

Catherine stared at her and wondered how her empty-headed friend could be so heartless and just plain ignorant.

Downstairs at the banquet, it became obvious that England's newly crowned monarchs were not speaking. Each held Court at opposite ends of the Presence Chamber.

Isobel excused Anne's refusal to take the Anglican sacra-ment. "The queen is Catholic. She was being true to her faith."

Philadelphia laughed. "Anne was not brought up a Catholic. She converted only a few years ago. What she did established her power as queen to show that her role as consort won't be an empty one."

Catherine was dismayed that all the talk was about what had occurred at the crowning. The threat of plague was being over-shadowed by the power struggle between James and Anne. She thought of her own husband and realized they too were having a power struggle. *Men like to be in control and rule the roost. If a wife asserts herself, she is punished.*

Cat spoke to Philadelphia about the threat of plague.

"Scrope tells me James wishes to go to Cecil's country es-tate, Theobalds, but Anne insists they go to Windsor. Another battle royal is brewing. It will be fascinating to see who wins."

"It won't be fascinating if plague comes to Whitehall while they play their silly power games."

"Scrope insists we go to Carlisle, and for once I think I shall allow him to have his way. There may not be a Border anymore, but Thomas is still Constable of Carlisle Castle."

Queen Anne summoned Isobel. "Lady Spencer, I want you to pack my wardrobe. We are leaving Whitehall at week's end. Select a half dozen of your best assistants to come with us."

Isobel curtsied. Since gossip said the royal couple was arguing about their destination, she did not ask questions.

Anne had made up her mind. She told Margretha, "James can go to Theobalds or he can go to the devil. I am the Queen of England with my own Court. My ladies and I are going to Windsor. Would you discreetly pass my invitation on to Lady Scrope, Lady Hunsdon, Lady Stewart—you know the ladies I consider to be friends."

"Patrick Hepburn's wife told me she is returning to Hertford, Your Highness, but I will quietly inform the other ladies."

The moment Queen Anne withdrew from the overheated Presence Chamber, Catherine retired. Upstairs, she paced back and forth, fanning herself. "Honestly, Maggie, I don't know whether to open these windows or keep them closed. The night air may carry the contagion. London is an unfit place to be in July. I hope Queen Anne decides to move us to Windsor soon."

The next few nights were spent tossing and turning in the sticky heat. The following morning, Catherine put fresh linen on the beds while Maggie went down to get them some breakfast. When she returned, she was out of breath from hurrying.

"Maggie, you look like you've seen a ghost. What's amiss?"

"It's Rose, the cook I was telling you about." She stopped to catch her breath. "She's come down with the plague!"

"Mother of God! Is she very ill? Is she expected to live?"

"They've carted her off to Bridewell, poor soul!"

"But that's a prison, not a hospital!"

"Nobody will harbor plague victims, let alone nurse them. They've issued new rules—any servant at Whitehall who gets sick will be sent to Bridewell."

"Start packing, Maggie. We cannot stay here. I'm going down to the palace storekeeper to see when David Hepburn is due to make his next delivery. We'll return with him to Spencer Park."

Chapter Thirty-three

An hour later, a worried Catherine returned to her chambers. "I'm afraid David Hepburn won't be coming to Whitehall anytime soon. He was directed to take the meat and butter to Windsor Castle, after the royal children were moved there. I suppose the best thing we can do is go to Windsor with the queen, then wait for David to take us home to Spencer Park."

Maggie rubbed her back and said wearily, "Windsor to Hertford is a forty-mile journey. London is much closer to Spencer Park."

"Are you all right, Maggie?"

"It's just a backache from climbing stairs in this heat."

"Sit down and rest. I shall do the packing." Catherine dragged out the trunks and began the tedious job of emptying the wardrobe. At lunchtime she went down to the kitchens to get them some food and something cool to drink.

Everyone working in the palace kitchens was talking about the dreaded scourge. Each had an opinion on how the contagion was spread. One said that it was the river Thames; another said that it was the air; two others insisted that nothing was so dangerous as the breath of those who were infected. All agreed about what signs to look for when someone was coming down with the pestilence: no appetite, headache, sweating, dull aching pain in the back and loins. Cat noticed with apprehension that every person in the kitchens was sweating profusely.

She took a freshly baked loaf of bread, some chicken, a pear compote and a jug of mead upstairs. When Maggie said she wasn't hungry, Catherine became alarmed. She poured her a cup of mead and was relieved when Maggie drank it down greedily. She forced herself to eat some bread and chicken breast but it made her nauseated. She decided to go and speak with her mother.

Cat found the Ladies of the Queen's Wardrobe packing. "Mother, I'm so relieved that you are readying everything for a move. I too am packing. When is the queen planning to leave?"

"Tomorrow, I believe," Isobel confided, "but I've been instructed to take only six ladies, and I don't know if we are going to Windsor or Theobalds, which is the king's preference."

Cat's spirit lifted. *Theobalds is in Hertfordshire, only a few miles from Spencer Park!* "I'll go and have a private word with Robert. As a Gentleman of the King's Bedchamber, he should be able to tell us where the Royal Court is going."

Catherine made her way to the monarch's royal apartments. The only men she encountered were guards who would not let her pass through to the king's bedchamber. "Can you please take a message to my uncle, Sir Robert Carey? I am in sore need of his advice."

"Sorry, my lady, but His Royal Highness and his Gentlemen of the Bedchamber left this morning for Theobalds."

Catherine's spirits sank. "Thank you." She went back to the Wardrobe Department and told Isobel what she had learned.

"Ah, then it is to be Windsor, after all. We will go by river, an easier journey than by road when I have so much to transport."

"I'd better go and finish packing." Cat almost mentioned that Maggie seemed under the weather, but she didn't want to worry her mother. Isobel had enough responsibilities.

When she returned to her chambers, Catherine's hopes that Maggie would be improved were dashed. "I'm so sorry you are feeling poorly. Is there anything I can get you, Maggie?"

"Just some water . . . I'm so thirsty. I'm sorry, lass."

Cat brought her a drink. "Sorry? There's nothing to be sorry about." Without a word, she filled a bowl with water and brought soap and towel. Cat knelt down before her faithful serving woman and sponged her hands and face, which were clammy with sweat. She chattered to keep her fears at bay. "It is this heat that is making you feel ill. It's making me quite nauseous."

"Perhaps ye're having a wee bairn." Maggie sounded worried.

"No, no, it's this dreadful heat. Mother is packing for the

queen. We are going to Windsor Palace tomorrow by river. That's probably better than being jostled in a hot carriage."

Catherine checked her jewel case to make sure she had everything, and then she locked it. Finally, she packed Maggie's clothes for her and piled all their luggage at the door.

When it was dark, she helped Maggie to bed, then retired. Cat couldn't sleep and got up twice in the dark to get Maggie a drink.

"I'm sorry to be so much trouble, lass."

"You are no trouble. How many times when I was a child did you bring me a drink in the night?"

"That was my job, my lamb."

"No, it was love, Maggie, and I love you." *Please, please, don't let her have the plague . . . I couldn't bear it!*

Cat spent the remaining hours of the night alternating between denial and fear. First she would tell herself that it was impossible for Maggie to have the contagion, then she would pray that Maggie's friend Rose hadn't infected her. She didn't sleep until dawn and, as a result, slept later than she intended.

When she checked on Maggie, she found that though she moved restlessly, she was asleep. Cat dressed and, seeing no need to disturb Maggie just yet, went along to the Wardrobe Department to arrange for her luggage to be taken to the queen's barge.

"Are you still here, Catherine? Queen Anne and her ladies left an hour ago. Arbella was with them. They told me you weren't coming to Windsor, that you were going home to Spencer Park."

"Who told you that, Mother? Arbella?"

"No, it was the queen's lady Margaretta, or whatever her name is. Anyway, it doesn't matter. The queen is sending the barge back for all the luggage. If your trunks haven't been taken to the Palace Water Stairs, I'll send a porter for them. You can come along with me; there is no time to lose."

"I can't. Maggie is still abed. We'll meet you by the river."

"Maggie in bed? Is she ill?"

"She wasn't feeling well yesterday, but I'm sure she'll be fine. It was just a backache."

"Backache? Dear God, that's a sure sign of plague!" Isobel clutched her heart. "You mustn't go near her. Don't go back to your chambers—just send for your luggage."

"I cannot abandon Maggie!" Cat was outraged at the suggestion.

"Well, you certainly cannot take her to Windsor and risk infecting Her Royal Highness. All you have to do is report her illness and she will be taken to Bridewell."

"Mother! Bridewell is a prison."

"It is a temporary hospital. Whitehall is under strict orders that any servant with symptoms of contagion must go to Bridewell."

Catherine recoiled. "Keep away from me, lest I infect you. It seems Margretha was right; I *am* going home to Spencer Park."

"You must get through the city gate before you can reach the road to Hertfordshire, and none may leave without a certificate of health. Come with me now, Catherine; it's the only way out."

"Goodbye, Mother. Our paths, as always, diverge."

Cat returned to her rooms and found Maggie awake, attempting to dress herself. "Let me help you." She lifted Maggie's petticoat over her head and heard a soft groan. "Are you feeling worse?"

"My head aches something fierce."

Cat brushed her hand across Maggie's forehead and found it warm. With stoic determination she pushed her fear away, sat Maggie down on the bed and with what water they had left, gave her a cool sponge bath. Then she helped her into her dress, pulled on her stockings and fastened her shoes.

Cat summoned a porter and paid him to take the luggage to the entrance closest to Whitehall's stables. She gave Maggie a drink of mead, set her locked jewel case beside her and told her to sit quietly until she got back. Then she went in search of Arbella's coach driver. Worried thoughts chased each other relentlessly in her head as she searched one servants' haunt after another. Just as she despaired of ever finding the man, she met him coming from the kitchens munching a meat pie. "Ah, there you are, Stoke. Arbella sent me to find you." She lowered her voice and said confidentially, "We don't think it's healthy to remain in London. Arbella asks that you ready her coach and take us to my estate in Hertford until all this threat of contagion is past."

"A wise move, my lady—they're droppin' like flies hereabouts."

As Cat climbed the stairs back to her rooms, her legs were

shaking from relief, even though she knew the next step would be fraught with difficulty. She opened the door and found Maggie sitting where she had left her. She had stopped sweating, her face was flushed and she shivered as if she was cold.

"I want you to wear my cloak." Cat pulled up the hood of the fashionable pink watered-silk cape. "Keep your face covered. We don't want anyone to know you are ill." She helped Maggie to her feet. "I've found us a coach, but we must get down to the courtyard." She picked up her jewel case and, clutching Maggie's hand, helped her from the room.

Whenever Maggie moaned, Catherine leaned her against the wall and waited until she could go on. There were three flights of stairs to descend, and in the middle of each, Maggie had to sit down on the steps until she gained enough strength to go farther. Though it seemed to take forever, Cat patiently allowed Maggie to go at her own pace. When they reached the ground floor of Whitehall, her old nurse looked like she could go no farther. "Lean on me, Maggie. Come on, love, just a few more steps."

When they got to the entrance, the coach was there before them and Stoke was loading their baggage. He opened the carriage door for them and somehow Maggie swayed and wobbled the last few yards.

When Stoke stared with open curiosity at the two females clutching each other, Cat said, "Lady Stuart has had a bit too much wine. Someone told her it would protect her from the contagion."

"Ah, well, get her inside and she can sleep it off."

Catherine settled Maggie in a corner of the coach and adjusted her hood so that her face was hidden. Cat was grateful that the movement of the carriage as they drove along the Strand rocked Maggie to sleep. The driver avoided the Ludgate by turning up Shoe Lane, but Cat was horrified at what she saw through the window. Red crosses were being painted over doorways, and people, both young and old, were being put into carts and taken away. As they got closer to the wall of London, she shuddered at the sight of two corpses lying in the street. When the coach stopped at the Aldergate, Cat held her breath and prayed. If the guards discovered that Maggie was ailing, they would take her away.

The minutes stretched out until she was ready to scream,

then Stoke knocked on the window. Cat opened it reluctantly, dreading what he would say.

"They won't let us through the gate without health certificates, my lady. Do either of ye have papers?"

Cat shook her head. "Go back and tell them I am Lady Stewart, traveling with Arbella Stuart, cousin to King James." As Stoke went to do her bidding, she could hear her own heartbeat thudding in her ears. Then the carriage seemed to fill with the scent of lavender, and Catherine was immediately reminded of Kate Howard, who had always worn that fragrance. "Help us, Kate," she murmured.

Stoke returned. "He says he doesn't care if you're the Virgin Queen resurrected; the law is the law."

Catherine's eardrums felt as if they would burst. Then she thought she heard a voice say *"Use the earrings."* A vision of Kate's ruby and diamond earrings came into her head. Quickly, she unlocked her jewel case and stared down at the gems that were so precious to her. *I cannot part with them.* She heard Maggie moan in her sleep and knew she would sacrifice all her jewels if it would help Maggie.

Catherine grabbed the earrings and stepped from the carriage. She knew all depended upon her performance. She must act as if she were a goddess who had stepped down from Mount Olympus to challenge a mere mortal. She'd had lessons from Queen Elizabeth on how to be imperial. "My good man, the King of England and his gentlemen passed through this gate yesterday on their way to Hertfordshire. We are part of the king's Royal Court. Inside is the king's first cousin, Lady Arbella Stuart. Do you not see the Stuart crest on the coach door?"

"Milady, I have orders to let no one pass either in or out of the city gates without a health certificate."

"Really?" Cat drawled. "Did the king and his gentlemen have health certificates? Of course they didn't. Take a good look at me, sir. Do I look as if I am ailing?" She lifted the skirts of her pink gown and twirled around. "I have something better than a silly piece of paper." She smiled seductively and opened her fingers to display the jewels on her palm. "Rubies and diamonds."

When the guard reached for them, she closed her fingers. He called to his fellow guard, "Open the gate."

Catherine opened her fingers and gave him a radiant smile,

but when she climbed back into the carriage she was trembling all over. *Thank you, Kate. Thank you for helping us.*

As the coach picked up speed, Maggie slumped over. Cat moved her so that she was lying down on the seat and began to make plans for what she would do when they arrived at Spencer Park. By now she was convinced that Maggie had the plague, and she knew that she must be isolated from other people.

As they passed through small villages, Cat was alarmed at the number of people who were lying in the ditches. She realized with dismay that the epidemic was not just in London. It seemed to be spreading everywhere.

It was early afternoon by the time the carriage came to a stop in Spencer Park's courtyard. Catherine stepped out. "Stoke, would you be good enough to bring the luggage?" As she reached the front door, Mr. Burke opened it.

"Welcome home, my lady. I am so very relieved you are well."

She waited until he had helped Stoke bring the luggage inside, then said, "Mr. Burke, I need to speak with you in private."

Burke told Stoke to go to the kitchen for a drink of ale, and then he followed Catherine to the library.

She closed the door, took a deep breath and turned to face him. "You won't welcome me, Mr. Burke. I fear that I have brought the plague to Spencer Park. It's Maggie." Her shoulders slumped. "She's in the carriage. I had nowhere else to take her."

"Regretfully, my lady, the plague arrived here before you. Last week, one of the maids came down with the contagion. Her family came and took her away, but sadly, they could not save her. I sent the entire staff home until this scourge passes. The only one who stayed is Cook, who says she survived a plague epidemic before. Let's get Maggie into the house."

"Are you not afraid, Mr. Burke?"

"Afraid of the plague, yes; afraid of death, no. You do understand that you have exposed yourself?"

"I had no choice. I love Maggie. We will isolate her away from your quarters and of course the kitchens. I will nurse her, but I can't get her into the house by myself."

"I will carry her in. Does your coach driver know?"

Cat flushed. "No, I lied to him. I must go and confess." She went to the kitchens, opened the door and called his name. Stoke came out holding a tankard of ale.

"Lady Stewart, they've already had a plague victim here. Are you sure you want to stay?"

"It seems to be everywhere. It's so frightening. The lady I brought with me is very ill, Stoke, and I fear it's the plague."

"Lady Arbella has the plague?"

"No, Arbella is safe at Windsor with the queen. The lady with me is my serving woman. I lied to you and I have no excuse."

Stoke stared at her in amazement. "You exposed yourself to help a servant? God bless you, my lady."

"I will keep her isolated. You may stay if you wish, Stoke. Thank you. Mr. Burke will pay you for your service to me."

"Thank you, my lady, but I'd best make my way to Windsor if I want to keep my job. Take care of yourself, ma'am."

They put Maggie to bed in the east wing nursery. "Ask Cook to make some barley water, Mr. Burke. Just knock on the door when it's ready. I don't want you to come inside this room again."

Maggie was burning with fever and muttering incoherently. Cat removed her dress but left on her petticoat. She gave her a sponge bath with cool water; though her skin was burning hot, Maggie was shivering. Cat spoke in a soothing voice. "You have chills and fever. I know you must be thirsty. Here is some nice barley water to make you feel better. Try and sip a little."

She lifted Maggie's head and put the cup to her lips, but she refused to drink. Patiently, Cat tried again and again, but it was to no avail. She decided to leave her in peace for a while and try again later. Cat answered a knock on the door and found Mr. Burke with another tray that held food for her. She took it and closed the door firmly.

Catherine tried to eat, but the lump in her throat made it difficult. She found it far easier to drink the watered wine. She sat down in a chair beside the bed and closed her eyes. Cat prayed for Maggie and made bargains with God. When she opened her eyes she saw that twilight had descended. *The Scots call it gloaming.* Once again she tried her best to get Maggie to drink, but her patient suddenly knocked the cup from her hand and began to thrash about and scream as if she were in terrible pain.

"What is it, love?"

Maggie had thrown off her covers and was tearing at her petticoat as if she could not bear the feel of it against her flesh.

Catherine lifted up her skirt and gasped in horror at the huge black lump that had arisen in her groin. *Dear God, this is the dreaded bubo, the plague boil!* Cat had never been as afraid in her life. She went to the window and threw it open. She felt so alone and helpless, her eyes flooded with tears. There was only one man who had ever taken away her fears and loneliness, and her heart and soul cried out for him. "Patrick! I don't know what to do. Patrick, I need you. You are my magic man."

Hepburn and his moss-troopers had had a productive month, with twelve-hour days riding the dales, keeping the peace. They had covered far more territory than in previous years when they had patrolled only the Scottish Middle March. They had ridden into England's northern shires in their efforts to erase the invisible Border that separated the two countries. As July came to a close, the men were weary, tired of sleeping on the ground and more than ready to return home to Crichton.

Before Hepburn and his moss-troopers made the long eighty-mile trek home, he took it upon himself to seek the hospitality of Carlisle Castle in Cumberland, where they would get a decent meal and a comfortable bed. Lord Thomas Scrope, Philadelphia's husband, was the castle constable, and though Patrick knew Scrope had gone to England with King James, he was sure of a welcome.

That evening, the Great Hall rang with the noises of men bent on enjoying themselves. They had eaten themselves to a convivial stodge, imbibed enough ale to guarantee them a hangover and were in the process of stealing one another blind in a game of dice. As Hepburn's dark glance roved around the hall he felt satisfaction in all he'd accomplished and was glad he'd brought his moss-troopers to Carlisle for a well-deserved respite.

He drained his tankard, swung his long legs from beneath the trestle table and quit the smoke-filled hall in search of fresh air. He climbed to the castle ramparts, enjoying a quiet moment as the gloaming deepened into total darkness.

Almost immediately his sense of satisfaction and contentment drained away, and he was left with an ominous feeling. Guardedly, he opened his mind, sending out feelers that searched and probed for the source of this foreboding. His sixth sense told him that the menace did not emanate from this castle, but came from afar.

Hepburn immediately thought of Catherine, who was constantly on his mind of late. Though he was filled with dread that some misfortune might befall her, he did not shy away from fervently seeking to learn if real danger threatened her. Patrick focused intently to conjure a vision of his wife. He saw only her beautiful face, and his hands gripped the crenellated stone of the ramparts as he saw that her eyelashes glistened with teardrops.

Her overwhelming sadness rolled over him, and he sensed that her heart was breaking. But his inward conviction portended more than sadness. She was surrounded by a black, evil menace that told him she was in mortal danger. He resolved to leave immediately and thanked the Fates that he was already in England. Hepburn asked himself why he felt Catherine's peril now, when he had never sensed it before. The answer was simple. *It is because I have finally stopped denying that I love her.*

Chapter Thirty-four

*C*atherine had no idea how to combat the contagion that raged in Maggie's body, but she knew that delirium was brought on by high fever and instinctively tried to cool her down. Every hour she gave her a cooling sponge bath. Because of the agony caused by the black swelling in Maggie's groin, Cat took great pains to lift her limbs gently. She tried again and again to coax Maggie to sip a cold drink, but the sick woman refused. When Cat tried to force down some cool water, Maggie choked and it came back up.

During the next two days the patient raved and shouted and thrashed about wildly. Finally, her words became incoherent gibberish, and Catherine was gripped with fear and hopelessness.

On the third day, Maggie had periods of calm and seemed to doze quietly. When Catherine checked on the plague boil, it looked as if the swelling had lessened. Cat's hope returned and she was able to close her eyes and rest a little. On the fourth day, however, when Maggie did not rouse, Catherine realized that she had sunk into a coma.

As her hope began to melt away like snow in summer, she sat down on the side of the bed and, holding Maggie's hand between both of hers, murmured to her beloved friend in a soft voice. She spoke of times she remembered from her childhood when her old nurse had quietened her fears. She spoke of joys they'd shared and told her how much she had enjoyed their time in Scotland. Finally, with tears streaming freely down her cheeks, she spoke her fears aloud. "You cannot leave me, Maggie. You're the only one who ever loved me. Don't go; please don't go."

· · ·

Hepburn, mounted on Valiant and leading a second horse, rode through the night. With each mile the menace seemed to increase. Though he had no idea what threatened Catherine, he was becoming more and more convinced that her life was in peril.

When dawn broke, Patrick saw the turrets of Richmond Castle. He knew he had covered fifty miles and tried not to think of the two hundred that lay before him. While he watered his horses, he took a dip in the river Swale, then broke his fast with some oatcakes and let his horses crop the grass along the riverbank.

After an hour's rest, he was back in the saddle. Though he was riding south, to where the climate was milder, Hepburn began to realize that the heat was unusual. Both he and his mount were sweating and he knew he must water the horses more often.

When he arrived at York, he learned to his great horror that the city was in the grip of the black plague. Victims had been locked out of the walled city and lay dying or dead in the fields and ditches. "Holy God, the black evil that hovers over Catherine is the bubonic plague!" Hepburn's gut knotted with fear. He crossed himself and rode hell-for-leather from the accursed place. He vowed to avoid cities henceforth and stopped for food and rest at Selby Abbey, reasoning that the monks who lived there in isolation would be free of the contagion. He bought bread and cheese and a flagon of wine and put them in his saddlebags, then he rode south, following the river Trent, and did not stop again until he passed the small hamlet of Sutton and entered Sherwood Forest.

He drew strength from his surroundings. The place was so sheltered and ancient, so peaceful and untouched by man, with its massive oaks and abundant wildlife, that he became tranquil enough to rest for a few hours. He knew that he had covered more than half the distance, but it had taken him two days. Patrick vowed to finish his journey in less than that.

He sat with his back against the bole of a tree and tried to envision where Catherine was. He felt certain that she had gone to Court for the coronation, but he recoiled from the thought that she was still in London. With the heat and the city's overcrowded slums, the plague would be running a rampage.

Hepburn removed his leopard ring that Catherine had worn

and, holding it between thumb and forefinger, focused the powers of his mind. "Come to me, Cat, come to me." When she did not respond, he knew that he had failed to reach her spirit. His trancelike state produced other visions, however, that were disturbing. He saw Mr. Burke holding a spade. He also saw a river and prayed it was the Lea and not the river Styx. Hepburn probed no farther for fear of what he would learn. "I shall go to Hertford."

Catherine held Maggie's hand long after she had stopped breathing. She sat motionless, not wanting to let go, not daring to move or think or feel. She had lost all sense of time. Mr. Burke's knock on the door roused her from her trance.

Cat gently laid the hand she held on Maggie's breast. She stood up slowly, vaguely aware that her back ached from bending over her patient. She moved to the door and, without opening it, said quietly, "Maggie has left me, Mr. Burke."

"Thank God her suffering is over. Her corpse is contagious, my lady. She must be buried with all haste. If you will choose her resting place, I will dig the grave immediately."

No! No! You cannot put her in the ground!

Catherine, my spirit is here with ye, my lamb.

Cat's hand went to her throat. "Thank you, Mr. Burke. I will wash her body and ready it for burial."

"I will have Cook heat water for your own bath, my lady. You must change your clothes after you have seen to Maggie."

Catherine went through the motions, tenderly washing her old nurse and dressing her in a pristine cotton night rail that Maggie had sewn with her own hands. The swelling in her groin had gone down, but the blackness had spread out across her belly and down her leg, as if it had poisoned her from within. Catherine brushed Maggie's gray hair back into a neat bun, then crossed her arms upon her breast. *Her body has already begun to stiffen.*

As a single tear slid down her cheek, she opened the door and went up to her own chamber. After she bathed, she opened her trunk and lifted out a black dress. Cat rejected it immediately. *Maggie doesn't like me in black!* Instead, she put on the white silk gown that she had worn for the coronation. As she began to brush her hair, she became aware of a searing headache that almost blinded her. She set the brush down, unable to fashion her tresses into an elegant style. *I must go to the library and find a prayer book. I will have to say the burial service.*

The only groom who'd remained to look after the stables fashioned a rough coffin, and he and Mr. Burke carried it to the orchard and lowered Maggie's body into the freshly dug grave. Catherine's fingers trembled as she took a handful of earth and sprinkled it onto Maggie's coffin. She opened the prayer book and said in a clear voice, "I am the resurrection and the life, saith the Lord; he that believeth in me shall never die." Her voice broke on a sob and it took her a minute to collect herself. Her head was pounding, and inside, her ears were screaming and the lump in her throat nigh choked her.

Catherine took a deep, quivering breath and forced herself to continue. "Forasmuch as it hath pleased Almighty God of his great mercy to take unto himself the soul of our dear Maggie here departed; we therefore commit her body to the ground; earth to earth, ashes to ashes, dust to dust; in sure and certain hope of the Resurrection to eternal life, through our Lord Jesus Christ—"

The prayer book slipped from her nerveless fingers and Cat, sucked into a swirling vortex, collapsed in a small heap.

The blood drained from Mr. Burke's face as he bent to pick her up. "I hope she has only fainted. I pray she hasn't caught—" He was too superstitious to utter the dreaded word in connection with Catherine.

Cook met him at the front door. "I've burned the sheets that Maggie lay on and put fresh linen on the bed. My lady is exhausted from tending her serving woman. She isn't sick!"

Mr. Burke laid his mistress on the clean bed in the nursery, and when she opened her eyes, he offered a prayer of thanks. "You fainted. Is there anything I can get you, Lady Catherine?"

She put her hand to her head and tried to rub away the pain. "I'm so thirsty, Mr. Burke. Would you get me some water?"

He ushered Cook from the room back to her kitchen domain. "I will tend her. I know you believe that this contagion only affects servants, but it is better to proceed with caution. I'll take her some cold well water."

Cat drank thirstily. "The shock of losing Maggie and burying her has left me feeling tired and listless, Mr. Burke. But I would rather sit in a chair than lie in bed." When she stood up,

Cat felt dizzy and somewhat disoriented. She gratefully sank down into the chair and reached for more water.

Catherine closed her eyes and slept. A few hours later, she was awakened by Mr. Burke when he brought her supper.

"Cook has prepared you some broth and a small breast of grouse. You need the nourishment to regain your strength, my lady."

Catherine lifted her hand to her flushed warm cheek. "I cannot eat." She tried to smile. "Dear Mr. Burke, you need not pretend. We both know that I have contracted the plague."

Hepburn jolted awake. He had been dreaming of Maggie. She had prodded his shoulder. *Lord Stewart, my wee Catherine needs ye!* He rubbed his eyes and got to his feet. Dawn was just breaking, so he knew he had slept for about two hours. Renewed energy coursed through him as he realized that if he rode hard, he could reach Spencer Park before dark.

He saddled the mare, reserving Valiant for later in the day, knowing he could count on the powerful black's speed and energy to get him to Hertford before dark. Patrick rode from the grounds of Thorney Abbey and headed toward Huntingdon.

He changed horses at Bassingbourn, and Valiant's hooves seemed to fly over the sunbaked ground, swallowing the miles like a rapacious beast. The sun had just begun its descent as he skirted the town of Hertford, and Hepburn rejoiced that he would reach Spencer Park before twilight.

At the stables there was only one groom in attendance. He had no trouble recognizing the new master even though he was garbed in rough leathers and sported a four-day beard. He took the reins of the lathered horses and blurted, "Lord Stewart, we have *plague!*"

Hepburn nodded grimly, his heart constricting at the dreaded words. "See to my horses; there's a good man." As he left the stables his dark glance swept about the property. The courtyard and the gardens had a neglected look, and the house seemed deserted, as if the servants had fled.

He went inside quietly and found no staff on duty. He smelled food and went straight to the kitchens. His abrupt entrance made Cook drop her soup ladle. "I'm home," he announced shortly. She poured him a mug of ale and he took it gratefully. "Where is Mr. Burke?" He drained the tankard and set it down.

Cook was afraid to impart bad news to the dark and powerful wild-looking Scot who towered before her. She pointed her finger and murmured hoarsely, "He's in the nursery, my lord."

Patrick walked a direct path to the east wing and opened the nursery door.

Cat roused from her warm, lethargic torpor and saw the dark figure that filled the doorway. *It's Death! He has come for me.*

"Catherine."

The voice rolled the *r* and she recognized Hepburn instantly. "No! Go away, go away! Don't come near me!"

He thought he had given her a permanent disgust of him, but her rejection didn't stop him. He strode to her chair and only then did he see Mr. Burke in the shadowed room. "Get me some light." He put his hand to Cat's forehead and found it hot.

She recoiled. "Don't touch me, Patrick, I'll infect you!"

His heart did a somersault. *Does she not want me to touch her because she's worried for me?* He took the candleholder from Mr. Burke and the light flooded over her face. He masked his horror when he saw that she was flushed a dark pink and her golden eyes glittered feverishly. "How long has she been sick?"

"She collapsed today—when we were burying Maggie."

"Maggie's dead? From plague?" he demanded.

"Lady Catherine nursed her. I hope and pray she is only suffering from exhaustion, and that Maggie hasn't infected her."

"I will infect you, Patrick," Cat said.

He gave the candles back to Burke and swept Cat up into his arms. "I'm taking her upstairs. I'll need tepid water for a bath. Tell Cook to pick some angelica and brew a tisane."

Hepburn looked down at the delicate female in the lovely white silk gown. "Sorry I stink of sweat and horse, Catherine."

She closed her eyes. He was too big, too dominant to fight, and she had no strength left.

He laid her on her own bed and carried in the slipper bath from the bathing room. Then he lit all the candles he could find. By this time Mr. Burke had brought up two buckets of water. Patrick took them from him and cautioned him not to come into the chamber. Burke went downstairs to get more water and made sure that Cook had picked the angelica herb.

Patrick half filled the bathing tub and removed Catherine's

white silk gown and her fine lawn undergarments. He was not a gentle man, but he tried to handle her carefully. He had forgotten how physically small and delicate she was and he could see that she had lost weight since the night he'd left Spencer Park. Guilt washed over him. It was an emotion he had seldom experienced. He examined her groin and her armpits, feeling for any sign of a bubo, and grunted with satisfaction when he found none.

As he lifted her and placed her in the tepid water, Cat whimpered, and he wished that his big hands were less calloused and clumsy. Patrick, with more patience than he had ever expended before, sponged her body over and over in a determined effort to bring down her fever.

Mr. Burke knocked on the door. "I have the tisane, my lord."

"Thank you. Leave it outside the door."

When he heard Burke's footsteps retreat, he opened the door and carried the jug and goblet to the bedside table. Patrick stood Cat on her feet, wrapped her in a big towel and sat down on the bed, holding her in his lap. He poured some of the tisane into the goblet and held it to her lips.

Cat turned her head away and said thickly, "No . . . I cannot."

"The choice is not yours; it is mine. You will drink."

When she looked up at him and opened her lips to refuse, he tipped the herbal tisane into her mouth. She choked a bit but some of it went down. Cat tried to push away the goblet, and he saw that she was not wearing her wedding ring. "Again . . . drink."

He hardened himself to her suffering, knowing that she would get a lot worse. "I must be cruel to be kind, Hellcat. Drink!"

Wearily, she closed her eyes and opened her lips, yielding to his command because she had no power to resist.

It took the better part of an hour before the goblet was drained. Though she felt no cooler to the touch, at least she was no hotter. He laid her down upon the bed. "Rest now, sweeting." Patrick never took his eyes from her until she drifted asleep.

Mr. Burke brought him food and left it at the door along with more water. Hepburn wolfed down the cold beef, the chunk of homemade cheese, a loaf of crusty bread and a pot of ale. Then he took the bucket of water into the adjoining chamber, stripped off his soiled leathers, washed the sweat from his body, then shaved. He opened the wardrobe and reached for the clean doublet. *I wore this on my wedding day. Why in the name of God did I not tell her that I loved her? Christ Almighty, I still haven't told her!*

He dressed quickly and returned to Catherine. Her face was extremely flushed from fever, but she still slept. Hepburn stretched his long length on the floor beside his wife.

Patrick roused a few hours later when Cat became restless and began to toss about. He poured more tisane into the goblet, unwrapped the towel from her body and lowered her into the water. Her eyes flew open and she cried out at the indignity of being immersed in cold water, but her protests were in vain.

With the big sponge, Patrick repeated the ablutions, then took her onto his lap and by fair means and foul, made her swallow the concoction. When she had drunk most of it, she was exhausted, and he held her in his arms, rocking her and willing his strength into her body. He wanted to whisper that he loved her, but resisted. *Now is not the time for soft love words. It's a time for strong words to make her fight.* "Back to bed, Hellcat, and don't snore!"

It was almost morning, and while she dozed he unpacked her trunks and hung her lovely clothes in the wardrobe. He moved the slipper bath out of the way to a corner of the room, then left and went to the head of the stairs. "Burke!"

When Mr. Burke came to the foot of the stairs, Patrick signaled for him to remain where he was. "Tell me what has happened here."

"A fortnight ago, one of the maids came down with the plague. Her family came for her, but the lass died. I sent the rest of the staff home, except for Cook, who has previously survived an epidemic. I sent messages to all the tenant farms to isolate themselves from us and from one another."

"Good man." Patrick nodded. "Where is David Hepburn?"

"On his last trip to Whitehall before the coronation, he was told to take the next shipment of beef and cheese to Windsor, where the royal children had been sent. He hasn't returned. When Maggie fell ill, Lady Stewart fled London and brought her here with the aid of Lady Arbella's coach driver. For more than four days my lady insisted on nursing her serving woman alone. Maggie died yesterday and we buried her immediately in the orchard."

"May God rest her soul. I need to go out and cut some rue. If Catherine awakens, don't come up to her. She has the contagion, I'm afraid. Check to see if there's dried dill in the kitchens and I'll join you there, Mr. Burke."

Hepburn searched the herb garden, found no rue and decided that wild rue would do just as well. He took off across a meadow then slowed at the hedgerow, looking for the plant's telltale yellow flowers. When he found it, he cut a huge bunch and hurried back to the house. In the kitchen, Burke had found the dill, and Patrick washed and stripped the blue-green leaves from the wild rue and put the two herbs into a pot with water and wine.

"I'll brew it for you, my lord." Cook handed him a huge slice of meat pie and watched him devour it. "Take her some broth."

"Thank you." With the pot of broth in one hand and a bucket of fresh water in the other, Patrick went back upstairs.

He found Catherine awake and moaning softly. Once more she was flushed with fever, yet she started to shiver. He propped her up against the pillows and wrapped a blanket about her. "This broth will warm you. You cannot get strong without nourishment."

Her eyes glazed over. "I'm going to die," she whispered.

He took hold of her shoulders possessively. "No, you are going to live," he said decisively. His grip tightened fiercely to reassure her and transfer some of his strength to her.

Patrick put a towel in front of her like a bib and held a spoonful of broth to her lips. With infinite patience he managed to coax some down her. She stopped shivering and he noticed a sheen of perspiration on her brow. He let her rest for a while, and then fed her once more. When she could take no more, he bathed her face. Then he sat on the bed and held her hand. It wrung his heart to see her this way. "Little love," he murmured.

While she slept, he bundled up her soiled clothes and set them outside the door. Using a bucket he emptied the bath and put the water down the jakes, and then he brought fresh sheets and towels from the linen cupboard. Mr. Burke brought up a steaming jug of wine boiled with dill and rue, and Patrick set it on the windowsill to cool.

Catherine's sleep became increasingly restless until finally she awoke and began to thrash her legs about. "I'm dying!"

He went on his knees and gathered her to him. "Hush, darling. I won't let you die."

She looked at him with wild, accusing eyes and tried to fight him off, whimpering, moaning, panting and raving.

The heat of her body branded his arms, and her moans wrenched his heart. When she began to kick him, he held her legs in a vice-like grip and examined her groin for a plague boil. He broke out in a relieved sweat when he found none and knew he needed to cool her body. He decided to put her in the empty tub, then pour the tepid water over her, but when he went to lift her, she screamed in agony and he realized she was in terrible pain.

Patrick brought the bucket of water to the bed and sponged her over and over. He managed to cool her enough that she stopped thrashing and her shouts lowered to incoherent mutters. Gingerly he lifted her arm, dreading what he knew he would find.

Patrick recoiled inwardly. As he gazed down at the ugly purple swelling in her armpit he felt total panic. Cat was going to die an agonizing death, and there was nothing he could do about it.

Chapter *Thirty-five*

H epburn cursed aloud. He did not waste time praying—he was too cynical to expect help from that quarter. He hardened his resolve. *I may not be able to keep her from dying, but I can do something to relieve her agony.*

He brought the jug from the windowsill to the bedside table and half filled a goblet. He sat down on the bed and pulled his struggling wife into his lap. Rue was a powerful herb that reduced pain. He had seen it work magic on men wounded in battle, and he was determined that it would ease Catherine's suffering.

Patrick held her wrists in an iron grip and forced the liquid down her. She began to retch. Quickly, he dragged the chamber pot from beneath the bed. He held her firmly, his hands feeling the convulsive spasms of her stomach as he lowered her head to aid her vomiting. Catherine retched, heaved and spewed.

Hepburn cursed vilely, venting his frustration yet at the same time steeling his emotions to dose her again in the hope that some of the brew would stay down. As he had dreaded, Cat began to retch, heave and spew once more. She gasped, choked, retched and heaved. Patrick lost all hope that she would survive. All that mattered to him now was that he stop her agony. He massaged her belly and when he felt the knotted cramp begin to ease, he forced down more rue. "Hang on, ride the wave of pain, stay with me, Hellicate!"

He held his breath and waited, willing the medicinal wine to stay down. Patrick knew that if it did not, he didn't have the heart to dose her again.

He held her in his lap until at last she stopped writhing, and he knew the pain had abated somewhat and was no longer racking her body. Though she was still hot as fire, he laid her gently in the bed and covered her. Just as the rue had stopped her agony, the wine would make her sleep. His wife made such a tiny mound in the great bed, it brought a lump to his throat.

Hepburn cleaned up the vomit and emptied the chamber pot. It was dark again and he wondered where the day had gone. He lit the candles and common sense urged him to rest while he had the chance. The light reflected something that was shining on the carpet. He walked across the room, bent down and picked it up.

It's Catherine's wedding ring! He envisioned her pulling it off and flinging it across the chamber. *She rejects the marriage, and she totally rejects me as a husband!*

Though it mauled his pride, he knew in his heart that he deserved it. He looked at the tiny gold circle resting in his calloused palm and contemplated slipping it back on her finger without her knowing. *How expedient,* his inner voice mocked. Hepburn sat down in the big chair beside the bed. Now that Cat was asleep, his mind was free to wander.

For over ten years he had vowed and pledged that the king would return full value for what he had taken from the Hepburns. When James had proposed that he repay him with marriage to an English heiress, he had accepted on condition that he could take his pick. *I made sure that I chose a wealthy heiress with vast landholdings in both England and Scotland. The fact that Catherine was exquisitely beautiful was most fortunate, but it was also irrelevant.* Hepburn thoroughly understood his own motives, but that did not make them right. He could see now that the contract drawn up between him and Jamie was unconscionable.

Poor innocent Catherine didn't stand a chance once I had marked her and her inheritance as mine. I stopped at nothing to seduce her and get my own way. I even used my occult power on her to gain my own ends. I bent Fate to my will, but Fate is having the last laugh. He rubbed his eyes wearily. His inner voice taunted: *You never counted on falling in love, did you, Hepburn?*

Patrick again looked at her wedding ring, and the pain in his heart was savage. He would never get the chance to tell her that he loved her, that she was dearer to him than life itself. She was too ill to even recognize him, too afflicted to understand the meaning of his words. *That is my punishment,* he thought bitterly. He covered his eyes and eventually gave himself up to Morpheus.

He fell into a dream so compelling that it seemed real.

Maggie appeared and began urgently pleading with him. "Ye must save her for the sake of the bairn. If Catherine dies, yer unborn son goes to the grave with her."

"There is no babe, Maggie. That is just wishful thinking. But you are right, if she dies, the chance of an heir dies with her."

"Ye have the power, Hepburn. Use it! But this time, ask naught in return!"

Patrick awoke at sunrise, the moment Catherine began to move. She was delirious and more fevered than before. His heart was heavy as he gave her a sponge bath and murmured comforting words he knew she could not comprehend. He glanced at her belly, which was so concave he believed it impossible that she carried a babe. When he lifted her arm to inspect the bubo and she cried out pitifully, he was covered with guilt at the pain he caused her.

The purple swelling in her armpit was slightly larger, and he told himself that the kindest thing he could do for the woman he loved was leave her in peace. *That's the craven way out,* his inner voice taunted. *Dose her with more rue. Fill the bathtub and immerse her again!*

I have no right to make her suffer more. I've brought her enough emotional anguish; I won't add to my sins by inflicting unnecessary physical pain. As he stood looking down at her, Maggie's words came to him. *Ye have the power, Hepburn. Use it!*

A spark of hope ignited. *If I go into a trance, perhaps I will be shown the way.*

The chamber suddenly darkened, and Patrick walked to the window, wondering what had happened to the brilliant morning sun. The sky had gone black, and as he opened the window a streak of lightning split the dark sky in half and a thunderbolt shook the house. He stared, mesmerized, as the violent storm danced and crashed about Spencer Park for the better part of an hour. The thunder was deafening, the lightning blinding in its savage intensity. It rolled, cracked and flashed over and over as if nature had gone mad and was ready to destroy the earth.

Without warning, large hailstones came pelting down, bouncing on the ground and pinging against the open windowpanes. The hail turned to torrential rain and the thunder and lightning moved away. Gradually, the rain lessened its intensity until it became a gentle shower, and finally it stopped altogether.

Patrick breathed deeply and, no longer transfixed, took a step back from the open window. The curtains billowed inward and he felt the cool wind on his face. The atmosphere was no longer oppressive. He felt his skin chill and realized that the sweltering, suffocating heat that had blanketed the country was being swept away by a force greater than itself.

Hepburn knew he had been given his answer. He went to the bed and gazed down at his suffering wife. The plague could only be swept away by a force greater than itself. He must destroy it by intense and violent means, but could she survive the torture? It might kill her, but if he did nothing, his beloved was doomed. He pushed the tangled hair back from her fevered brow. *Catherine has enough reckless courage to face anything!*

Patrick ran down the stairs and didn't stop until he reached the kitchens. He found Cook hiding in the pantry, terrified by the upheaval in the heavens. "The storm is over. It is safe to come out. Miraculously, it brought cold air to the region. Now we need a miracle for Catherine. I want to make a poultice. Do you have meal and mustard seed?"

"We have plenty of oatmeal, my lord." Cook handed him a pot and a sack of meal. "I'll crush some mustard seed."

Patrick trickled boiling water into the meal and sprinkled in the mustard. He stirred it until it made a thick hot paste, then he took the iron pot upstairs. He tore a square from a sheet and spooned on a huge dollop of the hot meal. Steeling his resolve and his emotions, he raised Cat's arm and applied the poultice.

She screamed like a banshee, and the hair on the nape of Hepburn's neck stood on end. As she clawed at him, he realized she would rip off the poultice. Quickly, he tore the sheet into wide strips and bound her arms to her body. "Forgive me, Catherine, forgive me," he muttered.

Her legs were still free to kick, so Patrick took hold of one and began to stroke his calloused palm along its slim length in an effort to soothe her agitation. She calmed like a wild beast that had used all its strength, just before it sought escape in death.

A few hours later, he unwrapped her bindings and applied

another hot poultice. The swelling was far larger and darker now, and Patrick focused his mind, visualizing all the poison being drawn from her body into the grotesque bubo.

Hepburn schooled himself to patience, as time seemed to crawl forward imperceptibly. It was the hardest thing he'd ever done.

Yet ahead of him lay a task he knew would be far more difficult.

Before the light faded from the late afternoon, he knew he must wait no longer. He carefully removed the bindings and the poultice. He visibly flinched at the size of the swelling. It had turned black and now filled the entire hollow of her armpit and was starting to discolor her delicate breast.

Patrick lit a candle, took his dagger from its sheath and held the blade in the flame for a full minute. As he let the metal cool, he gathered his courage. *May Fortune favor the bold!*

Hepburn raised her arm and plunged in the sharp point of his dirk. Catherine screamed twice before she fell unconscious. Like a volcano, the plague boil erupted, spurting its putrefaction everywhere. The black liquid exploded over her body, spread across the sheets and splashed up into his face. The stench of the poisonous effluence was vile. He squeezed out the remainder of the dark puss with his fingers. While she was still mercifully unconscious he bathed her and put fresh linen on the bed.

Finally, almost spent, he sat down beside her and clasped her hand tightly. Catherine's breathing was dangerously shallow, and he feared she was at the end of her endurance. He did not dare to take his eyes from her throughout the long hours of the night. *She cannot slip away—I have too firm a grip on her.*

As the light of dawn filtered into the room, Patrick caught his breath in abject fear. Catherine's hand was cold. He went down on his knees and said a humble prayer. *Please let her be alive. I will go and leave her in peace if you show mercy to Catherine.*

Still on his knees, he edged closer and peered into her face. Her skin was deathly pale and waxy, her eyes were closed and there was a bluish tinge about her mouth, but, by all the saints, she was still breathing. He reached out to gently touch her cheek and found her fever had abated. *Her life has stopped draining away!*

At his touch, she opened her eyes, and then her lashes fell as if they were too heavy.

"Catherine. Do you know me?" he murmured.

Her mouth opened. "Th . . . thirsty."

"Thank God!" His gaze swept the chamber, searching for a suitable drink. He had the wine with rue, but that herb was exceedingly bitter. There was still some angelica tisane, but that was to reduce fever and her body already seemed too cold. He reached for the ale he had been drinking yesterday, raised her head and held the tankard to her lips.

Cat drank thirstily, but the effort exhausted her strength.

He sat down on the bed and took her hand. "Catherine, you have survived the plague. Do you understand? You're going to recover. All you need now is food and rest." It wrung his heart to see how fragile she looked with the violet smudges beneath her eyes. "Try to sleep, and I'll be back with some nourishment soon."

Patrick bundled up the soiled sheets and towels and dropped them from the window so that he could burn them. He hurried downstairs to let the others know that Catherine had survived the nightmare. "I don't think she's infectious, but I'll do the nursing myself for the next few days. Try and think of something that will tempt her appetite."

"You haven't slept in days, my lord," Mr. Burke reminded him.

"I'm suddenly energized and hungry as a wolf. I'll be back soon." He went outside and set fire to the soiled linen. When the pile was reduced to ashes he strode down to the river Lea, breathing in the cool fresh air. He undressed and took a brisk swim, symbolically washing away his sins. When he emerged, it seemed that the cold water had cleansed his body and spirit at the same time.

For the next few days, Patrick spent every moment focused on making Catherine well. At first he fed her chamomile tea, barley broth, calf's-foot jelly and lots of honey to give her energy and satisfy her sweet tooth. Then she graduated to chicken, fish and fruit, and then finally she was able to eat small portions of bread and meat. He mixed up a soothing ointment by crushing calamint leaves into a wax honeycomb and spread it over the nasty wound in her armpit. When he tended it on the third day, he saw that it was almost healed. "I'm afraid you'll have a scar."

Catherine's eyes flooded, and he sat down on the bed and kissed her teardrops away. "Don't cry, love."

"I failed Maggie," she whispered. "I let her die." She pressed her face into his chest and began to sob.

"No, no," he soothed, "you did everything in your power to save her, Catherine. You loved her—you risked your life for her and almost lost it—none of us can do more than that." He hesitated, then lifted her chin with his fingers and looked into her eyes. "Maggie came to me in a vision and told me you needed my help."

Catherine nodded sadly. "She talks to me too."

Patrick knew his wife was much better, but she looked so fragile he was almost afraid to touch her. She was still deathly pale, with violet smudges beneath her eyes, and though her hair was a dull, disheveled tangle that diminished the exquisite, elegant beauty that usually shone from her, Patrick thought her the loveliest sight he'd ever seen.

Gingerly, she explored beneath her arm. "Is it ugly?"

"Nothing about you could ever be ugly, Catherine."

"Would you bring me my hand mirror?" she asked softly.

"Mirror?" Patrick began to panic. He could not let her see herself—she would be devastated. He went over to her dressing table, made a pretense of searching and shoved the hand mirror behind her jewel case. "I can't find it—it's not here." He saw her pull the bedcovers aside and quickly returned to her. "Oh, no, you cannot get out of bed today, Cat." His thoughts chased each other like quicksilver. "Tomorrow. I'll find you something pretty to wear, and tomorrow you can get up and look at yourself in the big mirror." He watched her sink back against her pillows and knew he'd postponed the reckoning for only one day. The feeling of panic remained. *When she sees herself, she will be horrified.*

After supper he sat and read to her from *Julius Caesar.* He knew some passages by heart. Finally, her lashes lowered and he thought she was asleep. He closed the book and set it aside.

"You look so haggard, Patrick. Come and lie beside me."

Hepburn felt extremely reluctant, wondering how he could lie beside her and not touch her. Yet how could he demur and not hurt her? He removed his boots and stretched out on top of the covers.

Catherine's fingers sought his and he enfolded her small

hand in his. He heard her sigh deeply before she drifted into slumber.

He lay in the darkness, staring up at the ceiling, knowing sleep would elude him while he was this close to his heart's desire. "I love you more than life, Catherine."

In the darkness, he did not see the smile that curved her lips.

Early next morning, Patrick slipped from the bed noiselessly and went downstairs to fix her a breakfast tray. From the garden he plucked her some apricots and picked her some roses. He had a plan, but knew he needed all the help he could get.

Cook gave him a lace tray cloth, and he set the roses in a small vase and the fruit on a delicate porcelain dish. She cut the freshly baked bread into small fingers and handed him a pot of honey. He poured a goblet of mead and took the tray upstairs.

He was relieved when he saw that though Cat was awake, she was still abed. Her face lit up when she saw the flowers. "Today we are celebrating your recovery."

Patrick plumped up her pillows, set the tray before her and took delight in watching her. Before she started to eat, she smelled the roses. Her appetite was so small, her movements so delicate, her sips of mead so minute, he was held in thrall.

"Next on the agenda is milady's bath." He carried the tub from the corner and Mr. Burke brought two buckets of water. Patrick took them from him at the door and half filled the slipper bath. He lifted her into the tub and pretended that he did not notice her blush. She was so thin he felt alarm, but he hid his concern.

She picked up the sponge. "I can do it myself."

Relief rushed over him. His hands were so rough and calloused he feared scratching her fragile skin. "I'll get you a bed robe." He went to the wardrobe and chose one he hoped would give her some needed color. "Here's a pretty pink one."

Catherine giggled. "That's not pink; it's peach."

He looked at her blankly. "Peach is a color?"

"Yes, a lovely color, the same as the roses you brought me."

He shook his head at the mysteries of the female mind. How the devil he was going to accomplish the next part, he hadn't the faintest notion, but he was determined to try. He wrapped her in a towel, gently patted her dry, sat her on the edge of the bed, and then helped her put on the *peach* bed gown. "Don't move."

Nervous, and feeling like a bull in a boudoir, he went to her dressing table and looked down uncertainly at the items upon it.

He picked up her brush, which was the smallest one he'd ever seen, and its matching comb. Then he scooped up a handful of hairpins. He cursed the clumsiness of his fingers as he dropped a couple and had to carefully retrieve them. *Send me divine help,* he prayed.

Tentatively, Patrick lifted a tress of her dark hair and began to gently brush it. Then he lifted another and repeated the motion. He did it over and over until some of the dullness began to disappear. *Now comes the hard part, Hepburn.* He looked down, appalled at his large clumsy hands with their thick fingers. *Hard? It's bloody impossible!*

Doggedly, he rolled a curl around his finger and pinned it to her head. He knew he was inept, and it took all his willpower to keep his hands from trembling like leaves in a gale. Patrick wanted with all his heart to make her hair look as elegant as he had always seen it. Catherine took such deep pride in her lovely black hair. It had truly been her crowning glory.

Some of the curls unraveled, but painstakingly he did them over again, holding the tiny hairpins in his mouth, until at last he had used them all. Even to his undiscerning eye, the hairdo looked somehow askew. Then he remembered the roses. He took them from the vase and, handling them with the greatest care so he wouldn't crush their delicate petals, pinned them into her curls.

Patrick swallowed hard and, taking her hand, led her to the dressing table and sat her down before the mirror.

Cat almost gasped with shocked dismay when she saw her sallow skin, thin cheeks, and huge dark smudges beneath her eyes, but she caught a glimpse of Patrick's anxious face in the mirror and then she looked at her hair. What he had done was amazing; the effect was bizarre in a beautiful sort of way. Her throat tightened as she realized he had done his utmost to make her appear more attractive before she looked at herself in the mirror. Her heart melted. What he had done this morning proved that her husband loved her! "I love you, Patrick," she whispered softly.

Hepburn flushed. "What you feel is gratitude. Because I saved your life, you believe you owe me love, but you do not, Catherine."

She shook her head at the mysteries of the male mind.

"Come," he said briskly, "let's show you off downstairs." He picked her up to carry her down. "You are insubstantial as thistledown. You must eat more, Catherine." He set her down at the bottom of the stairs and allowed her to walk to the kitchens.

When Cook bobbed a curtsy, Cat chided her. "Please don't do that. It is I who must thank you for staying at Spencer Park and risking your health."

"You are a sight for sore eyes, Lady Stewart." Mr. Burke held a chair so she could sit down.

"Dear Mr. Burke, how will we ever repay you for your selfless devotion? What you did for Maggie was beyond the call of duty."

"You both have my eternal thanks also," Patrick said sincerely. "I'll go and check on the horses. See if you can tempt her to eat something while I'm gone."

During the week that followed, Catherine gained strength and vitality and her face lost its wan look of fragility. At night Patrick lay beside her on top of the covers until she slept, then he quit the bed, keeping a safe distance between them, as he prowled about like a caged animal for most of the night.

During these long hours he could not stop thinking of the vow he had made. *I will go and leave her in peace if you will show mercy to Catherine.* Last night he had found it almost impossible to leave her in peace. A dozen times he'd had to stop himself from gathering her in his arms and kissing her senseless.

Maggie's words haunted him too. *Ye have the power, Hepburn. Use it! But this time ask naught in return!* The words kept repeating in his brain, *ask naught in return . . . ask naught in return.* Finally, Patrick knew what he must do. He had no idea if he could be truly selfless, but he knew he must try.

Taking pen and paper, he wrote out his confession to Catherine and gave back all he had gained from their marriage. He put the letter in an envelope, and before he sealed it, he put her wedding ring inside. He laid it on the bedside table and looked down at his sleeping wife. *God keep you safe, my little Hellicate.*

Chapter Thirty-six

*C*atherine awoke, turned her head on the pillow and smiled. Patrick was such an early riser; he was never there when she opened her eyes. She stretched and sighed happily, guessing that he wouldn't be far away.

Cat got out of bed and went to the window. She didn't see him, but a frisson of joy went through her as she saw David Hepburn had returned from Windsor. She dressed quickly, brushed and tied back her hair with a ribbon and went to the stairs. Until today, Patrick had always carried her down, making sure she didn't overexert herself. Today she would do it alone. She grasped the oak banister firmly and slowly descended the steps.

Catherine went outside to greet the young Scot. "David, I am so relieved to see that you are well. I've been extremely worried about my mother. Have you any news of her?"

"My lady, Windsor Castle completely escaped the dreaded contagion. It was a miracle, really. London and a lot of the towns were not so lucky, I'm afraid. Your mother and Lady Carey are both well, but they have been worried about you. I promised to send them a message to let them know how you are faring."

"Maggie and I were not as fortunate. We both caught the plague. Maggie died, but Patrick nursed me and saved my life."

"I'm so sorry for yer loss, my lady. It's miraculous to survive the plague. I'm thankful his lordship returned."

"So am I, David. You must be starving; come and have breakfast. Since the weather has turned cool, the contagion seems to have left these parts. Mr. Burke sent all the staff home to protect them, but they are gradually returning."

"Aye, I think the epidemic has started to abate everywhere."

Cat accompanied David to the kitchens. "I haven't seen my husband this morning. Does anyone know where he is?"

David quaffed some ale and wiped his mouth on his sleeve. "Valiant wasn't in the stables."

"He must be visiting the tenant farms. Until now we've all been in isolation."

Cook was in her glory, frying eggs and gammon for the ravenous young Scot, but when she put the huge platter before him, Catherine suddenly turned pale, stood up and excused herself.

She climbed the stairs slowly, hoping her nausea wouldn't erupt to befoul the steps. She had thought the debilitating symptoms of plague were behind her, and her happiness fled. As she reached her chamber, Cat thought she heard Maggie's voice. *It's the bairn!*

She went over to the window, breathed deeply and was relieved when the sick feeling passed. "I wonder if Maggie was right. Can it be possible that I am carrying a baby?" She thought about the last time she and Patrick had made love and began to count. "It was the beginning of May when Queen Anne visited. Tomorrow is the first day of September." She looked down at her slim form dubiously. "I can't possibly be four months gone with child."

Catherine experienced a pang of disappointment. Then the corners of her mouth lifted in a secret smile. "Now that I am well, there is no reason why we shouldn't try to make a baby."

She turned from the window and saw the envelope propped on the bedside table. She shuddered as if a goose had walked over her grave. She tore open the envelope and her wedding ring fell into her hand. *Patrick picked it up!* The echo of her vow came back to her. *Leave it! Hepburn will be the one who must pick it up, or it will lie there forever.* Cat blushed at her own arrogance.

With a premonition of dread, she slowly unfolded the letter and sank down on the edge of the bed. *You are a bastard, Hepburn, if you have left me again.* She looked at the wedding ring.

I should have vowed that not only would you pick it up but you would get on your knees and beg to put it back on my finger!

She was so angry, the words in the letter blurred and it took a couple of moments before she could read it.

Catherine:
Please accept my apology for what I did to you. The
contract drawn up between King James and me was
unconscionable. I deeply regret the hurt I caused you.
   I hereby renounce any claim to Spencer Park
through my marriage to you. I also wish it known that I
will never lay claim to any part of your Seton
inheritance in Scotland, nor will I ever accept the title
Earl of Winton.
   It is you I want, and you alone, without wealth,
landholdings or titles. I love you, Catherine, and my
heart's desire is that you love me in return. What you
feel at the moment is gratitude; please do not mistake it
for love.
   I made a vow that if you recovered from the plague,
I would leave you in peace. I am honoring that vow by
returning to Crichton Castle. Give yourself time to fully
heal in body, mind and soul. When you feel ready, send
me a letter telling me your wishes. If you want me for
your husband, I shall return. If you do not, I shall
remain in Scotland.
   Patrick Hepburn, Lord Stewart

Cat flung the letter away from her. "Lord Bloody Stewart," she cursed. "Remain in Scotland and see if I care!" She rubbed her temples in an effort to rid herself of fury.

She realized that she had used up all her energy by losing her temper. Cat lay down on her bed to rest. She decided that she would not think of the infuriating devil. Instead, she would concentrate on herself. First, she would remain calm at all times. When she was in blooming health, she would decide what to do.

During the next two weeks, Catherine's appetite increased, and when she looked in the mirror with a critical eye, she had to admit that her face no longer looked wan and peaked. Every day she performed the ritual of taking flowers to Maggie's grave in the orchard, where the trees were now heavy with pears and russet apples. She talked to Maggie, revealing her thoughts but keeping a tight rein on her emotions. Maggie didn't answer her, of course, but these visits brought comfort to Catherine.

She did not mention Patrick Hepburn, but avoided the subject as if it were taboo. Then one day she brought some purple

Michaelmas daisies that were the same color as Scottish heather and thistles and her emotions broke through. "I warrant you were right, Maggie; I think I'm having a bairn. I have morning sickness, and instead of being skeletal, my face and breasts are quite full. Damn Hepburn to hellfire! How dare he get me with child then leave me to face it all alone?"

Catherine was shocked by her own words. It was the first time she had admitted that she didn't want to be alone. Before she went back to the house, she went into the meadow to look at the wild horses. They approached her warily and then tore off on a mad gallop across the field, preferring their own company.

That night in her chamber she took out Patrick's letter and read it again. Some of the phrases jumped out at her: . . . *accept my apology . . . contract was unconscionable . . . I deeply regret . . . I hereby renounce any claim . . . I am honoring that vow . . .*

"Holy God, what have I done?" Cat ran to the mirror and took a good look at her reflection. "I don't want his love for me to turn him into someone who apologizes, and deeply regrets, and selflessly renounces his claims. What the hell sort of a man is that? I don't want him to change; I want Patrick Hepburn exactly as he is, wild and untamed!"

Catherine wanted him dominant, arrogant, ambitious and expedient. She wanted him lusty, irreverent and uncivilized. She wanted him in rough leathers and that bloody sheepskin, smelling of horses and issuing his orders. She wanted Hepburn to be *himself,* so that she could be exactly *herself,* a little hellcat! They were a perfect match. One made in either heaven or hell, and she didn't care which.

She hurried to the small desk and found a piece of paper. "Send me a letter telling me your wishes," he had written. Catherine dipped in the pen and then flung it down, blotching the paper with ink spatters. "To lowest hell with letters! I shall go and confront him myself. When Hepburn wed me, he endowed me with Crichton—and I have an irresistible urge to see my castle."

She went downstairs and asked Mr. Burke to find David Hepburn and send him to her in the library. She sat down at the mahogany desk, spread out a large map of England and Scotland and began to study it from top to bottom. She became so engrossed in her task that she would not have heard David's knock had it not been loud.

Cat lifted her eyes and gave him a radiant smile. "Come in, David; I need your help."

"I'm happy to see ye've recovered yer health, my lady."

"Yes, since my health seems to be blooming, I've decided to go to Scotland. I need your help deciding on our route."

David had the wariness of a Hepburn. "Our route, my lady?"

"Yes," she said impatiently. "Come and look at this map."

David ran a rough, thick finger from Hertford to Edinburgh. "'Tis too far fer a lady to ride, and it would take days by carriage. Moreover, plague may still be ravishing the country."

"Your thoughts mirror mine exactly, David." She purposely ignored the forbidding tone in his voice; she'd had experience handling a Hepburn. Her determined finger pushed his aside as it drew a direct line from Hertford to the coast. "A short ride to Maldon, where I'm sure we could find a ship to take us to Leith, would be the fastest route."

"Ye cannot go alone, Lady Stewart," he said firmly.

"I won't be alone; I'll be under your protection."

"His lordship would have my ba—"

"Your balls, David? If you haven't enough guts to escort me, I shall doubt if you have any balls!"

David flushed. "My lady, I will do as ye bid."

"Thank you. Pack tonight. I want an early start."

In the morning, as David loaded Catherine's baggage into the small coach, he asked, "Where is yer serving woman, my lady?"

"It is far too soon after Maggie's death to even contemplate replacing her, and I'm quite capable of doing for myself."

David exchanged a speaking look with Mr. Burke, who did his best to keep his face impassive. "Capable and willful," he muttered.

"Why, thank you. A compliment from a Hepburn is a rare thing."

David climbed up beside the driver, and Mr. Burke held the carriage door open. "Here's that ginger wine you asked for, my lady. I hope and pray it alleviates your seasickness."

She touched his hand. "Thank you, Mr. Burke. After the plague, *mal de mer* is a trifling ailment."

• • •

During the two-day sea voyage to Leith, Catherine rued her dismissal of the motion sickness. She put it down to one of the necessary discomforts connected with pregnancy as she gratefully sipped the ginger wine and laid the blame for her predicament at Patrick Hepburn's door, where it squarely belonged.

The small, swift vessel made port during the dark hours before dawn, and when Cat went up on deck in the morning, she recognized the town of Leith. She identified the look on David's face as apprehension and knew he was worried about taking her to Crichton.

"Hire a carriage, David. I want you to escort me to my grandfather at Seton."

"Ye're not going to Crichton, my lady?" He looked relieved.

"Not today, David. Once you have delivered me into the hands of the Earl of Winton, you are free to go to Crichton alone. Under no circumstances are you to tell my husband that I am in Scotland." She handed him an envelope. "Give him this, please."

He eyed it warily. "Will he kill the messenger?"

The corners of her mouth went up. "I warrant that Patrick is eagerly awaiting my letter, but to be on the safe side, once you hand it to him, you had better duck."

On the carriage ride to Seton, Catherine spoke to Maggie. *I would give anything in the world if you could be with me today. You loved Scotland with all your heart.* Cat swallowed the lump in her throat and smiled wistfully. *I shall simply have to enjoy it for both of us.*

When the carriage arrived at Seton and Geordie rode into the courtyard, he threw his bonnet into the air the moment he realized who it was. "My wee lass! I've missed ye somethin' fierce!"

Catherine opened the door and jumped straight into his arms.

Geordie swung her about until they were both giddy. "This calls fer a celebration. I'll round everybody up and we'll have—"

"No, Geordie, I want to spend the day with just you. I have so much to tell you. David needs to borrow a horse."

"Thanks fer deliverin' my wee lass. Ye'll find a mount in the stables." Geordie paid the coach driver, picked up her bags and headed toward the castle.

Cat turned to David. "I thank you with all my heart. Please keep my secret from Patrick. I want to surprise him."

After dinner that evening, Catherine and Geordie talked for hours. With Tattoo purring on her knee, she sipped watered whisky, rolling the smoky liquor over her tongue, as Geordie had taught her. She described King James's arrival at Whitehall, Queen Anne's stopover at Spencer Park and their coronation in Westminster Abbey.

Then she went on to tell him about the horrendous plague epidemic that had scourged England and taken Maggie's life. They took comfort from each other over the terrible loss.

"I caught the infection too and would have surely died if Patrick Hepburn had not arrived to nurse me back to health."

Geordie looked at her quizzically. "Do ye no' think it's time tae wed the laddie, and put him out o' his misery?"

"Wed him?" Cat asked in surprise. *My grandfather doesn't know we are married!*

"Before he went tae England wi' the king, he asked me if I objected to an alliance between our clans. I told him that was yer decision. When he arrived home two months later without a bride, everyone assumed ye had turned him down. Rumor had it he was in a foul temper fer weeks."

"How do you hear these rumors?"

"Well, Andrew wed that bonnie lass, Jenny Hepburn. 'Twas she who told us his lordship returned without a bride. If ye have changed yer mind about havin' him fer yer husband, I'll give ye a grand weddin', Catherine."

Cat was speechless. Did no one in Scotland know that she was Lady Stewart? Did that devil Hepburn not want any to know he was a married man? A strange frisson went through her. *Perhaps he's not as saintly as he sounds in the letter of apology he left me.*

She squeezed Geordie's hand. "I'll go to Crichton tomorrow and settle this question of our marriage once and for all."

"I don't want ye ridin' alone. I'll get Andrew to escort ye."

"I would far rather have you for escort, Granddad."

The grin almost split his weathered face.

"I shall go to bed and get my beauty sleep. I need to look my best tomorrow." She tucked the black cat beneath her arm and kissed Geordie good night. As she climbed the castle stairs, the anticipation of seeing Patrick soared higher with every step.

•   •   •

When David Hepburn arrived at Crichton, he was vastly relieved to learn that Patrick had gone hunting and had not yet returned. Later, in the Great Hall, he recounted graphic tales of the
great plague epidemic that had decimated England, but had
miraculously left Scotland unscathed. His rapt audience listened
open-mouthed at the heart-scalding stories he told, and all truly
believed that the invisible Border between the two countries,
which supposedly no longer existed, had magically protected
the Scots.

David asked Jock, "Did his lordship not tell ye he nursed his
lady through plague? He was a heartbeat away from being widowed."

"Patrick is wed?"

"King James wed Lord Stewart to Catherine Seton Spencer
the first day he arrived at Whitehall. Did he not tell ye?"

Jock shook his head. "Wed five months and never a hint
from the close-mouthed devil! The Hepburn ranges alone these
days."

The next morning, as the men of Crichton broke their fast in
the ancient hall that overlooked the Tyne Valley, David saw the
dogs first, and knew Hepburn was returned from his hunt.
Within minutes he saw Patrick astride Valiant, leading a packhorse that carried a great seven-point stag.

David finished his breakfast and straightened his shoulders.
It was far better to face up to an unpleasant duty immediately
and get it out of the way. He went down to the stables and
awaited the laird of Crichton.

The moment Patrick recognized the tall redhead, his brows
drew together in a dark frown. "David! What are you doing
here, man? Is aught amiss?"

"Nay, all was well when I left Spencer Park, my lord." He
tentatively reached into his doublet and took out the envelope.

The moment Patrick's eyes saw it they gleamed with triumph.
"You brought me a message!" He dismounted with one lithe
movement and seized the envelope. He tore it open expectantly,
but there was no letter inside. He shook the contents into his hand
and stared down in disbelief at the tiny gold circle that lay on his
palm. Hepburn looked at David and quickly masked his emotions,
but not before his young captain had seen the pain in his eyes.
Christ, she's sent back her wedding ring! Patrick was devastated.

Chapter Thirty-seven

*C*atherine stood in front of the oval mirror, critically assessing her appearance. Her face had lost its gaunt look and she fancied her fuller cheeks made her prettier. She had fashioned her hair into a French knot, leaving tiny kiss curls at her temples.

Her quilted white doublet was tight across her breasts, and she'd had a devil of a struggle to fasten the waist of her black velvet riding pants. She reckoned this was the last time she'd be able to wear these garments until after her child was born. With deliberation she carefully tucked Patrick's letter into her bodice and smiled her secret smile. "*En garde,* Lord Bloody Stewart!"

As Catherine made her way down to join Geordie for breakfast, Tattoo appeared and rubbed against her leg. "Hello, puss; where did you disappear to last night?"

"The black bugger sleeps wi' me now," Geordie confessed.

Catherine laughed. "I assume your bed partner chose you, rather than the other way about." She flushed slightly, remembering that she had done the same with Hepburn.

When they walked outside into the glorious autumn morning, their mounts were saddled and ready for them. Cat smiled her thanks at the groom who had remembered the glossy black filly she had ridden during her stay at Winton Castle last summer.

They cantered from the courtyard and headed south. Catherine slowed to a walk as her filly crossed Tyne Water, and Geordie followed suit so he wouldn't splash her elegant riding costume.

By the time they were halfway to Crichton, Cat was lost in thought as she rehearsed the things she would say to Hepburn. They were riding past a tall stand of firs when suddenly a horse and rider broke from the cover of the trees, frightening their mounts.

Geordie's horse reared and threw him onto the hard ground. Cat's filly lifted her heels and fled. It took her a few minutes to calm the animal and circle back to aid her grandfather. What she found was totally unexpected. Her cousin Malcolm had one powerful arm about Geordie's neck and a dagger in his other hand.

"Flee fer yer life, Catherine!" Geordie cried, and received a jab of the dagger point for his warning.

Judas! Patrick was right. Malcolm does want to be Earl of Winton. Impulsive as always, Cat tried to trample her cousin, but before she knew what had happened, the swine had taken a firm grip on her leg and yanked her from the saddle. "You bastard, leave him alone!" she screamed, as she reached for her own dagger. Her heart jumped into her throat as she realized she was not wearing it today. She knew with terrified certainty that both she and Geordie would die unless she could find a way to save them.

"You are a fool, Malcolm Lindsay! Even if you kill both of us, you won't inherit Seton."

Lindsay's eyes narrowed, the dagger poised in its descent. "Nothing will keep me from inheriting, you spoiled English slut!"

"If Geordie dies, I inherit. If I die, my husband, Patrick Hepburn, inherits Seton."

"Lying slut!" His arm tightened painfully about Geordie's throat. "Yer not wed to Hepburn."

"King James Stuart himself married us five months ago!"

At Crichton, as Hepburn stared down at the wedding ring on his palm, the sun reflected on the gold with a shimmering light. He closed his fingers over it and looked at David.

"Catherine is here! You brought her to Scotland!"

David hesitated and flushed. "She asked me not to tell ye."

"Christ Almighty, she's close by and in mortal danger!" As he swung back up into the saddle, he flung out his arm, pointing north, and ordered the pair of deerhounds, "Seek!"

David watched Hepburn gallop after his hunting hounds, then he ran into the stables to saddle his horse. He shouted to a couple of his fellow moss-troopers, "His lordship says there's trouble. He may need help."

Catherine screamed with terror as she watched Malcolm Lindsay raise the arm that held his dagger. Her warning had not deterred the evil, greedy swine; it had inflamed him to commit murder.

Malcolm thrust into Geordie's chest. He withdrew the dagger and was about to repeat his onslaught when a massive hound bounded across Catherine's path, leaped at the attacker and plunged its fangs into Malcolm's throat. His scream was cut off as his throat and mouth flooded with blood.

"Satan, Sabbath! Thank God!" Averting her eyes from the bloody attack, Catherine ran to her grandfather, who lay on the ground. "Geordie, can you stand up?"

"Leave him lie, Catherine!" Hepburn was out of the saddle in a flash. "Are you all right, Hellcat?"

Hand on her throat, she nodded quickly, weak with relief that Hepburn had materialized.

Patrick knelt beside Geordie to investigate his wound. "Your leather jac saved you. The blade went in only about an inch." He turned to see David arrive. "Get Lord Winton to Crichton. Better get his bleeding stopped."

Hepburn got up from his knees and Catherine ran into his arms. "Patrick, Malcolm intended to murder both of us! Satan saved us."

He brushed the tumbled curls back from her brow. "It was Sabbath who attacked. She's in pup and savagely protective at the moment." He felt her trembling. "Are you all right, sweetheart?"

She nodded and asked hesitantly, "Is he dead?"

"Yes, deerhounds always kill their prey." He raised his eyes to the moss-troopers who had just arrived. "Take that offal back to Seton, and explain to Andrew what happened here. Assure him that the earl is in no danger."

Standing in the circle of Hepburn's arms, Catherine felt completely safe and secure. Then she looked up into his eyes and found them suddenly black with anger.

He took her by the shoulders and shook her. "You reckless little bitch! No sooner do you cheat death by recovering from plague, than you journey to Scotland with only David for escort, impulsively risking your life again! Cat, I told you to send for me and I would come. What the hell is the matter with you?"

Hepburn was wearing the bloody sheepskin, and he had a two-day growth of beard. Cat went weak at the knees. "Don't be fierce with me, Patrick."

"Why? Because you're with child? Tell me the truth!"

"Yes." Her eyes widened. "You really do have the sight."

"I should beat you to a jelly for being so reckless, Hellcat. Don't move," he ordered. Patrick swung up onto Valiant and lifted her before him in the saddle.

She saw Tor fly into a fir tree. She shuddered, knowing what the scavenger raven would relish. *An eye for an eye!*

"Are you ready to put your wedding ring on?" Patrick asked.

Cat lifted her chin. "Don't you dare to assume I'm ready to forgive you for deserting me. *Again!*"

"We will take this argument up when we can be private. I intend to carry Lady Stewart over Crichton's threshold, and there had better be a smile on her lips, Hellcat."

When they arrived at the castle, Catherine knew better than to disobey the dominant devil. She smiled her secret smile, deciding to postpone their battle of wills until bedtime, when they would be private in the Master Tower. She shivered in anticipation.

All the Hepburn clan gathered in the Great Hall to welcome their laird's lady. Geordie sat, his chest tightly bandaged, already on his second whisky. He grinned at Catherine. "So, ye were tellin' the truth when ye said King Jamie wed ye?"

Hepburn cocked a dark brow. "We had better be married. She will make you a great-grandfather in less than five months."

"Wheesht, yer a lucky man, Hepburn. This calls fer a toast."

When everyone held either a dram of whisky or a tankard of ale, Geordie toasted the expected child as if it were a male.

Catherine was about to bend her elbow when Patrick removed the whisky from her hand. "I think not, Lady Stewart."

She held her tongue before the people of Crichton, and even managed a sweet smile, but her golden eyes glittered dangerously at the challenge he presented.

Patrick hid his amusement and bent his head to whisper in her ear. "Go up and take a nap. I want you to be rested so you can hold your own tonight, when we retire."

• • •

That night they dined with Geordie and Jock. Catherine knew that her grandfather was feeling no pain from all the whisky he had consumed, but worried that he might pay for it tomorrow. "You should be in bed. Your system had a nasty shock today."

Geordie winked at Jock and Patrick. "Ye want me in bed so ye'll have an excuse to retire early. Brides don't need excuses, Catherine. Off ye go, lass. Have at 'im!"

Unable to hide his grin, Hepburn took her hand and led her from the room. The moment they were alone, Cat pulled her fingers from his and marched ahead of him up the long flights of steps that led to his tower. Her bottom was so tempting he had to put his hands behind his back. When they arrived, he threw open the door.

Catherine, who had never seen Hepburn's chamber before, looked about her with avid curiosity. A pink granite fireplace dominated one wall, its mantel carved with Hepburn roses. The opposite wall had two long slits cut into the ancient stone. Their purpose was mainly defense, but they also acted as windows. They held no glass but had shutters that could be closed on cold nights.

She did not dare let her eyes linger on the massive bed, curtained with red velvet, but shifted her gaze to the wall that was lined with books and the tall cushioned chairs with leopards carved into their arms. Before the fire was a lynx-skin rug, and more animal furs were piled on the bed. *It suits the wild devil!*

"Well?"

She swung to face him. He stood waiting impassively with his hands behind his back. Cat pulled his letter from her doublet and flung it at him. "What's this drivel?"

He masked his surprise. "I thought it an honorable letter."

"'I hereby renounce any claim to Spencer Park,'" she quoted. "Why the hell would you do that? To keep me from claiming any part of Crichton? Surely you don't expect me to manage two thousand acres and all those cattle? Why the devil do you think I married you, Hepburn?"

"If you wish me to be the master of Spencer Park, I accept."

"You also vow to never lay claim to my Seton inheritance! Have you no ambition? Do you feel inadequate to manage

Seton and its longhorns? Would you prefer to spend your time at Jamie's Court?"

"If you wish me to manage Seton when you inherit, I accept."

" 'I will never accept the title Earl of Winton,' " she quoted. "Is the earldom not good enough for you, Hepburn?"

"That's where I draw the line, Catherine. I won't take your grandfather's title. Because it would come to me through marriage, it would be like buying a title—I have too much pride. If we have a son, he can inherit the earldom of Winton." He took a step toward her, not quite threatening but definitely challenging. "Are you ready to put your wedding ring back on?"

She lifted her chin. "Only if you give me back my earrings and my emerald betrothal ring!"

He reached into the pocket of his shirt and produced them.

"Anything else, Lady Stewart?"

"Yes! There will be no more *Margrethas* or I shall pay you back in kind and take a lover. I am not without admirers in Scotland!"

Hepburn was instantly incensed. "Name him!"

As she put on her earbobs and rings, her mind raced to find a name she could throw at him. "Sir Robert Carr, a royal favorite!"

Amusement lit Hepburn's face, then he bent over with laughter.

"Blessed are they who can laugh at themselves, for they shall never cease to be amused!" she hissed. "What's so bloody funny?"

Patrick's arms swept about her. He wasn't about to sully her innocence by explaining pederasty to her. He gazed down into her beautiful face. "I don't just love you, Catherine; I adore, worship and dote on you. You are my *treasure*." He bent and took possession of her tempting mouth. He lifted his lips a fraction. "I am going to make tender love to you all night, Hellicate."

"To lowest hell with *tender love,* Hepburn." She dug her nails into his shoulders. "I want you wild and untamed!"

Author's Note

For the benefit of telling a love story, I have taken license with some dates.

Lord Hunsdon actually died in 1596, rather than 1602, and William Herbert's father died in 1601, rather than 1602.

William Seymour, who eventually married Arbella Stuart, was much younger than she was. When Queen Elizabeth discovered Arbella plotting to marry Seymour and banished her from Court, William was only fourteen.

I have strived for accuracy with all other historical dates, events and places.

Virginia Henley

*V*elvet Cavendish had lived at St. Germain, France, at the impoverished Court of exiled Royalists since she was a child, but had recently come to London to live with her wealthy aunt Christian, Dowager Countess of Devonshire.

Velvet had been reluctant to live with the other branch of the family since they had chosen Cromwell over Charles, but at least she would be living in England and she and her father's new wife would not be at each other's throats. With great daring she found the courage before she left to voice a thought she'd kept hidden deep and never spoken aloud before. "What about my betrothal?"

Her father, Earl of Newcastle, rubbed the back of his neck. "I wouldn't count on it, Velvet. Circumstances have changed considerably over the years we've lived in exile. The Earl of Eglinton will not be eager for his heir to take a wife without a substantial dowry."

Deeply stung, she tossed her head. "Nor am I eager to wed Eglinton's heir. I am delighted the betrothal is null and void. I don't remember the callow youth," she lied.

"Of course, should King Charles be restored to the throne and we get back our confiscated estates, I have no doubt your union would once again become most desirable to Eglinton."

Velvet lifted her chin. "That will be too bad. I wouldn't have his son for husband if he were the last man alive!"

• • •

In her chamber at the dowager's great house in London, Velvet looked at her reflection in the mirror. Though most females would have thought the dress of plain gray cambric with starched white collar and cuffs extremely plain, she was most grateful that it was new and fit her perfectly.

She picked up the silver hairbrush, fashioned her unruly red-gold hair into neat ringlets, and pinned on a sheer linen cap. She hurried downstairs to take breakfast with Christian.

"Good morning, darling. You look lovely." *Oh dear, you look like a little milkmaid rather than an aristocratic Cavendish. Your years of penniless exile robbed you of your confidence. I must build up your self-esteem and try to restore some of that delicious precocious attitude you displayed as a child.*

She watched Velvet eat, bemused that she seemed to relish plain bread and honey. "My dear, you have the most radiant complexion. Your skin is translucent and seems to glow from the inside. What is your secret?"

Velvet flushed, pleased at the compliment. "I use cold water. Mother told me about using glycerin distilled with rose water when she was a girl. I wish I had some."

Her wants are so simple. "Well, we have glycerin, and the garden is filled with summer roses. Go out and gather some."

"Oh, thank you." Velvet wiped her mouth and folded her napkin, then dashed outside.

Christian watched her through the back windows. "Ods bodkin, you'd think I'd given her the Crown Jewels."

Greysteel Montgomery had learned the Dowager Countess of Devonshire was living at her grand house in Bishopsgate, the one where her late husband had entertained royalty on a lavish scale. He turned his horse over to a groom and went up the front steps. He presented his card to the butler.

"I'm here to see the Devonshire steward on business, but first I'd like to pay my respects to the dowager countess if she is receiving."

"Very good. This way, my lord." The butler showed him into the library, and in less than two minutes the dowager appeared.

She gave her visitor a quick appraisal and liked what she saw. The gentleman had a commanding presence, which set him apart. She glanced at his card. "Lord Montgomery?"

"My father is Alexander, Earl of Eglinton. I'm here to pay your steward for some sheep we recently acquired from you."

"Ah, yes, you were a captain with the Royalist army."

Velvet came into the library, her head bent over a flower basket. "Christian, it is such a pity that these lovely cream roses have specks of soot on—" She looked up and saw the dowager had a male visitor. "Oh, I beg your pardon . . ." Her voice trailed off as she stood and stared. The man had a military bearing with a ramrod straight back and broad muscular shoulders. His face was dark, hard, lean, and his gray eyes were so compellingly direct a shudder ran down her back. He was the most powerfully attractive male she had ever seen, and her physical response to him was immediate and profound.

Montgomery took one look at the female and felt as if time stood still. His heart too stopped beating momentarily and then began to thud. The young lady before him in the simple gown, carrying a profusion of cream roses, was a vision of sweet innocence. She had the face of an angel; he'd never seen anyone as lovely.

"Velvet, darling, this is Captain Montgomery—"

His dark brows drew together. "Velvet?"

Her violet eyes widened. "Greysteel?"

"Of course!" Christian's face lit up as she realized why his name was so familiar. "Greysteel Montgomery is your betrothed!"

Velvet's cheeks turned crimson. "He is no such thing!"

"It was so long ago. You were only about seven. Perhaps you have forgotten," Christian suggested.

"Yes, I had forgotten." *No, I never forgot. That was the day I decided to name myself Velvet and realized I was in love with Prince Charles. Your first glance told me you wanted to beat me. You were forced to betroth me because of my family's wealth, and you hated me for it. Now that wealth is gone and you don't wish to be reminded of the betrothal. You still hate me.*

"Perhaps you *have* forgotten, Mistress Cavendish. I was a thirteen-year-old youth. My looks have changed considerably."

Velvet stared at him haughtily, desperately trying to mask her physical response to him. Though there was no trace of youthfulness left in the dark, hard countenance, she could never forget his mesmerizing gray eyes, which had the ability to look into her mind and read all her secrets. Moreover, the arrogant devil knew she hadn't forgotten him.

"I'm sure the Earl of Eglinton considers the betrothal null and void, as does my own father, after all these years."

"It matters little what they consider." Greysteel set his jaw. "It is I who will decide about our betrothal."

"You must be mad!" she defied him. "Go to the devil!"

Her words stung him. She had made it plain she hadn't wanted him then, and she didn't want him now. *Set yourself against me and you will lose; your objections only make me more determined.*

"My lord, do forgive Velvet. She doesn't mean to be rude."

"Of course she does. She'd like to run me through with my own sword, but she doesn't quite dare."

"You read my thoughts exactly, sir," Velvet said sweetly.

Christian eyed the pair of antagonists with relish. The sexual sparks between them heated the air. "Lord Montgomery, may I suggest that you come to dinner Wednesday night? Perhaps you two can settle your differences—or continue your duel. Either would be vastly entertaining, I warrant."